WATCHING ME,
WATCHING YOU

WATCHING ME.

*Including 11 short stories
and her long-out-of-print
first novel,*

The Fat Woman's Joke

WATCHING YOU

by Fay Weldon

SUMMIT BOOKS

New York

ACKNOWLEDGMENTS

Angel, All Innocence was first published in the U.S. in *Mademoiselle*, May 1978; *Holy Stones* in *Mademoiselle*, June 1979; *Man with No Eyes* in *Chatelaine*, August 1978 under the title, *Father Figure*; *Weekend* in *Harper's* Magazine, August 1979.

Watching Me, Watching You was a commissioned television play in the *Leap in the Dark* series, BBC Bristol 1980, produced by Michael Croucher, directed by Colin Godman.

The Fat Woman's Joke was originally published in the United States under the title . . . *And the Wife Ran Away* in 1968.

Copyright © 1981 by Fay Weldon
All rights reserved including the right of reproduction in whole or in part in any form. Published by SUMMIT BOOKS, A Simon & Schuster Division of Gulf & Western Corporation, Simon & Schuster Building, Rockefeller Center, 1230 Avenue of the Americas, New York, New York 10020. SUMMIT BOOKS and colophon are trademarks of Simon & Schuster

Manufactured in the United States of America
10 9 8 7 6 5 4 3 2 1

Library of Congress Cataloging in Publication Data
Weldon, Fay.
    Watching me, watching you.

      Contents: Christmas tree—Breakages—Alopecia—[etc.]
      I. Weldon, Fay. The fat woman's joke. 1981.
II. Title.
PR6073.E374W3   1981   823'.914   81-9156
                                AACR2

ISBN 0-671-44817-X

Contents

WATCHING ME,
WATCHING YOU

———

Christmas Tree

The last thing Brian did before he came South was to plant out the Christmas Tree for his Mum and Dad. The tree had grown and flourished for years in the sooty square of Bradford backyard where all other growing things failed, except cabbages. Its needles were dark-green, thick and resilient upon the twig, and its branches grew in conventional Christmas Tree shape. Every year one or other of the Smith family would dig it out on Christmas Eve and replant it on Twelfth Night, and every year the tree repaid them by growing thicker, higher and glossier. Soot clearly suited it. So the tree had existed since 1948, when Brian was ten. Now he was twenty-five. It had given him, Brian worked out on that traumatic day, fifteen years' worth of pleasurable feelings.

'Never drops a needle on my carpet,' said his mother with pride, every year. 'Not like the ones you buy down the market.'

'They're dead before they get to you,' she would explain, every year. 'They boil the roots, you know. They don't want them growing, do they. No profit in that.'

Brian was spending a last Christmas with his Mum and Dad before leaving Bradford for good. There seemed no point in staying. His wife Audrey would not have him back, even though his daughter Helen was born that Boxing Day.

'I told you no and I meant no,' said Audrey. 'I told you if you went with that woman you needn't think you were coming back, and what I say I mean.'

Meaning what was said was a Northern habit, and in retrospect, admirable enough. At the time, however, it had seemed merely drastic. Audrey had shut him, Brian, the hero of his life, out of the cosy warmth of home; left him out in the cold exciting glitter of the unknown world, and he didn't know whether to be glad or sorry. His Mum was allowed to visit the new baby, but not his Dad. Audrey made strange distinctions. 'Pity it's not a boy,' said his Mum, cautiously. 'It's a funny looking little thing. But Helen's a pretty name and time can work wonders.'

The affair with Carlotta had ended. Brian had written a play for the local theatre—his first. It had transferred to London. Carlotta played the lead. Brian had gone down for rehearsals. Audrey had protested. 'You'll sleep with her if you go,' she said. 'I know you. Too big for your boots.'

That was another Northern crime, being too big for your boots. Almost as bad as having a swelled head, putting on airs or having eyes bigger than your stomach. Brian slept with Carlotta, and the affair lasted for the run of the play. Four months.

'That's the way it goes,' said Alec, his agent, later to be his friend. 'When actresses say for life they mean 'til the end of the run. That's show-biz.'

So Brian, who had believed he was a serious writer, and not in show-biz, returned bruised and contrite to Bradford, was thrown out by Audrey, stayed with his parents over Christmas, planted out the Christmas Tree, digging the pit wide and deep, spreading the roots to maximise nourishment and minimise stress—'That's the key to that tree's success,' said his Dad, this year as every other, 'taking care of the roots. Careful!'—and left, for London, all soft-centred harshness and painful integrity, to slam into the soft cultural underbelly of the South. And so he did.

In the year after he left Audrey Brian wrote two stage plays, one musical, four television plays for the BBC and three letters to Audrey. The applause was deafening and prolonged for everything except the letters, which were met by silence, and the silence hurt him more than the applause cheered him.

Writers tend to undervalue those who praise them, or complain that praise is patronising: whilst at the same time feeling aggrieved if they are not praised. They never win the battle with themselves, which is why, perhaps, they go on writing.

The theme of Brian's work was adoration, almost reverence, of the working classes, and his message a howl of hatred for the middle classes, and his solution violence.

'Wonderful!' said Alec. 'The more you insult them the more they'll love you.' And in those cosy pre-Open days it seemed uncomfortably true. Though that of course was not why Brian chose such themes. The themes—which was something Alec could not or would not understand—chose him. Looking around his middle-class, cheering audience, Brian suffered.

There were, of course, compensations. His words upon the page were simple and direct and attractive; and as he was upon the page, so was he in bed. The girls trailed in and out of his flat and wept when it was all, all over, and for the rest of their lives searched his work for their appearance in it, and frequently found themselves, portrayed not unsympathetically.

'I don't know how you do it,' said Alec, politely. Alec wore bifocals. He was happily married to a good cook, and a prey to romantic love of inaccessible young girls. He, at least, maintained that he was happily married. His wife had another story.

After the fourth letter, Brian forgot Audrey. He asked his parents down to London for first nights, or the taping of his Plays for Today, and they were pleased enough to stay in the grand hotels he booked them into, and his friends seemed genuinely to like them—'What a lucky man you are, Brian, to come from a family like that. Real people!'—and if they went back, shaking their heads over him and his rackety life, as if he were a neighbour's child and not their own, Brian was not there to see it.

They would bring him photographs of Helen, and even a father's kind eye was obliged to observe that she was a plain and puddingy child, and that made her the easier to ignore.

He worried about himself, all the same. Had he lost his roots, forsaken his origins, worse, joined the middle classes? He had an image of himself as the Christmas Tree back home, dug up and not put back, left in its pot, unwatered, living on borrowed time, on the goodness of the past.

'Do stop *going on*,' said Victoria of the green pubic hair and feather boa. 'I never knew anyone so guilty as you. Can't you just stop worrying?'

He couldn't. Victoria left.

'But you've got it all made,' said Harriet the theatrical turn, or was it Belinda, they played the silliest games, 'rich and famous, and the revolution just around the corner, and you won't even be the first to go, like us; but the last. You good little leftie, you.'

They went, pretty soon to be cooks on someone's charter yacht, somewhere in the sun. 'Perhaps I'm having my cake and eating it too,' he fretted to Lady Ann Scottwell, who had piano legs but wore the shortest of mini skirts, when a less secure girl would have worn trousers, and they somehow managed to make a plus out of a minus, erotically speaking. 'You might be a little naive about the revolution,' she murmured into his chest hair, cautiously. 'Daddy says it definitely isn't coming.'

That was 1968 and Daddy, it transpired, knew best.

Things went wrong. 'Violence, dear boy,' said Alec, who was going through a camp stage, 'is definitely unfashionable. There's too much of it about in real life. If things go on as they are, your entire audience will be legless and armless.'

Brian, who nowadays said in public that Alec, in the great school report of life, got good marks for contracts, but bad marks for integrity, tried to take no notice. But he felt, as the world changed about him, and goodies became baddies, confused—from Castro to the IRA to Israel, and even cigarette smoking became fashionable. He drank to clear the confusion.

The BBC actually rejected a script and a stage play at the Aldwych was taken off after two weeks. 'How about a film?' asked Alec. 'Hollywood calls.'

'Never,' said Brian.

'A television series? Good money. Good practice.' Brian put the phone down.

He knocked down a television producer in an Indian restaurant, appeared in Court, and was given a conditional discharge, but the *Evening Standard* picked up the story and ran a piece about Brian's recent succession of creative disasters, and referred to his 'emotional stalinism.'

'We'll sue,' said Brian to Alec.

'We won't,' said Alec to Brian. 'We'll work out what it means and see if it fits.' Alec was back on the straight and narrow path to glory.

Instead, Brian married Rea, a fragile blonde actress with a passionate nature, who stopped him drinking by only sleeping with him when he was sober. They went back to Bradford in search of Brian's roots, but found fly-overs and by-passes where the red brick back-to-backs of his childhood had been. His parents now lived on the seventeenth floor of a high-rise block. Rea did not like the place at all. Shopping baskets were filled with white sliced bread and Mr. Kipling cakes, and mothers slapped their children in the streets, and youths smoked and swore on corners. 'I think you'd better forget your roots,' said Rea. She did not want anything to do with Helen, who was still not pretty, in spite of her name.

Brian and Rea set up a fashionable home and gave fashionable dinners for writers with international reputations and New York publishers and notable film directors of a noncommercial kind, mostly from Europe, and filled the house with fashionable stripped pine and Victorian biscuit tins—'Oh the colours! Those faded reds and crimsons!'— and Brian, to give himself time to think, wrote a comedy about the upper classes and the encroaching Arabs, which did very well in the West End. 'Christ, you have sold out,' wrote Audrey, out of the blue. 'Making people laugh is a perfectly serious ambition,' he wrote back. He needed money. Rea was very expensive. He hadn't realised. She would import Batik silk just to make curtains—the yellows and browns—(ironwork had to be genuine Coalbrookdale: steak had to be fillet: clothes had to be Bonnie Cashin).

'How about doing the re-writes on a film? Rome, not Hollywood. Money's fantastic,' said Alec. 'All right,' said Brian.

Brian could not understand why, to his eye, the house looked more and more like an old junk-shop, the more Rea spent. And why she spoiled fillet steak with garlic and laughed him out of liking chips. He fell rather suddenly and startlingly out of love with Rea. She bought Christmas Trees without even the pretence of roots—merest branches posing as proper trees—and failed to deal properly with the needles, which of course would fall in profusion, so that he would find them all the year round, in piles of dust in corners and stuck, slant-wise and painful, into the fabric of his clothes. 'They've been dry-cleaned, Brian. Surely my duty to your clothes stops there?'

So that he felt out of sympathy with her, and rightly critical. She lived on the surface of her life: she lacked complexity. She either laughed at his moods and sensitivities, or, worse, failed to notice them. If he got drunk and hit her—which on one or two lamentable occasions happened, when he was busy re-writing the re-writes, and Rome would ring and the demand would be for this line in and this line out, taking the very last scrap of integrity from the script, and every drop of remaining dignity from himself—if he then lashed out at Rea, he had the impression that it was merely, for her, a scene in a play in which she thought she should never have accepted a part in the first place. He suffered. She would not even wear his black eye boldly, as his mother had worn his father's, but used make-up to disguise it. Everything, with Rea, was disguise, because there was no real self. She acted. She acted the part of wife, hostess, lover, connoisseur of impossible objects. She even acted being pregnant, but when it came to the point, had abortions, and then made him feel responsible by saying it was his lack of enthusiasm for the baby which induced her to have them.

'I didn't want to see you acting mother,' he said. 'That's true enough. At least I know what a real mother is. You don't. It's not your fault. You've had no mother.' Rea's mother had died when she was born. It was a source of some sorrow to her.

Rea had no mother, no roots, no soul. Brian felt it acutely. Times were bad between them.

Brian delivered scripts late, or sloppily written, or not at all. First drafts failed to get to second draft stage. There were arguments about broken contracts. Brian was half-pleased, half-humiliated. There seemed nothing to write about. Nothing, in a changing world, that a writer could put his finger on and cry, stop, that's it: and hold back the world for a minute or two, to allow it to look at itself.

'Tax man's at the door,' said Alec. And so he was, hammering away. 'Television series?'

'Not yet,' said Brian. 'Not quite yet.'

Brian found Rea in bed, in his and her bed, with a second-rate cameraman. 'That's it,' said Brian. 'Out!'

'Not on your nelly,' said Rea. 'You go, I'll stay.'

Rea countered, by solicitor's letter, his accusations of adultery with accusations of mental cruelty, which he could not understand, and physical cruelty, which he could. He let her have everything. 'You never were quite real to me,' he said to her, when he called to collect his clothes, in the bold New Year of 1976. 'You lived in a play.'

'You wrote it,' she said, sourly, and slammed the front door after him, and the shock made the brown Christmas Tree, stuck carelessly outside for the dustmen to collect, lose the last of its needles.

He felt the world was ending, in a sour dream. He was nearly forty, and had nothing.

'Except friends, fans, freedom, a reputation, and a queue of TV producers outside your door,' said Alec. Brian let one or two of them in. With Rea out of the way he could work properly again. He sent a large sum of money to his parents. They sent it back.

'We have everything we need,' they wrote. 'Our pensions are more than sufficient. You save it for a rainy day. You need it more than we do.'

He was hurt, feeling the reproach, and re-directed the money to Audrey. She kept it, but sent no thanks.

Brian felt old. The world was full of young men in jeans, and more than a few of them were competent writers, quicker, cheaper, more sober and harder-working than he, snatching the work from under his nose; and the best and brightest girls behaved as girls never had since the beginning of time, expecting him to make coffee and saying 'don't ring me, I'll ring you': and the theatre had lost its shape, and its giants, and the proscenium arch had gone, and everyone ran round pretending the writer was no one special, just someone with a job to do: and a stage play had become just a television play, with a live audience.

Unsatisfactory times. The young women still came. They preferred him, if anything to their contemporaries. They had a surface politeness. They would ask him what the matter was, on those mornings when he turned his face to the wall, and couldn't get up, and his phone would ring, and he couldn't bring himself to answer it. 'I've lost my roots,' he'd say. They could not of course believe him, and took his mournfulness as a slur upon their sexuality, and an insult to their femininity. But what he said was at last true. He could no longer send down feelers into his past, into the black, crumbling, moving soil of his childhood.

'Re-pot yourself,' snapped Alec, who had other stars in his stable now—young men who liked, nostalgically, to dress like Colin Wilson. Alec had never stopped. 'Find new soil.'

'I tried with Rea,' said Brian.

'Now's the time to write something really big,' said Alec. 'Some spectacular statement, to hit the contemporary button on the head.'

'It's been hit so often it's lost its spring,' said Brian.

But he thought perhaps Alec was right. And he felt he was resting, not idling. He knew, as he had always known, that the big work was there somewhere, waiting to emerge: the great work, that was to be to Brian Smith and the contemporary world, as Paradise Lost had been to Milton and his world. The master work, the summing up, knotting up, tying up and gift presentation of the human experience that everyone was hoping for, waiting for.

In two acts, of course, with a small cast and a single set to minimise expense, and one good interval to maximise bar and ice-cream sales.

'Don't be like that,' said Alec. 'Playwrighting is the art of the practical.'

'One thing you have taught me, Alec,' said Brian, 'is that a writer is gigolo to the Muse, not lover.' Perhaps he should change agents? But death seemed easier.

Brian spent the Christmas of 1978 in Alec's new home, in Belgravia. One of Alec's inaccessible young girls had proved accessible, and now Alec lived with her, while Alec's wife lived with her former boyfriend. 'Playing fathers and mothers,' murmured Brian into his Christmas pudding. 'Easier than husband and wife.'

But Alec's girl made a good brandy butter and her father actually worked for the Forestry Commission and the Christmas Tree in the corner had real roots, and was dark green and bouncy, and she planned to keep it in a tub out on the balcony all year, and Brian felt a real surge of affection for both of them, and a conviction that the Western World was not tottering about on its last legs, as everyone kept saying but just, as he was, having a little rest before undergoing a transfiguration into youth, health, vigour and purpose.

Almost as if this welling up of optimism attracted real reason for it, Brian fell in love in the spring of 1979.

He could not recall ever having felt such an emotion before. What he had thought was love, he now realised was a mixture of lust and anxiety lest the object of his lust should get away, together with a soupçon of practical worry about who was to iron his shirts and wash his socks, seasoned with a pinch of pleasure at having found someone who would listen, with attention and sympathy, to the continuing soap opera of his life. In the heat and glory of his new-found love, and in the renaissance that went with it, in the new awareness of the spiritual content of what goes on, or should go on, between man and woman, he wrote to Rea, and apologised.

Rea wrote a friendly letter back, saying she was pregnant and happy and a lot of their trouble had been his, Brian's, womb-envy. Having babies, she said, was the real creativity: compared to this the writing of plays and the making of films must seem thin indeed. But the best a man could do.

He read the letter out to Linda, the object of his love. She nodded and smiled. She had long fair hair, and a pink and white complexion and tiny teeth and a little mouth, and a plump bosom and a plump figure all over. Little white hands; tiny feet. She was twenty-two. She was a country girl. Her voice, when she spoke, which she did only when entirely necessary, was faint and frail and female and had a gentle, seductive Devon burr. She was working, when he met her, as a waitress in a hotel in Weston-Super-Mare, where Brian and a film crew were filming a chase sequence: a man on water skis being pursued by a beautiful CIA girl in a black wet-suit.

Brian had expected, more or less, to bed the wet-suit girl sometime during their stay at the hotel: but when he saw Linda, standing against the window of the breakfast room, the morning sun shining behind her hair, silhouetting her sweet, pensive face, he lost all interest in that petty ordinary ambition. Linda brought him his orange juice, and her eyes were downcast, and he thought this is what women ought to be, and why I have had such trouble with the others: this is how my mother must have looked when she was young. Linda raised her eyes, and there was a look in them which he remembered from the Statue of the Madonna in the classroom where he'd gone for a time, when he was seven, to the Catholic school: it was of understanding, forgiveness and invitation all at once. Blue eyes beneath an alabaster brow, and the ridiculous waitress's cap narrowing the forehead, as had the Virgin Mary's wimple. He loved her.

'Christ!' said Alec. 'Are you out of your mind?'

Brian hardly thought Alec was one to talk. 'Listen,' said Alec, 'my Lisa may have been a college girl but at least she was doing English Lit and got a perfectly respectable 2-2. This girl is a waitress!'

It was only a holiday job, in actual fact. Linda's parents, he had discovered, owned a garage in East Devon and Linda lived at home, helping out.

'I'm glad she's a waitress,' said Brian. 'I'm finally back where I belong. Amongst real people, who do real things, and live simple, honest hard-working lives.'

'Christ!' was all Alec would say.

During that long hot summer Brian wrote a four part love story for television so full of sensual delights that even enemies and critics were touched, and Alec was silent, and Audrey wrote, out of the blue. 'My God,' said Audrey, 'life was never like that for you and me. Wish it had been. My fault, perhaps. Helen's training as a nurse. Shouldn't you be using your television time to protest about low pay instead of all this full-frontal stuff?'

Still, it was better than nothing.

Linda came to live with him in London. She wouldn't and didn't sleep with him, though nobody believed it. She was virtuous. Her family didn't believe it either and cast her off. She spent her time writing letters home on thin blue lined paper with purple violets round the edge. She had unformed, careful writing and her spelling was bad. He found that charming. He still had trouble spelling, himself.

Forgiveness was a long time coming.

'I've let them down,' she whispered. 'They trusted me.'

'Perhaps we ought to be married,' said Brian, though he'd sworn publicly never to do anything like that again. She considered.

'I suppose that would be nice,' said Linda. 'They'd forgive me, then. Oh, I do so want you to meet them! I miss my mother and my brothers so much.'

They agreed to marry at Christmas. It couldn't be any earlier because Brian had to go to Los Angeles for three months, to work on a film. A thriller.

He half-wondered whether to take Linda, but she said firmly that she didn't want to come. 'I'll stay home and arrange the wedding,' she said. 'Honestly, I'd rather. I don't really fit in with your smart friends.'

'That's what's so wonderful about you,' he said. He could see that in Los Angeles, where girls were thin and leggy and bronzed, she might not appear to advantage. She liked to keep out of the sun, because it made her nose peel.

He had thought the wedding would be a Register Office affair, but Linda had set her heart on being married in a white dress with bell sleeves in the village church, and he agreed. 'It will cost you to do it properly,' she said, timorously. She had never asked for money before. He gave her a cheque. 'I haven't got a bank account,' she said.

'If you're going home,' he said, 'your parents can cash it for you.'

'They don't have banks,' she said, and he was surprised. What kind of people were they? 'It's only a little garage,' she apologised.

He was pleased. He thought the peasant soil might be some kind of equivalent to the proletarian earth that afforded his early nourishment. He flew off to L.A. over the Pole, first class, and did not even try to date the young woman who sat next to him, who wore sneakers and had a little silver snuff box full of vitamin pills and said she was in hospitals. 'Administration?' he asked.

'I own them,' she said, and what with East turning West beneath them, and the sun rising where it had only just set, and rather too much champagne, he felt the world was upside-down and longed for Linda's stolid charm, and her little feet in high strap heels, rather than those serviceable if sexy sneakers. Stolid? He was rather shocked by that particular choice of word. It was not how one usually described the Virgin Mary. Stolid.

In love with the Virgin Mary. But he was. He became almost nauseous when confronted with the ravishing Mary Magdalenas of Malibu Beach: human animals doing their copulatory dance under the Studio Ring Master's whip: the fantasies of an exhausted film industry, taken such definite flesh. He had no trouble resisting them.

It was not, he saw now, that he had ever been promiscuous. Just that no woman until now had ever succeeded in properly captivating him. 'Christ!' said Alec on the telephone, across half the world. But he'd put his commission up to fifteen per cent and since the spring, and the advent of Linda, Brian had been doing well enough and fulfilling his early promise, as money maker if not saviour of society.

Brian came home on December 14. The wedding was on December 15. Linda was already in Devon. The wedding was all organised, she told him when he rang from Heathrow. All that was required was Brian's appearance, wearing a suit, and with the ring, early the next morning. She'd even arranged the cars, which should have been the groom's task. The wedding reception was to be in the Women's Institute Hall, and they were to spend the night with Linda's parents, the Jones's, in the caravan in the garden. If it was raining, or snowing, they could squeeze into her bedroom.

Women's Institute? Caravan? In December? After Studio City, Malibu and Sunset Boulevard, it sounded strange. But Brian Smith marrying Linda Jones sounded profoundly, agreeably right.

He was relieved, too, if only by virtue of shortage of time, of the burden of providing friends and family to witness the wedding. He wanted a new life. He did not want the past clouding any issues. In East Devon, down in the South West, he would be born again.

Honest rural folk.

Linda's father met him at the station. The train was late. Mr. Jones paced up and down in an ill-fitting navy suit, and boots with buckled uppers. No more ill-fitting, Brian told himself, than my father's at prize day at the grammar school. The pale grey suits of the executives of Studio City, their smooth after-shaved jowls, their figures jogged into shape, made an unfair comparison. Linda's father was narrow like a ferret, sharp-eyed like a fox, untidy as an unpruned hedge in autumn, and had thick red hands with bleak oil beneath the nails. One eye wandered when he spoke.

'Best hurry,' said Mr. Jones, 'Linda's waiting,' and they climbed into an old C registration Mini, with the back seats taken out and piled with plastic fertilizer sacks and ropes, guarded by a snappy, noisy, ugly little dog. Barking prevented them from talking.

The garage had a single petrol pump, and was marked No Petrol, and was outside the last house in an undistinguished row of pre-war houses set back from the main road. Brian was rushed upstairs to change, the dog snapping at his heels, into a tiny room with four different flowered papers on the wall, and two beds and three wardrobes and six trays of sausage rolls on boards placed across the beds. He caught a glimpse of Linda as he fled from the dog; she was in brilliant Terylene white. He thought she blew him a kiss.

What am I doing, he thought, trying to find a place between the plastic beads and greeting cards and Mr Men stickers and the Christmas holly and bells which decked the mirror, so he could fix his tie. He was bronzed by the Californian sun; his face was narrow and handsome and clever. What am I doing? What desperation has landed me here? No, this is jet-lag speaking. I love Linda. Write it in plastic Christmas foam on what remains of the mirror. I love Linda. What has Linda's family to do with her, any more than mine to do with me? Roots. Aye, there's the rub. Red Devon soil hardened by winter. What good was that to him? He was used to soot. He was ready. A Rolls-Royce stood outside. Well, he was paying.

Into the first car he stepped, and Linda's father came with him. Best man. Linda's father had trodden in the mess left by the dog in the hall. Linda's father's shoe smelt. 'Over excited,' said Linda's mother. She was stout and dressed in green satin but otherwise might have been anyone. Linda's cross-eyed brother kicked the dog out of the house. Linda's wall-eyed brother hoovered up the mess, which was largely liquid.

'Don't do that!' cired Linda's mother. Linda smiled serenely beneath her white white veil. She was a virgin.

'My wedding day is the happiest day of my life,' she said, though whether to Brian as he passed, or as a statement of policy to God above, or simply to quell the riot he did not know. Mr. Jones nipped upstairs to clean his shoe.

The village church was big and handsome and very cold. A hundred people or so were gathered on the Bride's side of the church. The acoustics were bad, and there were many small children in the congregation. Brian stood dazed, facing the cross and banks of paper flowers. The vicar was elderly and dressed in a white gown. Brian heard sound and movement and presently Linda stood beside him, and he felt better and to the sound of children crying and protesting he and she were married, in God's sight.

Outside the church, later, there were many photographs taken. He thought he had never seen so many ugly and misshapen people gathered together in one place. He could not be sure whether this was so, and a phenomenon peculiar to this part of Devon, or whether it was just the sudden contrast to the people of Southern California.

Various people young and old, men and women, came up to congratulate him, and in the course of brief conversations let it be known that Linda was not a virgin, had had at least two relationships with married men, one abortion, one miscarriage and had married him for his money. Linda did not seem to be popular. He thought perhaps he was dreaming.

At the reception at the W.I. Hall, where sherry was served, and also the sausage rolls he had seen on the bed, the Vicar remarked on the cross and wall eyes of the Jones's boys, and accounted for it by village in-breeding. It's a genetic weakness, he said. Genetics, he added, bitterly, was a three syllable word, and words so long were not often heard in these parts.

Jet-lag became more pressing. He had to sleep. He remembered making a speech. Linda put on her going-away clothes and the Rolls took them back to the garage. The dog lay vomiting on the path.

'Now we can,' said Linda, quick! Before anyone comes home,' and she pulled him upstairs to the room with the many wallpapers and he removed her clothes except her veil and made love to her. That was what marriage was all about. He thought she probably wasn't a virgin, but just pretending. He wondered where his silver cuff-links were and couldn't see them. Then he fell asleep. When he woke she was unpacking wedding presents, and singing happily. 'This is the happiest day of my life! Oh, how I love you!' said Linda, and gave him a kiss. 'Look, a toaster, and a lovely casserole with yellow flowers. That's from Auntie Ann.'

She had not noticed any lack of sexual enthusiasm in him. Was that innocence, or insensitivity, or cunning? His cuff-links were decidedly gone. 'You must have left them in London,' said Linda. 'They'll turn up.'

They had been a present from Rea. For some reason he valued them. But Linda dismissed the matter. Now they were married she seemed much more definite. Her eyelids no longer drooped, in modesty and decorum. She looked him straight in the eye, and lied.

'The bill from the caterers hasn't been paid. Could you possibly give me a cheque? Three hundred pounds.'

'I thought you made the food yourselves.'

'No. It was all bought in. Every scrap.' She did not seem to mind that the lie was easily detected, nor the amount improbable. She gave him a little kiss on the nose. 'Husband! Go on, say wife.'

'Wife!'

'Will you come out with us on the Christmas Trees? It would please Dad.'

And so they did. Dad and the two boys and Brian, after dark on his wedding night, with light snow falling, took shovels and borrowed a neighbour's van and travelled ten miles inland, on to Forestry Commission land, where the pylons were slung from hill to hill, carrying electricity from the Nuclear Power Station to the good folk of Exeter, and there, beneath the wires, hair crackling and tooth fillings zinging, they pirated Christmas Trees. Good healthy well-shaped trees, three foot high, with a broad spread of vigorous roots. Brian dug, and laughed, and dug some more. It was theft, it was dangerous, there were dog patrols to stop such acts, but he felt, at last, that he was doing something sensible and useful. The Jones's family were pleased by the muscle and enthusiasm of their new relative. Father Jones, despite the snow, took off his coat, and carefully laid it down beside where Brian rested, and on impulse Brian felt in the inside pocket, and yes, there were his silver cuff-links. He left them where they were, and said nothing. What was there to say?

He didn't suppose the dog was trained to cause uproar: no one was clever enough for that: just that when the dog caused uproar, the cover seemed too good to miss. He thought Mrs Jones might well feed it on cascara, just to be on the safe side.

The hilarity of exhaustion and despair turned sour when they arrived back at the house with some fifty Christmas Trees and unloaded them in the backyard. Mrs Jones had an old tin bath ready outside the back door, filled with boiling water. The brother with the wall-eyes bound the living green of the trees with twine. Mrs Jones dumped the roots in the boiling water, and the cross-eyed brother re-loaded them into the van. Linda stood by and watched the murder. 'What are you doing? Why?' he shouted at them, but the wind was strong, and snow flicked off the ground, and the water bubbled, and the stereo in the house was on loud to cover their nefarious deed. Cliff Richard. He thought he could hear the trees screaming as they died. 'Just boiling them,' said Linda, surprised.

'But why, why?'

'It's just what we do.'

'It can't make any difference to you,' he cried. 'No profit lost to you if they grow.'

'People always boil the roots,' she said, looking at him as if he was daft. 'It's the done thing.'

He could see she took him for a fool, and despised him for it, and had tricked him and trapped him, for all he was bright and old, and she was thick and young.

He stumbled inside and up to the bedroom and fell asleep and slept, with the smell of boiling tree in his nostrils, and flakes of sausage-roll pastry in the sheets, and woke, with Linda next to him. Her skin was clammy. She wore a cerise nylon nightie, trimmed with fawn nylon lace. He went downstairs to the coin telephone in the hall and rang Alec. 'I think I've found the right place for me,' he said, and indeed he had. He had bound himself by accident to a monstrous family in a monstrous place and had discovered by accident what he felt to be the truth, long evident, long evaded, that human nature was irredeemable. It seemed a good base for a writer to work from. 'I think I'll stay down here for a while with my wife,' he said. My wife! All aspirations and ambition had been burned away: old wounds cauterised with so sudden and horrific a knife as to leave him properly cleansed, and purified. 'Next to nature,' said Brian with a dreadful animation rising in him: a writer's animation. 'With cows and cider and power lines and kind and honest country folk. I think I could really write down here.'

'Christ!' said Alec. He seemed to have fewer and fewer words to rub together, as his stable of writers found more and more.

Breakages

> 'We blossom and flourish
> Like leaves on a tree,
> And wither and perish
> But nought changeth thee —

sang David's congregation in its laggardly, quavery voice. Some trick of
acoustics made much of what happened in the church audible in the
vicarage kitchen, where tonight, as so often, Deidre sat and darned
socks and waited for Evensong to end.

The vicarage, added as a late Victorian afterthought, leaned up
against the solidity of the Norman church. The house was large, ram-
shackle, dark and draughty, and prey to wet rot, dry rot, woodworm
and beetle. Here David and Deidre lived. He was a vicar of the established church; she was his wife. He attended to the spiritual welfare of
his parishioners: she presided over the Mothers' Union and the Wom-
en's Institute and ran the Amateur Dramatic Society. They had been
married for twenty-one years. They had no children, which was a
source of acute disappointment to them and to Deidre's mother, and of
understandable disappointment to the parish. It is always pleasant, in a
small, stable and increasingly elderly community, to watch other
people's children grow up, and sad to be deprived of that pleasure.

'Oh no, please,' said Deidre, now to the Coronation Mug on the
dresser. It was a rare piece, produced in anticipation of an event which
had never occurred: the Coronation of the Duke of Windsor. The mug

was, so far, uncracked and unchipped, and worth some three hundred pounds, but had just moved to the very edge of its shelf, not smoothly and purposively, but with an uneven rocking motion which made Deidre hope that entreaty might yet calm it, and save it from itself. And indeed, after she spoke, the mug was quiet, and lapsed into the ordinary stillness she had once always associated with inanimate objects.

> 'Immortal, invisible,
> God only wise—
> In light inaccessible—'

Deidre joined in the hymn, singing gently and soothingly, and trying to feel happy, for the happier she felt the fewer the breakages there would be and perhaps one day they would stop altogether, and David would never, ever find out; that one by one, the ornaments and possessions he most loved and valued were leaping off shelves and shattering, to be secretly mended by Deidre with such skills as she remembered from the early days, before marriage had interrupted her training in china restoration, and her possible future in the Victoria and Albert Museum.

Long ago and far away. Now Deidre darned. David's feet were sensitive to anything other than pure, fine wool. Not for him the tough nylon mixtures that other men wore. Deidre darned.

The Coronation Mug rocked violently.

'Stop it,' said Deidre, warningly. Sometimes to appear stern was more effective than to entreat. The mug stayed where it was. But just a fraction further, and it would have fallen.

Deidre unpicked the last few stitches. She was in danger of cobbling the darn, and there is nothing more uncomfortable to sensitive skin than a cobbled darn.

'You do it on purpose,' David would complain, not without reason. Deidre's faults were the ones he found most difficult to bear. She was careless, lost socks, left lids unscrewed, taps running, doors open, saucepans burning: she bought fresh bread when yesterday's at half price would do. It was her nature, she maintained, and grieved bitterly when her husband implied that it was wilful and that she was doing it to annoy. She loved him, or said so. And he loved her, or said so.

The Coronation Mug leapt off its shelf, arced through the air and fell and broke in two pieces at Deidre's feet. She put the pieces at the very back of the drawer beneath the sink. There was no time for mending now. Tomorrow morning would have to do, when David was out parish-visiting, in houses freshly dusted and brightened for his arrival. Fortunately, David seldom inspected Deidre's drawer. It smelt, when opened, of dry rot, and reminded him forcibly of the large sums of money which ought to be spent on the repair of the house, and which he did not have.

'We could always sell something,' Deidre would sometimes venture, but not often, for the suggestion upset him. David's mother had died when he was four; his father had gone bankrupt when he was eight; relatives had reared him and sent him off to boarding school where he had been sexually and emotionally abused. Possessions were his security.

She understood him, forgave him, loved him and tried not to argue.

She darned his socks. It was, today, a larger pile than usual. Socks kept disappearing, not by the pair, but singly. David had lately discovered a pillowslip stuffed full of them pushed to the back of the wardrobe. It was his wife's deceit which worried him most, or so he said. Hiding socks! That and the sheer careless waste of it all. Losing socks! So Deidre tried tying the socks together for the wash, and thus, in pairs, the night before, spun and dried, they had lain in the laundry basket. In the morning she had found them in one ugly, monstrous knot, and each sock oddly long, as if stretched by a hand too angry to know what it was doing. Rinsing had restored them, fortunately, to a proper shape, but she was obliged to darn where the stretching had worn the fabric thin.

It was always like this: always difficult, always upsetting. David's things were attacked, as if the monstrous hand were on her side, yet it was she, Deidre, who had to repair the damage, follow its source as it moved about the house, mending what it broke, wiping tomato purée from the ceiling, toothpaste from the lavatory bowl, replanting David's seedlings, rescrewing lids, closing doors, refolding linen, turning off taps. She scarcely dared leave the house for fear of what might happen in her absence, and this David interpreted as lack of interest in his parish. Disloyalty, to God and husband.

Times were bad between them. Yet they loved each other. Man and wife.

Deidre's finger was bleeding. She must have cut it on the sharp edge of the broken Coronation Mug. She opened the table drawer and took out the first piece of cloth which came to hand, and wrapped her finger.

The cold tap started to run of its own accord, but she ignored it. Blood spread out over the cloth but presently, fortunately, stopped.

Could you die from loss of blood, from a small finger cut?

The invisible hand swept the dresser shelf, knocking all sorts of treasures sideways but breaking nothing. It had never touched the dresser before, as if awed, as Deidre was, by the ever increasing value of its contents—rare blue and white pieces, frog mugs, barbers' bowls, lustre cups, a debatedly Ming bowl, which a valuer said might well fetch five thousand pounds.

Enough to paint the vicarage, inside, and install central heating, and replaster walls and buy a new vacuum cleaner.

The dresser rattled and shook: she could have sworn it slid towards her.

David did not give Deidre a housekeeping allowance. She asked for money when she needed it, but David seldom recognised that it was in fact needed. He could not see the necessity of things like washing-up liquid, sugar, toilet rolls, new scourers. Sometimes she stole money from his pocket: once she took a coin out of the offertory on Sunday morning instead of putting a coin in it.

Why did she stoop to it? She loved him.

A bad wife, a barren wife, and a poor sort of person.

David came home. The house fell quiet, as always, at his approach. Taps stopped running and china rattling. David kissed her on her forehead.

'Deidre,' said David, 'what have you wrapped around your finger?'

Deidre, curious herself, unwrapped the binding and found that she had used a fine lace and cotton handkerchief, put in the drawer for mending, which once had belonged to David's grandmother. It was now sodden and bright, bright red.

'I cut my finger,' said Deidre, inadequately and indeed foolishly, for what if he demanded to know what had caused the wound? But David was too busy rinsing and squeezing the handkerchief under the tap to enquire. Deidre put her finger in her mouth and put up with the salt, exciting taste of her own blood.

'It's hopelessly stained,' he mourned. 'Couldn't you just for once have used something you wouldn't spoil? A tissue?'

David did not allow the purchase of tissues. There had been none in his youth: why should they be needed now, in his middle age?

'I'm sorry,' said Deidre, and thought, as she spoke, 'I am always saying sorry, and always providing cause for my own remorse.'

He took the handkerchief upstairs to the bathroom, in search of soap and a nailbrush. 'What kind of wife are you, Deidre?' he asked as he went, desperate.

What kind, indeed? Married in a register office in the days before David had taken to Holy Orders and a Heavenly Father more reliable than his earthly one. Deidre had suggested that they re-marry in Church, as could be and had been done by others, but David did not want to. Hardly a wife at all.

A barren wife. A fig-tree, struck by God's ill-temper. David's God. In the beginning they had shared a God, who was bleak, plain, sensible and kind. But now, increasingly, David had his own jealous and punitive God, whom he wooed with ritual and richness, incense and images, dragging a surprised congregation with him. He changed his vestments three times during services, rang little bells to announce the presence of the Lord, swept up and down aisles, and in general seemed not averse to being mistaken for God.

The water pipes shrieked and groaned as David turned on the tap in the bathroom, but that was due to bad plumbing rather than unnatural causes. She surely could not be held responsible for that, as well.

When the phenomena—as she thought of them—first started, or rather leapt from the scale of ordinary domestic carelessness to something less explicable and more sinister, she went to the doctor.

'Doctor,' she said, 'do mumps in adolescence make men infertile?'

'It depends,' he said, proving nothing. 'If the gonads are affected it well might. Why?'

No reason had been found for Deidre's infertility. It lay, presumably, like so much else, in her mind. She had had her tubes blown, painfully and unforgettably, to facilitate conception, but it had made no difference. For fifteen years twenty-three days of hope had been followed by five days of disappointment, and on her shoulders rested the weight of David's sorrow, as she, his wife, deprived him of his earthly immortality, his children.

'Of course,' he said sadly, 'you are an only child. Only children are often infertile. The sins of the fathers—' David regarded fecundity as a blessing; the sign of a woman in tune with God's universe. He had married Deidre, he vaguely let it be known, on the rebound from a young woman who had gone on to have seven children. Seven!

David's fertility remained unquestioned and unexamined. A sperm count would surely have proved nothing. His sperm was plentiful and he had no sexual problems that he was aware of. To ejaculate into a test-tube to prove a point smacked uncomfortably of onanism.

The matter of the mumps came up during the time of Deidre's menopause, a month or so after her, presumably, last period. David had been in the school sanitarium with mumps: she had heard him saying so to a distraught mother, adding, 'Oh mumps! Nothing in a boy under fourteen. Be thankful he has them now, not later.'

So he was aware that mumps were dangerous, and could render a man infertile. And Deidre knew well enough that David had lived in the world of school sanatoria after the age of fourteen, not before. Why had he never mentioned mumps? And while she wondered, and pondered, and hesitated to ask, toothpaste began to ooze from tubes, and rose-trees were uprooted in the garden, and his seedlings trampled by unseen boots, and his clothes in the wardrobe tumbled in a pile to the ground, and Deidre stole money to buy mending glue, and finally went to the doctor.

'Most men,' said the doctor, 'confuse impotence with infertility and believe that mumps cause the former, not the latter.'

Back to square one. Perhaps he didn't know.

'Why have you *really* come?' asked the doctor, recently back from a course in patient-doctor relations. Deidre offered him an account of her domestic phenomena, as she had not meant to do. He prescribed Valium and asked her to come back in a week. She did.

'Any better? Does the Valium help?'

'At least when I see things falling, I don't mind so much.'

'But you still see them falling?'

'Yes.'

'Does your husband see them too?'

'He's never there when they do.'

Now what was any thinking doctor to make of that?

'We could try hormone replacement therapy,' he said.

'No,' said Deidre. 'I am what I am.'

'Then what do you want me to do?'

'If I could only feel angry with my husband,' said Deidre, 'instead of forever understanding and forgiving him, I might get it to stop. As it is, I am releasing too much kinetic energy.'

There were patients waiting. They had migraines, eczema and boils. He gave her more Valium, which she did not take.

Deidre, or some expression of Deidre, went home and churned up the lawn and tore the gate off its hinges. The other Deidre raked and smoothed, resuscitated and blamed a perfectly innocent child for the gate. A child. It would have taken a forty stone giant to twist the hinges so, but no one stopped, fortunately, to think about that. The child went to bed without supper for swinging on the vicar's gate.

The wound on Diedre's finger gaped open in an unpleasant way. She thought she could see the white bone within the bloodless flesh.

Deidre went upstairs to the bathroom, where David washed his wife's blood from his grandmother's hankie. 'David,' said Deidre, 'perhaps I should have a stitch in my finger?'

David had the toothmug in his hand. His jaw was open, his eyes wide with shock. He had somehow smeared toothpaste on his black lapel. 'The toothmug has recently been broken, and very badly mended. No one told me. Did you do it?'

The toothmug dated from the late eighteenth century and was worn, cracked and chipped, but David loved it. It had been one of the first things to go, and Deidre had not mended it with her usual care, thinking, mistakenly, that one more crack amongst so many would scarcely be noticed.

'I am horrified,' said David.

'Sorry,' said Deidre.

'You always break my things, never your own.'

'I thought that when you got married,' said Deidre, with the carelessness of desperation, for surely now David would start an inspection of his belongings and all would be discovered, 'things stopped being yours and mine, and became ours.'

'Married! You and I have never been married, not in the sight of God, and I thank Him for it.'

There. He had said what had been unsaid for years, but there was no relief in it, for either of them. There came a crash of breaking china from downstairs. David ran down to the kitchen, where the noise came from, but could see no sign of damage. He moved into the living room. Deidre followed, dutifully.

'You've shattered my life,' said David. 'We have nothing in common. You have been a burden since the beginning. I wanted a happy, warm, loving house. I wanted children.'

'I suppose,' said Deidre, 'you'll be saying next that my not having children is God's punishment?'

'Yes,' said David.

'Nothing to do with your mumps?'

David was silent, taken aback. Out of the corner of her eye Deidre saw the Ming vase move. 'You're a sadistic person,' said David eventually. 'Even the pains and humiliations of long ago aren't safe from you. You revive them.'

'You knew all the time,' said Deidre. 'You were infertile, not me. You made me take the blame. And it's too late for me now.'

The Ming vase rocked to the edge of the shelf: Deidre moved to push it back, but not quickly enough. It fell and broke.

David cried out in pain and rage. 'You did it on purpose,' he wept. 'You hate me.'

Deidre went upstairs and packed her clothes. She would stay with her mother while she planned some kind of new life for herself. She would be happier anywhere in the world but here, sharing a house with a ghost.

David moved through the house, weeping, but for his treasures, not for his wife. He took a wicker basket and in it laid tenderly—as if they were the bodies of children—the many broken and mended vases and bowls and dishes which he found. Sometimes the joins were skilful and barely detectable to his moving forefinger: sometimes careless. But everything was spoilt. What had been perfect, was now second-rate and without value. The finds in the junk-shops, the gifts from old ladies, the few small knick-knacks which had come to him from his dead mother—his whole past destroyed by his wife's single-minded malice and cunning.

He carried the basket to the kitchen, and sat with his head in his hands.

Deidre left without saying another word. Out of the door, through the broken garden gate, into the night, through the churchyard, for the powers of the dead disturbed her less than the powers of the living, and to the bus station.

David sat. The smell of rot from the sink drawer was powerful enough, presently, to make him lift his head.

The cold tap started to run. A faulty washer, he concluded. He moved to turn it off, but the valve was already closed. 'Deidre!' he called, 'what have you done with the kitchen tap?' He did not know why he spoke, for Deidre had gone.

The whole top of the dresser fell forward to the ground. Porcelain shattered and earthenware powdered. He could hear the little pings of the Eucharist bell in the church next door, announcing the presence of God.

He thought perhaps there was an earthquake, but the central light hung still and quiet. Upstairs heavy feet bumped to and fro, dragging, wrenching and banging. Outside the window the black trees rocked so fiercely that he thought he would be safer in than out. The gas taps of the cooker were on and he could smell gas, mixed with fumes from the coal fire where Deidre's darning had been piled up and was now smouldering. He closed his eyes.

He was not frightened. He knew that he saw and heard these things, but that they had no substance in the real world. They were a distortion of the facts, as water becomes wine in the Communion service, and bread becomes the flesh of the Saviour.

When next he opened his eyes the dresser was restored, the socks still lay in the mending basket, the air was quiet.

Sensory delusions, that was all, brought about by shock. But unpleasant, all the same. Deidre's fault. David went upstairs to sleep but could not open the bedroom door. He thought perhaps Deidre had locked it behind her, out of spite. He was tired. He slept in the spare room, peacefully, without the irritant of Deidre's warmth beside him.

In the morning, however, he missed her, and as if in reply to his unspoken request she reappeared, in the kitchen, in time to make his breakfast tea. 'I spent the night in the hospital,' she said. 'I went to casualty to have a stitch put in my finger, and I fainted, and they kept me in.'

Her arm was in a sling.

'I'm sorry,' he said. 'You should have told me it was a bad cut and I'd have been more sympathetic. Where did you put the bedroom key?'

'I haven't got it,' she said, and the teapot fell off the table and there was tea and tea-leaves everywhere, and, one-armed, she bungled the business of wiping it up. He helped.

'You shouldn't put breakables and spillables on the edge of tables,' he reproached her. 'Then it wouldn't happen.'

'I suppose not.'

'I'm sorry about what I may have said last night. Mumps are a sore point. I thought I would die from the itching, and my friends just laughed.'

Itching? Mumps?

'Mumps *is* the one where you come out in red spots and they tie your hands to stop you scratching?'

'No. That's chicken-pox,' she said.

'Whatever it was, if you're over fourteen you get it very badly indeed and it is humiliating to have your hands tied.'

'I can imagine.'

He wrung out the dish-cloth. The tap, she noticed, was not dripping.

'I'm sorry about your things,' she said. 'I should have told you.'

'Am I such a frightening person?'

'Yes.'

'They're only things,' he said, to her astonishment. The house seemed to take a shift back into its ordinary perspective. She thought, that though childless, she could still live an interesting and useful life. Her friends with grown-up children, gone away, complained that it was as if their young had never been. The experience of child-rearing was that, just that, no more, no less. An experience without much significance, presently over; as lately she had experienced the behaviour of the material world.

David insisted that Deidre must surely have the bedroom key, and was annoyed when she failed to produce it. 'Why would I lock you out of the bedroom?' she asked.

'Why would you do anything!' he remarked dourly. His gratitude for her return was fading: his usual irritation with her was reasserting itself. She was grateful for familiar ways, and as usual animated by them.

He went up the ladder to the bedroom window, and was outraged. 'I've never seen a room in such a mess,' he reported, from the top of the ladder, a figure in clerical black perched there like some white-ruffled crow. 'How you did all that, even in a bad temper, I can't imagine.'

The heavy wardrobe was on its side, wedged against the door: the bed was upside down: the chairs and light bulb broken, and the bed-clothes tumbled and knotted, had the same stretched and strained appearance as David's socks; and the carpet had been wrenched up, tossing furniture as it lifted, and wrung out like a dish-cloth.

When the wardrobe had been moved back into place, the door was indeed found to be locked, with the key on the inside of the door, but both preferred not to notice that.

'I'm sorry,' said Deidre, 'I was upset about our having no children. That, and my time of life.'

'All our times of life,' he said. 'And as to your having no children, if it's anyone's fault, it's God's.'

Together they eased the carpet out of the window and down onto the lawn, and patiently and peaceably unwrung it. But the marks of the wringing stayed, straying for ever across the bedroom floor, to remind them of the dangers of, for him, petulance, and for her, the tendency to blame others for her own shortcomings.

Presently the Ming vase was mended, not by Deidre but by experts. He sold it and they installed central heating and had a wall knocked out there, a window put in here, and the washer on the kitchen tap mended, and the dry rot removed so that the sink drawer smelled like any other, and the broken floorboard beneath the dresser replaced. The acoustics in the kitchen changed, so that Deidre could no longer hear David's services as she sat by the fire, so she attended church rather more often; and David, she soon noticed, dressed up as God rather less, and diverted his congregation's attention away from himself and more towards the altar.

Alopecia

It's 1972.

'Fiddlesticks,' says Maureen. Everyone else says 'crap' or 'balls', but Maureen's current gear, being Victorian sprigged muslin, demands an appropriate vocabulary. 'Fiddlesticks. If Erica says her bald patches are anything to do with Brian, she's lying. It's alopecia.'

'I wonder which would be worse,' murmurs Ruthie in her soft voice, 'to have a husband who tears your hair out in the night, or to have alopecia.'

Ruthie wears a black fringed satin dress exactly half a century old, through which, alas, Ruthie's ribs show even more prominently than her breasts. Ruthie's little girl Poppy (at four too old for playgroup, too young for school), wears a long, white (well, yellowish) cotton shift which contrasts nicely with her mother's dusty black.

'At least the husband might improve, with effort,' says Alison, 'unlike alopecia. You wake up one morning with a single bald patch and a month or so later there you are, completely bald. Nothing anyone can do about it.' Alison, plump mother of three, sensibly wears a flowered Laura Ashley dress which hides her bulges.

'It might be quite interesting,' remarks Maureen. 'The egg-head approach. One would have to forgo the past, of course, and go all space-age, which would hardly be in keeping with the mood of the times.'

'You are the mood of the times, Maureen,' murmurs Ruthie, as expected. Ruthie's simple adulation of Maureen is both gratifying and embarrassing, everyone agrees.

Everyone agrees, on the other hand, that Erica Bisham of the bald patches is a stupid, if ladylike, bitch.

Maureen, Ruthie and Alison are working in Maureen's premises off the Kings Road. Here Maureen, as befits the glamour of her station, the initiator of Mauromania, meets the media, expresses opinions, answers the phone, dictates to secretaries (male), selects and matches fabrics, approves designs and makes, in general, multitudinous decisions—although not, perhaps, as multitudinous as the ones she was accustomed to make in the middle and late sixties, when the world was young and rich and wild. Maureen is forty but you'd never think it. She wears a large hat by day (and, one imagines, night) which shades her anxious face and guards her still pretty complexion. Maureen leads a rich life. Maureen once had her pubic hair dyed green to match her fingernails—or so her husband Kim announced to a waiting (well, such were the days) world: she divorced him not long after, having lost his baby at five months. The head of the foetus, rumour had it, emerged green, and her National Health Service GP refused to treat her any more, and she had to go private after all—she with her Marxist convictions.

That was 1968. If the state's going to tumble, let it tumble. The sooner the better. Drop out, everyone! Mauromania magnifique! And off goes Maureen's husband Kim with Maureen's au pair—a broad-hipped, big-bosomed girl, good breeding material, with an ordinary coarse and curly brush, if somewhat reddish.

Still, it had been a good marriage as marriages go. And as marriages go, it went. Or so Maureen remarked to the press, on her way home (six beds, six baths, for recep., American kitchen, patio, South Ken) from the divorce courts. Maureen cried a little in the taxi, when she'd left her public well behind, partly from shock and grief, mostly from confusion that beloved Kim, Kim, who so despised the nuclear family, who had so often said that he and she ought to get divorced in order to have a true and unfettered relationship, that Maureen's Kim should have speeded up Maureen's divorce in order to marry Maureen's au pair girl before the baby arrived. Kim and Maureen had been married for fifteen years. Kim had been Kevin from Liverpool before seeing the light or at any rate the guru. Maureen had always been just Maureen from Hoxton, east London: remained so through the birth, rise and triumph of Mauromania. It was her charm. Local girl makes good.

Maureen has experience of life: she knows by now, having also been married to a psychiatrist who ran off with all her money and the marital home, that it is wise to watch what people do, not listen to what they say. Well, it's something to have learned. Ruthie and Alison, her (nominal) partners from the beginning, each her junior by some ten years, listen to Maureen with respect and diffidence.

'Mind you,' says Maureen now, matching up purple feathers with emerald satin to great effect, 'if I was Brian I'd certainly beat Erica to death. Fancy having to listen to that whining voice night after night. The only trouble is he's become too much of a gentleman. He'll never have the courage to do it. Turned his back on his origins, and all that. It doesn't do.'

Maureen has known Brian since the old days in Hoxton. They were evacuees together: shared the same bomb shelter on their return from Starvation Hall in Felixstowe—a boys' public school considered unsafe for the gentry's children but all right for the East Enders.

'It's all Erica's fantasy,' says Ruthie, knowledgeably. 'A kind of dreadful sexual fantasy. She *wants* him to beat her up so she trots round London saying he does. Poor Brian. It comes from marrying into the English upper classes, old style. She must be nearly fifty. She has that kind of battered-looking face.'

Her voice trails away. There is a slight pause in the conversation.

'Um,' says Alison.

'That's drink,' says Maureen, decisively. 'Poor bloody Brian. What a ball-breaker to have married.' Brian was Maureen's childhood sweetheart. What a romantic, platonic idyll! She nearly married him once, twice, three times. Once in the very early days, before Kim, before anyone, when Brian was selling books from a barrow in Hoxton market. Once again, after Kim and before the professor, by which time Brian was taking expensive photographs of the trendy and successful— only then Erica turned up in Brian's bed, long-legged, disdainful, beautiful, with a model's precise and organised face, and the fluty tones of the girl who'd bought her school uniform at Harrods, and that was the end of that. Not that Brian had ever exactly proposed to Maureen; not that they'd ever even been to bed together: they just knew each other and each other's bed partners so well that each knew what the other was thinking, feeling, hoping. Both from Hoxton, east London: Brian, Maureen; and a host of others, too. What was there, you might ask, about that particular acre of the East End which over a period of a few years gave birth to such a crop of remarkable children, such a flare-up of human creativity in terms of writing, painting, designing, entertaining? Changing the world? One might almost think God had chosen it for an experiment in intensive talent-breeding. Mauromania, God-sent.

And then there was another time in the late sixties, when there was a short break between Brian and Erica—Erica had a hysterectomy against Brian's wishes; but during those two weeks of opportunity Maureen, her business flourishing, her designs world famous, Mauromania a label for even trendy young queens (royal, that is) to boast, rich beyond counting—during those two special weeks of all weeks Maureen fell head over heels classically in love with Pedro: no, not a fisherman, but as good as—Italian, young, open-shirted, sloe-eyed, a designer. And Pedro, it later transpired, was using Maureen as a means to laying all the models, both male and female (Maureen had gone into menswear). Maureen was the last to know, and by the time she did Brian was in Erica's arms (or whatever) again. A sorry episode. Maureen spent six months at a health farm, on a diet of grapes and brown rice. At the end of that time Mauromania Man had collapsed, her business manager had jumped out of a tenth-floor window, and an employee's irate mother was bringing a criminal suit against Maureen personally for running a brothel. It was all quite irrational. If the employee, a runaway girl of, it turned out, only thirteen, but looking twenty, and an excellent seam-stress, had contracted gonorrhoea whilst in her employ, was that Maureen's fault? The judge, sensibly, decided it wasn't, and that the entire collapse of British respectability could not fairly be laid at Maureen's door. Legal costs came to more than £12,000: the country house and stables had to be sold at a knock-down price. That was disaster year.

And who was there during that time to hold Maureen's hand? No one. Everyone, it seemed, had troubles enough of their own. And all the time, Maureen's poor heart bled for Pedro, of the ridiculous name and the sloe eyes, long departed, laughing, streptococci surging in his wake. And of all the old friends and allies only Ruthie and Alison lingered on, two familiar faces in a sea of changing ones, getting young-er every day, and hungrier year by year not for fun, fashion, and excite-ment, but for money, promotion, security, and acknowledgment.

The staff even went on strike once, walking up and down outside the workshop with placards announcing hours and wages, backed by Maoists, women's liberationists and trade unionists, all vying for their trumpery allegiance, puffing up a tiny news story into a colossal media joke, not even bothering to get Maureen's side of the story—absenteeism, drug addiction, shoddy workmanship, falling markets, constricting profits.

But Ruthie gave birth to Poppy, unexpectedly, in the black and gold ladies' rest-room (customers only—just as well it wasn't in the staff toilets where the plaster was flaking and the old wall-cisterns came down on your head if you pulled the chain) and that cheered everyone up. Business perked up, staff calmed down as unemployment rose. Poppy, born of Mauromania, was everyone's favourite, everyone's mascot. Her father, only seventeen, was doing two years inside, framed by the police for dealing in pot. He did not have too bad a time—he got three A-levels and university entrance inside, which he would not have got outside, but it meant poor little Poppy had to do without a father's care and Ruthie had to cope on her own. Ruthie of the ribs.

Alison, meanwhile, somewhat apologetically, had married Hugo, a rather straight and respectable actor who believed in women's rights; they had three children and lived in a cosy house with a garden in Muswell Hill: Alison even belonged to the PTA! Hugo was frequently without work, but Hugo and Alison managed, between them, to keep going and even happy. Now Hugo thinks Alison should ask for a rise, but Alison doesn't like to. That's the trouble about working for a friend and being only a nominal partner.

'Don't let's talk about Erica Bisham any more,' says Maureen. 'It's too draggy a subject.' So they don't.

But one midnight a couple of weeks later, when Maureen, Ruthie and Alison are working late to meet an order—as is their frequent custom these days (and one most unnerving to Hugo, Alison's husband)—there comes a tap on the door. It's Erica, of course. Who else would tap, in such an ingratiating fashion? Others cry 'Hi!' or 'Peace!' and enter. Erica, smiling nervously and crookedly; her yellow hair eccentric in the extreme; bushy in places, sparse in others. Couldn't she wear a wig? She is wearing a Marks & Spencer nightie which not even Ruthie would think of wearing, in the house or out of it. It is blood-stained down the back. (Menstruation is not yet so fashionable as to be thus demonstrable, though it can be talked about at length.) A strong smell of what? alcohol, or is it nail-varnish? hangs about her. Drinking again. (Alison's husband, Hugo, in a long period of unemployment, once veered on to the edge of alcoholism but fortunately veered off again, and the smell of nail-varnish, acetone, gave a warning sign of an agitated, overworked liver, unable to cope with acetaldehyde, the highly toxic product of alcohol metabolism.)

'Could I sit down?' says Erica. 'He's locked me out. Am I speaking oddly? I think I've lost a tooth. I'm hurting under my ribs and I feel sick.'

They stare at her—this drunk, dishevelled, trouble-making woman.

'He,' says Maureen finally. 'Who's he?'

'Brian.'

'You're going to get into trouble, Erica,' says Ruthie, though more kindly than Maureen, 'if you go round saying dreadful things about poor Brian.'

'I wouldn't have come here if there was anywhere else,' says Erica.

'You must have friends,' observes Maureen, as if to say, Don't count us amongst them if you have.

'No.' Erica sounds desolate. 'He has his friends at work. I don't seem to have any.'

'I wonder why,' says Maureen under her breath; and then, 'I'll get you a taxi home, Erica. You're in no state to be out.'

'I'm not drunk, if that's what you think.'

'Who ever is,' sighs Ruthie, sewing relentlessly on. Four more blouses by one o'clock. Then, thank God, bed.

Little Poppy has passed out on a pile of orange ostrich feathers. She looks fantastic.

'If Brian does beat you up,' says Alison, who has seen her father beat her mother on many a Saturday night, 'why don't you go to the police?'

'I did once, and they told me to go home and behave myself.'

'Or leave him?' Alison's mother left Alison's father.

'Where would I go? How would I live? The children? I'm not well.' Erica sways. Alison puts a chair beneath her. Erica sits, legs planted wide apart, head down. A few drops of blood fall on the floor. From Erica's mouth, or elsewhere? Maureen doesn't see, doesn't care. Maureen's on the phone, calling radio cabs who do not reply.

'I try not to provoke him, but I never know what's going to set him off,' mumbles Erica. 'Tonight it was Tampax. He said only whores wore Tampax. He tore it out and kicked me. Look.'

Erica pulls up her nightie (Erica's wearing no knickers) and exposes her private parts in a most shameful, shameless fashion. The inner thighs are blue and mottled, but then, dear God, she's nearly fifty.

What does one look like, thigh-wise, nearing fifty? Maureen's the nearest to knowing, and she's not saying. As for Ruthie, she hopes she'll never get there. Fifty!

'The woman's mad,' mutters Maureen. 'Perhaps I'd better call the loony wagon, not a taxi?'

'Thank God Poppy's asleep.' Poor Ruthie seems in a state of shock.

'You can come home with me, Erica,' says Alison. 'God knows what Hugo will say. He hates matrimonial upsets. He says if you get in between, they both start hitting you.'

Erica gurgles, a kind of mirthless laugh. From behind her, mysteriously, a child steps out. She is eight, stocky, plain and pale, dressed in boring Ladybird pyjamas.

'Mummy?'

Erica's head whips up; the blood on Erica's lip is wiped away by the back of Erica's hand. Erica straightens her back. Erica smiles. Erica's voice is completely normal, ladylike.

'Hallo, darling. How did you get here?'

'I followed you. Daddy was too angry.'

'He'll be better soon, Libby,' says Erica brightly. 'He always is.'

'We're not going home? Please don't let's go home. I don't want to see Daddy.' .

'Bitch,' mutters Maureen, 'she's even turned his own child against him. Poor bloody Brian. There's nothing at all the matter with her. Look at her now.'

For Erica is on her feet, smoothing Libby's hair, murmuring, laughing.

'Poor bloody Erica,' observes Alison. It is the first time she has ever defied Maureen, let alone challenged her wisdom. And rising with as much dignity as her plump frame and flounced cotton will allow, Alison takes Erica and Libby home and instals them for the night in the spare room of the cosy house in Muswell Hill.

Hugo isn't any too pleased. 'Your smart sick friends,' he says. And, 'I'd beat a woman like that to death myself, any day.' And, 'Dragging that poor child into it: it's appalling.' He's nice to Libby, though, and rings up Brian to say she's safe and sound, and looks after her while Alison takes Erica round to the doctor. The doctor sends Erica round to the hospital, and the hospital admits her for tests and treatment.

'Why bother?' enquires Hugo. 'Everyone knows she's mad.'

In the evening, Brian comes all the way to Muswell Hill in his Ferrari to pick up Libby. He's an attractive man: intelligent and perspicacious, fatherly and gentle. Just right, it occurs to Alison, for Maureen.

'I'm so sorry about all this,' he says. 'I love my wife dearly but she has her problems. There's a dark side to her nature—you've no idea. A deep inner violence—which of course manifests itself in this kind of behaviour. She's deeply psychophrenic. I'm so afraid for the child.'

'The hospital did admit her,' murmurs Alison. 'And not to the psychiatric ward, but the surgical.'

'That will be her hysterectomy scar again,' says Brian. 'Any slight tussle—she goes quite wild, and I have to restrain her for her own safety—and it opens up. It's symptomatic of her inner sickness, I'm afraid. She even says herself it opens to let the build-up of wickedness out. What I can't forgive is the way she drags poor little Libby into things. She's turning the child against me. God knows what I'm going to do. Well, at least I can bury myself in work. I hear you're an actor, Hugo.'

Hugo offers Brian a drink, and Brian offers (well, more or less) Hugo a part in a new rock musical going on in the West End. Alison goes to visit Erica in hospital.

'Erica has some liver damage, but it's not irreversible: she'll be feeling nauseous for a couple of months, that's all. She's lost a back tooth and she's had a couple of stitches put in her vagina,' says Alison to Maureen and Ruthie next day. The blouse order never got completed—re-orders now look dubious. But if staff haven't the loyalty to work unpaid overtime any more, what else can be expected? The partners (nominal) can't do everything.

'Who said so?' enquires Maureen, sceptically. 'The hospital or Erica?'

'Well,' Alison is obliged to admit, 'Erica.'

'You are an innocent, Alison.' Maureen sounds quite cross. 'Erica can't open her poor sick mouth without uttering a lie. It's her hysterectomy scar opened up again, that's all. No wonder. She's a nymphomaniac: she doesn't leave Brian alone month in, month out. She has the soul of a whore. Poor man. He's so upset by it all. Who wouldn't be?'

Brian takes Maureen out to lunch. In the evening, Alison goes to visit Erica in hospital, but Erica has gone. Sister says, oh yes, her husband came to fetch her. They hadn't wanted to let her go so soon but Mr Bisham seemed such a sensible, loving man, they thought he could look after his wife perfectly well, and it's always nicer at home, isn't it? Was it *the* Brian Bisham? Yes she'd thought so. Poor Mrs Bisham—what a dreadful world we live in, when a respectable married woman can't even walk the streets without being brutally attacked, sexually assaulted by strangers.

It's 1974.

Winter. A chill wind blowing, a colder one still to come. A three-day week imposed by an insane government. Strikes, power-cuts, black-outs. Maureen, Ruthie and Alison work by candle-light. All three wear fun-furs—old stock, unsaleable. Poppy is staying with Ruthie's mother, as she usually is these days. Poppy has been developing a squint, and the doctor says she has to wear glasses with one blanked-out lens for at least eighteen months. Ruthie, honestly, can't bear to see her daughter thus. Ruthie's mother, of a prosaic nature, a lady who buys her clothes at C & A Outsize, doesn't seem to mind.

'If oil prices go up,' says Maureen gloomily, 'what's going to happen to the price of synthetics? What's going to happen to Mauromania, come to that?'

'Go up market,' says Alison, 'the rich are always with us.'

Maureen says nothing. Maureen is bad tempered, these days. She is having some kind of painful trouble with her teeth, which she seems less well able to cope with than she can the trouble with staff (over-paid), raw materials (unavailable), delivery dates (impossible), distribution (unchancy), costs (soaring), profits (falling), re-investment (non-existent). And the snow has ruined the penthouse roof and it has to be replaced, at the cost of many thousands. Men friends come and go: they seem to get younger and less feeling. Sometimes Maureen feels they treat her as a joke. They ask her about the sixties as if it were a different age: of Mauromania as if it were something as dead as the dodo—but it's still surely a label which counts for something, brings in foreign currency, ought really to bring her some recognition. The Beatles got the MBE; why not Maureen of Mauromania? Throw-away clothes for throw-away people?

'Ruthie,' says Maureen. 'You're getting careless. You've put the pocket on upside-down, and it's going for copying. That's going to hold up the whole batch. Oh, what the hell. Let it go through.'

'Do you ever hear anything of Erica Bisham?' Ruthie asks Alison, more to annoy Maureen than because she wants to know. 'Is she still wandering round in the middle of the night?'

'Hugo does a lot of work for Brian, these day,' says Alison carefully. 'But he never mentions Erica.'

'Poor Brian. What a fate. A wife with alopecia! I expect she's bald as a coot by now. As good a revenge as any, I dare say.'

'It was nothing to do with alopecia,' says Alison. 'Brian just tore out chunks of her hair, nightly.' Alison's own marriage isn't going so well. Hugo's got the lead in one of Brian's long runs in the West End. Show business consumes his thoughts and ambitions. The ingenue lead is in love with Hugo and says so, on TV quiz games and in the Sunday supplements. She's under age. Alison feels old, bored and boring.

'These days I'd believe anything,' says Ruthie. 'She must provoke him dreadfully.'

'I don't know what you've got against Brian, Alison,' says Maureen. 'Perhaps you just don't like men. In which case you're not much good in a fashion house. Ruthie, that's another pocket upside-down.'

'I feel sick,' says Ruthie. Ruthie's pregnant again. Ruthie's husband was out of prison and with her for exactly two weeks; then he flew off to Istanbul to smuggle marijuana back into the country. He was caught. Now he languishes in a Turkish jail. 'What's to become of us?'

'We must develop a sense of sisterhood,' says Alison, 'that's all.'

Alison's doorbell rings at three in the morning. It is election night, and Alison is watching the results on television. Hugo (presumably) is watching them somewhere else, with the ingenue lead—now above the age of consent, which spoils the pleasure somewhat. It is Erica and Libby. Erica's nose is broken. Libby, at ten, is now in charge. Both are in their night-clothes. Alison pays off the taxi-driver, who won't take a tip. 'What a world,' he says.

'I couldn't think where else to come,' says Libby. 'Where he wouldn't follow her. I wrote down this address last time I was here. I thought it might come in useful, sometime.'

It is the end of Alison's marriage, and the end of Alison's job. Hugo, whose future career largely depends on Brian's goodwill, says, you have Erica in the house or you have me. Alison says, I'll have Erica. 'Lesbian, dyke,' says Hugo, bitterly. 'Don't think you'll keep the children, you won't.'

Maureen says, 'That was the first and last time Brian ever hit her. He told me so. She lurched towards him on purpose. She *wanted* her nose broken; idiot Alison, don't you understand? Erica nags and provokes. She calls him dreadful, insulting, injuring things in public. She flays him with words. She says he's impotent: an artistic failure. I've heard her. Everyone has. When finally he lashes out, she's delighted. Her last husband beat hell out of her. She's a born victim.'

Alison takes Erica to a free solicitor, who—surprise, surprise—is efficient and who collects evidence and affidavits from doctors and hospitals all over London, has a restraining order issued against Brian, gets Libby and Erica back into the matrimonial home, and starts and completes divorce proceedings and gets handsome alimony. It all takes six months, at the end of which time Erica's face has altogether lost it battered look.

Alison turns up at work the morning after the alimony details are known and has the door shut in her face. Mauromania. The lettering is flaking. The door needs re-painting.

Hugo sells the house over Alison's head. By this time she and the children are living in a two-room flat.

Bad times.

'You're a very destructive person,' says Maureen to Alison in the letter officially terminating her appointment. 'Brian never did you any harm, and you've ruined his life, you've interfered in a marriage in a really wicked way. You've encouraged Brian's wife to break up his perfectly good marriage, and turned Brian's child against him, and not content with that you've crippled Brian financially. Erica would never have been so vindictive if she hadn't had you egging her on. It was you who made her go to law, and once things get into lawyers' hands they escalate, as who better than I should know? The law has nothing to do with natural justice, idiot Alison. Hugo is very concerned for you and thinks you should have mental treatment. As for me, I am really upset. I expected friendship and loyalty from you, Alison; I trained you and employed you, and saw you through good times and bad. I may say, too, that your notion of Mauromania becoming an exclusive fashion house, which I followed through for a time, was all but disastrous, and symptomatic of your general bad judgment. After all, this is the people's age, the sixties, the seventies, the eighties, right through to the new century. Brian is coming in with me in the new world Mauromania.'

Mauromania, meretricious!

A month or so later, Brian and Maureen are married. It's a terrific wedding, somewhat marred by the death of Ruthie—killed, with her new baby, in the Paris air crash, on her way home from Istanbul, where she'd been trying to get her young husband released from prison. She failed. But then, if she'd succeeded, he'd have been killed too, and he was too young to die. Little Poppy was at the memorial serivce, in a sensible trouser-suit from C & A, bought for her by Gran, without her glasses, both enormous eyes apparently now functioning well. She didn't remember Alison, who was standing next to her, crying softly. Soft beds of orange feathers, far away, another world.

Alison wasn't asked to the wedding, which any way clashed with the mass funeral of the air-crash victims. Just as well. What would she have worn?

It's 1975.

It's summer, long and hot. Alison walks past Mauromania. Alison has remarried. She is happy. She didn't know that such ordinary everyday kindness could exist and endure. Alison is wearing, like everyone else, jeans and a T-shirt. A new ordinariness, a common sense, a serio-cheerfulness infuses the times. Female breasts swing free, libertarian by day, erotic by night, costing nobody anything, or at most a little modesty. No profit there.

Mauromania is derelict, boarded up. A barrow outside is piled with old stock, sale-priced. Coloured tights, fun-furs, feathers, slinky dresses. Passers-by pick over the stuff, occasionally buy, mostly look, and giggle, and mourn, and remember.

Alison, watching, sees Maureen coming down the steps. Maureen is rather nastily dressed in a bright yellow silk shift. Maureen's hair seems strange, bushy in parts, sparse in others. Maureen has abandoned her hat. Maureen bends over the barrow, and Alison can see the bald patches on her scalp.

'Alopecia,' says Alison, out loud. Maureen looks up. Maureen's face seems somehow worn and battered, and old and haunted beyond its years. Maureen stares at Alison, recognising, and Maureen's face takes on an expression of half-apology, half-entreaty. Maureen wants to speak.

But Alison only smiles brightly and lightly and walks on.

'I'm afraid poor Maureen has alopecia, on top of everything else,' she says to anyone who happens to enquire after that sad, forgotten figure, who once had everything—except, perhaps, a sense of sisterhood.

Man with No Eyes

Edgar, Minette, Minnie and Mona.

In the evenings three of them sit down to play Monopoly. Edgar, Minette and Minnie. Mona, being only five sleeps upstairs, alone, in the little back bedroom, where roses, growing up over the porch and along under the thatch, thrust dark companionable heads through the open lattice window. Edgar and Minnie, father and daughter, face each other across the table. Both, he in his prime, she in early adolescence, are already bronzed from the holiday sun, blue eyes bright and eager in lean faces, dull red hair bleached to brightness by the best summer the Kent coast has seen, they say, since 1951 — a merciful God allowing, it seems, the glimmer of His smile to shine again on poor humiliated England. Minette, Edgar's wife, sits at the kitchen end of the table. The ladderback chair nearest the porch remains empty. Edgar says it is uncomfortable. Minnie keeps the bank. Minette doles out the property cards.

Thus, every evening this holiday, they have arranged themselves around the table, and taken up their allotted tasks. They do it almost wordlessly, for Edgar does not care for babble. Who does? Besides, Mona might wake, think she was missing something, and insist on joining in.

How like a happy family we are, thinks Minette, pleased, shaking the dice. Minette's own face is pink and shiny from the sun and her nose is peeling. Edgar thinks hats on a beach are affected (an affront, as it were, to nature's generosity) so Minette is content to pay the annual penalty summer holidays impose on her fair complexion and fine mousy hair.

Her mouth is swollen from the sun, and her red arms and legs are stiff and bumpy with midge bites. Mona is her mother's daughter and has inherited her difficulty with the sun, and even had a slight touch of sunstroke on the evening of the second day, which Edgar, probably rightly, put down to the fact that Minette had slapped Mona in the cheek, in the back of the car, on the journey down.

'Cheeks afire,' he said, observing his flushed and feverish child. 'You really shouldn't vent your neuroses on your children, Minette.'

And of course Minette shouldn't. Edgar was right. Poor little Mona. It was entirely forgivable for Mona, a child of five, to become fractious and unbiddable in the back of a car, cooped up as she was on a five-hour journey; and entirely unforgivable of the adult Minette, sitting next to her, to be feeling so cross, distraught, nervous and unmaternal that she reacted by slapping. Minette should have, could have diverted: could have sung, could have played Here is the Church, this Little Pig, something, anything, rather than slapped. Cheeks afire! As well they might be. Mona's with upset at her mother's cruel behaviour: Minette's, surely, with shame and sorrow.

Edgar felt the journey was better taken without stops, and that in any case no coffee available on a motorway was worth stopping for. It would be instant, not real. Why hadn't Minette brought a thermos, he enquired, when she ventured to suggest they stop. Because we don't *own* a thermos, she wanted to cry, in her impossible mood, because you say they're monstrously over-priced, because you say I always break the screw; in any case it's not the coffee I want, it's for you to stop, to recognise our existence, our needs—but she stopped herself in time. That way quarrels lie, and the rare quarrels of Edgar and Minette, breaking out, shatter the neighbourhood, not to mention the children. Well done, Minette.

'Just as well we didn't go to Italy,' said Edgar, on the night of Mona's fever, measuring out, to calm the mother-damaged, fevered cheek, the exact dosage of Junior Aspirin recommended on the back of the packet (and although Minette's doctor once instructed her to quadruple the stated dose, if she wanted it to be effective, Minette knows better than to say so), dissolving it in water, and feeding it to Mona by the spoonful though Minette knows Mona much prefers to suck them—'if this is what half an hour's English sun does to her.'

Edgar, Minette, Minnie and Mona. Off to Italy, camping, every year for the last six years, even when Mona was a baby. Milan, Venice, Florence, Pisa. Oh what pleasure, riches, glory, of countryside and town. This year, Minette had renewed the passports and replaced the sleeping bags, brought the Melamine plates and mugs up to quota, checked the Gaz cylinders, and waited for Edgar to reveal the date, usually towards the end of July, when he would put his ethnographical gallery in the hands of an assistant and they would pack themselves and the tent into the car, happy families, and set off, as if spontaneously, into the unknown; but this year the end of July went and the first week of August, and still Edgar did not speak, and Minette's employers were betraying a kind of incredulous restlessness at Minette's apparent lack of decision, and only then, on 6 August, after a studied absent-mindedness lasting from 31 July to 5 August, did Edgar say 'Of course we can't afford to go abroad. Business is rock-bottom. I hope you haven't been wasting any money on unnecessary equipment?'

'No, of course not,' says Minette. Minette tells many lies: it is one of the qualities which Edgar least likes in her. Minette thinks she is safe in this one. Edgar will not actually count the Melamine plates; nor is he likely to discern the difference between one old lumpy navy-blue sleeping bag and another unlumpy new one. 'We do have the money set aside,' she says cautiously, hopefully.

'Don't be absurd,' he says. 'We can't afford to drive the car round the corner, let alone to Venice. It'll only have sunk another couple of inches since last year, beneath the weight of crap as much as of tourists. It's too depressing. Everything's too depressing.' Oh Venice, goodbye Venice, city of wealth and abandon, and human weakness, glorious beneath sulphurous skies. Goodbye Venice, says Minette in her heart, I loved you well. "So we shan't be having a holiday this year? she enquires. Tears are smarting in her eyes. She doesn't believe him. She is tired, work has been exhausting. She is an advertising copywriter. He is teasing, surely. He often is. In the morning he will say something different.

'You go on holiday if you want,' he says in the morning. 'I can't. I can't afford a holiday this year. You seem to have lost all sense of reality, Minette. It's that ridiculous place you work in.' And of course he is right. Times are hard. Inflation makes profits and salaries seem ridiculous. Edgar, Minette, Minnie and Mona must adapt with the times. An advertising agency is not noted for the propagation of truth. Those who work in agencies live fantasy lives as to their importance in the scheme of things and their place in a society which in truth despises them. Minette is lucky that someone of his integrity and taste puts up with her. No holiday this year. She will pay the money set aside into a building society, though the annual interest is less than the annual inflation rate. She is resigned.

But the next day, Edgar comes home, having booked a holiday cottage in Kent. A miracle. Friends of his own it, and have had a cancellation. Purest chance. It is the kind of good fortune Edgar always has. If Edgar is one minute late for a train, the train leaves two minutes late.

Now, on the Friday, here they are, Edgar, Minette, Minnie and Mona, installed in this amazing rural paradise of a Kentish hamlet, stone-built, thatched cottage, swifts flying low across the triangular green, the heavy smell of farmyard mixing with the scent of the absurd roses round the door and the night-stocks in the cottage garden, tired and happy after a day on the beach, with the sun shining and the English Channel blue and gentle, washing upon smooth pebbles.

Mona sleeps, stirs. The night is hot and thundery, ominous. Inflation makes the Monopoly money not so fantastic as it used to be. Minette remarks on it to Edgar.

'Speak for yourself,' he says. Minette recently got a rise, promotion. Edgar is self-employed, of the newly impoverished classes.

They throw to see who goes first. Minette throws a two and three. Minnie, her father's daughter, throws a five and a six. Minnie is twelve, a kindly, graceful child, watchful of her mother, adoring her father, whom she resembles.

Edgar throws a double six. Edgar chooses his token—the iron—and goes first.

Edgar, Minette, Minnie and Mona.

Edgar always wins the toss. Edgar always chooses the iron. (He is as good at housekeeping and cooking as Minette, if not better.) Edgar always wins the game. Minnie always comes second. Minette always comes last. Mona always sleeps. Of such stuff are holidays made.

Monopoly, in truth, bores Minette. She plays for Minnie's sake, to be companionable, and for Edgar's, because it is expected. Edgar likes winning. Who doesn't?

Edgar throws a double, lands on Pentonville Road, and buys it for £60. Minette hands over the card; Minnie receives his money. Edgar throws again, lands on and buys Northumberland Avenue. Minnie throws, lands on Euston Road, next to her father, and buys it for £100. Minette lands on Income Tax, pays £200 into the bank and giggles, partly from nervousness, partly at the ridiculous nature of fate.

'You do certainly have a knack, Minette,' says Edgar, unsmiling. 'But I don't know if it's anything to laugh about.'

Minette stops smiling. The game continues in silence. Minette lands in jail. Upstairs Mona, restless, murmurs and mutters in her sleep. In the distance Minette can hear the crackle of thunder. The windows are open, and the curtains not drawn, in order that Edgar can feel close to the night and nature, and make the most of his holiday. The window squares of blank blackness, set into the white walls, as on some child's painting, frighten Minette. What's outside? Inside, it seems to her, their words echo. The rattle of the dice is loud, loaded with some kind of meaning she'd rather not think about. Is someone else listening, observing?

Mona cries out. Minette gets up. 'I'll go to her,' she says.

'She's perfectly all right,' says Edgar. 'Don't fuss.'

'She might be frightened,' says Minette.

'What of?' enquires Edgar dangerously. 'What is there to be frightened of?' He is irritated by Minette's many fears, especially on holiday, and made angry by the notion that there is anything threatening in nature. Loving silence and isolation himself, he is impatient with those city-dwellers who fear it. Minette and Mona, his feeling is, are city-dwellers by nature, whereas Edgar and Minnie have the souls, the patience, the maturity of the country-dweller, although obliged to live in the town.

'It's rather hot. She's in a strange place,' Minette persists. 'She's in a lovely place,' says Edgar, flatly. 'Of course, she may be having bad dreams.'

Mona is silent again, and Minette is relieved. If Mona is having bad dreams, it is of course Minette's fault, first for having slapped Mona on the cheek, and then, more basically, for having borne a child with such a town-dweller's nature that she suffers from sunburn and sunstroke.

'Mona by name,' says Minette, 'moaner by nature.'

'Takes after her mother,' says Edgar. 'Minette, you forgot to pay £50 last time you landed in jail, so you'll have to stay there until you throw a double.'

'Can't I pay this time round?'

'No you can't,' says Edgar.

They've lost the rule book. All losses in the house are Minette's responsibility, so it is only justice that Edgar's ruling as to the nature of the game shall be accepted. Minette stays in jail.

Mona by name, moaner by nature. It was Edgar named his children, not Minette. Childbirth upset her judgment, made her impossible, or so Edgar said, and she was willing to believe it, struggling to suckle her young under Edgar's alternately indifferent and chiding eye, sore from stitches, trying to decide on a name, and unable to make up her mind, for any name Minette liked, Edgar didn't. For convenience' sake, while searching for a compromise, she referred to her first-born as Mini—such a tiny, beautiful baby—and when Edgar came back unexpectedly with the birth certificate, there was the name Minnie and Minette gasped with horror, and all Edgar said was, 'But I thought that was what *you* wanted, it's what *you* called her, the State won't wait for ever for *you* to make up your mind; I had to spend all morning in that place and I ought to be in the gallery; I'm exhausted. Aren't you grateful for anything? You've got to get that baby to sleep right through the night somehow before I go mad.' Well, what could she say? Or do? Minnie she was. Minnie Mouse. But in a way it suited her, or at any rate she transcended it, a beautiful loving child, her father's darling, mother's too.

Minette uses Minnie as good Catholics use the saints—as an intercessionary power.

Minnie, see what your father wants for breakfast. Minnie, ask your father if we're going out today.

When Mona was born Minette felt stronger and happier. Edgar, for some reason, was easy and loving. (Minette lost her job: it had been difficult, looking after the six-year-old Minnie, being pregnant again by accident—well, forgetting her pill—still with the house, the shopping and the cleaning to do, and working at the same time: not to mention the washing. They had no washing machine, Edgar feeling, no doubt rightly, that domestic machinery was noisy, expensive, and not really, in the end, labour saving. Something had to give, and it was Minette's work that did, just in time to save her sanity. The gallery was doing well, and of course Minette's earnings had been increasing Edgar's tax. Or so he believed. She tried to explain that they were taxed separately, but he did not seem to hear, let alone believe.) In any case, sitting up in childbed with her hand in Edgar's, happy for once, relaxed, unemployed—he was quite right, the work did overstrain her, and what was the point—such meaningless, anti-social work amongst such facile, trendy non-people—joking about the new baby's name, she said, listen to her moaning. Perhaps we'd better call her Moaner. Moaner by name,

Moaner by nature. Imprudent Minette. And a week later, there he was, with the birth certificate all made out. Mona.

'Good God, woman,' he cried. 'Are you mad? *You* said you wanted Mona. I took *you* at your word. I was doing what *you* wanted.'

'I didn't say that.' She was crying, weak from childbirth, turmoil, the sudden withdrawal of his kindness, his patience.

'Do you want me to produce witnesses?' He was exasperated. She became pregnant again, a year later. She had an abortion. She couldn't cope, Edgar implied that she couldn't, although he never quite said so, so that the burden of the decision was hers and hers alone. But he was right, of course. She couldn't cope. She arranged everything, went to the nursing home by mini-cab, by herself, and came out by mini-cab the next day. Edgar paid half.

Edgar, Minette, Minnie and Mona. Quite enough to be getting on with.

Minette started going to a psychotherapist once a week. Edgar said she had to; she was impossible without. She burned the dinner once or twice—'how hostile you are,' said Edgar, and after that cooked all meals himself, without reference to anyone's tastes, habits, or convenience. Still, he did know best. Minette, Minnie and Mona adapted themselves splendidly. He was an admirable cook, once you got used to garlic with everything, from eggs to fish.

Presently, Minette went back to work. Well, Edgar could hardly be expected to pay for the psychotherapist, and in any case, electricity and gas bills having doubled even in a household almost without domestic appliances, there was no doubt her earnings came in useful. Presently, Minette was paying all the household bills—and had a promotion. She became a group head with twenty people beneath her. She dealt with clients, executives, creative people, secretaries, assistants, with ease and confidence. Compared to Edgar and home, anyone, anything was easy. But that was only to be expected. Edgar was real life. Advertising agencies—and Edgar was right about this—are make-believe. Shut your eyes, snap your fingers, and presto, there one is, large as life. (That is, if you have the right, superficial, rubbishy attitude to make it happen.) And of course, its employees and contacts can be easily manipulated and modified, as dolls can be, in a doll's house. Edgar was not surprised at Minette's success. It was only to be expected. And she never remembered to turn off the lights, and turned up the central heating much too high, being irritatingly sensitive to cold.

Even tonight, this hot sultry night, with the temperature still lingering in the eighties and lightning crackling round the edges of the sky, she shivers.

'You can't be cold,' he enquires. He is buying a property from Minnie. He owns both Get Out of Jail cards, and has had a bank error in his favour of £200. Minnie is doing nicely, on equal bargaining terms with her father. Minette's in jail again.

'It's just so dark out there,' she murmurs.

'Of course, it is,' he said. 'It's the country. You miss the town, don't you?' It is an accusation, not a statement.

The cottage is on a hillside: marsh above and below, interrupting the natural path from the summit to the valley. The windows are open front and back as if to offer least interruption, throwing the house and its inhabitants open to the path of whatever forces flow from the top to the bottom of hills. Or so Minette suspects. How can she say so? She, the town-dweller, the obfuscate, standing between Edgar and the light of his expectations, his sensitivity to the natural life-forces which flow between the earth and him.

Edgar has green fingers, no doubt about it. See his tomatoes in the window-box of his Museum Street gallery? What a triumph!

'Couldn't we have the windows closed?' she asks.

'What for?' he enquires. 'Do *you* want the windows closed, Minnie?'

Minnie shrugs, too intent on missing her father's hotel on Northumberland Avenue to care one way or the other. Minnie has a fierce competitive spirit. Edgar, denying his own, marvels at it.

'Why do you want to shut out the night?' Edgar demands.

'I don't,' Minette protests. But she does. Yes, she does. Mona stirs and whimpers upstairs: Minette wants to go to her, close her windows, stop the dark rose heads nodding, whispering distress, but how can she? It is Minette's turn to throw the dice. Her hand trembles. Another five. Chance. You win £10, second prize in beauty contest.

'Not with your nose in that condition,' says Edgar, and laughs. Minnie and Minette laugh as well. 'And your cheeks the colour of poor Mona's. Still, one is happy to know there is a natural justice.'

A crack of thunder splits the air; one second, two seconds, three seconds—and there's the lightning, double-forked, streaking down to the oak-blurred ridge of hills in front of the house.

'I love storms,' says Edgar. 'It's coming this way.'

'I'll just go and shut Mona's window,' says Minette.

'She's perfectly all right,' says Edgar. 'Stop fussing and for God's sake stay out of jail. You're casting a gloom, Minette. There's no fun in playing if one's the only one with hotels.' As of course Edgar is, though Minnie's scattering houses up and down the board.

Minette lands on Community. A £20 speeding fine or take a Chance. She takes a Chance. Pay £150 in school fees.

The air remains dry and still. Thunder and lightning, though monstrously active, remain at their distance, the other side of the hills. The front door creaks silently open, of its own volition. Not a whisper of wind—only the baked parched air.

'Ooh,' squeaks Minnie, agreeably frightened.

Minette is dry-mouthed with terror, staring at the black beyond the door.

'A visitor,' cries Edgar. 'Come in, come in,' and he mimes a welcome to the invisible guest, getting to his feet, hospitably pulling back the empty ladderback chair at the end of the table. The house is open, after all, to whoever, whatever, chooses to call, on the way from the top of the hill to the bottom.

Minette's mouth is open: her eyes appalled. Edgar sees, scorns, sneers.

'Don't, Daddy,' says Minnie. 'It's spooky,' but Edgar is not to be stopped.

'Come in,' he repeats. 'Make yourself at home. Don't stumble like that. Just because you've got no eyes.'

Minette is on her feet. Monopoly money, taken up by the first sudden gust of storm wind, flies about the room. Minnie pursues it, half-laughing, half-panicking.

Minette tugs her husband's inflexible arm.

'Stop,' she beseeches. 'Don't tease. Don't.' No eyes! Oh, Edgar, Minette, Minnie and Mona, what blindness is there amongst you now? What threat to your existence? An immense peal of thunder crackles, it seems, directly overhead: lightning, both sheet and fork, dims the electric light and achieves a strobe-lighting effect of cosmic vulgarity, blinding and bouncing round the white walls, and now, upon the wind, rain, large-dropped, blows in through open doors and windows.

'Shut them,' shrieks Minette. 'I told you. Quickly! Minnie, come and help—'

'Don't fuss. What does it matter? A little rain. Surely you're not frightened of storms?' enquires Edgar, standing just where he is, not moving, not helping, like some great tree standing up to a torrent. For once Minette ignores him and with Minnie gets door and windows shut. The rain changes its nature, becomes drenching and blinding; their faces and clothes are wet with it. Minnie runs up to Mona's room, to make that waterproof. Still Edgar stands, smiling, staring out of the window at the amazing splitting sky. Only then, as he smiles, does Minette realise what she has done. She has shut the thing, the person with no eyes, in with her family. Even if it wants to go, would of its own accord drift down on its way towards the valley, it can't.

Minette runs to open the back door, Edgar follows, slow and curious.

'Why do you open the back door,' he enquires, 'having insisted on shutting everything else? You're very strange, Minette.'

Wet, darkness, noise, fear make her brave.

'You're the one who's strange. A man with no eyes!' she declares, sharp and brisk as she sometimes is at her office, chiding inefficiency, achieving sense and justice. 'Fancy asking in a man with no eyes. What sort of countryman would do a thing like that? You know nothing about anything, people, country, nature. Nothing.'

I know more than he does, she thinks, in this mad excess of arrogance. I may work in an advertising agency. I may prefer central heating to carrying coals, and a frozen pizza to a fresh mackerel, but I grant the world its dignity. I am aware of what I don't know, what I don't understand, and that's more than you can do. My body moves with the tides, bleeds with the moon, burns in the sun: I, Minette, I am a poor passing fragment of humanity: I obey laws I only dimly understand, but I am aware that the penalty of defying them is at best disaster, at worst death.

Thing with no eyes. Yes. The Taniwha. The Taniwha will get you if you don't look out! The sightless blundering monster of the bush, catching little children who stumble into him, devouring brains, bones, eyes and all. On that wild Australasian shore which my husband does not recognise as country, being composed of sand, shore and palmy forest, rather than of patchworked fields and thatch, lurked a blind and eyeless thing, that's where the Taniwha lives. The Taniwha will get you if you don't watch out! Little Minette, Mona's age, shrieked it at her infant enemies, on her father's instructions. That'll frighten them, he said, full of admonition and care, as ever. They'll stop teasing, leave you alone. Minette's father, tall as a tree, legs like poles. Little Minette's arms clasped round them to the end, wrenched finally apart, to set him free to abandon her, leave her to the Taniwha. The Taniwha will get you if you don't watch out. Wish it on others, what happens to you? Serve you right, with knobs on.

'You know nothing about anything,' she repeats now. 'What country person, after dark, sits with the windows open and invites in invisible strangers? Especially blindness.'

Well, Edgar is angry. Of course he is. He stares at her bleakly. Then Edgar steps out of the back door into the rain, now fitful rather than torrential, and flings himself upon his back on the grass, face turned to the tumultuous heavens, arms outspread, drinking in noise, rain, wind, nature, at one with the convulsing universe.

Minnie joins her mother at the door.

'What's he doing?' she asks, nervous.

'Being at one with nature,' observes Minette, cool and casual for Minnie's benefit. 'He'll get very wet, I'm afraid.'

Rain turns to hail, spattering against the house like machine-gun bullets. Edgar dives for the safety of the house, stands in the kitchen drying his hair with the dish towel, silent, angrier than ever.

'Can't we go on with Monopoly?' beseeches Minnie from the doorway. 'Can't we, Mum? The money's only got a little damp. I've got it all back.'

'Not until your father puts that chair back as it was.'

'What chair, Minette?' enquires Edgar, so extremely annoyed with his wife that he is actually talking to her direct. The rest of the holiday is lost, she knows it.

'The ladderback chair. You asked in something from the night to sit on it,' cries Minette, over the noise of nature, hung now for a sheep as well as a lamb, 'now put it back where it was.'

Telling Edgar what to do? Impudence.

'You are mad,' he says seriously. 'Why am I doomed to marry mad women?' Edgar's first wife Hetty went into a mental home after a year of marriage and never reemerged. She was a very trying woman, according to Edgar.

Mad? What's mad in a mad world? Madder than the dice, sending Minette to jail, back and back again, sending Edgar racing round the board, collecting money, property, power: placing Minnie in between the two of them, but always nearer her father than her mother? Minnie, hot on Edgar's heels, learning habits to last a lifetime?

All the same, oddly, Edgar goes to the ladderback chair, left pulled back for its unseen guest, and puts it in its original position, square against the table.

'Stop being so spooky,' cries Minnie, 'both of you.'

Minette wants to say 'and now tell it to go away—' but her mouth won't say the words. It would make it too much there. Acknowledgment is dangerous; it gives body to the insubstantial.

Edgar turns to Minette. Edgar smiles, as a sane person, humouring, smiles at an insane one. And he takes Minette's raincoat from the peg, wet as he already is, and races off through the wind to see if the car windows have been properly closed.

Minette is proud of her Bonnie Cashin raincoat. It cost one hundred and twenty pounds, though she told Edgar it was fifteen pounds fifty, reduced from twenty-three pounds. It has never actually been in the rain before and she fears for its safety. She can't ask Edgar not to wear it. He would look at her in blank unfriendliness and say 'But I thought it was a raincoat. You described it as a raincoat. If it's a raincoat why can't you use it in the rain? Or were you lying to me? It isn't a raincoat after all?'

Honestly, she'd rather the coat shrunk than go through all that. Silly garment to have bought in the first place: Edgar was quite right. Well, would have been had he known. Minette sometimes wonders why she tells so many lies. Her head is dizzy.

The chair at the top of the table seems empty. The man with no eyes is out of the house: Edgar, coat over head, can be seen through the rain haze, stumbling past the front hedge towards the car. Will lightning strike him? Will he fall dead? No.

If the car windows are open, whose fault? Hers, Minnie's?

'I wish you'd see that Mona shut the car door after her.' Her fault, as Mona's mother. 'And why haven't you woken her? This is a wonderful storm.'

And up he goes to be a better mother to Mona than Minette will ever be, waking his reluctant, sleep-heavy younger daughter to watch the storm, taking her on his knee, explaining the nature and function of electrical discharge the while: now ignoring Minette's presence entirely. When annoyed with her, which is much of the time, for so many of Minette's attitudes and pretensions irritate Edgar deeply, he chooses to pretend she doesn't exist.

Edgar, Minette, Minnie and Mona, united, watching a storm from a holiday cottage. Happy families.

The storm passes: soon it is like gunfire, flashing and banging on the other side of the hills. The lights go out. A power-line down, somewhere. No one shrieks, not even Mona: it merely, suddenly, becomes dark. But oh how dark the country is.

'Well,' says Edgar presently, 'where are the matches? Candles?'

Where, indeed. Minette gropes, useless, trembling, up and down her silent haunted home. How foolish of Minette, knowing there was a storm coming, knowing (surely!) that country storms meant country power cuts, not to have located them earlier. Edgar finds them; he knew where they were all the time.

They go to bed. Edgar and Minette pass on the stairs. He is silent. He is not talking to her. She talks to him.

'Well,' she says, 'you're lucky. All he did was make the lights go out. The man with no eyes.'

He does not bother to reply. What can be said to a mad woman that's in any way meaningful?

All night Edgar sleeps on the far edge of the double bed, away from her, forbidding even in his sleep. So away from her, he will sleep for the next four or even five days. Minette lies awake for an hour or so, and finally drifts off into a stunned and unrefreshing sleep.

In the morning she is brisk and smiling for the sake of the children, her voice fluty with false cheer, like some Kensington lady in Harrods Food Hall. Sweeping the floor, before breakfast, she avoids the end of the table, and the ladderback chair. The man with no eyes has gone, but something lingers.

Edgar makes breakfast. He is formal with her in front of the children, silent when they are on their own, deaf to Minette's pleasantries. Presently she falls silent too. He adorns a plate of scrambled eggs with buttercups and adjures the children to eat them. Minette has some vague recollection of reading that buttercups are poisonous: she murmurs something of the sort and Edgar winces, visibly. She says no more.

No harm comes to the children, of course. She must have misremembered. Edgar plans omelette, a buttercup salad and nettle soup for lunch. That will be fun, he says. Live off the land, like we're all going to have to, soon.

Minette and Mona giggle and laugh and shriek, clutching nettles. If you squeeze they don't sting. Minette, giggling and laughing to keep her children company, has a pain in her heart. They love their father. He loves them.

After lunch—omelette with lovely rich fresh farm eggs, though actually the white falls flat and limp in the bowl and Minette knows they are at least ten days old, but also knows better than to say so, buttercup salad, and stewed nettles, much like spinach—Edgar tells the children that the afternoon is to be spent at an iron age settlement, on Cumber Hill. Mona weeps a little, fearing a hilltop alive with iron men, but Minnie explains there will be nothing there—just a few lumps and bumps in the springy turf, burial mounds and old excavations, and a view all round, and perhaps a flint or two to be found.

'Then why are we going?' asks Mona, but no one answers. 'Will there be walking? Will there be cows? I've got a blister.'

'Mona by name, moaner by nature,' remarks Edgar. But which comes first, Minette wonders. Absently, she gives Minnie and Mona packet biscuits. Edgar protests. Artificial sugar, manufactured crap, ruining teeth, digestion, morale. What kind of mother is she?

'But they're hungry,' she wants to say and doesn't, knowing the reply by heart. How can they be? They've just had lunch.

In the car first Mona is sick, then Minnie. They are both easily sick, and neatly, out of the car window. Edgar does not stop. He says, 'You shouldn't have given them those biscuits. I knew this would happen,' but he does slow down.

Edgar, Minette, Minnie and Mona. Biscuits, buttercups and boiled nettles. Something's got to give.

Cumber Hill, skirted by car, is wild and lovely: a smooth turfed hilltop wet from last night's rain, a natural fort, the ground sloping sharply away from the broad summit, where sheep now graze, humped with burial mounds. Here families lived, died, grieved, were happy, fought off invaders, perished: left something of themselves behind, numinous beneath a heavy sky.

Edgar parks the car a quarter of a mile from the footpath which leads through stony farmland to the hill itself, and the tracks which skirt the fortifications. It will be a long walk. Minnie declines to come with them, as is her privilege as her father's daughter. She will sit in the car and wait and listen to the radio. A nature programme about the habits of buzzards, she assures her father.

'We'll be gone a couple of hours,' warns Minette.

'That long? It's only a hill.'

'There'll be lots of interesting things. Flints, perhaps. Even fossils. Are you sure?'

Minnie nods, her eyes blank with some inner determination.

'If she doesn't want to come, Minette,' says Edgar, 'she doesn't. It's her loss.'

It is the first direct remark Edgar has made to Minette all day. Minette is pleased, smiles, lays her hand on his arm. Edgar ignores her gesture. Did she really think his displeasure would so quickly evaporate? Her lack of perception will merely add to its duration.

Their walking sticks lie in the back of the car—Minette's a gnarled fruit-tree bough, Edgar's a traditional blackthorn (antique, with a carved dog's head for a handle, bought for him by Minette on the occasion of his forty-second birthday, and costing too much, he said by five pounds, being twenty pounds) and Minnie's and Mona's being stout but mongrel lengths of branch from some unnamed and undistinguished tree. Edgar hands Mona her stick, takes up his own and sets off. Minette picks up hers and follows behind. So much for disgrace.

Edgar is brilliant against the muted colours of the hill—a tall, long-legged rust-heaped shape, striding in orange holiday trousers and red shirt, leaping from hillock to hillock, rock to rock, black stick slashing against nettle and thistle and gorse. Mona, trotting along beside him, stumpy-legged, navy-anoraked, is a stocky, valiant, enthusiastic little creature, perpetually falling over her stick but declining to relinquish it.

Mona presently falls behind and walks with her mother, whom she finds more sympathetic than her father as to nettle-sting and cow-pats. Her hand is dry and firm in Minette's. Minette takes comfort from it. Soon Edgar, relieved of Mona's presence, is so far ahead as to be a dark shape occasionally bobbing into sight over a mound or out from behind a wall or tree.

'I don't see any iron men,' says Mona. 'Only nettles and sheep mess. And cow splats, where I'm walking. Only I don't see any cows either. I expect they're invisible.'

'All the iron men died long ago.'

'Then why have we come here?'

'To think about things.'

'What things?'

'The past, the present, the future,' replied Minette.

The wind gets up, blowing damply in their faces. The sun goes in; the hills lose what colour they had. All is grey, the colour of depression. Winter is coming, thinks Minette. Another season, gone. Clouds, descending, drift across the hills, lie in front of them in misty swathes. Minette can see neither back nor forward. She is frightened: Edgar is nowhere to be seen.

'There might be savage cows in there,' says Mona, 'where we can't see.'

'Wait,' she says to Mona, 'wait,' and means to run ahead to find Edgar and bring him back; but Edgar appears again as if at her will, within earshot, off on a parallel path to theirs, which will take him on yet another circumnavigation of the lower-lying fortifications.

'I'll take Mona back to the car,' she calls. He looks astonished.

'Why?'

He does not wait for her answer: he scrambles over a hillock and disappears.

'Because,' she wants to call after him, 'because I am forty, alone and frightened. Because my period started yesterday, and I have a pain. Because my elder child sits alone in a car in mist and rain, and my younger one stands grizzling on a misty hilltop, shivering with fright, afraid of invisible things, and cold. Because if I stay a minute longer I will lose my way and wander here for ever. Because battles were fought on this hilltop, families who were happy died and something remains behind, by comparison with which the Taniwha, sightless monster of the far-off jungle, those white and distant shores, is a model of good-will.'

Minette says nothing: in any case he has gone.

'Let's get back to the car,' she says to Mona.

'Where is it?' enquires Mona, pertinently.

'We'll find it.'

'Isn't Daddy coming?'

'He'll be coming later.'

Something of Minette's urgency communicates itself to Mona: or some increasing fear of the place itself. Mona leads the way back, without faltering, without complaint, between nettles, over rocks, skirting the barbed-wire fence, keeping a safe distance from the cows, at last made flesh, penned up on the other side of the fence.

The past. Minette at Mona's age, leading her weeping mother along a deserted beach to their deserted cottage. Minette's father, prime deserter. Man with no eyes for Minette's distress, her mother's despair. Little Minette with her arms clutched rigidly round her father's legs, finally disentangled by determined adult arms. Whose? She does not know. Her father walking off with someone else, away from the wailing Minette, his daughter, away from the weeping mother, his wife. Later, it was found that one of Minette's fingers was broken. He never came back. Sunday outings, thereafter, just the two of them, Minette and mother, valiantly striving for companionable pleasure, but what use is a three-legged stool with two legs? That's what they were.

The present? Mist, clouds, in front, behind; the wind blowing her misery back in her teeth. Minette and Mona stumble, hold each other up. The clouds part. There's the road: there's the car. Only a few hundred yards. There is Minnie, red hair gleaming, half-asleep, safe.

'England home and safety!' cries Minette, ridiculous, and with this return to normality, however baffling, Mona sits down on the ground and refuses to go another step, and has to be entreated, cajoled and bluffed back to the car.

'Where's Daddy?' complains Minnie. It is her children's frequent cry. That and 'Are you all right, Mummy?'

'We got tired and came back,' says Minette.

'I suppose he'll be a long time. He always is.'

Minette looks at her watch. Half-past four. They've been away an hour and a half.

'I should say six o'clock.' Edgar's walks usually last for three hours. Better resign herself to this, than to exist in uneasy expectation.

'What will we do?'

'Listen to the radio. Read. Think. Talk. Wait. It's very nice up here. There's a view.'

'I've been looking at it for three hours,' says Minnie, resigned. 'Oh well.'

'But I'm hungry,' says Mona. 'Can I have an iced lolly?'

'Idiot,' says Minnie to her sister. 'Idiot child.'

There is nothing in sight except the empty road, hills, mist. Minette can't drive. Edgar thinks she would be a danger to herself and others if she learned. If there was a village within walking distance she would take the chidren off for tea, but there is nothing. She and Minnie consult the maps and discover this sad fact. Mona, fortunately, discovers an ant's nest. Minnie and Minette play I-Spy. Minette, busy, chirpy, stands four square between her children and desolation.

Five o'clock. Edgar reappears, emerging brilliantly out of the mist, from an unexpected direction, smiling satisfaction.

'Wonderful,' he says. 'I can't think why you went back, Minette.'

'Mummy was afraid of the cows,' says Mona.

'Your mother is afraid of everything,' says Edgar. 'I'm afraid she and nature don't get along together.'

They pile back into the car and off they go. Edgar starts to sing, 'One man went to mow.' They all join in. Happy families. A cup of tea, thinks Minette. How I would love a cup of immoral tea, a plate of fattening sandwiches, another of ridiculous iced cakes, in one of the beamed and cosy tea-shops in which the Kentish villages abound. How long since Minette had a cup of tea? How many years? Edgar does not like tea—does not approve of eating between meals. Tea is a drug, he says: it is the rot of the English: it is a laughable substance, a false stimulant, of no nutritive value whatsoever, lining the stomach with tannin. Tea! Minette, do you want a cup of tea? Of course not. Edgar is right. Minette's mother died of stomach cancer, after a million comforting cups. Perhaps they did instead of sex? The singing stops. In the back of the car, Minette keeps silent; presently cries silently, when Mona, exhausted, falls asleep. Last night was disturbed.

The future? Like the past, like the present. Little girls who lose their father cry all their lives. Hard to blame Edgar for her tears: no doubt she makes Edgar the cause of them. He says so often enough. Mona and Minette shall not lose their father, she is determined on it. Minette will cry now and for ever, so that Minnie and Mona can grow up to laugh— though no doubt their laughter, as they look back, will be tinged with pity, at best, and derision, at worst, for a mother who lives as theirs did. Minnie and Mona, saved from understanding.

I am of the lost generation, thinks Minette, one of millions. Interleaving, blotting up the miseries of the past, to leave the future untroubled. I would be happier dead, but being alive, of necessity, might as well make myself useful. She sings softly to the sleeping Mona, chats brightly to Minnie.

Edgar, Minette, Minnie and Mona. Nothing gives.

That night, when Mona is in bed, and Minnie has set up the Monopoly board, Edgar moves as of instinct into the ladderback chair, and Minette plays Monopoly, Happy Families, with the Man with no Eyes.

Holy Stones

He flew El Al, as befitted a guest of Israel. He would have flown first class, as he imagined befitted his age and his station in life—he was forty-one and a successful journalist—but flying El Al made that impossible.

The fact disappointed Adam but did not surprise him. That was the way, by and large, the cookie crumbled. Life, which gave with one hand, took away with the other. There was always something to mar perfection—a wart on a face, a flaw in a character, an uneasy grating, if not in a voice then in what that voice said.

'It seems there's not first class on El Al,' he apologised to Elsie, his new young wife. 'Israel has more important things to do than provide luxuries for the likes of us.'

'I don't mind,' said Elsie, happily. 'It just means we can sit closer together.'

And they squashed in beside each other and sat, knees touching, his and hers both in jeans. Elsie was twenty-three.

Adam's first wife Elaine, mother of his three children, had long ago sunk into obsession and misery, and now they were divorced, leaving Adam with a sense of tragedy behind him, and solicitors' letters and bills still falling through the letter box. But the past was now finally redeemable—its events had, after all, led him to Elsie and happiness.

The plump girl in the seat in front of Adam stuck her little black high-heeled shoes out into the aisle. Her legs were bare, except for a thin gold chain around her right ankle.

Elsie giggled at it and nudged Adam. 'Does that mean she's a prostitute? I never know.' Elsie had a double first in classics. No one would ever know that, either; at any rate not on first acquaintance. Elsie had large pale luminous eyes in a sweet, pale face, and pale silky hair, and a slight, slender body and long drooping fingers and a tender crotch. Adam loved to watch the shock on the faces of his friends as the girl they took to be Adam's latest lay turned out to be as bright as she was pretty, as aristocratic by birth as she was egalitarian in speech and manner, and as prepared to marry Adam as he was prepared to marry her.

Someone had told him, half joking, half serious, when he was alone and miserable and looking for love, after his divorce and before Elsie, that he was in fact too old to fall in love: that he would do better to draw up a check list of desirable attributes in a wife, and check off the girls he knew, and propose to the one who did best. No sooner had the check list been devised than he fell in love. Elsie would have come top, anyway.

The anklet girl in the seat in front was the kind Adam had loved to sleep with in the days when he searched for true love. White-skinned, small, plump, tottering about on absurd heels—needing only a little dinner, a little push, and down they'd fall, on their backs upon his bed, awed by his station in life, the evidence of his column in the Sunday papers, their remembrance of his face smiling down from his advertising posters: their parts, in general, sweetly moistened by his position in the world as much as by his expert fingers. He accepted it. They didn't matter. In the morning, or even with any luck sooner, he'd say goodbye and mean it. Then the office. Then lunch with some girl he took seriously, whom he liked and respected and admired, and hoped to love; but somehow alas never did; and worse, felt too self-conscious, too judged, to take to bed without the presence of such grace. It seemed he was doomed to the half-sorry, half-exciting rites of lust.

But now Adam and Elsie. He had true love. And that was the end of philandering, of bachelor pad, of the calling of taxis at 2 A.M., of the hairpins and pants and scents that collected under his divan: of female tears alternating with female toughness, of the occasional parting with money—though mostly the pick-ups did it for love; a transitory love, of course, evaporating at the door, though deceptive enough at the time, for Adam had the talent of plucking out of the very air, or so it seemed, a sexual vigour which turned his soft lips hard and bruising, and blanked and slowed his usually bright and flickering eyes—as if he were the particular focusing point of some cosmic energy, predatory and fecundating, asserting its male right over the female. Girls who had been with Adam, however defended by pills and coils, worried lest they'd been made pregnant.

The anklet girl turned and caught Adam's eye. She had dark frizzy hair and a receding chin and slightly buck teeth, but her skin was white and her eyes large and beautiful beneath arched over-plucked brows. He wondered what she was doing and where she was going. There was a Christian tour on board, bound for Jerusalem, but the girls who belonged to that had the dull skin and dead eyes of the un-sexed. She could not be with them. He imagined she was Jewish.

What did the anklet mean? That she was someone else's property? That she was symbolically tethered? He did not know, any more than did Elsie. All he knew and cared, or so he told himself, was that now he had Elsie, whom he desired, admired, respected and loved, and needed no one else. He returned the anklet girl's smile, but coldly.

Adam pointed out to Elsie the armed security guard, posing as an ordinary passenger: a young man rather too strong and handsome for the shabby businessman's suit he wore. 'There's one or two on every El Al flight,' he told her. 'In case of hijacks.'

Elsie was impressed, frightened and reassured all at once. She grew pink and pale and pink again. She changed colour easily; he could read her feelings on her face. She was transparent to him. It made him happy, and safe from the fear, always with him, of being the object of mockery.

When the plane's engines roared, Elsie clutched Adam. She was frightened of flying. As it rose from the ground her hand left his arm and moved up to finger the little crucifix that hung from a thin gold chain round her neck. She had had it hidden beneath her T-shirt. Adam's happiness evaporated, and with it the feeling of safety, to be replaced by a sense of desolation, which he half understood and half did not, and the prescience of the end of love. 'I wish you wouldn't wear that,' he said, when the seat belt light went off.

'It's only for good luck,' she said, and he bit back the retort that such a statement proved, if proof was necessary, the confusion in her mind between superstition and spirituality. Adam had a dislike of religions, both political and spiritual: he saw how faith in the irrational, how belief in the hero, had through the centuries led the self-righteous to murder, massacre and grief. 'It's not all that important,' said Elsie, raising her arms and with them her small, delicate breasts, and unfastening the chain. She stuffed the bauble into the pocket of her jeans. He felt happier again.

He hoped very much that Israel would teach Elsie a lesson or two as to the dangers of irrational belief. Adam's check list, finally drawn up with the help of Mrs Bramble—a painter of note and mother of six, who lived in rural confusion in Sussex, and whose talent and life-style were the frequent subject of articles on rural haute-Bohème in the smarter magazines—had not included a section on religion. That, in retrospect, had been a bad mistake. 'Now we must be honest.' Mrs Bramble had said, doing her best, pen poised over virgin paper. 'Brutal and dreadful but realistic. What do you require of a girl?'

'She must be attractive,' said Adam. The inquisition made him shy.

'What does that mean?'

'She must turn me on.'

'What turns you on?' Little by little Mrs Bramble bullied a firm description out of him.

Age: Under thirty.

Height: Two inches, or more, shorter than Adam.

Build: Slim, broad-shouldered, small breasted, long legged, with prominent pubis.

Colouring: Pale.

Eyes: Large, but not deep set.

Intelligence: High but not quite as high as Adam's.

She must play a good game of tennis, ski and swim and accompany him jogging.

She must turn brown not red in the sun.

She must not sweat under the arms.

She must be sought-after by other men: he must win her in the face of competition.

She must either be born to wealth or have achieved it herself.

She must come from a titled family or have achieved some measure of fame or notoriety herself.

'I'm sorry about all this,' Adam said to Mrs Bramble. 'It's just what turns me on. Does it sound ridiculous?'

Mrs Bramble held a baby under one arm and removed bread from the oven with her free hand. Hens walked in and out of the kitchen, picking up crumbs and pieces of food from the floor, which was just as well, as otherwise they would have stayed there for days. Five children fell upon hot bread, and divided it and devoured it, as might a pride of lions. Mrs Bramble wore an artist's smock, and a smear of fresh red paint was still wet upon it and coming off on the baby. She did her painting before the children awoke. 'Not ridiculous,' she said, doubtfully. 'Just rather specialised. There are so many different kinds of women in the world. I only hope you haven't limited yourself too much. What about her domestic qualities?'

'Just so long as she isn't like Elaine. Elaine was obsessively tidy. That was a real drag. But she must be a good cook and a competent hostess. I'm not looking for a housekeeper, don't think that. I want a companion, not a servant.'

'Fertile? Do you want that on the list?'

'I'm easy,' said Adam. 'I do have three already.' He seldom saw his children. Elaine was busy turning them against him. This, more than anything, made him bitter. He had loved his children, or so he had believed. But could such a one way flow of emotion be termed love? Now he began to doubt it.

'I'm sure we're leaving something important off the list,' he said, but they could not think what it was, and there was an accident with the baby's nappy, and Mrs Bramble lost her concentration. Sometimes he thought that if only Mrs Bramble was ten years younger and a little less fecund, he could quite happily have married her—at other times not.

A week after drawing up the check list he picked up Elsie at a bookstall on a railway station. He'd thought she was a typist, or something like that. He'd been attracted to her at once, and fell into conversation with her, and when she agreed without demur to go out to dinner with him, had assumed she was some kind of prostitute. 'No,' she said simply, a week later. 'I just heard your voice and I'd known it for ever, and I looked up and recognised you as the man I was going to marry.'

Ah, it was a miracle. He thought that night, as he entered her, but I love her. And then, but how can I love a cheap pick-up? And then again, as he felt, along with the accustomed surge of energy and relief, and the exercise of somehow punitive power, an overwhelming tenderness and happiness for himself and her—but I do! I love her, whatever and whoever she is.

He kept her the whole night and the next morning, and for lunch, and marvels unfolded. He discovered that her uncle was a peer and an aunt a millionairess, he remembered the mild scandal of the brief affair she'd had with married royalty at the age of sixteen. She had money of her own. She'd been at the station because she was running away from a long-standing, worn-out affair with a leading playwright, and had lost her purse.

She could swim, ski, jog, play tennis, cook cordon bleu, converse, was well-read but not as well-read as Adam; she was narrow rather than wide shouldered but he decided that after all he preferred that. He feared she might be cleverer than he was, but she laughed and told him not to worry. Hers was an academic intelligence—about the real world she was usually pretty stupid. She could not get from point A to point B without getting lost—which became to him a source of combined pleasure and irritation. She would lose her clothes, umbrellas, books and was untidy. He tidied up after her and was glad to do so.

Elaine had been untidy and cheerful to begin with, but over the years, little by little, had become obsessively orderly and distressingly afraid of germs. He sometimes thought that her progressive reluctance to make love had been a simple fear of germs. It certainly had not been the reason she gave in her divorce petition—which he had unsuccessfully defended—that of his consistent infidelity. For one thing he had not—had he?—started going with other women until he had been driven to it, out of the sheer insistence of the sexual frustration imposed by his wife. Had she claimed her reluctance was because she was frightened of getting VD, he would just about have believed that. He took Elaine's jealousy as a sign that she did not really love him: jealousy, after all, betokened possessiveness, not love.

He hoped Elsie would be faithful to him, and certainly intended to be faithful to her: he could see that their particular brand of love depended upon sexual exclusivity.

They passed over the Alps. Elsie's hand lay in his. He squeezed it. 'Wear the crucifix if you like,' he said generously. She took it out of her jeans pocket and put it on again. He sighed. 'Religion is the refuge of fools,' he said.

'But I am foolish,' she said happily. 'You like me foolish.' He could not deny it.

'How can someone as educated as you are, as sophisticated, believe in something so patently absurd as all that rigmarole?'

'Jesus isn't absurd.'

'Do you actually believe that Jesus is the son of God, was crucified, dead and buried and ascended on the third day and sitteth at the right hand of God the Father Almighty maker of heaven and earth?'

'I do! I do!' She giggled and laughed and seemed vastly amused.

'On the right hand? Not the left hand?' asked Adam, disagreeably.

"No. The Holy Ghost is on the left.'

'If he's a ghost he won't take up much room. They could both sit on the same hand.'

'You're silly sometimes,' she said, and looked quite cross, but not as cross as he did.

It was her wearing of the crucifix, when he first met her, that had persuaded him she was nothing but a cheap and superstitious tart: he had told her so later, and had thought she seemed shaken, and certainly hoped that she was. But still she wore it, from time to time.

And as the plane circled and lowered and landed, she fingered the crucifix again, and the hand which should have been in his was not and his heart sank, and he knew again that everything was lost. His mother had died when he was four; small incidents could still, suddenly and unexpectedly, bring back the overwhelming sense of loss, desolation and finality. He understood the feeling for what it was—as something which belonged to the past, not the present, and could not bear with it and deal with it, and wait for the pain to go away, as one might the pain of a stubbed toe.

He waited, and it passed. But he knew that though the symptom was cured, the ailment was not. The flaw had been discovered.

They travelled Israel in minibus, in the company of other journalists, escorted by a kindly, elderly, cultured ex-ambassador. 'The country's full of them,' said Adam to Elsie, 'Israel believes in having its embassies everywhere.' In the more troubled zones their escort was a bronzed young army captain with a machine-gun tucked under his arm, in the companionable way that such weapons are carried by their owners.

Elsie trembled under Adam's hand at the sight of that. Her colour came and went. Her fingers went up to her throat but he had taken off the crucifix in the hotel the night before, while making love, so now Elsie's fingers had to seek out Adam's hand instead.

He squeezed them, gratified. The anklet girl, surprisingly enough, was one of their party and a reporter from a Scottish newspaper. She could not be as stupid as she looked. Adam took care not to fall into conversation with her.

It was very hot. Elsie's skin was moist and cool. The anklet girl had wet patches under the arms of her creamy silk blouse.

'Such an energetic, practical country,' observed Adam. 'Israel pays lip-service to religion, to keep its benefactors happy, but thank God it's not more than that. They've put all that superstition behind them.'

'Thank God they're not religious!' mocked Elsie, dancing round in the desert, stirring the glazed air, laying cool, hopeful lips on his. She would not take seriously his rage with the established religions of the world.

They went to the Dead Sea, where the sky and the land and the sea seem made all of the same substance, so that only the touch of the hand can determine which is which, passing through air, resting on ground, sinking in water.

They put on swimming costumes and bobbed up and down in the chemical liquid, which edged the surrounding rocks with white, like sugar frosting an iced glass.

'Like the beginning of the world,' said Adam. 'Well, this is the cradle of civilisation, after all.'

'I can see why they believe in Jehovah,' said Elsie, who was better at balancing in the water than was Adam. 'A great bearded face looming over the hills wouldn't seem at all out of the way. I'm sure He did loom, too.'

Adam's eyes smarted. He felt he was weeping though he knew he was not.

The anklet girl, coming down later with the rest of the party, declined to swim at all, but wore a bikini out of which her plump white body stirred and swelled, reminding Adam of times past.

They were taken to the Golan Heights, whence the Israeli army looks out over the Syrian plain and waits for attack. They crawled through dugouts and were allowed to use the giant telescope, which swept the desert and far, far away caught the glint of Syrian weapons. Nearer were the pretty white canopies of the UN tents, and the wreathed standards of the peace-keeping force, flying bold and high. 'It's been like this for ever,' said Adam. 'Armies of one kind or another, back and forth across the desert. It breeds paranoia.'

'The Lord God of Hosts is with *us*,' said Elsie, 'can't you feel it in the air?'

Over dinner in Haifa Adam confided that he found Israel a distressing place. He had the sense of a culture being destroyed from within, and not, as it is thought, from without. The Arab Jews would outbreed their European compatriots and the sands of the desert would sweep back and drown art, and music, and books and learning. Civilisation. And superstition would rule once again over reason. 'I think it's the most wonderful country in the world,' said Elsie. They couldn't buy hot food in the hotel that day but only cold, it being the Sabbath. Adam was infuriated. Elsie entranced. She talked about the power of religious ritual, and the necessity of sacrifice.

They went to Jerusalem, that nexus of rare beliefs. In Adam's mind the yellow stones of Herod's temple—currently being excavated to a depth of twenty feet—were slippery with the blood of innocents. Jew killed by Christian killed by Muslims. The Canaanites and the Philistines, the Crusaders and the Saracens, the Israelis and the Palestinians, all bent on slaughter in the name of God.

Elsie peered down into the shadowed chasms of the excavation. 'To think that Jesus himself might have walked those streets!'

She looked up at the great lintel which marked the gates of the palace. 'And we know he passed under that!'

'Stones!' he ranted, 'Holy stones! You piled them up and down they fell, and you piled them up again, as monument to a different folly. But you used the very same stones, yellow ochre, spattered with blood.' His eyes were tired by the glazed yellowy look of everything his eyes fell upon. Sand, sky, or building.

They went to Bethlehem, where the Catholics, the Greek Orthodox and an assortment of other sects had their different versions of the birthplace of Jesus, and their own individual shrines erected, where hands could be best outstretched for the alms of the muttering dull-eyed faithful. Elsie blanched a little but solved the problem by going out onto the hill-side of the Shepherds, holding her lovely face up to the serene heavens and saying, 'There in the East is where the Star appeared.'

She had even, in her first year at college, included astronomy as one of her minor subjects.

She insisted on stumbling up to Via Dolorosa, in the company of troops of murmuring Christian pilgrims and their greedy, ignorant guides. The journalists looked on from the safety of the bus. Adam was embarrassed. The pilgrims fell upon their knees, uttered incantations, wailed, rolled their eyes and moaned at the Stations of the Cross. At least Elsie kept on her feet and her lips closed. 'There's no historical evidence that these are the exact stations of the Cross,' said Adam, 'even supposing these events took place at all.'

'Of course they did, silly,' she laughed, indulgently.

Little stalls sold religious relics of gross vulgarity and sentimentality which managed to combine the worst of Victorian England, Renaissance Italy and contemporary New York. Adam said as much, and then felt himself turn cold as Elsie bought a brooch portraying the Virgin

and Child, in gilt and orange and red and blue. 'Who's that for?' he
asked. 'The maid?'

'I think it's lovely,' said Elsie, simply. 'It's a memento of a time when
I was happy. I know it's in bad taste, but the Virgin has such a lovely
expression on her face. Don't you think so?'

But he couldn't even look.

After the Via Dolorosa they went to the Wailing Wall. Tall pale
men dressed in all black, with long ringlets beneath high hats and dark
starry eyes, stood for long periods, faces only inches away from the
wall at which they stared, and from time to time pushed folded pieces
of paper into gaps in the stone. 'It's appalling,' said Adam. 'I suppose
you realise Muslim houses have been razed to the ground to provide an
open space so that those fellows up there'—and he pointed up to where
an Israeli machine-gun glinted on the battlements—'can keep an eye on
things?'

Elsie led him away from the Wailing Wall, where he seemed to get
over-excited, and up the path behind it, and on beneath a sign erected by
the Chief Rabbi requesting the faithful not to pass, lest by mistake they
tread upon the Holy of Holies and defile it, and up into the sacred
places of Muslims, where the temple of the Knights Templar stood in
white palladian beauty, welcome relief from the pervading ochre of sky
and earth and stone, and there sudden and gaudy, in brilliant shiny
ceramic, gold and crimson and vermilion, stood the great Mosque itself,
burning in the sun.

The anklet girl followed them up the path. Her blouse was perma-
nently marked with sweat. He thought he could almost smell her
stench.

Elsie led Adam inside, taking off her shoes without demur, into the
cool, domed sweetness within. There was, to his surprise, no altar, no
pews, no aisle. The great circling vault existed to house a slab of stone—
the kind that tops a hill, any hill. Smooth, sloping and important, as if
set there by some almighty hand, but in fact merely left as the softer soil
around was eroded by wind and storm, over centuries.

'That's the holiest stone of all,' said Adam bitterly. 'Where Abraham
nearly sacrificed Isaac, or Mohammed rose to heaven, depending on
which story you like to believe, and who owns it at the time.'

But she wasn't listening. He saw her fall on her knees, and with some
difficulty, for there was a protective wrought-iron barrier between the
object of worship and the worshipper, ease her long slender neck forward so that her lips could reach the stone. Then she kissed it.

Adam turned and caught the eye of the anklet girl. She stood behind him in the shadows, watching. He smiled, she smiled back. Soon he would manage to get her alone. She would not prove difficult. Half an hour's privacy, behind a holy stone or in a wadi or in some hotel room somewhere, was all that was required. He felt he needed the violence and relief of a new sexual encounter.

He thought he saw passing over Elsie's face, later on that week, the same expression as had come to mar his first wife's looks: softness hardening into sadness, gentleness into reproach, kindness into self-pity. He blamed Elsie for his loss of his love for her and he blamed Mrs Bramble, for forgetting to put at least some stricture or other in regard to religion in the check list. His sense of himself as a tragic figure increased; he, who had been prepared to worship a wife, had married a woman who worshipped strange gods instead of her husband.

Threnody

I don't want to take up too much of your time and attention, Miss Jacobs. I am sure there are many others in a far worse state than me. I met a couple of them on the way here, in fact, in the High Street. An old woman walked behind me shouting that Sainsbury's was the worst den of iniquity in the world and that the police station was a brothel. And a beautiful young woman passed me, weeping. Her face was so wet I thought for a minute it was raining. Well, I am in neither of those sorry states. I am prepared to take the world at its face value, and nothing distresses me very much any more. Look at me! My skirt and blouse are neat: my hair is combed: I am not distressed. I look what I am; a solicitor's wife, aged thirty-five, well set up for the slow run down to old age and death.

Depressed? No. I don't think so. Realistic, perhaps. Do I look depressed? I notice I am sitting in the bright light from the window, while you sit almost in the dark. I find that uncomfortable. I am not used to it. Usually the self remains obscure while others are brilliantly lit. Self knowledge is hard to come by. That is why I am here. I want to say the things I do not like to say at home, for fear of making the milk curdle and the children anxious. I have blisters on my tongue, from biting words back.

Start at the beginning? Very well.

My mother named me Threnody. No. It isn't written on my card. I am known as Anne; well, who wants a name like Threnody? My husband Eric certainly does not. The name was a mistake on my mother's part. She thought Threnody meant some kind of happy, lilting melody. In fact, it means dirge, or lament. My mother's friend Elsie, who was to bring me up, pointed this out, but only after the deed was done. I don't hold the error against my mother. It was 1940, after all. Bombs fell and food was short, and I dare say she thought that Davis was a dull and ordinary surname, and that I deserved all the help I could get, and that was why she plucked Threnody out of the air, and used it for a name, instead of fishing Jane or Mary or Helen out of the common pool. And if more excuses were needed for my mother, she was only twenty when I was born, and my father was not available for consultation. According to Elsie, too, she had a milk ulcer. That helps no one think straight. I had one with Robert. He's my younger. And the Registrar would have been too busy entering deaths—Elsie said the week I was born was the week of the worst of the London bombings—to have had time or energy to help my mother out.

Yes. Elsie spoke a lot to me about my early childhood: yes. Perhaps I remember with her memory. See with her eyes. The world according to Elsie. We have grown apart for various reasons but I remain fond of her. I think those war years were the best of Elsie's life. She had three children and her husband was in the navy, and she lived next door to my mum and me, when I was a baby, in Riley Street. By all accounts it was a casual, slap-dash street; a woman's world, for the husbands were away fighting Germany. Meals were seldom served on time, and came straight out of saucepans, not from serving dishes, and children shared beds with mothers and were the happier for it.

Yes, of course, Miss Jacobs. All these attitudes and assumptions of mine will be examined in the course of time. I know that and am prepared to change them. That's why I'm here. In the meantime I am just giving you the broad outline, so you know the kind of person I am. A solicitor's wife, burdened by the fact that her mother named her Threnody. A dirge or lament.

Where were we, before you interrupted? Though I must say you are very silent. It must be quite a good way to make money. Sitting there like a voyeur, saying nothing in particular, getting on with your knitting. Yes, a very good way indeed. I must try it some time. Set myself up so nice and cosy.

No. It doesn't make me feel better to have lost my temper with you. It makes me feel worse. Fourteen sessions before I was honest with you about my feelings? Is that good or bad? If it's neither good nor bad, why fucking well mention it? Can I now get on with my story, please? Christ, isn't that what I pay you for?

Riley Street in the war. Local schools had closed and such mothers as had stood out against evacuation now had the company of their children all day long. Bombs fell by night, of course, but quite a lot of the women claimed that air-raids were preferable to their husband's attentions. According to Elsie. Yes. All this is according to Elsie. I was only a child, not Einstein. I do not have total recall.

Elsie wasn't like the others. Elsie liked sex. So did my mother. I don't think they were real lesbians, not in the modern sense. No, certainly I have no sense of disgust. Why should I? I can see it all clearly. The general feeling between them of a sensuous common bond; the slap-happy life of early nights and late risings, and cheerful neighbours and cups of tea, and time passing and no one caring, and mother-skin touching child-skin in the glow of the coal fire, and no one ever bothering to sweep up, and the money from the army coming through the letter box every week, so there was no hassle getting it out of husbands—and every night the bombers going over and real physical fear and the need for relief from it—well, I can see how all these things would combine so that Jan's and Elsie's lips were all but bound to meet, if only casually, and more in the expectation of comfort than in any actual desire for sexual gratification.

What do you mean, protest too much? I see that you're wearing a nice new jumper. Is that the one you've been knitting at my expense? You are not, if you don't mind me saying so, too good a knitter. You can't mind me saying so. I pay you not to mind.

Yes, I know that children like to deny their parents' sexual experiences; I have even heard my little Rosalind say Mummy and Daddy only did it the twice; once for Robert and once for me, and it made me laugh, though the way Eric's going these days, she wouldn't be so far out. But for me, you see, it was true. I haven't mentioned my father much since I've been seeing you, for the I would have thought obvious reason that he died before I was born. He never even got to know I had been named Threnody. My mother wrote a letter to him and posted it, confessing all, but she needn't have bothered. He died before he could read it. He was on the African front. He was trapped in a blazing tank. No. Not a nice way to go. But that was the war. People got burned alive or asphyxiated or cut into bits or crushed flat or starved to death or died of disease: a nice clean bullet hole was rare. Killed in Action. If you disintegrated altogether and just weren't there any more you were posted Missing, Presumed Killed. They must have found bits of my father, I suppose. How do you mourn a father you never saw? He and my mother met, married and conceived me all in the space of two months, as was not unusual at the time. Then my father was sent back to the front, buttons shining, leaving my poor young mother to cope.

I know it wasn't his fault. What are you implying? My difficulties with Eric are because of my father? My *father*? What father? Look, I don't have difficulties with Eric; he has difficulties with himself. What are you *talking* about?

No. That my mother had this relationship with Elsie is not fantasy. One day when I'm feeling strong enough I'll tell you how I know.

Poetry? Write poetry? Me? Do solicitor's wives write poetry? I suppose I wasn't always a solicitor's wife, though it seems hard to believe.

As a baby I had a transparent look—Elsie said so. My mother didn't quite believe in my existence, according to Elsie, and that was the reason for my transparency. I think my mother was lucky: she was not quite able to believe in the desperate reality of anything. Why should she? She was Eve in the Garden of Eden, happy in Riley Street, until when I was four she bit into the apple of knowledge, and we were all cast out into outer darkness. Yesterday I sent a poem off to the Cheltenham Festival competition. I must be mad.

Talking about must be mad, I have to keep secret from everyone the fact that I come to see you. Eric says people will not just think, but know I'm mad, if they don't already. I expect he's right. He's always right. I married him because he was so right, and generally in charge. Never mind. Mustn't grumble. Elsie used to say mustn't grumble.

The apple my mother bit into was the apple of love. Had it just been sex no harm would have been done. Love doesn't just move mountains it sends them toppling down upon the innocent.

I don't want to come here any more. I can't afford it. I can't face it. It's doing more harm than good. My mother went dancing. She and Elsie had a row about it. I remember it. I was four. Elsie didn't want her to go. My mother had a pair of the new black glassy nylons and she put them on and Elsie called her names, but she went off to the dance and met a U.S. serviceman called Gus and they fell in love. Gus wanted my mum to put her past behind her, and that included me. Threnody. Dirge or lament.

I remember him saying to my Mum when she brought him home,

'Funny names you English give your kids,' and I remember Elsie saying, 'Not as funny as Gus. What's it short for? Disgusting?'

My mum married Gus in Seattle and Elsie got one thousand pounds from Gus' family to take me in.

Sold to the nice lady next door. For the sum of one thousand pounds.

Well, Elsie was nice. Nicer than my mum I dare say. My Mum was a flibbertygibbet. The lady at No. 8 said so.

God, I feel about six. No, four. Christ!

1977/8

Historically, women have always abandoned their children in favour of their husbands. All through the days of empire, middle-class mothers left their little ones with nannies and schools and followed their men and thought themselves virtuous for doing so. Working-class women, of course, behaved more naturally. Perhaps my Mum was just being up-market.

Yes, I feel myself again. Surprisingly mature. I am runnerup in the Cheltenham Poetry Prize. Eric brought half a bottle of champagne. Had I won, it would have been a whole bottle. He's like that.

I remember when the war came to an end. Bells and flags and kissing in the streets. And then all up and down Riley Street husbands returned and children were pushed out of their mother's beds and lived for ever with a sense of Paradise Lost. Meals became meat and two veg again: male voices demanded quiet and clean socks: and the pot plants began to flourish again. They do, I am quite convinced, in houses where normal sex is frequently practised. You are right: lately mine have been dying off. That's coincidence. Please let me get on, Miss Jacobs. Always butting in. If you're not too silent you're too talkative.

As for me, I belonged to nobody and had my own fate. Threnody. Dirge or lament. I had a little back bedroom at the top of Elsie's house and everyone was kind to me, and yes, I have always said I had a very happy childhood. I liked my name in those days. I was always good at turning misfortune into advantage. 'It's a Russian name,' I'd say to my friends. 'My father, who died the day I was born, was a prince. My mother was a princess. She was abducted by secret agents: she is imprisoned in a castle!' No. She never wrote to me.

I suppose in fact I was always a little ashamed of Elsie. I thought she was coarse and vulgar. I was very sensitive. I swelled up terribly if bitten by a wasp. I couldn't wear wool next to my skin. Remember the vagrant girl in the Hans Andersen story? They knew she was a princess because when she slept on a hundred mattresses she could still feel the pea underneath.

Ted? Elsie's husband? Ted my foster-father? Oh, Ted. Him. Well.

Elsie had another baby when I was eleven and Ted didn't like me very much in those days—I'm not surprised. If there were beans and chips I'd say isn't there any salad, that kind of thing—and they needed my bedroom so Elsie wrote to my mum, but the letter was returned Gone Away. My father's family? Elsie went along to the Registrar because all she knew, all anyone knew, about my father was his name, Arthur Davis, but the Registrar was gone with all his files. V2 rocket. Direct hit. That's war. People appear, and disappear, and history with them.

If anything goes wrong at home Eric says, 'Of course, you can't be expected to concentrate. You're a poet, after all.' It's all your fault, Miss Jacobs. Encouraging me to be something I'm not. I'd have thought you weren't supposed to do things like that.

I think I was a very pretty child. Well, that's the feeling I have. I loved nice dresses and button shoes. I remember Elsie saying, when I said I wanted to go to grammar school, 'Christ, that child gives herself airs.' But Ted backed me, surprisingly enough, and paid for my uniform without even complaining. He'd quite come round to me by the time I was thirteen. Yes, I was frightened of him. I'd wedge a chair beneath my door handle at night. No. I wasn't exactly frightened of him, more of the way Elsie didn't ever let me be in the room alone with him.

Anyway, Elsie was rescued from the threat of me by the government. They brought out a scheme for the residential education of war-disadvantaged children, so I was wrenched out of the grammar school where I was doing English lit and learning to be a journalist and put into this institution and taught shorthand typing and office management.

Institution? Well, actually, it wasn't too bad. It was a stately home, which had been requisitioned from some ducal family in the war. Gold stucco flaked on to the filing cabinets and the canteen was set up beneath faded tapestries, and stone cherubs lay on their backs in the weeds and smiled. It suited my mood.

I slept alone in the servants' attic, beneath a sloping roof, and icicles formed outside my dormer window, but I knew it was better than Riley Street.

Yes, I made lots of friends at college. I entertained them. They were mostly very plain—being disadvantaged does tend to make people plain—and I felt in some way responsible for them. I always felt I had a future: but they only seemed to have pasts. They still write to me. One of them became a countess, for all her cross eyes. You can never tell.

Of course I see good looks as the way a woman gets on. Her face is her future. Would you be sitting there knitting shrouds—I assume you're knitting shrouds—if you hadn't been born with a face like a flat iron?

Flat iron? No, I have no particular association with flat irons. It just reminds me of your fucking face. Or vice versa. Look, I'm sorry. Yes, there's something coming up.

Ted. Foster-father Ted. I learned office routine, bookkeeping, short-hand typing. I'd given up wanting to be a journalist. You could be a secretary until you got married; but if you were a journalist that was a career. If you had a career you couldn't be married, and vice versa. And I wanted to be married, oh yes. I wanted to marry out of Riley Street for ever and into stately homes, however decayed. I settled for Eric, in the end, and Georgian country. Madness!

Love? What do you mean? Of course I love my husband. You're supposed to, aren't you? That's what it's all about.

Ted. Why do you keep bringing me back to Ted? It was better when you sat silent and gently snored; did you know you snored?—now I seem to hear your gratey whiny voice in my ears all day and all night. 'Ted—whine, sniffle—what about—whine, sniffle—Ted, whine, sniffle.' It was nothing. It was the kind of thing that happens to girls all the time. Ted came to visit me at the stately home. Stump, stump, stump up the wide staircase in brown boots. He was a good looking man. Horrible, and old, and bristly, with a moustache. And angry, always. Not as if I'd done something wrong, but as if I *was* something wrong. Do you know? No, you wouldn't. You're always right.

Ted. He described himself as my uncle, and they allowed him up into my attic bedroom and he made love to me. Rape? I don't know. That's another word like love. I don't know what it means. I didn't want him to and yet I let him. I hated him and feared him and despised him and I wanted him to wrong me. He knew it was wrong, and I knew it was wrong, and he knew that I knew, and I acquiesced in this monstrous ugly act: I think perhaps it has made me passive. More passive than I need be. In order to accept that deed and incorporate it in my sweet vision of myself, I had to accept and incorporate everything else. The monstrous crime. Incest: in the spirit if not the deed.

Yes, of course I'm rationalising, Miss Jacobs, whatever that means. If you'll excuse me I'll leave this session now. I know it's early, but I'm sure your other clients are clamouring at the door. They always are. I'm surprised you can tell us apart. Perhaps you can't.

Why are you suggesting I start a business of some kind? I don't *want* to be independent. I think women should be looked after and it's the husband's place to do it. You know that.

Thank you. I had a good Christmas. I hope you did. Eric decided the turkey wasn't properly cooked, so everything had to go back into the oven, and it was all rather spoiled. Eric fears food poisoning. I don't. I hope for it. I have blisters on my tongue again. Haven't had those for ages. And I'm getting back pains.

Listen, I've got the premises for the Press, and raised the money for the lease. I'll print leaflets and wedding invitations, and circulars and handbooks and when I've managed to scrape together a little capital, even try doing volumes of poetry. I have quite a gift for handprinting, it seems.

I have been thinking about the Ted episode. He justified himself, as he adjusted his dress. Gentlemen were required to do that in public conveniences, at that time. Gentlemen will kindly adjust their dress. Meaning, don't forget your flies. He didn't. Some men make love without even taking off their trousers. Did you know? Well, you are *Miss* Jacobs. For all I know you're a virgin and have no idea what I'm talking about half the time.

Incidentally I have an Arts Council grant for the poetry editions. They needn't think they can dictate to me culturally, just because I take their money.

Ted's justification was that while he'd been away in the war Elsie had been having it off with my mother, so he owed her no fidelity. He thought a balance had been righted. And I'm sure he thought sex with me was his just reward for the money he had expended on me. Well, men do, don't they. But it was hit and run, really. He didn't write or phone and I was glad and I put it out of my mind, or thought I did. No. I felt no guilt towards Elsie. Should I have? But there has been a barrier between my life before and my life after; between my present and my past. I have become someone to whom the early life, the magic of infancy and total love, has been lost. I suppose that is how the traumatised live. Most of us are traumatised. Will knowing it make any difference?

1979

Miss Jacobs, I am in love. I shall tell you about it presently. A woman of 37 in love! Ridiculous. Heart pounding, mouth dry, loins melting. Oh! No. I shan't say any more about it. Not yet. Wonderful. I am so happy. Do you like my new jeans?

Eric. It was as much my fault as his. Now I am in love I can afford to forgive him. Look at my own part in it all. I was a tough little thing, really. After I left college I pushed my accent up a notch or so, acquired a fantasy Mummy and Daddy, and a country home and a horsy head square or two, and shared a Knightsbridge flat with a gaggle of secretaries who had all these things by natural right. Manners and attitudes brushed off. I meant to catch a man: the best man I could. I got a job with a firm of West End solicitors. I don't think anyone doubted me. I had the same clear honest eyes then as I have now. People believe what you say you are, if you say it loud and clear. So I did. Anne Threnody-Davis. Hyphenated. Madness!

Eric was the youngest partner in the law firm. Twenty-eight, unmarried, public school, private income, good background. There was, in those days, a very special kind of war between men and women. The women's virginity was the trophy. The men's desire was to seduce the women, prove her bad, and then abandon her as she deserved. The woman's was to snare and fascinate by sexual wiles, but exact marriage as the price of bed. Well I wasn't a virgin, was I, but I sure as shit tried.

Yes. My language has become freer. I think it's the company I'm keeping more than anything you've done for me. Freudian or sub-Freudian analysis doesn't go down too well in the circles I move in, I can tell you. But the Press is going very well. Do you think I should change its name to the Threnody Press? I'd like to do that. A kind of half-way acknowledgment. Eric won't like it, though.

I manoeuvred Eric into marrying me: sitting in his office as cool and sweet as could be, making up imaginary suitors for myself until he was so sick with anxiety and lust he proposed marriage. Once engaged, my various deceptions were quickly and horribly exposed. Served me right. I know I was a victim of a system which led women to weak survival by deceit but even so I behaved badly. I think Eric could have accepted

Riley Street and Elsie and Ted with perfect equanimity if I'd been open and honest about it. But I was ashamed of it, and so he was too. He kept his word and married me but I knew he really didn't want to. He fell a third out of love with me when he discovered Threnody was my Christian name and not attached to Davis by a hyphen, and the second third when he actually made love to me on our wedding night and I confessed I wasn't a virgin, and the last third when we just somehow didn't get on in bed together, anyway. Look, I was only eighteen.

We both did our best. We lived in the country so I could put my past behind me, including the name Threnody. We had a nice house and nice children and I kept them both well. We entertained. I was a model wife. I went through all the motions; and we are always polite to each other. I felt so guilty about those initial deceptions that I thereafter behaved impeccably. But I died. I was dead. And even you couldn't revive me. Not so bad a crime? How can you say that? Think of the harm I've done! The damage. I killed my father: I drove my mother away; I stole poor Elsie's husband, I cheated my husband and my children of the life they should have had. You can say what you like to me. But that is the truth.

The truth of what I feel, not the truth of what happened, all right, but that is the greater truth and how am I to live with that? That I'm not just dirt: but poisonous dirt as well. I must be punished, obliterated. You know you have made me suicidal? Sheila says she hopes you know what you are doing. Sheila is the person I am in love with.

What's the matter? Why did you cough like that? Do you think you have failed? I *know* you have succeeded. I don't think you meant to, mind you. But I know my true nature now. I am lesbian. I am going to come out. What is coming out? Don't you *know*? Where have you been the last few years? Coming out is declaring your sexual nature to the world. The theory being that if everyone does it, then straight society will stop being so censorious, and isolated gays will stop being so miserable, and realise what an ordinary, lovely, everyday thing same-sex-sexuality is. You might even start wondering about your own nature, Miss Jacobs. What do you mean, caution? No haste? God, you are so boring. Don't you realise I am in love?

Good heavens, yes ages and ages ago I said that. Sex isn't as dangerous as love. Mountains move and topple on the innocent. But I'm not deserting my children. Sheila is so good with them. They'll move in with us. It may be a bit difficult with Robert—I mean, he may be my son but he's still male, and male is the enemy, when you come down to it. But of course Eric will be reasonable when I tell him. We'll be so much happier apart. I really think he's a bit gay too, you see. People like me and him do tend to drift together, Sheila says.

Sheila says a lot, as Elsie did. What are you implying? No, I don't think so. In fact, Sheila doesn't believe in small talk. She's quite tall; nearly six-foot, and really striking looking. She has a sort of husky, languorous voice. It really turns me on. I was publishing the newsletter for the lesbian commune she runs—well, she doesn't run it; it's a group thing: no male hierarchical organisation.

What do you mean, the world according to Sheila? As it used to be the world according to Elsie? What are you trying to *say*? You're jealous. I think you're jealous because I'm happy and you're not. Yes. I know about my outer shell. My carapace. Sheila says all women married to men grow them, in self defence. We must use our sisters to help crack the shell, Sheila says, so the true self can emerge.

How much money have I given you, over the years? When I think how it could have helped the commune! You know the trouble I was having with the back? Sheila says it's because I've been playing heterosexual. She says she dare say if she submitted to male sexual aggression nightly she'd have a bad back too. Not *nightly*? Well, all right. You have a funny air, Miss Jacobs, crouched in your dark corner, of being girded for battle. Yes, I do see all male sex as assault, frankly. No, not an expression of love. Love between men and women can't be the love between equals, because men believe women are their inferiors. They can't help it. It's in the language. He before she. *Man* kind. *His*-story, John and Mary. The love men show towards women is at its best patronising. The penis is after all a weapon of mastery. Good heavens, look at rockets. Missiles. Whee! What a humdinger of an ejaculation! Wow.

I'm afraid Eric isn't being co-operative at all. He's being vindictive. Sheila says gays are, if they're under cover.

Sex with Sheila. It's wonderful. How can I explain to you? Peaceful. There is so much time. No fear of the other's failure, which will later be revenged. No fear of your own. Everything waits. The seasons. The earth in its orbit. Everything. It's love, as I have never known it. Eric won't give me a divorce. He has thrown me out. Well, he's a solicitor. He has friends. He is claiming custody of the children. He will only let me see them in the presence of a third party. Specifically not Sheila! It's barbaric, monstrous! Male vengeance. The man whose pride has been injured. That's all it is. Not *feeling*.

But I have the Threnody Press, which is just about now breaking even, and I have Sheila. I have no savings, no house, no children, no possessions: and many of my friends don't understand the truth and have taken Eric's side: but a few understand. Especially Paula. She's very supportive. And I have my dignity, and I have love, and when I have recovered from these blows, I will be happy. I am very calm, and very confident.

They are so kind to us at the commune. My sisters. Sheila and I have our own room: We're not in the dormitories. There are a lot of things I have to get used to. It is good of you to let me see you for nothing, even though it is only once a week. I would have thought, considering— well, never mind. You live as a woman in the old male world—you have to have your props. Money, status, possessions. We're different. Even our clothing we have in common.

Sheila has moved back into the dormitory. We talked it out. She feels there is something destructive in our exclusiveness. I see what she means. I think. No, I'm not depressed. It's just I haven't had time to mend my sandal thongs.

Of course it's a feather in Sheila's cap to have seduced a married woman with children. It's happening all the time. All over the country women are realising their true natures, coming out, leaving husband and children. It's nothing to do with fashion. If we are strong, if we hold together, as sisters, all will be well—

What do you mean, I use words without meaning? Miss Jacobs, I think I am going mad. Eric owns half the Threnody Press. He says I may keep it if I buy out his share. But that's two thousand pounds. I haven't got it. It will have to be sold. I am destroyed.

Miss Jacobs, Sheila says that emotions are political. That I should hand mine over to the group for discussion and direction, and not to you. But I don't know. I do love Sheila. I'm sure I do. I must, mustn't I? I mean, that's what's supposed to happen. Now when did I say that before? Round and round: circles within circles, little wheels within big wheels. Cogs grinding. Dear God, forgive me my sins.

Miss Jacobs, I met Paula in the street. I thought she was a good friend, even though she was heterosexual, but she was getting a bit funny and I asked her straight out why, and she said it's not that she thought it was disgusting or anything like that: just that she couldn't trust me any more. She couldn't relax in my company. She said it was as if I were one of the men, weighing her up for her attractiveness or otherwise, dismissing her because of her body, not her self. As if I would! But it's true that now when I look at the lips of women I wonder what kissing them would be like.

No. Pre-Sheila, I never had thoughts like that.

Do you mind if I cry? Sheila doesn't like me crying, and I have blisters on my tongue again. Why do I cry? Because of the children. Sheila says why shouldn't Eric take care of them for a change: much as she liked them they were something of a nuisance: it was difficult to be properly sexually spontaneous when kids were around. I remarked that heterosexuals waited 'til they'd gone to bed, and Sheila said yes, and look how miserable they are!

No. I don't see eye to eye with Sheila all the time, not any more. I think that's your fault. Eric has custody of the children. The case has been taken up by the Society for Lesbian Mothers. There's been a lot of press about, and even television interviews. God, I did look a mess. I'd no idea. Anyway now everyone knows. Everyone. If I even put my head out of the door people stare.

It all reminds me of Ted, I don't know why. Stump, stump, stump, up the stairs, dreadful but inevitable. My doom.

My name is Threnody. It means dirge or lament. My mother didn't make a mistake. She had a foreknowledge, that's all.

Sheila wants Ellen to be included in our relationship. Ellen's twenty-two. Sheila says I've been a real drag lately, miserable and depressing and self-centred and unable to break out of my sexist conditioning, so that she's sometimes wondered if I weren't just a heterosexual playing sick fashionable games. I cried, which really made her angry, but the blisters on my tongue have gone. She said Rose Ellen would be good for all of us, being cheerful and positive—twenty-two, is what I think she means—and a bit confused politically, Sheila says, but fantastic in bed! Well, she should know. What does that mean anyway? Good in bed! She said to me Threnody by name, and Threnody by nature. A real drag, Sheila said. The world according to Sheila.

I accept that. Threnody, I fully accept my name. What did I do about Rose Ellen? I packed my one suitcase, which is all I have left of my life, and I went out into the world. Rose Ellen is *not* fantastic in bed: or at any rate she doesn't turn me on in the least, and she is very, very stupid. I have the suitcase in your waiting room. I shall go and stay with Paula if she'll have me now. You wanted me punished, I seem to remember. You didn't? It was what *I* wanted? Are you sure? I certainly feel much better. I mean quite dreadful, as befits my circumstances, which is totally ruined, everything lost: but nothing on either side of that, except a most wonderful cheerfulness. I shan't see you now for some time. I can't afford you. I mean, emotionally afford *not* paying for you, if you see what I mean. No, frankly, I don't think I have manoeuvred this whole situation just to get of treatment. Goodbye, and thank you. I mean really, thank you from the bleeding, beating heart of Threnody.

I see you have some new knitting. I love the colours. Much brighter! I hope it wasn't me who depressed you? I was going to post you the money I owe you but Tim said why not come and visit you and do it in person. I said you'd probably not be able to find the time to fit me in, but he said of course you would and he was right. Tim is often right, but not always, the way Eric was. Did I tell you about Tim? I don't know if seeing you did me the slightest good: perhaps all that was required was for me to meet the right person? Tim is a doctor. He was a widower when I met him. Now he is married to me. We have five children between us. Three of his and two of mine. Mine come at weekends. I am quite good friends with Eric now. He married again very soon after the divorce a local farmer's daughter. Perhaps he was never the snob I thought he was, and it was me all the time? But since this is a social visit and I'm not paying you, I don't suppose you'll see the need to go into all that. In any case Tim likes me as I am and does not see the need for alteration. Do you know what he said to me the other day? He said, 'Don't tell me your mother made a mistake when she called you Threnody. She didn't. So far as I am concerned,' said Tim, 'the word Threnody now means a happy, lilting melody, and not dirge, or lament, at all.'

So you see Miss Jacobs, all is well. What did you say? Nothing is ever as good as one hopes, or as bad as one fears? What a very sort of *intermediate* remark.

Angel, All Innocence

There is a certain kind of unhappiness, experienced by a certain kind of woman married to a certain kind of man, which is timeless: outrunning centuries, interweaving generations, perpetuating itself from mother to daughter, feeding off the wet eyes of the puzzled girl, gaining fresh strength from the dry eyes of the old woman she will become—who, looking back on her past, remembers nothing of love except tears and the pain in the heart which must be endured, in silence, in case the heart stops altogether.

Better for it to stop, now.

Angel, waking in the night, hears sharp footsteps in the empty attic above and wants to wake Edward. She moves her hand to do so, but then stills it for fear of making him angry. Easier to endure in the night the nightmare terror of ghosts than the day-long silence of Edward's anger.

The footsteps, little and sharp, run from a point above the double bed in which Angel and Edward lie, she awake, he sleeping, to a point somewhere above the chest of drawers by the door; they pause briefly, then run back again, tap-tap, clickety-click. There comes another pause and the sound of pulling and shuffling across the floor; and then the sequence repeats itself, once, twice. Silence. The proper unbroken silence of the night.

Too real, too clear, for ghosts. The universe is not magic. Everything has an explanation. Rain, perhaps? Hardly. Angel can see the moon shine through the drawn blind, and rain does not fall on moonlit nights.

Perhaps, then, the rain of past days collected in some blocked gutter, to finally splash through on to the rolls of wallpaper and pots of paint on the attic floor, sounding like footsteps through some trick of domestic acoustics. Surely! Angel and Edward have not been living in the house for long. The attic is still unpainted, and old plaster drops from disintegrating laths. Edward will get round to it sooner or later. He prides himself on his craftsman's skills, and Angel, a year married, has learned to wait and admire, subduing impatience in herself. Edward is a painter—of pictures, not houses—and not long out of art school, where he won many prizes. Angel is the lucky girl he has loved and married. Angel's father paid for the remote country house, where now they live in solitude and where Edward can develop his talents, undisturbed by the ugliness of the city, with Angel, his inspiration, at his side. Edward, as it happened, consented to the gift unwillingly, and for Angel's sake rather than his own. Angel's father Terry writes thrillers and settled a large sum upon his daughter in her childhood, thus avoiding death duties and the anticipated gift tax. Angel kept the fact hidden from Edward until after they were married. He'd thought her an ordinary girl about Chelsea, sometime secretary, sometime barmaid, sometime artist's model.

Angel, between jobs, did indeed take work as an artist's model. That was how Edward first clapped eyes upon her; Angel, all innocence, sitting nude upon her plinth, fair curly hair glinting under strong lights, large eyes closed beneath stretched blue-veined lids, strong breasts pointed upwards, stubby pale bush irritatingly and coyly hidden behind an angle of thigh that both gave Angel cramps and spoiled the pose for the students. So they said.

'If you're going to be an exhibitionist,' as Edward complained to her later in the coffee bar, 'at least don't be coy about it.' He took her home to his pad, that handsome, dark-eyed, smiling young man, and wooed her with a nostalgic Sinatra record left behind by its previous occupant; half mocking, half sincere, he sang love words into her pearly ear, his warm breath therein stirring her imagination, and the gentle occasional nip of his strong teeth in her flesh promising passion and pain beyond belief. Angel would not take off her clothes for him: he became angry and sent her home in a taxi without her fare. She borrowed from her flatmate at the other end. She cried all night, and the next day, sitting naked on her plinth, had such swollen eyelids as to set a student or two scratching away to amend the previous day's work. But she lowered her thigh, as a gesture of submission, and felt a change in the studio ambience from chilly spite to warm approval, and she knew Edward had forgiven her. Though she offered herself to multitudes, Edward had forgiven her.

'I don't mind you being an exhibitionist,' Edward said to her in the coffee bar, 'in fact that rather turns me on, but I do mind you being coy. You have a lot to learn, Angel.' By that time Angel's senses were so aroused, her limbs so languid with desire, her mind so besotted with his image, that she would have done whatever Edward wished, in public or in private. But he rose and left the coffee bar, leaving her to pay the bill.

Angel cried a little, and was comforted by and went home with Edward's friend Tom, and even went to bed with him, which made her feel temporarily better, but which she was to regret for ever.

'I don't mind you being a whore,' Edward said before the next studio session, 'but can't you leave my friends alone?'

It was a whole seven days of erotic torment for Angel before Edward finally spent the night with her: by that time her thigh hung loosely open in the studio. Let anyone see. Anyone. She did not care. The job was coming to an end anyway. Her new one as secretary in a solicitor's office began on the following Monday. In the nick of time, Just as she began to think that life and love were over, Edward brought her back to their remembrance. 'I love you,' he murmured in Angel's ear. 'Exhibitionist slut, typist, I don't care. I still love you.'

Tap-tap, go the footsteps above, starting off again: clickety-click. Realer than real. No, water never sounded like that. What then? Rats? No. Rats scutter and scamper and scrape. There were rats in the barn in which Angel and Edward spent a camping holiday together. Their tent had blown away: they'd been forced to take refuge in the barn. All four of them. Edward, Angel, Tom and his new girlfriend Ray. Angel missed Edward one night after they all stumbled back from the pub to the barn, and searching for him in the long grass beneath an oak tree, found him in tight embrace with Ray.

'Don't tell me you're hysterical as well as everything else,' complained Edward. 'You're certainly irrational. You went to bed with Tom, after all.'

'But that was before.'

Ah, before, so much before. Before the declarations of love, the abandoning of all defence, all prudence, the surrendering of common sense to faith, the parcelling up and handing over of the soul into apparent safe-keeping. And if the receiving hands part, the trusted fingers lose their grip, by accident or by design, why then, one's better dead.

Edward tossed his Angel's soul into the air and caught it with his casual hands.

'But if it makes you jealous,' he said, 'why I won't . . . Do you want to marry me? Is that it? Would it make you happier?'

What would it look like when they came to write his biography? Edward Holst, the famous painter, married at the age of twenty-four— to what? Artist's model, barmaid, secretary, crime-writer's daughter? Or exhibitionist, whore, hysteric? Take your choice. Whatever makes the reader happiest, explains the artist in the simplest terms, makes the most successful version of a life. Crude strokes and all.

'Edward likes to keep his options open,' said Tom, but would not explain his remark any further. He and Ray were witnesses at the secular wedding ceremony. Angel thought she saw Edward nip Ray's ear as they all formally kissed afterwards, then thought she must have imagined it.

This was his overture of love: turning to Angel in the dark warmth of the marriage bed, Edward's teeth would seek her ear and nibble the tender flesh, while his hand travelled down to open her thighs. Angel never initiated their lovemaking. No. Angel waited, patiently. She had tried once or twice, in the early days, letting her hand roam over his sleeping body, but Edward not only failed to respond, but was thereafter cold to her for days on end, sleeping carefully on his side of the bed, until her penance was paid and he lay warm against her again.

Edward's love made flowers bloom, made the house rich and warm, made water taste like wine. Edward, happy, surrounded Angel with smiles and soft encouragement. He held her soul with steady hands. Edward's anger came unexpectedly, out of nowhere, or nowhere that Angel could see. Yesterday's permitted remark, forgiven fault, was today's outrage. To remark on the weather to break an uneasy silence, might be seen as evidence of a complaining nature: to be reduced to tears by his first unexpected biting remark, further fuel for his grievance.

Edward, in such moods, would go to his studio and lock the door, and though Angel (soon learning that to weep outside the door or beat against it, moaning and crying and protesting, would merely prolong his anger and her torment) would go out to the garden and weed or dig or plant as if nothing were happening, would feel Edward's anger seep-ing out from under the door, darkening the sun, poisoning the earth; or at any rate spoiling her fingers in relation to the earth, so that they trembled and made mistakes and nothing grew.

The blind shakes. The moon goes behind a cloud. Tap, tap, overhead. Back and forth. The wind? No. Don't delude yourself. Nothing of this world. A ghost. A haunting. A woman. A small, desperate, busy woman, here and not here, back and forth, out of her time, back from the grave, ill-omened, bringing grief and ruin: a message that nothing is what it seems, that God is dead and the forces of evil abroad and unstoppable. Does Angel hear, or not hear?

Angel, through her fear, wants to go to the bathroom. She is three months' pregnant. Her bladder is weak. It wakes her in the night, crying out its need, and Angel, obeying, will slip cautiously out of bed, trying not to wake Edward. Edward needs unbroken sleep if he is to paint well the next day. Edward, even at the best of times, suspects that Angel tossing and turning, and moaning in her sleep, as she will, wakes him on purpose to annoy.

Angel has not yet told Edward that she is pregnant. She keeps putting it off. She has no real reason to believe he does not want babies: but he has not said he does want them, and to assume that Edward wants what other people want is dangerous.

Angel moans aloud: afraid to move, afraid not to move, afraid to hear, afraid not to hear. So the child Angel lay awake in her little white bed, listening to her mother moaning, afraid to move, afraid not to move, to hear or not to hear. Angel's mother was a shoe-shop girl who married the new assistant manager after a six-week courtship. That her husband went on to make a fortune, writing thrillers that sold by the million, was both Dora's good fortune and tragedy. She lived comfortably enough on alimony, after all, in a way she could never have expected, until dying by mistake from an overdose of sleeping pills. After that Angel was brought up by a succession of her father's mistresses and au-pairs. Her father Terry liked Edward, that was something, or at any rate he had been relieved at his appearance on the scene. He had feared an element of caution in Angel's soul: that she might end up married to a solicitor or stockbroker. And artists were at least creative, and an artist such as Edward Holst might well end up rich and famous. Terry had six Holst canvases on his walls to hasten the process. Two were of his daughter, nude, thigh slackly falling away from her stubby fair bush. Angel, defeated—as her mother had been defeated. 'I love you, Dora, but you must understand. I am not *in* love with you.' As I'm in love with Helen, Audrey, Rita, whoever it was: off to meetings, parties, off on his literary travels, looking for fresh copy and new backgrounds, encountering always someone more exciting, more interesting, than an ageing ex shoe-shop assistant. Why couldn't Dora understand? Unreasonable of her to suffer, clutching the wretched Angel to her alarmingly slack bosom. Could he, Terry, really be the only animation of her flesh? There was a sickness in her love, clearly; unaccompanied as it was by the beauty which lends grace to importunity.

Angel had her mother's large, sad eyes. The reproach in them was in-built. Better Dora's heart had stopped (she'd thought it would: six months' pregnant, she found Terry in the housemaid's bed. She, Dora, mistress of servants! What bliss!) and the embryo Angel never emerged to the light of day.

The noise above Angel stops. Ghosts! What nonsense! A fallen lath grating and rattling in the wind. What else? Angel regains her courage, slips her hand out from beneath Edward's thigh preparatory to leaving the bed for the bathroom. She will turn on all the lights and run. Edward wakes; sits up.

'What's that? What in God's name's that?'

'I can't hear anything,' says Angel, all innocence. Nor can she, not now. Edward's displeasure to contend with now; worse than the universe rattling its chains.

'Footsteps, in the attic. Are you deaf? Why didn't you wake me?'

'I thought I imagined it.'

But she can hear them, once again, as if with his ears. The same pattern across the floor and back. Footsteps or heartbeats. Quicker and quicker now, hastening with the terror and tension of escape.

Edward, unimaginably brave, puts on his slippers, grabs a broken banister (five of these on the landing—one day soon, some day, he'll get round to mending them—he doesn't want some builder, paid by Angel, bungling the job) and goes on up to the attic. Angel follows behind. He will not let her cower in bed. Her bladder aches. She says nothing about that. How can she? Not yet. Not quite yet. Soon. 'Edward, I'm pregnant.' She can't believe it's true, herself. She feels a child, not a woman.

'Is there someone there?'

Edward's voice echoes through the three dark attic rooms. Silence. He gropes for and switches on the light. Empty, derelict rooms: plaster falling, laths hanging, wallpaper peeling. Floorboards broken. A few cans of paint, a pile of wallpaper rolls, old newspapers. Nothing else.

'It could have been mice,' says Edward, doubtfully.

'Can't you hear it?' asks Angel, terrified. The sound echoes in her ears: footsteps clattering over a pounding heart. But Edward can't, not any more.

'Don't start playing games,' he murmurs, turning back to warmth and bed. Angel scuttles down before him, into the bathroom; the noise in her head fades. A few drops of urine tinkle into the bowl.

Edward lies awake in bed: Angel can feel his wakefulness, his increasing hostility towards her, before she is so much as back in the bedroom.

'Your bladder's very weak, Angel,' he complains. 'Something else you inherited from your mother?'

Something else, along with what? Suicidal tendencies, alcoholism, a drooping bosom, a capacity for being betrayed, deserted and forgotten?

Not forgotten by me, Mother. I don't forget, I love you. Even when my body cries out beneath the embraces of this man, this lover, this husband, and my mouth forms words of love, promises of eternity, still I don't forget. I love you, Mother.

'I don't know about my mother's bladder,' murmurs Angel rashly.

'Now you're going to keep me awake all night,' says Edward. 'I can feel it coming. You know I've nearly finished a picture.'

'I'm not going to say a word,' she says, and then, fulfilling his prophesy, sees fit to add, 'I'm pregnant.'

Silence. Stillness. Sleep?

No, a slap across nostrils, eyes, mouth. Edward has never hit Angel before. It is not a hard slap: it contains the elements of a caress.

'Don't even joke about it,' says Edward, softly.

'But I am pregnant.'

Silence. He believes her. Her voice made doubt impossible.

'How far?' Edward seldom asks for information. It is an act which infers ignorance, and Edward likes to know more than anyone else in the entire world.

'Three and a half months.'

He repeats the words, incredulous.

'Too far gone to do anything,' says Angel, knowing now why she did not tell Edward earlier, and the knowledge making her voice cold and hard. Too far gone for the abortion he will most certainly want her to have. So much for the fruits of love. Love? What's love? Sex, ah, that's another thing. Love has babies: sex has abortions.

But Angel will turn sex into love—yes, she will—seizing it by the neck, throttling it till it gives up and takes the weaker path. Love! Edward is right to be frightened, right to hate her.

'I hate you,' he says, and means it. 'You mean to destroy me.'

'I'll make sure it doesn't disturb your nights,' says Angel. Angel of the bristly fair bush, 'if that's what you're worrying about. And you won't have to support it. I do that, anyway. Or my father does.'

Well, how dare she! Angel, not nearly as nice as she thought. Soft-eyed, vicious Angel.

Slap, comes the hand again, harder. Angel screams, he shouts; she collapses, crawls about the floor—he spurns her, she begs forgiveness; he spits his hatred, fear, and she her misery. If the noise above continues, certainly no one hears it, there is so much going on below. The rustlings of the night erupting into madness. Angel is suddenly quiet, whimpering, lying on the floor, she squirms. At first Edward thinks she is acting, but her white lips and taloned fingers convince him that something is wrong with her body and not just her mind. He gets her back on the bed and rings the doctor. Within an hour Angel finds herself in a hospital with a suspected ectopic pregnancy. They delay the operation and the pain subsides; just one of those things, they shrug. Edward has to interrupt his painting the next afternoon to collect her from the hospital.

'What was it? Hysteria?' he enquires.

'I dare say!'

'Well, you had a bad beginning, what with your mother and all,' he concedes, kissing her nose, nibbling her earlobe. It is forgiveness; but Angel's eyes remain unusually cold. She stays in bed, after Edward has left it and gone back to his studio, although the floors remain unswept and the dishes unwashed.

Angel does not say what is in her mind, what she knows to be true. That he is disappointed to see both her and the baby back, safe and sound. He had hoped the baby would die, or failing that, the mother would die and the baby with her. He is pretending forgiveness, while he works out what to do next.

In the evening the doctor comes to see Angel. He is a slight man with a sad face: his eyes, she thinks, are kind behind his pebble glasses. His voice is slow and gentle. I expect his wife is happy, thinks Angel, and actually envies her. Some middle-aged, dowdy, provincial doctor's wife, envied by Angel! Rich, sweet, young and pretty Angel. The efficient secretary, lovable barmaid, and now the famous artist's wife! Once, for two rash weeks, even an art school model.

The doctor examines her, then discreetly pulls down her nightie to cover her breasts and moves the sheet up to cover her crotch. If he were my father, thinks Angel, he would not hang my naked portrait on his wall for the entertainment of his friends. Angel had not known until this moment that she minded.

'Everything's doing nicely inside there,' says the doctor. 'Sorry to rush you off like that, but we can't take chances.'

Ah, to be looked after. Love. That's love. The doctor shows no inclination to go.

'Perhaps I should have a word with your husband,' he suggests. He stands at the window gazing over daffodils and green fields. 'Or is he very busy?'

'He's painting,' says Angel. 'Better not disturb him now. He's had so many interruptions lately, poor man.'

'I read about him in the Sunday supplement,' says the doctor.

'Well, don't tell him so. He thought it vulgarised his work.'

'Did you think that?'

Me? Does what I think have anything to do with anything?

'I thought it was quite perceptive, actually,' says Angel, and feels a surge of good humour. She sits up in bed.

'Lie down,' he says. 'Take things easy. This is a large house. Do you have any help? Can't afford it?'

'It's not that. It's just why should I expect some other woman to do my dirty work?'

'Because she might like doing it and you're pregnant, and if you can afford it, why not?'

'Because Edward doesn't like strangers in the house. And what else have I got to do with my life? I might as well clean as anything else.'

'It's isolated out here,' he goes on. 'Do you drive?'

'Edward needs peace to paint,' says Angel. 'I do drive but Edward has a thing about women drivers.'

'You don't miss your friends?'

'After you're married,' says Angel, 'you seem to lose contact. It's the same for everyone, isn't it?'

'Um,' says the doctor. And then, 'I haven't been in this house for fifteen years. It's in a better state now than it was then. The house was divided into flats, in those days. I used to visit a nice young woman who had the attic floor. Just above this. Four children, and the roof leaked; a husband who spent his time drinking cider in the local pub and only came home to beat her.'

'Why did she stay?'

'How can such women leave? How do they afford it? Where do they go? What happens to the children?' His voice is sad.

'I suppose it's money that makes the difference. With money, a woman's free,' says Angel, trying to believe it.

'Of course,' says the doctor. 'But she loved her husband. She couldn't bring herself to see him for what he was. Well, it's hard. For a certain kind of woman, at any rate.'

Hard, indeed, if he has your soul in his safe-keeping, to be left behind at the bar, in the pub, or in some other woman's bed, or in a seat in the train on his literary travels. Careless!

'But it's not like that for you, is it?' says the doctor calmly. 'You have money of your own, after all.'

Now how does he know that? Of course, the Sunday supplement article.

'No one will read it,' wept Angel, when Edward looked up, stony-faced from his first perusal of the fashionable columns. 'No one will notice. It's tucked away at the very bottom.'

So it was. 'Edward's angelic wife Angel, daughter of best-selling crime-writer Terry Toms, has smoothed the path upwards, not just with the soft smiles our cameraman has recorded, but by enabling the emergent genius to forswear the cramped and inconvenient, if traditional, artist's garret for a sixteenth-century farmhouse in greenest Gloucestershire. It is interesting, moreover, to ponder whether a poor man would have been able to develop the white-on-white techniques which have made Holst's work so noticeable: or whether the sheer price of paint these days would not have deterred him.'

'Edward, I didn't say a word to that reporter, not a word,' she said, when the ice showed signs of cracking, days later.

'What are you talking about?' he asked, turning slow, unfriendly eyes upon her.

'The article. I know it's upset you. But it wasn't my fault.'

'Why should a vulgar article in a vulgar newspaper upset me?'

And the ice formed over again, thicker than ever. But he went to London for two days, presumably to arrange his next show, and on his return casually mentioned that he'd seen Ray while he was there.

Angel had cleaned, baked, and sewed curtains in his absence, hoping
to soften his heart towards her on his return: and lay awake all the night
he was away, the fear of his infidelity so agonising as to make her
contemplate suicide, if only to put an end to it. She could not ask for
reassurance. He would throw the fears so neatly back at her. 'Why do
you think I should want to sleep with anyone else? Why are you so
guilty? Because that's what you'd do if you were away from me?'

Ask for bread and be given stones. Learn self-sufficiency: never
show need. Little, tough Angel of the soft smiles, hearing some other
woman's footsteps in the night, crying for another's grief. Well, who
wants a soul, tossed here and there by teasing hands, over-bruised and
over-handled. Do without it!

Edward came home from London in a worse mood than he'd left,
shook his head in wondering stupefaction at his wife's baking—'I
thought you said we were cutting down on carbohydrates'—and shut
himself into his studio for twelve hours, emerging just once to say—
'Only a mad woman would hang curtains in an artist's studio, or else a
silly rich girl playing at artist's wife, and in public at that'—and thrust-
ing the new curtains back into her arms, vanished inside again.

Angel felt that her mind was slowing up, and puzzled over the last
remark for some time before realising that Edward was still harking
back to the Sunday supplement article.

'I'll give away the money if you like,' she pleaded through the key-
hole. 'If you'd rather. And if you want not to be married to me I don't
mind.' That was before she was pregnant.

Silence.

Then Edward emerged laughing, telling her not to be so ridiculous,
bearing her off to bed, and the good times were restored. Angel sang
about the house, forgot her pill, and got pregnant.

'You have money of your own, after all,' says the doctor. 'You're
perfectly free to come and go.'

'I'm pregnant,' says Angel. 'The baby has to have a father.'

'And your husband's happy about the baby?'

'Oh yes!' says Angel. 'Isn't it a wonderful day!'

And indeed today the daffodils nod brightly under a clear sky. So far,
since first they budded and bloomed, they have been obliged to droop
beneath the weight of rain and mist. A disappointing spring. Angel had
hoped to see the countryside leap into energy and colour, but life
returned only slowly, it seemed, struggling to surmount the damage of
the past: cold winds and hard frosts, unseasonably late. 'Or at any rate,'

adds Angel, softly, unheard, as the doctor goes, 'he *will* be happy about the baby.'

Angel hears no more noises in the night for a week or so. There had been misery in the attic rooms, and the misery had ceased. Good times can wipe out bad. Surely!

Edward sleeps soundly and serenely: she creeps from bed to bathroom without waking him. He is kind to her and even talkative, on any subject, that is, except that of her pregnancy. If it were not for the doctor and her stay in the hospital, she might almost think she was imagining the whole thing. Edward complains that Angel is getting fat, as if he could imagine no other cause for it but greed. She wants to talk to someone about hospitals, confinements, layettes, names—but to whom?

She tells her father on the telephone—'I'm pregnant.'

'What does Edward say?' asks Terry, cautiously.

'Nothing much,' admits Angel.

'I don't suppose he does.'

'There's no reason *not* to have a baby,' ventures Angel.

'I expect he rather likes to be the centre of attention.' It is the nearest Terry has ever got to a criticism of Edward.

Angel laughs. She is beyond believing that Edward could ever be jealous of her, ever be dependent upon her.

'Nice to hear you happy, at any rate,' says her father wistfully. His twenty-year-old girlfriend has become engaged to a salesman of agricultural machinery, and although she has offered to continue the relationship the other side of marriage, Terry feels debased and used, and was obliged to break off the liaison. He has come to regard his daughter's marriage to Edward in a romantic light. The young bohemians!

'My daughter was an art school model before she married Edward Holst . . . you've heard of him? It's a real Rembrandt and Saskia affair.' He even thinks lovingly of Dora: if only she'd understood, waited for youth to wear itself out. Now he's feeling old and perfectly capable of being faithful to an ex shoe-shop assistant. If only she weren't dead and gone!

An art school model. Those two weeks! Why had she done it? What devil wound up her works and set poor Angel walking in the wrong direction? It was in her nature, surely, as it was in her mother's to follow the paths to righteousness, fully clothed.

Nightly, Edward studied her naked body, kissing her here, kissing her there, parting her legs. Well, marriage! But now I'm pregnant, now

I'm pregnant. Oh, be careful. That hard lump where my soft belly used to be. Be careful! Silence, Angel. Don't speak of it. It will be the worse for you and your baby if you do.

Angel knows it.

Now Angel hears the sound of lovemaking up in the empty attic, as she might hear it in hotels in foreign lands. The couplings of strangers in an unknown tongue—only the cries and breathings universal, recognisable anywhere.

The sounds chill her: they do not excite her. She thinks of the mother of four who lived in this house with her drunken, violent husband. Was that what kept you by his side? The chains of fleshly desire? Was it the thought of the night that got you through the perils of the day?

What indignity, if it were so.

Oh, I imagine it. I, Angel, half-mad in my unacknowledged pregnancy, my mind feverish, and the doctor's anecdotes feeding the fever—I imagine it! I must!

Edward wakes.

'What's that noise?'

'What noise?'

'Upstairs.'

'I don't hear anything.'

'You're deaf.'

'What sort of noise?'

But Edward sleeps again. The noise fades, dimly. Angel hears the sound of children's voices. Let it be a girl, dear Lord, let it be a girl.

'Why do you want a girl?' asks the doctor, on Angel's fourth monthly visit to the clinic.

'I'd love to dress a girl,' says Angel vaguely, but what she means is, if it's a girl, Edward will not be so—what is the word?—hardly jealous, difficult perhaps. Dreadful. Yes, dreadful.

Bright-eyed Edward: he walks with Angel now—long walks up and over stiles, jumping streams, leaping stones. Young Edward. She has begun to feel rather old, herself.

'I am a bit tired,' she says, as they set off one night for their moon-lit walk.

He stops, puzzled.

'Why are you tired?'

'Because I'm pregnant,' she says, in spite of herself.

'Don't start that again,' he says, as if it were hysteria on her part. Perhaps it is.

That night, he opens her legs so wide she thinks she will burst. 'I love you,' he murmurs in her nibbled ear, 'Angel, I love you. I do love you.' Angel feels the familiar surge of response, the holy gratitude, the willingness to die, to be torn apart if that's what's required. And then it stops. It's gone. Evaporated! And in its place, a new strength. A chilly icicle of non-response, wonderful, cheerful. No. It isn't right; it isn't what's required: on the contrary. 'I love you,' she says in return, as usual; but crossing her fingers in her mind, forgiveness for a lie. Please God, dear God, save me, help me save my baby. It is not me he loves, but my baby he hates: not me he delights in, but the pain he causes me, and knows he does. He does not wish to take root in me: all he wants to do is root my baby out. I don't love him. I never have. It is sickness. I must get well. Quickly.

'Not like that,' says Angel, struggling free—bold, unkind, prudish Angel—rescuing her legs. 'I'm pregnant. I'm sorry, but I am pregnant.'

Edward rolls off her, withdraws.

'Christ, you can be a monster. A real ball-breaker.'

'Where are you going?' asks Angel, calm and curious. Edward is dressing. Clean shirt; cologne. Cologne!

'To London.'

'Why?'

'Where I'm appreciated.'

'Don't leave me alone. Please.' But she doesn't mean it.

'Why not?'

'I'm frightened. Here alone at night.'

'Nothing ever frightened you.' Perhaps he is right.

Off he goes; the car breaking open the silence of the night. It closes again. Angel is alone.

Tap, tap, tap, up above. Starting up as if on signal. Back and forward. To the attic bed which used to be, to the wardrobe which once was; the scuffle of the suitcase on the floor. Goodbye. I'm going. I'm frightened here. The house is haunted. Someone upstairs, downstairs. Oh, women everywhere, don't think your misery doesn't seep into walls, creep downstairs, and then upstairs again. Don't think it will ever be done with, or that the good times wipe it out. They don't.

Angel feels her heart stop and start again. A neurotic symptom, her father's doctor had once said. It will get better, he said, when she's married and has babies. Everything gets better for women when they're married with babies. It's their natural state. Angel's heart stops all the same, and starts again, for good or bad.

Angel gets out of bed, slips on her mules with their sharp little heels, and goes up the attic stairs. Where does she find the courage? The light, reflected up from the hallway, is dim. The noise from the attic stops. Angel hears only—what?—the rustling noise of old newspapers in a fresh wind. That stops, too. As if a film were now running without sound. And coming down towards Angel, a small, tired woman in a nightie, slippers silent on the stairs, stopping to stare at Angel as Angel stares at her. Her face marked by bruises.

'How can I see that,' wonders Angel, now unafraid, 'since there isn't any light?'

She turns on the switch, hand trembling, and in the light, as she'd known, there is nothing to be seen except the empty stairs and the unmarked dust upon them.

Angel goes back to the bedroom and sits on the bed.

'I saw a ghost,' she tells herself, calmly enough. Then fear reasserts itself: panic at the way the universe plays tricks. Quick, quick! Angel pulls her suitcase out from under the bed—there are still traces of wedding confetti within—and tap-tap she goes, with sharp little footsteps, from the wardrobe to the bed, from the chest of drawers and back again, not so much packing as retrieving, salvaging. Something out of nothing!

Angel and her predecessor, rescuing each other, since each was incapable of rescuing herself, and rescue always comes, somehow. Or else death.

Tap, tap, back and forth, into the suitcase, out of the house.

The garden gate swings behind her.

Angel, bearing love to a safer place.

Spirit of the House

Some time after the trouble with Jenny began, Christine wrote off to a professor of psychical research in California, whose name she had discovered in a magazine article. 'Whenever Jenny comes into the room,' Christine wrote, 'I feel cold. So I know there's something wrong with her. But what it is?' She had an answer sooner than she expected, and more alarming, too. The professor wrote that the presence of evil was often registered, by sensitives, in this manner; and was there a bad smell as well?

Now Jenny did indeed quite often smell strongly of carbolic but Christine felt that this was not in itself significant. The soap provided for employees up at the Big House was a job-lot of hard, orange, carbolic tablets, brought cheap from an army surplus store, and Jenny washed herself with it, hard and often. Christine always took Mornay's Lavender to work with her, the more sweetly to wash her pretty hands. She liked to smell nice, and her husband Luke liked her to smell nice, and how he could put up with Jenny smelling of carbolic, Christine could not tell. Let alone love her.

But carbolic was not, in itself, a bad smell. Nothing, after all, like the stench of sulphur and decomposition associated with the presence of the devil. True enough, though, and bad enough, that the feeling of cold wafted around Jenny like an odour. She could be said to smell cold. Christine discontinued her correspondence with the Californian professor for fear of discovering worse. She prayed instead.

'Dear God, let him get over her. Dear God, let her not harm the baby. Dear God, let them believe me.'

But God seemed not to be listening. Luke went on loving Jenny, Jenny went on looking after Baby Emmy, and no one believed Christine when she said that Jenny was not to be trusted.

Christine had been married to Luke for nineteen years. She loved her husband with an energetic and consuming passion, well able to withstand his occasional lapses into the adoration of passing girls. She would treat him, when he was thus enamoured, with a fond indulgence, saying, 'Well, men are like that, aren't they?' and waiting for common sense and reason to return, and uxorious content to shine once again from his gentle eyes. But Jenny was different—Christine had suspected something unwholesome about her from the very first. In retrospect it was hard to tell, of course, quite when she had begun to think it— before Luke started mooning after Jenny, or after. But surely it was before—a sickly, chilly menace, a sudden shiver down the spine? Evil, the professor had written. Or perhaps he only wrote that, knowing what she wanted to hear? Americans were strange.

Jenny was stranger. Now Christine feared for Luke, body and soul, and feared for Emmy, Lord Mader's baby daughter, even more. Jenny was Emmy's nanny. Little, pretty, safe words, adding up to something monstrous.

And of course if Christine murmured against Jenny, the other members of the staff assumed that Christine was jealous, and discredited what she said. Jenny was quiet, gentle, pale and young. Christine was noisy and volatile and ruddy and in her middle years. And Christine's husband, everyone knew, was in love with Jenny, trailing after her, gazing after her.

'But look,' Christine felt like saying, 'he's been in love a dozen times in as many years. It's just the way he is. I don't mind. He's a genius, you see. A mathematical genius, not one of your artistic geniuses, but a genius all the same. My feeling about Jenny is nothing to do with what Luke feels or doesn't feel for her.'

But the rest of the staff were dull, if good-hearted, and had their preconceptions about the world, which nothing now would shake: it was almost as if the chilly presence of Jenny had cemented in these preconceptions, where once they had stood free, able to change and move. Their vision narrowed to what they already knew. Christine concluded that Jenny had a strange deadening power over everyone, excepting only, for some reason, herself.

Jenny had a white, dead face and large, pale eyes she magnified with round owl spectacles, and short plain hair and a child's body. The face was thirty, the body was thirteen. Perhaps that was her power—the desire of the grown man for the pre-pubertal girl? A sickly and insidious love! And did the women perhaps remember themselves at thirteen and set Jenny free now, to do what they would have liked then?

Christine herself, at forty, was plump and maternal and pretty and busy. There could be nothing unhealthy in anyone's desire for her, and many did desire her, but she seldom noticed. She loved Luke.

Christine, the Doris Day of Mader House! Wonderful Mader House, Stately Home, giving the lucky villagers of Maderley full employment! With its Elizabethan chimneys, and Jacobean mullions, Georgian casements and Victorian tiles, it still remained imposing, if hardly gracious. Its lands and gardens, its ancient oaks, its Disneyland and zoo, its Sunday lunches with Lord and Lady Mader (fifty pounds a place-setting), made it popular with millions. Lord Mader was often indisposed and his young brother Martin sent in his place, but the third Lady Mader was always there. She was young and did as she was told, as did the villagers.

The latest, newest Lady Mader had, it is true, given birth to little Emmy instead of to a son, but as Lord Mader observed, coming to terms with his disappointment, if any Lady Mader's first-born was male the child was doomed to die before the age of twenty-one. There was a family tradition that it was so. Take for example Lucien, eldest son by his second wife. Lucien was on hard drugs and wouldn't make twenty, let alone twenty-one. Said Lord Mader, peering myopically at Emmy, bending over the family cradle, hands clasped firmly behind his back. He never touched his offspring, if he could help it.

The Maders, their disparagers murmured, had fallen from being a powerful and wealthy family to a handful of publicity-seeking degenerates. Even Christine, who loved to be loyal, increasingly saw truth in this observation. Yves, the present Lord, was thrice married. His first wife had been barren, and for that reason divorced. Lucien, son by his second wife, was a junkie, and Lucien's little sister Deborah now played the lead in skin-flicks. Yet these seemed matters of mirth rather than shame to Yves. A further son, Piers, was in real estate, and considered too boring for discussion. Left a widower by his second wife's suicide, Yves promptly married Mara, a twenty-year-old Greek heiress, and sired little Emmy.

Yves had selected Jenny from over two hundred applicants for the post of Nanny. He prided himself on being a good judge of character.

'Does he love the baby?' people would ask Christine. 'Oh yes, she'd reply, adding in her heart, as much as he loves anything, which isn't very much.' The pressure of the words grew and grew and she was frightened that one day she would say them aloud.

'And the mother?'

'She's not very much at home, but I'm sure she does.' Christine was nice. She wanted to think well of everyone.

Mara loved treats and outings and hunting, and occasions on which she could wear a tiara, and the Mader family jewels—or, rather, replicas of same. The originals had been sold in the thirties; and Maderley House itself would have followed in the fifties, had not Yves discovered that the people's fascination with their aristocracy could be turned to excellent financial account; whereupon he flung open the gates, and filled up the moat, and turned the stables into restaurants, and himself into a public show.

The show business side of Maderley was in Christine's charge—it was she who organised the guides, the cleaners, the caterers, even the vets for sick animals. She saw to brochures, catalogues and souvenirs. She took the takings to the bank. She had the status in the household of someone dedicated, who is despised for their dedication. She was underpaid, and mocked for being so by those who underpaid her, and did not notice.

Christine's husband Luke sat in the Great Library and worked out efficient mathematical formulae for the winning of the pools. Yves had once met, over dinner, a Nobel Prize winner, a mathematician, who had convinced him of the practicality of working out such formulae, computer-aided. Yves promptly had a computer-terminal installed in the Great Library, and Luke installed likewise. Visitors gawped at both between two and three on Wednesdays. Luke had a first-class honours degree in mathematics from Oxford. He had been a Maderley child with a peculiar gift for numbers and few social skills. He had returned to the village, married to Christine, a girl from far away, to write textbooks for graduates, which he did slowly, with difficulty, and for very little money.

The Great Library! There Christine fed the computer with data about visitors, gate takings, capital costs and so forth. And here Luke puzzled over his formulae, and here Jenny liked to sit in the winter sun beneath the mullioned windows, and rock the baby's pram, and watch Luke at work. The baby never cried. Sometimes it whimpered. The cover was pulled up well over its face.

Christine had tried to say something to Yves about Jenny and the baby.

'Yves'—his employees were instructed to call him by his Christian name—'can I talk to you about Jenny?'

'What do you want to say?' He was unfriendly. She knew he did not like trouble. It was her function, after all, to keep it away from him. She had once asked for a rise in her wages, and the same shuttered, cold look had fallen across his face, as it now did, when she wanted to talk about Jenny. 'I don't think she's very good with the baby,' said Christine, tentatively, and wanted to go on and say, 'My Lord, I have seen bruises on the baby's arm. I don't like the way the baby whimpers instead of crying. I don't like the thinness of the baby's wrists. A baby's wrists should be chubby and creased, not bony.' But she didn't speak. She hesitated, looking at his cold face, and was lost.

'You mean she's too good with your husband, Christine,' was all Yves said. 'You sort out your own problems, don't come running to me.'

Christine, later that day, came across Yves with Jenny. They were together in the library. He had his hands on her thin shoulders: he, who seldom touched anyone. What were they saying?

Christine heard the baby make its little mewling cry, but Yves did not even glance into the pram.

Christine said to Mrs Scott the housekeeper. 'I'm worried about that baby. I don't think she gets enough to eat.'

Mrs Scott said, 'You don't know anything about babies. You've never had one. Jenny's a trained Norland nanny. She knows what she's doing.'

Jenny sat next to Mrs Scott at the staff lunch that day. They seemed very companionable.

Christine watched Luke watching Jenny being companionable with Mrs Scott, and the staff watched Christine watching Luke watching Jenny, and sniggered.

Christine telephoned the Norland nanny organisation, and they had no record of a Jenny Whitstone on their books.

Christine watched Jenny hold the baby's bottle an inch or so from the baby's mouth, so that the baby stopped whimpering and rooted with its mouth towards the warm, sweet smell and found it, and Christine watched Jenny tug out the bottle after the first few mouthfuls and put it back on the shelf. The baby moaned.

'What did you do that for?' asked Christine.

'I don't want the baby getting too fat,' said Jenny. 'It's a terrible thing to be fat.'

And Jenny eyed Christine's plump form with cold distaste.

Luke stopped making love to Christine altogether.

'It wouldn't be fair to you,' said Luke. 'How can I make love to you when I'm thinking of her? I wish I could, but I can't.'

'Why, why do you love her?' begged Christine.

But he didn't know, couldn't say.

It seemed to Christine that Luke felt cold in bed, as if his flesh was dying.

She spoke to the guides about Jenny, at their Monday morning meeting, where such things were discussed as meal breaks and the positioning of the silken ropes which guarded certain rooms and passages from the touch and view of ordinary people. 'Where did she come from?' Christine asked. 'Does anyone know?'

No one seemed to. It was as if she had always been there, along with the house itself, along with the family: the worm, or whatever it was, that nibbled away at the souls of the rich, so that born angels, they grew up devils.

For what could become of them but this? Generation succeeding generation: heartless mothers, distant fathers, and the distress of this made light of, by a surfeit of manners and money?

'The scale's all wrong,' Christine said in her heart. 'The house is just too big for people.'

Life's battles, life's events, triumphs and disasters—all were rendered puny by the lofty ceilings. Words of love and grief alike, hate and joy, all were muted beneath the arching vaults of the great hall, were sopped up and made one by ancient panelling. The stair was too high for the child to climb, or the old woman to descend. Marriages were lost in a bed so big it made passion trivial: the sexual act ridiculous under the cold eyes of ceiling cherubs. And animals! The love of dumb beasts put before the love of people; the death of a horse marking the year more than the death of a child; kennels always warmer than the nurseries. Manners replacing morals.

'They're born like anyone else,' Christine said in her heart, never aloud. 'And then I don't know what happens, but they end up monsters.'

So, now, it seemed to Christine, the damage which little Emmy could expect in the course of the next twenty years, was being, at the hands of Jenny, inflicted upon her in as many months.

'I know why you love her,' she said presently to Luke, 'it's because she's the spirit of the House. And it's sickening and disgusting, and everyone loves it. Except me.'

'That isn't why I love her.' said Luke. 'And if you feel like that about the House, why go on working here?'

'What else could I do round here? There's no employment except at Maderley.'

But in spite of what she said, she stayed and she knew she stayed because she too, like Luke, was still under the spell of the Big House, and felt honoured by the company of Yves, whom she was privileged to call by his Christian name, and because she did not want to leave Emmy and Luke to the mercies of Jenny.

Lady Mara was due back from the Bahamas. The whole house gleamed with polish and glowed with flowers.

But Emmy was listless, and blinked a good deal, and flinched and grizzled the day Lady Mara came back.

'She isn't very pretty,' said Mara, disappointed, peering into the pram, and after that seldom asked to see the child at all. She rode to hounds a good deal, along with farmers and carpet manufacturers.

'I wish you wouldn't,' complained Yves. 'Only the bourgeoisie go hunting these days.' But Mara was regaining her spirit, and learning how to do not what she was told, and she persisted, slashing at grasses with her riding crop, as if she'd like to slash at life itself.

Presently, Christine came across Jenny in the Great Library. Jenny had taken Emmy, for once, out of her pram. Jenny stood there, among ten thousand books, which were beautifully bound but never read, turning her owl eyes up to where the sunlight glanced through the windows, so that her spectacles dazzled, and seemed to retain the blinding shine even when she turned her head out of the sunlight to face Christine. Jenny, with her child's thighs in their tight, faded jeans, and budding breasts beneath a white T-shirt, and a dazzle where her face should be.

Jenny, with her soft, flat, slightly nasal voice, which could turn sharp and cruel and hard. Christine had often heard it. 'Christ, you little monster!' And slap, slap, thump, and then the weary grizzle again from Emmy.

Christine had never managed to get pregnant.

'Well,' the doctor had said, 'I dare say you have a child already, in your husband.'

Christine, cooking, nurturing, caring, worrying, had agreed with the doctor and not minded too much about their lack of children. Christine, after all, was the breadwinner. Perhaps what Luke saw in Jenny, suggested Christine, trying again, was his own unborn daughter? An incestuous love, given permission to live and thrive.

It was Yves who had given permission. Yes, he had.

'We all love Jenny,' Yves had said. 'Jenny saves us from our children.' Everyone except Christine, everyone's look said, watching Christine watching Luke watching Jenny, everyone loves Jenny.

Christine tried Yves' younger brother Martin, born by Caesarean while his mother lay dying from an overdose of sleeping pills and whisky, self-inflicted. Martin was the estate manager of Maderley, and kind and reliable, by virtue of an inborn insensitivity to the world about him. When Yves spoke to Martin it was in the same way he spoke to the upper servants—with a derisive politeness. Martin stuttered, so that Christine's conversation with him took a long time, and she was busy, needed at the toll-gate with new parking tickets.

'Sir, I don't think Jenny is what she says. She isn't a Norland nurse at all. I checked up.'

'No one round here is what they claim to be,' said Martin, sadly. 'And the baby is Lady Mara's business, not ours.'

'Couldn't you say something to Yves?'

'Not really,' said Martin. 'If you feel strongly about it, say something yourself.'

'I have, but he just got angry and wouldn't listen.'

'The baby looks like any other baby to me,' said Martin. 'Not that I know much about them, of course.' Martin was commonly known to be impotent and one of his eyes turned inwards—a squint which had been left untreated in infancy, and so remained.

'Yves is a very good judge of character,' said Martin. 'If he employed Jenny she must be all right.'

The next day Christine saw Jenny wheeling the baby in the grounds, and Martin was with her. Even Martin! Martin, saying goodbye to Jenny, pecked her on the cheek, and she turned her face so that once again her glasses glinted and dazzled and the space beneath the pram hood seemed black, like the mouth of hell.

When Jenny wheeled the baby into the kitchen that day Christine bent to pick the baby up.

'Don't pick up the baby,' said Jenny sharply. 'She's sleeping quietly.' But to Christine the baby looked not so much asleep, as dead. And then an eyelash fluttered against the white cheek and Christine knew she was wrong. She went on counting sandwiches—two hundred ham, one hundred cheese—for the special Maderley tea, four pounds a head, served in the converted stable block.

'But *how* do you love her, *why* do you love her?'

She knew that she was nagging: she couldn't help it. She kept Luke awake at night now, working away at the truth. It was only while he slept that his body grew cold, and the pain of his answers was preferable to the chilly numbness of his sleep; she knew that, sleeping, he drifted off somewhere away from her, over the safe, surrounding walls of her love and, moth-like, floated towards the chilly, blinding light which used Jenny as its beacon.

It was at that time that she wrote to the professor of physical research, and had confirmation of her fears. Jenny was evil.

'Lady Mara?'

'What is it, Christine?'

Lady Mara, broken arm in a sling—her horse had lurched and reared at nothing in particular, a sudden bright light in the grounds was all she could think of—was lately very much the grande dame. She would have bathed in asses' milk if she could.

'Lady Mara, I'm worried about the baby.'

'The baby is nothing to do with you. You look after the visitors and let Jenny look after the baby.'

Lady Mara was only twenty-one. The same age as Yves' daughter, the one who presented her body at rude, amazing angles for the benefit of the camera, a publisher and a million wistful men. But a title and wealth, and the assumption of power, of the right to tell other people what to do and what to say, add up to more than years. Mara stared coldly. Christine fumbled. Christine was impertinent. If she didn't stop meddling she might have to go. There were more than enough only too ready to take her place. Mara said nothing. There was no need to. Christine fell silent.

Yves and Mara went away to attend a wedding. Five thousand

pounds, they had heard, were to be spent on flowers for the marquees alone. Who would miss a wedding like that?

Christine found her husband Luke weeping in the conservatory. 'What's the matter, Luke?'

But he was frozen into silence. Presently, he thawed, as if warmed by Christine's presence, her arm round his shaking shoulders, and spoke.

'I asked her. I plucked up courage and asked her. I said I wanted to sleep with her more than anything in the world.'

'And?' How cold the pit of the stomach, where words strike their message home.

'She laughed at me. She told me I was old and flabby. She said I was weak. She said I was a failure. Am I these things, Christine?'

'Of course not.' But he was.

'I have no right to do this to you, Christine.' He cried again in her maternal arms. 'But I love her more than ever.'

Christine went to see Jenny in her bedroom. 'You leave my husband alone,' said Christine, 'or I'll kill you.'

'Get him to leave me alone,' said Jenny, laughing, a cold, dead laugh. How could you kill what was already dead?

The baby murmured in its cot. Christine looked at little Emmy. Her eyes were black, and swollen. Christine lifted the baby out of its cot.

'You leave that baby alone,' snapped Jenny. 'You poor jealous frustrated barren old bitch.'

It was the cry of the world, but it was not true. Christine's spirit was warm, loving and fecund.

Christine unwrapped little Emmy from her soft blankets and found that her back was bruised and her right leg hung oddly. Christine cradled the baby carefully in her arms and ran down long, long corridors, hung with family portraits, and down the great staircase, and into the reception area, where the tickets were taken, and rang all the bells she could, and Martin came, and Luke and three of the guides and Mrs Scott the housekeeper, and a cleaner; and Jenny followed after but stopped halfway down the stairs, in a little patch where the sun shone in, so she glowed all over, the source and not the reflection of light.

'Look,' said Christine, showing what was in her arms. 'Look! See what she's done to the baby?'

'It was an accident,' called Jenny, in her soft, nasal voice. 'You're all my friends. You know I wouldn't do it on purpose.'

But the sun had shone in upon the wrong stair. She was just too far away, her voice just a little too faint. Jenny's words meant nothing to the cluster of people gazing at the baby. Lord Mader's baby, with its swollen eyes and its blue-black back.

'I'll get an ambulance,' said Christine.

'Think of the publicity,' said Martin, but he spoke without much conviction. 'Yves won't like it.'

'Perhaps we'd better telephone him and get permission,' said Mrs Scott.

'Let me take the baby,' called Jenny. 'It's me Emmy loves. You're all strangers to her. She'll get better if I hold her.'

And what Jenny said was true, but she couldn't make up her mind to lose the sun and step another stair down into the hall, and she faltered and was lost.

Martin rang Yves. Christine had his number: flicked through her efficient files and found it at once.

'Yves,' said Martin, stuttering his message out. 'You'd better come back here. The baby's got a bruise on its back.'

'How big a bruise? Big as a sixpence?'

'Bigger.'

'Big as half a crown?'

'A fiver wouldn't cover it,' said Martin. 'Christine thinks we should call an ambulance.'

'Christine would,' said Yves, sourly. 'Well, stop her. We'll be right back.'

But Christine called the ambulance all the same. They took the baby away and just as well, because Yves and Mara didn't return until the next day.

Emmy had a fractured skull, two broken ribs, a broken thigh and a damaged kidney, but they patched her up quite well, and returned her after eight weeks looking quite pretty, so that her mother picked her up and murmured endearments and nuzzled into her baby neck, and fortunately Emmy smiled at that moment and didn't cry, which would have spoiled everything.

Christine lost her job, and Yves abandoned his hopes of breaking the Great Proletariat Pools Swindle and fired Luke too.

'You'd think they'd be grateful for my saving their baby,' said Christine. 'But the upper classes are just plain twisted.'

'The Greeks used to kill the bearer of bad news,' said Luke, 'so think yourself lucky.'

The sight of the damaged baby made him fall out of love with Jenny, and now he slept warm at night, and Christine beside him. Jenny did not lose her job, but she was no longer allowed to look after the baby. For a time she did what Christine had been doing, for twice the money and with the help of an assistant.

'What a great judge of character Yves is!' said Christine sourly. Everyone she asked, and ask she did, everyone, agreed with her. The Maders were degenerate and decadent. She could say the words aloud now, not just in her heart.

Later she heard that Jenny had taken another post as nanny to two little boys whose mother had died, and that Yves had written her an excellent reference.

'Your employees reflect back on you,' said Luke. 'That's what it is.'

Christine wondered whether to telephone the father of the two little boys and warn him, but knew she would never be believed. And perhaps, who was to say, there was someone like her in every little pocket of the world? Someone to save while others destroyed, or looked away. Wherever Jenny went, there would be someone like Christine.

'I loved her because she was evil,' said Luke, at last, explaining. 'She anaesthetised my moral nerve endings and that was wonderful. And you were right: she was the spirit of the house.'

Watching Me, Watching You

The ghost liked the stairs best, where people passed quickly and occasionally, holding their feelings in suspense between the closing of one door and the opening of another. Mostly, the ghost slept. He preferred sleep. But sometimes the sense of something important happening, some crystallisation of the past or omen for the future, would wake him, and he would slither off the stair and into one room or another of the house to see what was going on. Presently, he wore an easy path of transition into a particular room on the first floor—as sheep will wear an easy path in the turf by constant trotting to and fro. Here, as the seasons passed, a plane tree pressed closer and closer against the window, keeping out light and warmth. The various cats which lived out their lives in the house seldom went into this small damp back room, and seemed to feel the need to race up and down that portion of the stairs the ghost favoured, though sitting happily enough at the bottom of the stairs, or on the top landing.

Many houses contain ghosts. (It would be strange if they didn't.) Mostly they sleep, or wake so seldom their presence is not noticed, let alone minded. If a glass falls off a shelf in 1940, and a door opens by itself in 1963, and a sense of oppression is felt in 1971, and knocking sounds are heard on Christmas Day, 1980—who wants to make anything of that? Four inexplicable happenings in a week call for exorcism—the same number spread over forty years call for nothing more than a shrug and a stiff drink.

66 Aldermans Drive, Bristol. The house had stood for a hundred and

thirty years, and the ghost had slept and occasionally sighed and slithered sideways, and otherwise done little else but puff out a curtain on a still day for all but ten of those. He entered the house on the shoulders of a parlour-maid. She had been to a seance in the hope of raising her dead lover, but had raised something altogether more elusive, if at least sleepier, instead. The maid had stayed in the house until she died, driving her mistress to suicide and marrying the master the while, and the ghost had stayed too, long after all were dead, and the house empty, with paper peeling off the walls, and the banisters broken, and carpets rotting on the floors, and dust and silence everywhere.

The ghost slept, and woke again to the sound of movement, and different voices. The new people were numerous: they warmed gnarled winter hands before gas-fires, and the smell of boiled cabbage and sweat wafted up the stairs, and exhaustion and indifference prevailed. In the back room on the first floor, presently, a girl gave birth to a baby. The ghost sighed and puffed out the curtains. In this room, earlier, the maid's mistress had hanged herself, making a swinging shadow against the wall in the gas-light shining from the stairs. The ghost had a sense of justice, or at any rate balance. He slept again.

The house emptied. Rain came through broken tiles into the back room. A man with a probe came and pierced into the rotten beams of roof and floor, and shook his head and laughed. The tree thrust a branch through the window, and a sparrow flew in, and couldn't get out, and died, and after mice and insects and flies had finished with it, was nothing more than two slender white bones, placed crosswise.

It was 1965. The front door opened and a man and a woman entered, and such was their natures that the ghost was alert at once. The man's name was Maurice: he was burly and warm-skinned; his hands were thick and crude, labourer's hands, but clean and soft. His hair was pale and tightly curled; he was bearded; his eyes were large and heavily hooded. He looked at the house as if he were already its master: as if he cared nothing for its rotten beams and its leaking roof.

'We'll have it,' he said. She laughed. It was a nervous laugh, which she used when she was frightened. She had a small cross face half-lost in a mass of coarse red hair. She was tiny waisted, big-bosomed and long-legged; her limbs lean and freckly. Her fingers were long and fragile. 'But it's falling down,' said Vanessa. 'How can we afford it?'

'Look at the detail on the cornices!' was all he said. 'I'm sure they're original.'

'I expect we can make something of it,' she said.

She loved him. She would do what she could for him. The ghost sensed cruelty, somewhere: he bustled around, stirring the air.

'It's very draughty,' she complained.

They looked into the small back room on the first floor and even he shivered.

'I'll never make anything of this room,' she said.

'Vanessa,' he said. 'I trust you to do something wonderful with everything.'

'Then I'll make it beautiful,' she said, loud and clear, marking out her future. 'Even this, for you.'

The plane tree rubbed against the window pane.

'It's just a question of lopping a branch or two,' he said.

One night, after dark, when builders' trestles were everywhere, and the sour smell of damp lime plaster was on the stairs, Maurice spread a blanket for Vanessa in the little back room.

'Not here,' she said.

'It's the only place that isn't dusty,' he said.

He made love to her, his broad, white body covering her narrow, freckled one altogether.

'Today the divorce came through,' he said.

Other passions split the air. The ghost felt them. Outside in the alley which ran behind the house, beneath the plane tree, stood another woman. Her face was round and sweet, her hair was short and mousy, her eyes bright, bitter and wet. In the house the girl cried out and the man groaned; and the watcher's face became empty, drained of sweetness, left expressionless, a vacuum into which something had to flow. The ghost left with her, on her shoulders.

'I have fibrositis now,' said Anne, 'as well as everything else.' She said it to herself, into the mirror, when she was back home in the basement of the house in Upton Park, where once she and Maurice had lived and built their life. She had to say it to herself, because there was no one else to say it to, except their child Wendy, and Wendy was only four and lay asleep in a pile of blankets on the floor, her face and hands sticky and unwashed. Anne threw an ashtray at the mirror and cracked it, and Wendy woke and cried. 'Seven years bad luck,' said Anne. 'Well, who's counting?'

Sweetness had run out: sourness took its place: she too had marked out her future.

The ghost found a space against the wall between the barred windows of the room, and took up residence there, and drowsed, waking sometimes to accompany Anne on her midnight vigils to 66 Aldermans Drive. Presently he wore an easy route for himself, slipping and slithering between the two places, and no longer needed her for the journey. Sometimes he was here, sometimes there.

In Aldermans Drive he found a painted stairwell and a mended banister, but stairs which were still uncarpeted, and a cat which howled and shot upstairs. The ghost moved in to the small room and the door pushed open in his path and shadows swung and shifted against the wall.

Vanessa was wearing jeans. She and Maurice were papering the room with bright patterned paper. They were laughing: she had glue in her hair.

'When we're rich,' she was saying, 'I'll never do this kind of thing again. We'll always have professionals in to do it.'

'When we're rich!' He yearned for it.

'Of course we'll be rich. You'll write a bestseller; you're far better than anyone else. Genius will out!'

If he felt she misunderstood the nature of genius, or was insensitive to what he knew by instinct, that popularity and art are at odds, he said nothing. He indulged her. He kissed her. He loved her.

'What are those shadows on the wall?' she asked.

'We always get those in here,' he said. 'It's the tree against the window.'

'We'll have to get it lopped,' she said.

'It seems a pity,' he said. 'Such a wonderful old tree.'

He trimmed another length of paper.

'How can the tree be casting shadows?' she asked. 'The sun isn't out.'

'Some trick of reflected light,' said Maurice. The knife in his hand slipped, and he swore.

'It doesn't matter,' said Vanessa, looking at the torn paper, it doesn't have to be perfect. It's only Wendy's room. And then only for weekends. It's not as if she was going to be here all the time.'

'Perhaps you and I should have this room,' said Maurice, 'and Wendy could have the one next door. It overlooks the crescent. It has a view, and a balcony. She'll love it.'

'So would I,' said Vanessa.

'I don't want Wendy to feel second-best,' said Maurice. 'Not after all we've put her through.'

'All that's happened to her,' corrected Vanessa, tight lipped.

'And don't say "only Wendy",' he rebuked her. 'She is my child, after all.'

'It isn't fair! Why couldn't you be like other people? Why do you have to have a past?'

They worked in silence for a little, and the ghost writhed palely in the anger in the air, and then Vanessa relented and smiled and said, 'Don't let's quarrel,' and he said, 'You know I love you,' and the fine front room was Wendy's and the small back room was to house their marriage bed.

'I'm sure I closed the door,' said Vanessa presently, 'but now it's open.'

'The catch is weak,' said Maurice. 'I'll mend it when I can. There's just so much to do in a home this size,' and he sighed and the sigh exhaled out of the open window into the street.

'Goodbye,' said Vanessa.

'Why did you say goodbye?' asked Maurice.

'Because the net curtains flapped and whoever came in through the door was clearly going out by the window,' said Vanessa, thinking she was joking, too young and beautiful and far from death to mind an unseen visitor or so. The ghost whirled away on the remnant of Maurice's sigh, over the roof-tops and the brow of the hill, and down into Upton Park, where it was winter, no longer summer, and little Wendy was six, and getting out of bed, bare cold toes on chilly lino.

The ghost's observations were now from outside time. So a man might stand on a station overpass and watch a train go through beneath. Such a man could see, if he chose, any point along the train—in front of him the future, behind him the past, directly beneath him, changing always from past to future, his main rumbling, noisy perception of the present. The ghost keeps his gaze steadily forward.

The clock says five to nine; Anne is asleep in bed. Wendy shakes her awake.

'My feet are cold,' says the little girl.

'Then put on your slippers,' mourns the mother, out of sleep. It has been an uneasy, unsatisfying slumber. Once she lay next to Maurice and fancied she drew her strength out of his slumbering body, hot beside her, like some spiritual water-bottle. She clings to the fancy in her mind: she refuses to sleep as she did when a child, composed and decent in solitude, providing her own warmth well enough.

'Won't I be late for school?' asks Wendy.

'No,' says Anne, in the face of all evidence to the contrary.

'It is ever so cold,' says Wendy. 'Can I light the gas-fire?'

'No you can't,' says Anne. 'We can't afford it.'

'Daddy will pay the bill,' says Wendy, hopefully. But her mother just laughs.

'I'm frightened,' says Wendy, all else having failed. 'The curtains are waving about and the window isn't even open. Can I get into your bed?'

Anne moves over and the child gets in.

An egg teeters on the edge of the table, amidst the remnants of last night's chips and tomato sauce, and falls and smashes. Anne sits up in bed, startled into reaction.

'How did that happen?' she asks, aloud. But there is no one to reply, for Wendy has fallen asleep, and the ghost is spinning and spinning, nothing but a whirl of air in the corner of the eye, and no one listens to him, anyway.

Further forward still, and there's Vanessa, sitting up in bed, bouncy brown-nippled breasts half covered by fawn lace. It is a brass bed, finely filigreed. Maurice wears black silk pyjamas. He sits on the edge of the bed, while Vanessa sips fresh orange juice, and opens his letters.

'Any cheques?' asks Vanessa.

'Not today,' he says. Maurice is a writer. Cheques bounce through the letter box with erratic energy: bills come in with a calm, steady beat. It is a tortoise and hare situation, and the tortoise always wins.

'Perhaps you should change your profession,' she suggests.

'Be an engineer or go into advertising. I hate all this worry about money.'

A mirror slips upon its string on the wall, hangs sidewise. Neither notice.

'Is that a letter from Anne?' asks Vanessa. 'What does she want now?'

'It's her electricity bill,' he says.

'She's supposed to pay that out of her monthly cheque. She only sends you these demands to make you feel unhappy and guilty. She's jealous of us. How I despise jealousy! What a bitch she is!'

'She has a child to look after,' says Maurice. 'My child.'

'If I had your child would you treat me better?' she asks.

'I treat you perfectly well,' he says, pulling the bedclothes back, rubbing black silk against beige lace, and the mirror falls off the wall altogether, startling them, stopping them.

'This whole room will have to be stripped out,' complains Vanessa.

'The plaster is rotten. I'll get arthritis from the damp.' Vanessa notices, sometimes, as she walks up and down the stairs, that her knees ache.

Wendy is ten. Anne's room has been painted white, and there are cushions on the chairs, and dirty washing is put in the basket, not left on the floor, and times are a little better. A little. There is passion in the air.

'Vanessa says I can stay all week not just weekends, and go to school from Aldermans Drive!' says Wendy. 'Live with Dad, and not with you.'

'What did you say?' asks Anne, trying to sound casual.

'I said no thank you,' says Wendy. 'There's no peace over there. They always have the builders in. Bang, bang, bang! And Dad's always shut away in a room, writing. I prefer it here, in spite of everything. Damp and draughts and all.'

The damp on the wall between the barred windows is worse. It makes a strange shape on the wall; it seems to change from day to day. The house belongs to Maurice. He will not have the roof over their heads mended. He says he cannot afford to. In the rooms above live tenants, protected by law, who pay next to nothing in rent. How can he spare the money needed to keep the house in good order—and why, according to Vanessa, should he?

'We're just the rejects of the world,' says Anne to Wendy, and Wendy believes her, and her mouth grows tight and pouty instead of firm and generous, as it could have been, and her looks are spoiled. Anne is right, that's the trouble of it. Rejects!

'How my shoulder hurts,' says Anne. She should have stayed at home, never crossed the city to stand beneath the plane-tree in the alley behind Aldermans Drive, allowed herself her paroxysms of jealousy, grief, and solitary sexual frenzy. She has had fibrositis ever since. But she felt what she felt. You can help what you do, but not what you feel.

The ghost looks further forward to Aldermans Drive and finds the bed gone in the small back room, and a dining table in its place, and candles lit, and guests, and smooth mushroom soup being served. The candles throw shadows on to the wall: this way, that way. One of the guests tries to make sense of them, but can't. She has wild blonde hair and a fair skin and a laughing mouth, unlike Maurice's other women. Her name is Audrey. She is an actress. Maurice's hair is falling out. His temples are quite bare, and he has a moustache now instead of a beard, and he seems distinguished, rather than aspiring. His hand smooths Audrey's little one, and Vanessa sees. Maurice defies her jealousy: he smiles blandly, cruelly, at his wife.

He turns to Audrey's husband, who is eighteen years older than Audrey, and says, 'Ah youth, youth!' and offers back Audrey's hand, closing the husband's fingers over the wife's so that nobody could possibly take offence, and Vanessa feels puzzled at her own distress, and her glass of red wine tips over on its own account.

'Vanessa! Clumsy!' reproaches Maurice.

'But I didn't!' she says. No one believes her. Why should they? They pour white wine on the stain to neutralise the red, and it works, and looking at the tablecloth, presently, no one would have known anything untoward had happened at all.

'We must have security,' Vanessa weeps from time to time. 'I can't stand the uncertainty of it all! You must stop being a writer. Or write something different. Stop writing novels. Write for television instead.'

'No, you must stop spending the money,' he shouts. 'Stop doing up this house. Changing this, changing that.'

'But I want it to be nice. We must have a nursery. I can't keep the baby in a drawer.'

Vanessa is pregnant.

'Why not? It's what Anne had to do, thanks to you.'

'Anne! Can't you ever forget Anne?' she shrieks. 'Does she have to be on our backs for ever? She has ruined our lives.'

But their lives aren't ruined. The small back room becomes a nursery. The baby sleeps there. He is a boy, his name is Jonathan. He sleeps badly and cries a lot and is hard to love. His eyes follow the shadows on the wall, this way, that way.

'There's nothing wrong with his eyes,' says the doctor, visiting, puzzled at the mother's fears. 'But his chest is bad.'

Vanessa sits by the cot and rocks her feverish child.

'For you and I—'she sings, as she sings when she is nervous, driving away fear with melody—

'—have a guardian angel—on high with nothing to do—

—but to give to you and to give—to me—

—love for ever—true—.'

Maurice is in the room. Vanessa is crying.

'But why won't you go back to work?' he demands. 'It would take the pressure off me. I could write what I want to write, not what I have to write.'

'I want to look after my baby myself,' she weeps. 'It's a man's job to support his family. And you're not exactly William Shakespeare. Why don't you write films? That's where the money is.'

The baby coughs. The doctor says the room is too damp for its good.

'I never liked this room,' says Vanessa, as she and Maurice carry out the cot. 'And you and I always quarrel in it. The quarrelling room. I hate it. But I love you.'

'I love you,' he says, crossing his fingers.

The ghost looks forward. Aldermans Drive has become one of the most desirable streets in Bristol, all new paint and French kitchenware and Welsh dressers seen through lighted windows. The property is in Maurice's name, as seems reasonable, since he earns the money. He writes films, for Hollywood.

Anne's bed turns into a foam settee by day: she has a cooker instead of a gas ring: the window bars have gone: the panes are made of reinforced glass. She has had a telephone installed. Wendy has platform heels and puts cream on her spots.

The ghost looks further forward, and Anne has a boyfriend. A man sits opposite her in a freshly covered armchair. Broken springs have been taped flat. Sometimes she lets him into her bed, but his flesh is cool and none too firm, and she remembers Maurice's body, hot-water bottle in her bed, and won't forget. Won't. Can't.

'Is it wrong to hate people?' asks Anne. 'I hate Vanessa, and with reason. She is a thief. Why do people ask her into their houses? Is it that they don't realise, or that they don't care? She stole my husband: she tried to steal my child. Maurice has never been happy with her. He never wanted to leave me. She seduced him. She thought he'd be famous one day; how wrong she was! He's sold out, you know! One day he'll come back to me, what's left of him, and I'll be expected to pick up the bits.'

'But he's married to her. They have a child. How can he come back to you?' He is a nice man, a salesman, thoughtful and kind.

'So was I married to him. So do I have his child.'

How stubborn she is!

'You're obsessive.' He is beginning to be angry. Well, he has been angry often enough before, and still stayed around for more. 'While you take Maurice's money,' he says, 'you will never be free of him.'

'Those few miserable pennies! What difference can they make? I live in penury, while she lives in style. He is Wendy's father; he has an obligation to support us. He was the guilty party, after all.'

'The law no longer says guilty or not guilty, in matter of divorce.'

'Well, it should!' She is passionate. 'He should pay for what he did to me and Wendy. He destroyed our lives.'

The ghost is lulled by the turning wheel of her thoughts, so steady on its axis: he drowses; responds to a spasm of despair, an act of decision on the man's part, one morning, as he leaves Anne's unsatisfactory bed. He dresses silently: he means to go: never to come back. He looks in the mirror to straighten his tie and sees Anne's face instead of his own.

He cries out and Anne wakes.

'I'm sorry,' she says. 'Don't go.'

But he does, and he doesn't come back.

The gap between what could be, and what is, defeats him.

Anne has a job as a waitress. It is a humiliation. Maurice does not know she is earning. Anne keeps it a secret, for Vanessa would surely love an excuse to reduce Anne's alimony, already whittled away by inflation.

The decorators are back in Aldermans Drive. The smell of fresh plaster has the ghost alert. Paper is being stripped from walls: doors driven through here: walls dismantled there. The cat runs before the ghost, like a leaf before wind, looking for escape; finding none, cornered in the small back room, where animals never go if they can help it, and the shadows swing to and fro, and the tiny crossed bones from a dead sparrow are ledged beneath the wainscot.

'Get out of here, cat!' cries Vanessa. 'I hate cats, don't you? Maurice loves them. But they don't like me: forever trying to trip me on the stairs, when I had to go to the baby, in the night.'

'I expect they were jealous,' says the man with her. He is young and handsome, with shrewd, insincere eyes and a lecher's mouth. He is a decorator. He looks at the room with dislike, and at Vanessa, speculatively.

'The worst room in the house,' she laments. 'It's been bedroom, dining room, nursery. It never works! I hope it's better as a bathroom.'

He moves his hand to the back of her neck but she laughs and sidesteps.

'The plaster's shockingly damp,' he says, and as if to prove his opinion the curtain rail falls off the wall altogether, making a terrible clatter and clash, and the cat yowls and Vanessa shrieks, and Maurice strides up the stairs to see what is happening, and what was in the air between Vanessa and Toby evaporates. The ghost is on Anne's side—if ghosts take sides.

How grand and boring the house is now! There is a faint scent of chlorine in the air; it comes from the swimming pool in the basement. The stair walls are mirrored: a maid polishes away at the first landing but it's always a little misty. She marvels at how long the flowers last, when placed on the little Georgian stair-table bought by Vanessa for Maurice on his fifty-second birthday. The maid is in love with Maurice, but Maurice has other fish to fry.

Further forward still: something's happening in the bathroom! The bath is deep blue and the taps are gold, and the wallpaper rose, but still the shadows swing to and fro, against the wall.

Audrey has spilt red wine upon her dress. She is more beautiful than she was. She is intelligent. She is no longer married or an actress: she is a solicitor. Maurice admires that very much. He thinks women should be useful, not like Vanessa. He is tired of girls who have young flesh and liquid eyes and love his bed but despise him in their hearts. Audrey does not despise him. Vanessa has forgotten how.

Maurice is helping Audrey sponge down her dress. His hand strays here and there. She is accustomed to it: she does not mind.

'What are those shadows on the wall?' she asks.

'Some trick of the light,' he says.

'Perhaps we should use white wine to remove the red,' she says. 'Remember that night so long ago? It was in this room, wasn't it! Vanessa had it as a dining room, then. I think I fell in love with you that night.'

'And I with you,' he says.

Is it true?—He can hardly remember.

'What a lot of time we've wasted,' he laments, and this for both of them, is true enough. They love each other.

'Dear Maurice,' she says, 'I can't bear to see you so unhappy. It's all Vanessa's doing. She stopped you writing. You would be a great writer if it wasn't for her, not just a Hollywood hack! You still could be!'

He laughs, but he is moved. He thinks it might be true. If it were not for Vanessa he would not just be rich and successful, he would be rich, successful and renowned as well.

'Vanessa says this room is haunted,' he says, seeing the shadows himself, almost defined at last, a body hanging from a noose: a woman destroyed, or self-destroyed. What's the difference? Love does it. Love and ghosts.

'What's the matter?' Audrey asks. He's pale.

'We could leave here,' he says. 'Leave this house. You and me.'

A shrewd light gleams in her intelligent, passionate eyes. How he loves her!

'A pity to waste all this,' says Audrey. 'It is your home, after all. Vanessa's never liked it. If anyone leaves, it should be her.'

The flowers on the landing are still fresh and sweet a week later. Maurice will keep the table they stand upon—a gift from Vanessa to him, after all. If you give someone something, it's theirs forever. That is the law, says Audrey.

Vanessa moves her belongings from the bathroom shelf. She wants nothing of his, nothing. Just a few personal things—toothbrush, paste, cleansing cream. She will take her child and go. She cannot remain under the same roof, and he won't leave.

'You must see it's for the best, Vanessa,' says Maurice, awkwardly. 'We haven't really been together for years, you and I.'

'All that bed-sharing?' she enquires. 'That wasn't together? The meals, the holidays, the friends, the house? The child? Not together?'

'No,' he says. 'Not together the way I feel with Audrey.'

She can hardly believe it. So far she is shocked, rather than distressed. Presently, distress will set in: but not yet.

'I'll provide for you, of course,' he says, 'you and the child. I always looked after Anne, didn't I? Anne and Wendy.' Vanessa turns to stare at him, and over his shoulder sees a dead woman hanging from a rope, but who is to say where dreams begin and reality ends? At the moment she is certainly in a nightmare. She looks back to Maurice, and sees the horror of her own life, and the swinging body fades, if indeed it was ever there. The door opens, by itself.

'You never did fix the catch,' she says.

'No,' he replies. 'I never got round to it.'

The train beneath the overpass was nearly through. The past had caught up with the present and the present was dissolving into the future, and the future was all but out of sight.

It was 1980. The two women, Anne and Vanessa, sat together in the room in Upton Park. The damp patch was back again, but hidden by one of the numerous posters which lined the walls calling on women to live, to be free, to protest, to re-claim the right, demand wages for housework, to do anything in the world but love. The personal, they proclaimed, was the political. Other women came and went in the room.

'However good the present is,' said Anne, 'the past cannot be undone. I wasted so much of my life. I look back and see scenes I would rather not remember. Little things; silly things, even. Wendy being late for school, a lover looking in a mirror. Damp on a wall. I used to think this room was haunted.'

'I used to think the same of Aldermans Drive,' said Vanessa, 'but now I realise what it was. What I sensed was myself now, looking back; me now watching me then, myself remembering me with sorrow for what I was and need never have been.'

They talked about Audrey.

'They say she's unfaithful to him,' said Anne. 'Well, he's nearly sixty and she's thirty-five. What did he expect?'

'Love,' said Vanessa, 'like the rest of us.'

Geoffrey and
the Eskimo Child

Geoffrey thought that perhaps Tania should see a psychotherapist. She was having nightmares, the substance of which eluded her but the attendant feeling—tone (as she learned to call it)—was clear enough. Terror.

That was in 1962 and their joint income was low. Geoffrey was studying sociology at the London School of Economics, and Tania, who already had her degree, was working for a market research organisation in a rather humble capacity.

'Can we afford it?' mourned Tania. 'Isn't psychotherapy an unimaginable luxury? Isn't it immoral to accept a form of treatment which can never, by virtue of it being on a one-to-one basis, be available to the many, but only to the privileged few?'

She was very earnest, in those days.

Geoffrey reasoned that if Tania needed psychotherapy she should have it: that her happiness was important to him: that she was a valuable member of the community and would be able to pass on the benefit of self-awareness to many others in the course of her life. Their children, too, would benefit, when the time came to have them. Psychotherapy was like a stone dropping into a pool: the ripples spread and spread, with an ever widening circumference.

'Can't you make up your own mind, Tania?' asked Erica. 'Do you always have to ask Geoffrey what to do?' But it seemed that Tania did.

Erica was Tania's friend. Once Erica had been Geoffrey's mistress, but that was long ago. Now she did not seem to like Geoffrey very much, so Tania did not pay attention to those parts of Erica's conversation which appertained to her husband.

Geoffrey drove Tania to the psychotherapist for the initial visit, and took her out for a drink afterwards, and was rather nonplussed when she didn't tell him what had passed between the psychotherapist and herself. However, being reasonable and kind, he did not press the matter but allowed his wife her privacy.

'We can be one flesh,' he acknowledged, 'but we have to remain two minds. Otherwise, where's the mutual benefit, and stimulation? The cross-fertilisation?'

'I'm on the pill,' Tania had remarked to the therapist, who was a pleasant woman.

'What pill?'

'The contraceptive pill,' Tania had replied, and explained all about it. It had been tried out on Puerto Rican women and proved safe. The therapist had seemed rather baffled by this new development in the world, of which so far she had apparently been unaware, but was able nevertheless to relate Tania's nightly terrors to the nightly taking of the pill and the denial of her own femininity, and fear of ensuing punishment.

Tania did not, and could not, accept such an absurd explanation, and presently stopped her visits. She went on taking the pill, and the nightmares faded, and were forgotten, absorbed into the past along with everything else.

Geoffrey got a First and was rewarded with a rather insecure job as a junior lecturer at the London School of Economics. He was a Marxist, but of the stable kind which never degenerates into Trotskyism or Maoism, and his seniors believed that with time he would grow out of even that. Tania went into journalism. More money now came into the household, but both had spendthrift habits and neither approved of private property anyway, so they did not buy a house but continued to live in rented accommodation. Geoffrey spent a proportion of their joint income each year equipping sports halls for the local skinheads.

'We have everything we need,' he said, 'and these lads have nothing.'

'God, Geoffrey's a fool!' said Erica. Tania did not have her in the house for quite some time.

Geoffrey and Tania put off having children. Time enough for that.

Tania stayed on the pill, year in, year out, through health scares and out the other side of them, with regular physical check-ups and the dosage changing for maximum safety. Geoffrey saw to that.

'Contraception is both our responsibility,' said Geoffrey. He was an orphan himself: he wanted children, but not until Tania was ready.

Even as far back as 1968, when the whole Western world was gasping, heaving, and setting off in a different direction, in hot pursuit of youth, Geoffrey was conscious of the unfairness of woman's lot in society. In *his* revolutionary meetings, men were expected to make the coffee too, and women allowed to make policy decisions. And when the Women's Movement started, Geoffrey helped with the general organisation and setting up of meetings and the printing of pamphlets, and tried to deter his fellow men from standing up first when discussion time came, and the platform had finished, and prefixing their remarks with—'I'm all for Women's Liberation. I always help my wife with the washing up.'

'I *do* washing up,' said Geoffrey. 'We share household chores. We split our lives down the middle. When we have children—a pigeon pair would be nice: a boy and a girl, and then I'll have a vasectomy—it will be the same. We will take turns at tribulation as well as joy. We will share the chores of earning, cooking, washing, bill-paying, hoovering, cleaning the lavatory. All men should act likewise!'

Tania was thirty-two. It was no longer possible to deny that she was growing older, and that giving birth to a first child no longer the simple matter it once would have been. And man's procreative life, of course, goes on longer than woman's, and male sperm, being re-created daily, do not grow feeble or tired, as do female eggs, which are laid down before birth and have to hang about for release—and the danger of having a baby with something wrong with it presumably increased with every year that passed.

'Poppycock!' murmured Erica when Tania announced that time had run out and that she was coming off the pill. 'If doctors can't think of one way to frighten women, they'll think of another.' But no one listened to Erica. She disliked babies and had no intention of ever having one. She boasted of having had three terminations.

There were other worries, too. There was so much to be done in the world, and so many people in it, were they *entitled* to have children? Was the world a fit place to bring children into? This latter was Tania's worry. Geoffrey's, freely expressed, was whether, when it came to actuality and not just declamation, their domestic sharing, which worked so well without children, would continue to work when a child arrived? Or, if there was any conflict of interest, say an ill child needing a parent to stay home, which parent would it be? Geoffrey now had a job as a sociologist at the Camden Town Hall and was in charge of a department, which he ran with enthusiasm and energy, cutting away—perhaps a little ruthlessly—the dead wood of old staff and old ideas. He was relentlessly *young*; he wore jeans to work before anyone else dared, and had already abandoned collar and tie when others were still cautiously wondering if they could possibly abandon their vests. Tania had become a freelance journalist of note: she was a leading member of Women in Media: and an expert in women's affairs.

'Obviously,' said Geoffrey, 'I have a department to run, and you, Tania, can be flexible in your working arrangements, but that is hardly the point!'

'We'll work it out somehow,' said Tania, throwing away her pills. 'It's a matter of the efficient division of labour, that's all. We'll each do the best we can!'

Tania was much envied by her friends and colleagues, inasmuch as she was married to Geoffrey, who was one of the few genuinely unchauvinist men around, was not impotent but nevertheless apparently monogamous, and wasn't even boring. Geoffrey's mind worked marvellously, his tongue freely, and he passed lightly over this subject and that, seeming to know everything and everyone, lighting up rooms as he came into them. He could make people laugh, with his mock macho stances: he could listen quietly and at length if he had to, and his interest in others was genuine, and profound. He kept his fits of melancholy for home, and warned Tania when they were coming, so she could go away for a couple of days if they were bad, or just to the pictures if it was a transitory mood and not likely to outlast the evening. In these gloomy states, he was angry and rejecting of her: reproaches and rebukes sparking out of black silence. Tania had long since learned to discount them: not to include them in her vision of him, beloved Geoffrey, her good husband.

Both Tania and Geoffrey were surprised when Tania did not get pregnant at once. Tania was perhaps, for a month or so, secretly a little relieved. Relief quickly faded, to be replaced by a nagging anxiety. They were disconcerted to be told, by friends, that her fertility might not reassert itself for a year or so, and they saw themselves now in a race against time. Every month that passed seemed to increase the danger both to Tania and to the as yet unconceived baby, which now seemed as real as they were—a gap in the room where a high-chair should be, a space in the hall where there was no pram.

After a year of trying to become pregnant, and failing, Tania visited the staff doctor at the newspaper where she worked. He explained that five per cent of couples are sterile, a problem masked for women who had been taking the contraceptive pill since the beginning of their sexual relationships. He was not suggesting Tania was infertile, simply saying it was a possibility which must be faced.

'Good God,' protested Geoffrey, 'it might be *me* who's infertile (he hasn't even considered that), the man's a cretin!'

After much discussion as to the rights and wrongs of such a step, Tania agreed to visit a doctor in private practice, who had a more enlightened view of conception.

'It's always a conflict between individual right and public good,' Tania tried to explain to Erica, but Erica had no time for such excuses.

'It always happens,' lamented Erica. 'The drift to the right as people grow older!' Erica had no sympathy for Tania's pale face and haunted eyes, and Geoffrey's new quietness of demeanour, as month succeeded month, Tania's blood flowed, and disappointment and a sense of failure ensued in both of them. Geoffrey had no family himself, having been brought up by a solitary aunt. Tania's elderly father made up all of her relatives. He and she perched, being without children, on a dead branch of a family tree, and it crackled with misery.

Geoffrey's sperm count was normal; there was no apparent reason for Tania's failure to conceive. She had her fallopian tubes blown up with air—a rather disagreeable and expensive operation: she took pills to increase her fertility, which also increased her chances of multiple birth, but these measures did not work. She and Geoffrey confined intercourse to days of the month when she was most likely to conceive: she took Vitamin E, drank rose hip tea, and went to a hypnotist and after that an acupuncturist, all to no avail. Her body maintained the relentless, pulsing, bleeding course it had become so accustomed to.

When Tania was thirty-six, and worn out by hope disappointed, she gave up. 'I shall be an aunt,' she said, 'everyone's favourite aunt, since nature insists I cannot be a mother. And besides, there are certainly more than enough children in the world already, and quite enough work to be getting on with.'

Geoffrey and she agreed that the world was in a perilous state: cadmium in the fish, lead in the water, and radiation in the very air you breathed, and they concentrated their talents and energies into making it a safer place for future generations. It seemed a noble enough task.

Tania was offered the editorship of the newspaper.

'We must consider this really carefully,' said Geoffrey. 'It does mean a total commitment on your part. Is this what you really want from your life? Or perhaps it's time now for us to have a little rest and relaxation? You are looking rather tired, these days.'

Geoffrey was on a strict and successful diet. His jeans met easily enough. He still had all his hair. He looked ten years younger than his age: Tania looked perhaps a year or two older than hers, and had a tendency to eat cream eclairs and put sugar in her coffee.

'You must stop this consolation eating,' said Erica, who was thin and sinewy. 'It is obscene for someone as fortunate as you to need consolation,' and Tania realised the truth of this, lost a stone, and was herself again.

Tania turned down the editorship and she and Geoffrey adopted a half-Vietnamese half-American little girl, aged four when they first saw her, and five when they took possession of her. In the interval, the delicate Vietnamese features Geoffrey had so loved seemed to have given way to a certain American jowliness and clumsiness. But Tania loved her. They named her Star. In the interval, too, Tania became pregnant and gave birth to identical girl twins.

'You should never have the taken the fertility pill,' said Erica. 'Two! It's unnatural! Monozygotic—more of a mutation than anything else!'

The doctor—their local G.P. and not one in private practice, for care of three children was expensive, and the whole family now had to live on one salary, Geoffrey's, instead of two—said 'Nonsense! A completely random chance. Nothing to do with the fertility drug at all,' and might have been right, for all anyone knew.

It was out of the question for Geoffrey to share household chores; it took him all his energy to bring in enough money to keep the household going. It was out of the question for Tania to earn; one disturbed five-year-old (little Star lied, fought and stole, and had to have the reassurance of Tania's constant attention) and twin babies took up all her time and energy.

'I knew you'd both revert to type,' said Erica, and Tania wished she'd go away. It was not as if Erica ever washed out a bottle or offered to soothe a crying infant. All she seemed to do was pop round when Tania was feeding Sally and Susan and ask Geoffrey round to the pub for a drink. He'd go, too.

'Of course Erica has turned lesbian,' he said, eventually. 'Well, I can understand that. Why should a woman make do with a man, when she can have another woman?'

And Erica faded out of the picture. Well, is there a marriage in the world in which each partner is for ever true, in word, deed and fantasy, to the other?

The world outside continued to deteriorate. Oil prices soared: energy crises ensued: police states threatened, at home and abroad: certifiable madmen headed previously dignified states: even Geoffrey's job looked not so secure as before. But Tania was happy enough with her family.

'We must look after the next generation,' said Geoffrey, when Star was nine and the twins were four. 'It's all we can do for the world. We must adopt a child whom no one else wants.'

'Can we afford it?'

'Good heavens,' said Geoffrey. 'Families of nine manage very well on half what I earn!'

'But it's so nice,' said Tania, 'to have everyone out of nappies, and just a little time to myself.'

'Darling,' said Geoffrey, 'I know what it's like for you. Any time you want, I'll stay home and look after the kids while you go out to work. I'm pretty tired of the rat-race, I can tell you.'

'I don't know,' said Tania doubtfully. 'I seem to have rather got out of the way of things. And where would I find a job that paid as much as yours, or had such nice long holidays? No, things are pretty good as they are. We'll carry on a little longer.'

Geoffrey quickly took Tania to a children's home to see a child who had passed through his office files, and was being put up for adoption. She was the prettiest, blondest, most delicate little creature ever put in care, said Geoffrey, and Tania was obliged to agree. Her name was Jenny. She was six. She smiled at Geoffrey and looked coldly at Tania.

'Oh Geoffrey, we can't,' cried Tania, having woken in the middle of that night from a recurrence of her old trouble—nightmares. 'It will upset Star too much and make the twins jealous. An older or a younger child, but not one in the middle, please. Not a blonde, when the others are so dark, not a girl, when we have three girls already, and not a girl with this particular history, and most of all not *now*.'

'Night fears!' said Geoffrey. 'Perhaps you should try primal scream therapy?'

But Tania now hardly had the time, let alone the energy, to scream. They took in little Jenny who had remained un-snapped up by adoptors, in spite of her prettiness, because of her psychiatric history. She was mildly autistic, given to sudden shouts and fits of swearing and aggression, and her very presence in the house made Star revert to her earlier state of distress and the twins to adopt an irritating private language of their own. Tania, by dedication and with help from Geoffrey, had the household reasonably peaceful within six months, but was always aware of Jenny's hostility.

The night of the nightmare Tania must have conceived. Certainly the dates were about right, though why she should make a connection between the two events she was not quite sure. She was delighted to be pregnant, to have this second affirmation of her femininity after the dreadful years, and Geoffrey was proud as a peacock. He had not been able to have a vasectomy after all, because new evidence had come to light about possible side-effects and premature senility. Nor did she any longer wish vasectomy upon him. The long years of infertility had changed them both, made them value what they had together, and given an underlying seriousness to the act of sex.

They even discussed the possibility of becoming Catholics. They understood the Pope's stand on contraception, but could not quite accept the doctrine of the Assumption of the Virgin Mary, and so did not in the end undergo conversion.

'Anyway,' said Tania, 'your work colleagues would laugh at you. I'm sure they're all atheists!'

'Atheists, vedantists, Marxists and idiots,' said Geoffrey. He was disenchanted with work.

There was quite a scare when it looked as if Tania was having twins again but it did not happen. She gave birth to a son, Simon. But something rather strange happened to her insides at the same time—perhaps the earlier blowing and scraping and medicating was to blame, although the doctor laughed and said nonsense—but at any rate Tania was told she would not be able to conceive any more, and would do well to have a hysterectomy.

Geoffrey cried, and Tania put it off as long as she could, but in the end the strain of losing blood, and the care of five children, two of them disturbed and one of them a baby, told too much, and she had her hysterectomy. The event seemed to depress Geoffrey very much. His moodiness got worse, and he did not even bother to take it to the pub, out of Tania's way. He worried more and more about the lead, the strontium, the ozone layer, earthquakes, volcanoes, the government, plots against him at work and the onset of nuclear war, and received an offer of redundancy pay from his employers, which he hotly and bitterly declined.

Tania went on looking after the children.

Simon grew to be a lively, clever child, but Geoffrey saw signs of doom written in his eyes, and when Tania was forty-three, and Simon two, he said it was time to adopt another child.

'Oh no, oh no!' begged Tania. She was worried about a swollen vein in her leg, and thought it might be the beginning of a varicose vein.

'Good God,' said Geoffrey, 'you're lucky to have a leg! Lots of people don't even have legs to have varicose veins in!' and Tania was obliged to admit it was true.

She did a lot of walking and lugging shopping about. They had sold the car because it was polluting the air with lead fumes, and adding to the general distress of the world.

'I don't think anyone's going to let us adopt a child,' said Tania, firmly. 'Anyone in their right mind would say we had enough!'

She mourned the loss of that female part of her which seemed to have gone with her womb. She felt strange without it: a person. And though Geoffrey told her that was what everyone must try to be, a person, except in bed when you were allowed to be male or female, she was not altogether comforted. She had hormone therapy now, to counteract the effect of being without a womb, and took oestrogen by mouth again, as once she had before, in her young, carefree days, when she did what she wanted, and not what she had to.

Geoffrey asked around, and indeed, it looked as if another adoption would be hard to arrange, even if they undertook to take in a deviant fourteen-year old male half-caste, the most difficult kind of child to place.

He felt it was Tania's fault.

'You sit there at these interviews looking tired and exhausted on purpose,' he said. 'I'm sure you do. It's unconscious, of course. I'm not accusing you of open negativism, but the results are the same. Poor little Simon has to have a brother. The only boy! He's going to be so lonely, and have trouble with his role identification.'

'He can identify with me,' said Tania. 'I'm a person, aren't I?'

She tried not to make remarks like this, but at the time Star was staying out all night and Jenny had reverted to wetting the bed and biting the sheets to ribbons and the twins were playing truant from school and she was tired.

'Education is the prison of the mind,' said Geoffrey, who seemed unalarmed by such symptoms, 'the twins are showing courage and sense in staying away from their school!'

Tania wondered if it were so: she still saw their way ahead as she had her own—through the educational system and the passing of examinations, to the pinnacle of free thought and free expression of that thought. As for helping the less advantaged members of the community, Geoffrey did that on a large scale, she on an individual one. Well, that was how it went: how it had turned out.

She knew that Geoffrey was right: she saw that while she had life and strength and good-will she must feed it back, in her small way, into the community. How else was the world to be saved?

But she knew that to bring another child into the family would do little Simon no good at all. He was the youngest; her perfect son; passionately she wished him a safe and peaceful upbringing.

'Tania,' said Geoffrey, 'if everyone of good-will doesn't do their utmost now, there won't be a world to bring him up in!'

The nuclear threat hung over him like a cloud. Erica made a brief appearance.

'One would almost think Geoffrey was earmarked for his own personal missile,' she whispered, in a voice grown impossibly soft and sexy. She seemed less sinewy and athletic as she grew older: just rather slender and vulnerable. She had time to paint her toe-nails. She hadn't veered to the political right with age, just to the soft left of the woman's movement. No truck there with the separatists, those who looked ahead to a world without men.

Geoffrey explained to Erica how the war between good and evil was hotting up, and how all those on the side of good must be very, very busy indeed about their business.

'You really ought to try and cheer him up, Tania,' said Erica. She was mysterious about her own life, but Tania had the distinct feeling she was heterosexual again. She herself remained, perforce, very much a person. Geoffrey had rather gone off sex, lately. Their nights were usually disturbed by one or other of the five children, and sleep seemed the highest pleasure.

But Geoffrey did not give up the thought of adopting another child.

'The balance of the household isn't right,' he complained. 'I can feel it isn't. We must have another boy, and you don't have the wherewithal any more to provide one yourself. Tania, I'll help you with everything. You know I will.'

'You're very good,' said Tania. 'You always help with the washing up.'

He lay awake wondering how to acquire a baby. She had nightmares, again. What had the psychotherapist said, long, long ago? The daily denial of femininity? It began to make sense. She took another oestrogen pill. If ever she forgot, she had hot flushes and became depressed.

'Have I ever before asked you to make a sacrifice for me?' asked Geoffrey. 'I'm asking you, begging you, now, in the name of our love, and everything we have struggled for together: our common beliefs and aspirations. You in your way, I in mine. We must have another son!'

Tania gave in. One day shortly afterwards Geoffrey came home from work in the middle of the day, carrying an Eskimo baby, two hours old.

'Eskimo!' exclaimed Tania, looking at the serene little face framed in its greyish open-mesh social-welfare blanket, as Geoffrey handed the infant to her.

'It was meant,' said Geoffrey. 'It was a sign that I was right! An Eskimo—one of the most oppressed and endangered human species in the world!'

If you have been married for a long, long time, what seems strange to the outside world seems quite normal to husband and wife. Tania could accept Geoffrey's reasoning. She could see that it was *meant*.

God's will, that a pregnant Eskimo girl should stow away in a crate of scientific instruments on an aircraft bound from Alaska to Heathrow. God's will that by a series of miracles she and the baby should survive, should end up in the vast offices of Camden Social Services, that she should give birth, there and then, in the space of five minutes, to a healthy nine pound baby boy, hand the baby to Geoffrey, and die.

As Geoffrey had a wife at home ready and willing to look after a newborn baby, and the doctor said of course, any home was better than an institution for an orphaned baby and the sooner he was in a woman's arms the better, Geoffrey left with the baby as the undertaker arrived.

The Social Services department was like that, said Geoffrey. Sometimes nothing seemed to happen for weeks—then everything all at once.

Tania reared the Eskimo baby, and thought perhaps Geoffrey had been right. The presence of this particular child seemed to soothe the others. Geoffrey remained moody and ready to blame, however.

When the baby was a year old he determined to take them all on holiday in Crete. Tania was at first dubious of the wisdom of such a plan but Geoffrey persisted and presently she and the children were looking forward to the holiday, with happiness and animation. The money spent on the holiday had nearly been spent on a nuclear shelter. It had been a toss up. Not quite a toss up: Geoffrey had held out his clenched fists to the Eskimo baby; one hand was marked Shelter, and the child had chosen Holiday.

It took Tania a week to prepare for the journey. The requisites of six children require a good deal of parental organising, although Geoffrey did what he could to help. They were to drive to the airport, and be there by two. At twenty past twelve Star discovered she had started her first period, to Sally and Susan's consternation. The party's departure was delayed by fifteen minutes, which meant that Geoffrey would have to drive fast to the airport to make up for lost time, but he did not seem particularly disconcerted. When the family was re-settled nicely in the car, and the engine started, Geoffrey seemed to remember something, switched off the engine, said 'Just a minute,' and went inside.

Fifteen minutes later, as he had not returned, Tania disentangled herself from various living limbs and went to look for him. She found him in the back garden. He had shot himself dead, with a gun he should not have had.

She could give no explanation to the coroner: she could give no explanation to herself. Geoffrey had drifted into some kind of melancholy, she supposed, so gradually that she had not noticed. Perhaps if she had, she could have saved him? But she had been busy, she tried to excuse herself; and about his business, more than her own. No one seemed inclined to blame her, so she blamed herself. There was no insurance, no property, just six children and rent to be paid.

Tania worried in case Geoffrey could not, as a suicide, be buried in consecrated ground, but there seemed no longer any time or indeed opportunity for such worry, at the great overworked institutions which look after the disposal of the dead. He had once said, in joking casual conversation, that he wanted to be burned *and* buried, so she arranged for his cremation and the burial of his ashes.

There was quite a large gathering around the open grave, as the coffin containing the casket was lowered into the ground. (This particular bureaucracy, too, worked in strange ways: easier to go along with it, than arrange for a rational casket-size coffin.) For a child who had started out an orphan, Geoffrey had accumulated a large family of friends, colleagues and relatives. It had been a successful life, so far as it had gone. Erica was there, by the graveside, with a year old baby in her arms. If the child looked like Geoffrey, and Tania rather thought it might, it seemed not to matter.

She looked at her children—at Star, Susan, Sally, Jenny and Simon, and at the stocky little baby who rested placidly on her hip, and wondered what was to become of them all.

'Geoffrey,' she asked in her heart, into the still, sniffy quiet around the grave, as the first token lumps of soil were thrown, 'What am I going to do now?'

But Geoffrey didn't reply.

Weekend

By seven-thirty they were ready to go. Martha had everything packed into the car and the three children appropriately dressed and in the back seat, complete with educational games and wholewheat biscuits. When everything was ready in the car Martin would switch off the television, come downstairs, lock up the house, front and back, and take the wheel.

Weekend! Only two hours' drive down to the cottage on Friday evenings: three hours' drive back on Sunday nights. The pleasures of greenery and guests in between. They reckoned themselves fortunate, how fortunate!

On Fridays Martha would get home on the bus at six-twelve and prepare tea and sandwiches for the family: then she would strip four beds and put the sheets and quilt covers in the washing machine for Monday: take the country bedding from the airing basket, plus the books and the games, plus the weekend food—acquired at intervals throughout the week, to lessen the load—plus her own folder of work from the office, plus Martin's drawing materials (she was a market researcher in an advertising agency, he a freelance designer) plus hairbrushes, jeans, spare T-shirts, Jolyon's antibiotics (he suffered from sore throats), Jenny's recorder, Jasper's cassette player and so on—ah, the so on!—and would pack them all, skilfully and quickly, into the boot. Very little could be left in the cottage during the week. ('An open invitation to burglars': Martin) Then Martha would run round the house tidying and wiping, doing this and that, finding the cat at one neighbour's and delivering it to another, while the others ate their tea; and would usually, proudly, have everything finished by the time they had eaten their fill. Martin would just catch the BBC2 news, while Martha cleared away the tea table, and the children tossed up for the best positions in the car. 'Martha,' said Martin, tonight, 'you ought to get Mrs Hodder to do more. She takes advantage of you.'

Mrs Hodder came in twice a week to clean. She was over seventy. She charged two pounds an hour. Martha paid her out of her own wages: well, the running of the house was Martha's concern. If Martha chose to go out to work—as was her perfect right, Martin allowed, even though it wasn't the best thing for the children, but that must be Martha's moral responsibility—Martha must surely pay her domestic stand-in. An evident truth, heard loud and clear and frequent in Martin's mouth and Martha's heart.

'I expect you're right,' said Martha. She did not want to argue. Martin had had a long hard week, and now had to drive. Martha couldn't. Martha's license had been suspended four months back for drunken driving. Everyone agreed that the suspension was unfair: Martha seldom drank to excess: she was for one thing usually too busy pouring drinks for other people or washing other people's glasses to get much inside herself. But Martin had taken her out to dinner on her birthday, as was his custom, and exhaustion and excitement mixed had made her imprudent, and before she knew where she was, why there she was, in the dock, with a distorted lamp-post to pay for and a new bonnet for the car and six months' suspension.

So now Martin had to drive her car down to the cottage, and he was always tired on Fridays, and hot and sleepy on Sundays, and every rattle and clank and bump in the engine she felt to be somehow her fault.

Martin had a little sports car for London and work: it could nip in and out of the traffic nicely: Martha's was an old estate car, with room for the children, picnic baskets, bedding, food, games, plants, drink, portable television and all the things required by the middle classes for weekends in the country. It lumbered rather than zipped and made Martin angry. He seldom spoke a harsh word, but Martha, after the fashion of wives, could detect his mood from what he did not say rather than what he did, and from the tilt of his head, and the way his crinkly, merry eyes seemed crinklier and merrier still—and of course from the way he addressed Martha's car.

'Come along, you old banger you! Can't you do better than that? You're too old, that's your trouble. Stop complaining. Always complaining, it's only a hill. You're too wide about the hips. You'll never get through there.'

Martha worried about her age, her tendency to complain, and the width of her hips. She took the remarks personally. Was she right to do so? The children noticed nothing: it was just funny lively laughing Daddy being witty about Mummy's car. Mummy, done for drunken driving. Mummy, with the roots of melancholy somewhere deep beneath the bustling, busy, everyday self. Busy: ah so busy!

Martin would only laugh if she said anything about the way he spoke to her car and warn her against paranoia. 'Don't get like your mother, darling.' Martha's mother had, towards the end, thought that people were plotting against her. Martha's mother had led a secluded, suspicious life, and made Martha's childhood a chilly and a lonely time. Life now, by comparison, was wonderful for Martha. People, children, houses, conversations, food, drink, theatres—even, now, a career. Martin standing between her and the hostility of the world—popular, easy, funny Martin, beckoning the rest of the world into earshot.

Ah, she was grateful: little earnest Martha, with her shy ways and her penchant for passing boring exams—how her life had blossomed out! Three children too—Jasper, Jenny and Jolyon—all with Martin's broad brow and open looks, and the confidence born of her love and care, and the work she had put into them since the dawning of their days.

Martin drives. Martha, for once, drowses.

The right food, the right words, the right play. Doctors for the tonsils: dentists for the molars. Confiscate guns: censor television: encourage creativity. Paints and paper to hand: books on the shelves: meetings with teachers. Music teachers. Dancing lessons. Parties. Friends to tea. School plays. Open days. Junior orchestra.

Martha is jolted awake. Traffic lights. Martin doesn't like Martha to sleep while he drives.

Clothes. Oh, clothes! Can't wear this: must wear that. Dress shops. Piles of clothes in corners: duly washed, but waiting to be ironed, waiting to be put away.

Get the piles off the floor, into the laundry baskets. Martin doesn't like a mess.

Creativity arises out of order, not chaos. Five years off work while the children were small: back to work with seniority lost. What, did you think something was for nothing? If you have children, mother, that is your reward. It lies not in the world.

Have you taken enough food? Always hard to judge.

Food. Oh, food! Shop in the lunch-hour. Lug it all home. Cook for the freezer on Wednesday evenings while Martin is at his car-maintenance evening class, and isn't there to notice you being unrestful. Martin likes you to sit down in the evenings. Fruit, meat, vegetables, flour for home-made bread. Well, shop bread is full of pollutants. Frozen food, even your own, loses flavour. Martin often remarks on it.

Condiments. Everyone loves mango chutney. But the expense!

London Airport to the left. Look, look, children! Concorde? No, idiot, of course it isn't Concorde.

Ah, to be all things to all people: children, husband, employer, friends! It can be done: yes, it can: super woman.

Drink. Home-made wine. Why not? Elderberries grown thick and rich in London: and at least you know what's in it. Store it in high cupboards: lots of room: up and down the step-ladder. Careful! Don't slip. Don't break anything.

No such thing as an accident. Accidents are Freudian slips: they are wilful, bad-tempered things.

Martin can't bear bad temper. Martin likes slim ladies. Diet. Martin rather likes his secretary. Diet. Martin admires slim legs and big bosoms. How to achieve them both? Impossible. But try, oh try, to be what you ought to be, not what you are. Inside and out.

Martin brings back flowers and chocolates: whisks Martha off for holiday weekends. Wonderful! The best husband in the world: look into his crinkly, merry, gentle eyes; see it there. So the mouth slopes away into something of a pout. Never mind. Gaze into the eyes. Love. It must be love. You married him. *You.* Surely *you* deserve true love?

Salisbury Plain. Stonehenge. Look, children, look! Mother, we've seen Stonehenge a hundred times. Go back to sleep.

Cook! Ah cook. People love to come to Martin and Martha's dinners. Work it out in your head in the lunch-hour. If you get in at six-twelve, you can seal the meat while you beat the egg white while you feed the cat while you lay the table while you string the beans while you set out the cheese, goat's cheese, Martin loves goat's cheese, Martha tries to like goat's cheese—oh, bed, sleep, peace, quiet.

Sex! Ah sex. Orgasm please. Martin requires it. Well, so do you. And you don't want his secretary providing a passion you neglected to develop. Do you? Quick, quick, the cosmic bond. Love. Married love.

Secretary! Probably a vulgar suspicion: nothing more. Probably a fit of paranoics, `a la mother, now dead and gone.

At peace.

R.I.P.

Chilly, lonely mother, following her suspicions where they led.

Nearly there, children. Nearly in paradise, nearly at the cottage. Have another biscuit.

Real roses round the door.

Roses. Prune, weed, spray, feed, pick. Avoid thorns. One of Martin's few harsh words.

'Martha, you can't not want roses! What kind of person am I married to? An anti-rose personality?'

Green grass. Oh, God, grass. Grass must be mown. Restful lawns, daisies, bobbing, buttercups glowing. Roses and grass and books. Books.

Please Martin do we have to have the two hundred books, mostly twenties' first editions, bought at Christie's book sale on one of your afternoons off? Books need dusting.

Roars of laughter from Martin, Jasper, Jenny and Jolyon. Mummy says we shouldn't have the books: books need dusting!

Roses, green grass, books and peace.

Martha woke up with a start when they got to the cottage, and gave a little shriek which made them all laugh. Mummy's waking shriek, they called it.

Then there was the car to unpack and the beds to make up, and the electricity to connect, and the supper to make, and the cobwebs to remove, while Martin made the fire. Then supper—pork chops in sweet and sour sauce ('Pork is such a *dull* meat if you don't cook it properly': Martin) green salad from the garden, or such green salad as the rabbits had left. ('Martha, did you really net them properly? Be honest now!': Martin) and sauté potatoes. Mash is so stodgy and ordinary, and instant mash unthinkable. The children studied the night sky with the aid of their star map. Wonderful, rewarding children!

Then clear up the supper: set the dough to prove for the bread: Martin already in bed: exhausted by the drive and lighting the fire. ('Martha, we really ought to get the logs stacked properly. Get the children to do it, will you?': Martin) Sweep and tidy: get the TV aerial right. Turn up Jasper's jeans where he has trodden the hem undone. ('He can't go around like *that*, Martha. Not even Jasper': Martin)

Midnight. Good night. Weekend guests arriving in the morning.

Seven for lunch and dinner on Saturday. Seven for Sunday breakfast, nine for Sunday lunch. ('Don't fuss, darling. You always make such a fuss': Martin) Oh, God, forgotten the garlic squeezer. That means ten minutes with the back of a spoon and salt. Well, who wants *lumps* of garlic? No one. Not Martin's guests. Martin said so. Sleep.

Colin and Katie. Colin is Martin's oldest friend. Katie is his new young wife. Janet, Colin's other, earlier wife, was Martha's friend. Janet was rather like Martha, quieter and duller than her husband. A nag and a drag, Martin rather thought, and said, and of course she'd let herself go, everyone agreed. No one exactly excused Colin for walking out, but you could see the temptation.

Katie versus Janet.

Katie was languid, beautiful and elegant. She drawled when she spoke. Her hands were expressive: her feet were little and female. She had no children.

Janet plodded round on very flat, rather large feet. There was something wrong with them. They turned out slightly when she walked. She had two children. She was, frankly, boring. But Martha liked her: when Janet came down to the cottage she would wash up. Not in the way that most guests washed up—washing dutifully and setting everything out on the draining board, but actually drying and putting away too. And Janet would wash the bath and get the children all sat down, with chairs for everyone, even the littlest, and keep them quiet and satisfied so the grown-ups—well, the men—could get on with their conversation and their jokes and their love of country weekends, while Janet stared into space, as if grateful for the rest, quite happy.

Janet would garden, too. Weed the strawberries, while the men went for their walk; her great feet standing firm and square and sometimes crushing a plant or so, but never mind, oh never mind. Lovely Janet; who understood.

Now Janet was gone and here was Katie.

Katie talked with the men and went for walks with the men, and moved her ashtray rather impatiently when Martha tried to clear the drinks round it.

Dishes were boring, Katie implied by her manner, and domesticity was boring, and anyone who bothered with that kind of thing was a fool. Like Martha. Ash should be allowed to stay where it was, even if it was in the butter, and conversations should never be interrupted.

Knock, knock. Katie and Colin arrived at one-fifteen on Saturday morning, just after Martha had got to bed. 'You don't mind? It was the moonlight. We couldn't resist it. You should have seen Stonehenge! We didn't disturb you? Such early birds!'

Martha rustled up a quick meal of omelettes. Saturday nights' eggs. ('Martha makes a lovely omelette': Martin) ('Honey, make one of your mushroom omelettes: cook the mushrooms separately, remember, with lemon. Otherwise the water from the mushrooms gets into the egg, and spoils everything.') Sunday supper mushrooms. But ungracious to say anything.

Martin had revived wonderfully at the sight of Colin and Katie. He brought out the whisky bottle. Glasses. Ice. Jug for water. Wait. Wash up another sinkful, when they're finished. 2 A.M.

'Don't do it tonight, darling.'

'It'll only take a sec.' Bright smile, not a hint of self-pity. Self-pity can spoil everyone's weekend.

Martha knows that if breakfast for seven is to be manageable the sink must be cleared of dishes. A tricky meal, breakfast. Especially if bacon, eggs, and tomatoes must all be cooked in separate pans. ('Separate pans means separate flavours!': Martin)

She is running around in her nightie. Now if that had been Katie— but there's something so *practical* about Martha. Reassuring, mind; but the skimpy nightie and the broad rump and the thirty-eight years are all rather embarrassing. Martha can see it in Colin and Katie's eyes. Martin's too. Martha wishes she did not see so much in other people's eyes. Her mother did, too. Dear, dead mother. Did I misjudge you?

This was the second weekend Katie had been down with Colin but without Janet. Colin was a photographer: Katie had been his accessoriser. First Colin and Janet: then Colin, Janet and Katie: now Colin and Katie!

Katie weeded with rubber gloves on and pulled out pansies in mistake for weeds and laughed and laughed along with everyone when her mistake was pointed out to her, but the pansies died. Well, Colin had become with the years fairly rich and fairly famous, and what does a fairly rich and famous man want with a wife like Janet when Katie is at hand?

On the first of the Colin/Janet/Katie weekends Katie had appeared out of the bathroom. 'I say,' said Katie, holding out a damp towel with evident distaste, 'I can only find this. No hope of a dry one?' And Martha had to run to fetch a dry towel and amazingly found one, and handed it to Katie who flashed her a brilliant smile and said, 'I can't bear damp towels. Anything in the world but damp towels,' as if speaking to a servant in a time of shortage of staff, and took all the water so there was none left for Martha to wash up.

The trouble, of course, was drying anything at all in the cottage. There were no facilities for doing so, and Martin had a horror of clothes lines which might spoil the view. He toiled and moiled all week in the city simply to get a country view at the weekend. Ridiculous to spoil it by draping it with wet towels! But now Martha had bought more towels, so perhaps everyone could be satisfied. She would take nine damp towels back on Sunday evenings in a plastic bag and see to them in London.

On this Saturday morning, straight after breakfast, Katie went out to the car—she and Colin had a new Lamborghini; hard to imagine Katie in anything duller—and came back waving a new Yves St. Laurent towel. 'See! I brought my own, darlings.'

They'd brought nothing else. No fruit, no meat, no vegetables, not even bread, certainly not a box of chocolates. They'd gone off to bed with alacrity, the night before, and the spare room rocked and heaved: well, who'd want to do washing-up when you could do that, but what about the children? Would they get confused? First Colin and Janet, now Colin and Katie?

Martha murmured something of her thoughts to Martin, who looked quite shocked. 'Colin's my best friend. I don't expect him to bring anything,' and Martha felt mean. 'And good heavens, you can't protect the kids from sex for ever; don't be so prudish,' so that Martha felt stupid as well. Mean, complaining, and stupid.

Janet had rung Martha during the week. The house had been sold over her head, and she and the children had been moved into a small flat. Katie was trying to persuade Colin to cut down on her allowance, Janet said.

'It does one no good to be materialistic,' Katie confided. 'I have nothing. No home, no family, no ties, no possessions. Look at me! Only me and a suitcase of clothes.' But Katie seemed highly satisfied with the me, and the clothes were stupendous. Katie drank a great deal and became funny. Everyone laughed, including Martha. Katie had been married twice. Martha marvelled at how someone could arrive in their mid-thirties with nothing at all to their name, neither husband, nor children, nor property and not mind.

Mind you, Martha could see the power of such helplessness. If Colin was all Katie had in the world, how could Colin abandon her? And to what? Where would she go? How would she live? Oh, clever Katie.

'My teacup's dirty,' said Katie, and Martha ran to clean it, apologising, and Martin raised his eyebrows, at Martha, not Katie.

'I wish *you'd* wear scent,' said Martin to Martha, reproachfully. Katie wore lots. Martha never seemed to have time to put any on, though Martin brought her bottle after bottle. Martha leapt out of bed each morning to meet some emergency—miaowing cat, coughing child, faulty alarm clock, postman's knock—when was Martha to put on scent? It annoyed Martin all the same. She ought to do more to charm him.

Colin looked handsome and harrowed and younger than Martin, though they were much the same age. 'Youth's catching,' said Martin in bed that night. 'It's since he found Katie.' Found, like some treasure. Discovered; something exciting and wonderful, in the dreary world of established spouses.

On Saturday morning Jasper trod on a piece of wood ('Martha, why isn't he wearing shoes? It's too bad': Martin) and Martha took him into the hospital to have a nasty splinter removed. She left the cottage at ten and arrived back at one, and they were still sitting in the sun, drinking, empty bottles glinting in the long grass. The grass hadn't been cut. Don't forget the bottles. Broken glass means more mornings at the hospital. Oh, don't fuss. Enjoy yourself. Like other people. Try.

But no potatoes peeled, no breakfast cleared, nothing. Cigarette ends still amongst old toast, bacon rind and marmalade. 'You could have done the potatoes,' Martha burst out. Oh, bad temper! Prime sin. They looked at her in amazement and dislike. Martin too.

'Goodness,' said Katie. 'Are we doing the whole Sunday lunch bit on Saturday? Potatoes? Ages since I've eaten potatoes. Wonderful!'

'The children expect it,' said Martha.

So they did. Saturday and Sunday lunch shone like reassuring beacons in their lives. Saturday lunch: family lunch: fish and chips. ('So much better cooked at home than bought': Martin) Sunday. Usually roast beef, potatoes, peas, apple pie. Oh, of course. Yorkshire pudding. Always a problem with oven temperatures. When the beef's going slowly, the Yorkshire should be going fast. How to achieve that? Like big bosom and little hips.

'Just relax,' said Martin. 'I'll cook dinner, all in good time. Splinters always work their own way out: no need to have taken him to hospital. Let life drift over you, my love. Flow with the waves, that's the way.'

And Martin flashed Martha a distant, spiritual smile. His hand lay on Katie's slim brown arm, with its many gold bands.

'Anyway, you do too much for the children,' said Martin. 'It isn't good for them. Have a drink.'

So Martha perched uneasily on the step and had a glass of cider, and wondered how, if lunch was going to be late, she would get cleared up and the meat out of the marinade for the rather formal dinner that would be expected that evening. The marinaded lamb ought to cook for at least four hours in a low oven; and the cottage oven was very small, and you couldn't use that and the grill at the same time and Martin liked his fish grilled, not fried. Less cholesterol.

She didn't say as much. Domestic details like this were very boring, and any mild complaint was registered by Martin as a scene. And to make a scene was so ungrateful.

This was the life. Well, wasn't it? Smart friends in large cars and country living and drinks before lunch and roses and bird song—'Don't drink *too* much,' said Martin, and told them about Martha's suspended driving license.

The children were hungry so Martha opened them a can of beans and sausages and heated that up. ('Martha, do they have to eat that crap? Can't they wait?' Martin)

Katie was hungry: she said so, to keep the children in face. She was lovely with children—most children. She did not particularly like Colin and Janet's children. She said so, and he accepted it. He only saw them once a month now, not once a week.

'Let me make lunch,' Katie said to Martha. 'You do so much, poor thing!'

And she pulled out of the fridge all the things Martha had put away for the next day's picnic lunch party—Camembert cheese and salad and salami and made a wonderful tomato salad in two minutes and opened the white wine—'not very cold, darling. Shouldn't it be chilling?'—and had it all on the table in five amazing competent minutes. 'That's all we need, darling,' said Martin. 'You are funny with your fish-and-chip Saturdays! What could be nicer than this? Or simpler?'

Nothing, except there was Sunday's buffet lunch for nine gone, in place of Saturday's fish for six, and would the fish stretch? No. Katie had had quite a lot to drink. She pecked Martha on the forehead. 'Funny little Martha,' she said. 'She reminds me of Janet. I really do like Janet.' Colin did not want to be reminded of Janet, and said so. 'Darling, Janet's a fact of life,' said Katie. 'If you'd only think about her more, you might manage to pay her less.' And she yawned and stretched her lean, childless body and smiled at Colin with her inviting, naughty little girl eyes, and Martin watched her in admiration.

Martha got up and left them and took a paint pot and put a coat of white gloss on the bathroom wall. The white surface pleased her. She was good at painting. She produced a smooth, even surface. Her legs throbbed. She feared she might be getting varicose veins.

Outside in the garden the children played badminton. They were bad-tempered, but relieved to be able to look up and see their mother working, as usual: making their lives for ever better and nicer: organising, planning, thinking ahead, side-stepping disaster, making preparations, like a mother hen, fussing and irritating: part of the natural boring scenery of the world.

On Saturday night Katie went to bed early: she rose from her chair and stretched and yawned and poked her head into the kitchen where Martha was washing saucepans. Colin had cleared the table and Katie had folded the napkins into pretty creases, while Martin blew at the fire, to make it bright. 'Good night,' said Katie.

Katie appeared three minutes later, reproachfully holding out her Yves St. Laurent towel, sopping wet. 'Oh, dear,' cried Martha. 'Jenny must have washed her hair!' And Martha was obliged to rout Jenny out of bed to rebuke her, publicly, if only to demonstrate that she knew what was right and proper. That meant Jenny would sulk all weekend, and that meant a treat or an outing mid-week, or else by the following week she'd be having an asthma attack. 'You fuss the children too much,' said Martin. 'That's why Jenny has asthma.' Jenny was pleasant enough to look at, but not stunning. Perhaps she was a disappointment to her father? Martin would never say so, but Martha feared he thought so.

An egg and an orange each child, each day. Then nothing too bad would go wrong. And it hadn't. The asthma was very mild. A calm, tranquil environment, the doctor said. Ah, smile, Martha smile. Domestic happiness depends on you. 21 × 52 oranges a year. Each one to be purchased, carried, peeled and washed up after. And what about potatoes. 12 × 52 pounds a year? Martin liked his potatoes carefully peeled. He couldn't bear to find little cores of black in the mouthful. ('Well, it isn't very nice, is it?': Martin)

Martha dreamt she was eating coal, by handfuls, and liking it.

Saturday night. Martin made love to Martha three times. Three times? How virile he was, and clearly turned on by the sounds from the

spare room. Martin said he loved her. Martin always did. He was a
courteous lover; he knew the importance of foreplay. So did Martha.
Three times.

Ah, sleep. Jolyon had a nightmare. Jenny was woken by a moth.
Martin slept through everything. Martha pottered about the house in
the night. There was a moon. She sat at the window and stared out into
the summer night for five minutes, and was at peace, and then went
back to bed because she ought to be fresh for the morning.

But she wasn't. She slept late. The others went out for a walk.
They'd left a note, a considerate note: 'Didn't wake you. You looked
tired. Had a cold breakfast so as not to make too much mess. Leave
everything 'til we get back.' But it was ten o'clock, and guests were
coming at noon, so she cleared away the bread, the butter, the crumbs,
the smears, the jam, the spoons, the spilt sugar, the cereal, the milk (sour
by now) and the dirty plates, and swept the floors, and tidied up quickly, and grabbed a cup of coffee, and prepared to make a rice and fish
dish, and a chocolate mousse and sat down in the middle to eat a lot of
bread and jam herself. Broad hips. She remembered the office work in
her file and knew she wouldn't be able to do it. Martin anyway thought
it was ridiculous for her to bring work back at the weekends. 'It's your
holiday,' he'd say. 'Why should they impose?' Martha loved her work.
She didn't have to smile at it. She just did it.

Katie came back upset and crying. She sat in the kitchen while Martha worked and drank glass after glass of gin and bitter lemon. Katie
liked ice and lemon in gin. Martha paid for all the drink out of her
wages. It was part of the deal between her and Martin—the contract by
which she went out to work. All things to cheer the spirit, otherwise
depressed by a working wife and mother, were to be paid for by Martha. Drink, holidays, petrol, outings, puddings, electricity, heating: it
was quite a joke between them. It didn't really make any difference: it
was their joint money, after all. Amazing how Martha's wages were
creeping up, almost to the level of Martin's. One day they would over-
take. Then what?

Work, honestly, was a piece of cake.

Anyway, poor Katie was crying. Colin, she'd discovered, kept a photograph of Janet and the children in his wallet. 'He's not free of her.
He pretends he is, but he isn't. She has him by a stranglehold. It's the
kids. His bloody kids. Moaning Mary and that little creep Joanna. It's
all he thinks about. I'm nobody.'

But Katie didn't believe it. She knew she was somebody all right.

Colin came in, in a fury. He took out the photograph and set fire to it, bitterly, with a match. Up in smoke they went. Mary and Joanna and Janet. The ashes fell on the floor. (Martha swept them up when Colin and Katie had gone. It hardly seemed polite to do so when they were still there.) 'Go back to her,' Katie said. 'Go back to her. I don't care. Honestly, I'd rather be on my own. You're a nice old fashioned thing. Run along then. Do your thing, I'll do mine. Who cares?'

'Christ, Katie, the fuss! She only just happens to be in the photograph. She's not there on purpose to annoy. And I do feel bad about her. She's been having a hard time.'

'And haven't you, Colin? She twists a pretty knife, I can tell you. Don't you have rights too? Not to mention me. Is a little loyalty too much to expect?'

They were reconciled before lunch, up in the spare room. Harry and Beryl Elder arrived at twelve-thirty. Harry didn't like to hurry on Sundays; Beryl was flustered with apologies for their lateness. They'd brought artichokes from their garden. 'Wonderful,' cried Martin. 'Fruits of the earth? Let's have a wonderful soup! Don't fret, Martha. I'll do it.'

'Don't fret.' Martha clearly hadn't been smiling enough. She was in danger, Martin implied, of ruining everyone's weekend. There was an emergency in the garden very shortly—an elm tree which had probably got Dutch elm disease—and Martha finished the artichokes. The lid flew off the blender and there was artichoke purée everywhere. 'Let's have lunch outside,' said Colin. 'Less work for Martha.'

Martin frowned at Martha: he thought the appearance of martyrdom in the face of guests to be an unforgivable offence.

Everyone happily joined in taking the furniture out, but it was Martha's experience that nobody ever helped to bring it in again. Jolyon was stung by a wasp. Jasper sneezed and sneezed from hay fever and couldn't find the tissues and he wouldn't use loo paper. ('Surely you remembered the tissues, darling?': Martin)

Beryl Elder was nice. 'Wonderful to eat out,' she said, fetching the cream for her pudding, while Martha fished a fly from the liquefying Brie—('You shouldn't have bought it so ripe, Martha': Martin) 'except it's just some other woman has to do it. But at least it isn't *me*.' Beryl worked too, as a secretary, to send the boys to boarding school, where she'd rather they weren't. But her husband was from a rather grand family, and she'd been only a typist when he married her, so her life was a mass of amends, one way or another. Harry had lately opted out of the stockbroking rat race and become an artist, choosing integrity rather than money, but that choice was his alone and couldn't of course be inflicted on the boys.

Katie found the fish and rice dish rather strange, toyed at it with her fork, and talked about Italian restaurants she knew. Martin lay back soaking in the sun: crying, 'Oh, this is the life.' He made coffee, nobly, and the lid flew off the grinder and there were coffee beans all over the kitchen expecially in amongst the row of cookery books which Martin gave Martha Christmas by Christmas. At least they didn't have to be brought back every weekend. ('The burglars won't have the sense to steal those': Martin)

Beryl fell asleep and Katie watched her, quizzically. Beryl's mouth was open and she had a lot of fillings, and her ankles were thick and her waist was going, and she didn't look after herself. 'I love women,' sighed Katie. 'They look so wonderful asleep. I wish I could be an earth mother.'

Beryl woke with a start and nagged her husband into going home, which he clearly didn't want to do, so didn't. Beryl thought she had to get back because his mother was coming round later. Nonsense! Then Beryl tried to stop Harry drinking more home-made wine and was laughed at by everyone. He was driving, Beryl couldn't, and he did have a nasty scar on his temple from a previous road accident. Never mind.

'She does come on strong, poor soul,' laughed Katie when they'd finally gone. 'I'm never going to get married,'—and Colin looked at her yearningly because he wanted to marry her more than anything in the world, and Martha cleared the coffee cups.

'Oh don't *do* that,' said Katie, 'do just sit *down*, Martha, you make us all feel bad,' and Martin glared at Martha who sat down and Jenny called out for her and Martha went upstairs and Jenny had started her first period and Martha cried and cried and knew she must stop because this must be a joyous occasion for Jenny or her whole future would be blighted, but for once, Martha couldn't.

Her daughter Jenny: wife, mother, friend.

THE
FAT WOMAN'S
JOKE

___

I   What Esther Sussman liked about Earls Court was that she
    didn't know anyone who lived there. The legs which passed the
bars of her basement window, day and night, belonged to nobody she
had ever seen or would ever see again. Between four and six every
morning the street would empty, and then the silence would disturb
her, and she would wake, and get up, and make herself a cup of cocoa
and eat a piece of chocolate cake, icing first. There is nothing, she
would think, more delicious than the icing of bought chocolate cake,
eaten in the silence and privacy of the night.

During the day she would read science fiction novels. In the evenings she watched television. And she ate, and ate, and drank, and
ate.

She ate frozen chips and peas and hamburgers, and sliced bread with
bought jam and fishpaste, and baked beans and instant puddings, and
tinned porridge and tinned suet pudding, and cakes and biscuits from
packets. She drank sweet coffee, sweet tea, sweet cocoa and sweet
sherry.

This is the only proper holiday, she thought, that I have had for
years; and then she thought, but this is not a holiday, this is my life until
I die; and then she would eat a biscuit, or make a piece of toast, and melt
some ready-sliced cheese on top of it, remembering that the act of cooking had once been almost as absorbing as the act of eating.

The flat was dark and damp, as was only right and fitting, and the
furniture was nailed to the floor in case some passing tenant saw fit to

sell or burn it. Esther, in fact, found it pleasant to have her whereabouts controlled by a dozen nails. The less freedom of choice she had the better. She had not felt so secure since she spent her days in a pram.

She lived in this manner for several weeks. From time to time she would put on an old black coat over her old black dress and go to Smith's for more science fiction paperbacks, and to the supermarket for more food. When the cupboards were full of food she felt pleased. When her stocks ran low she became uneasy.

Phyllis was the last of Esther's circle to seek her out. She came tripping prettily down the steps one afternoon; thirty-one and finely boned, beautifully dressed in a red tiny-flowered trouser suit with hat to match—neat, sexy and rich; invincibly lively and invincibly stupid.

She dusted off the seat of the arm-chair before she sat down. She took off her hat and laid it on the table. She stared sadly at Esther with her round silly eyes; Esther kept her own lowered, and sliced a round of hot buttered toast into fingers. When drops of butter fell on to her black dress she rubbed them in with her hand.

'Oh Esther,' said Phyllis, 'why didn't you tell me? If I had known you'd needed help, I would have been here at once. If you'd left your address—'

'I don't need help. What sort of help should I need?'

'Going off like that without a word to anyone. I thought we were supposed to be friends? Now what are friends for if not for help at times like these?'

'Times like what?' Butter ran down Esther's chin. She salvaged it with her tongue.

'It took me weeks finding you, and you know how busy I am. I tried to make Alan tell me where you were but he just wouldn't, and your lawyer didn't know a thing, and your mother was fantastically evasive, and in the end I ran into Peter and he told me. Do you think that girl-friend of his is suitable? I mean, really suitable? She treats him like dirt. He's too young to know how to cope. I wish you'd stop eating, Esther, you'll be like a balloon.'

Esther surveyed her plump hands and wrists and laughed. It was a grimy flat, and the butter mingled with the dirt round her nails.

'Are you sure you wouldn't like some toast, Phyllis? Toast is one of the triumphs of our civilisation. It must be made with very fresh bread, thickly cut; then toasted very quickly and buttered at once, so the butter is half-melted. Unsalted butter, of course; you sprinkle it with salt afterwards. Sea salt, preferably.'

Esther found to her surprise she was crying. She wiped her face with the back of her hand, smearing a streak of oily grime across her cheek, where the white fat lay thickly larded beneath the skin.

'No thank you. No toast. And that lovely boy Peter. He needs you at this crisis of his life. If ever a boy needed his mother, it's Peter at this moment. And what about poor Alan? It breaks my heart to see all this senseless misery. I don't understand any of it. Your lovely marriage, all in ruins.'

'Marriage is too strong an institution for me,' said Esther. 'It is altogether too heavy and powerful.' And indeed at that moment she felt it to be a single steady crushing weight, on top of which bore down the entire human edifice of city and state, learning and religion, commerce and law; pomp, passion and reproduction besides. Beneath this mighty structure the little needles of feeling which flickered between Alan and her were dreadful in their implication. When she challenged her husband, she challenged her known universe.

'What an odd thing to say. Marriage to me is a source of strength, not a weight upon me. I'm sure that's how one ought to look at it. And you are going back to Alan, aren't you? Please say you are.'

'No. This is my home now. I like it. Nothing happens here. I know what to expect from one day to the next. I can control everything, and I can eat. I like eating. Were I attracted to men, or indeed attractive to them, I would perhaps find a similar pleasure in some form of sexual activity. But as it is, I just eat. When you eat, you get fat, and that's all. There are no complications. But husbands, children—no, Phyllis, I am sorry. I am not strong enough for them.'

'You are behaving so oddly. Have you seen a doctor? I know this divine man in Wimpole Street. He's done marvels for me.'

'I wish you would have something to eat, Phyllis. It makes me nervous, to see you just sitting there, not eating, staring, understanding only about a quarter of what I say.'

'No. I have to watch my figure.'

'I suppose you really do believe that your happiness is consequent upon your size? That an inch or two one way or the other would make you truly loved? Equating prettiness with sexuality, and sexuality with happiness? It is a very debased view of femininity you take, Phyllis. It would be excusable in a sixteen-year-old—if my nose were a different shape, if my bosom were larger, if my freckles were gone, then the whole world would be different. But in a woman of your age it is vulgar.'

'I am sorry, but I see it differently. It is just common-sense to make the most of oneself. In any case, everything is different for you. You don't seem to have to follow the rules, as the rest of us do. To be frank, you are an appalling sight at this very moment; you have let yourself go—but I have known you look quite ravishing. I think Gerry always rather fancied you. And I will say this for Gerry, he has good taste. Otherwise the humiliation would be unendurable. Yet it's odd; they are always women of a totally different type from me. Why do you think that is?'

Esther rose from her chair, her flesh unfolding beneath the loose fabric of her dress. She crossed to the cupboard and presently selected a tin of condensed mushroom soup which she opened, poured into a saucepan, and heated on the stove. Phyllis talked to her friend's broad back like a hummingbird chirping away at a rhinoceros.

'I don't mind about Gerry's fancies, really. It's a very small part of marriage, isn't it? If there's anything I've learned in my life it's that one comes to terms with this kind of thing in the end.'

'I come to terms with nothing.'

'Besides, it's probably just all talk with him. They do say that the men who talk most, do least.'

'They'll say anything to comfort themselves.'

'Oh.' Phyllis abandoned the subject. 'Esther, I don't understand what went wrong between you and Alan, so suddenly. Why are you living down here in this horrible place? And why did *you* leave, not him? I don't believe he turned you out. He's such a good man. He's not impetuous, like Gerry. You always seemed so right for each other, so settled and content. He never even talked about other women, not when you were in the room anyway. Sometimes after I'd been with you both I'd go home and cry because Gerry and I could never be close like you and Alan. The only time Gerry and I are ever close is when we're in bed, and even then I don't really enjoy it. It just seems the most important thing in the world. Can you understand that? And now that you two have split up, it just seems like the end of the world to me. Everything has suddenly become frightening. Esther, you've made me afraid.'

'You are right to feel afraid. Are you sure you don't want some of this soup? It is very good—although perhaps a little salty. That's the trouble with condensed soups. You have to choose between having them too weak or too salty.'

'Why am I right to feel afraid, Esther? What is there to be afraid of? I think and think but I can't make it out. You make me feel all kinds of things are going on underneath which I don't understand. It can't be Gerry, because I know he'll never leave me. He'll just go on having sordid affairs with sordid women, but they mean nothing to him. He tells me so, all the time. He's a hot-blooded man, you see, so it's understandable. It's just something a woman like me has to learn to put up with. And in a way, I suppose it has its advantages. He couldn't blame me if I did look round for my amusements, could he?'

'He would, though.'

'Well it wouldn't be reasonable of him—of course he's not a very reasonable person. That's why I love him. If only I could find an attractive man I'd have a lovely passionate affair with him. But there aren't any attractive men left. Why do you think that is? Esther, you haven't answered my question. Why do you think I am right to feel afraid?'

'Because you are growing old. Because lurking somewhere beneath the surface of your brain is a vision of loneliness, and it will be a terrible moment when it breaks through, and you realise that your future is not green pastures, but the knackers yard. We are all separate people, and we are all alone. It is a ridiculous thing to say that no man is an island. We are all islands. You can die, and Gerry won't. Gerry can die, and you won't. Our lives just go on, separate as they have always been. There are no end of things you can be afraid of, if you put your mind to it. Do have some soup. If I emptied a tin of cream in it might improve matters. And a little tomato sauce would cover up the tinny taste.'

'You say the most terrible things and then you expect me to eat.'

'Of course. You can't put off being useless and old and unwanted for ever. Soon, little Phyllis, you will stop painting your toe-nails. Already I suspect you no longer wear your best knickers to parties. It will all be over for you as it is for me, and love and motherhood and romance will be no more than dreams remembered, and rather bad dreams at that. Your real life will begin as mine has now. This is what it's like. Food. Drink. Sleep. Books. They are all drugs. None are as effective as sex, but they are calmer and safer. Nuts?'

'Nuts? Who? Oh—I see.'

Esther was offering Phyllis a bowl of nuts.

'Nuts are lovely,' said Esther. 'Your teeth go through the middle, and they're white and pure and clean inside, and slightly salty and dirty and sexy outside. They make your mouth just a little sore, so you have to take another mouthful to find out if they really do or not.'

'Esther, if you eat so much you will make yourself ill. You've gone completely to pieces. You must make an effort to pull yourself together. You will have to go on a diet again. You and Alan were on a diet just before all this started. I never thought you'd go through with it, but you did, and I respect you for it. But now you've undone all the good you did.'

Esther looked at Phyllis with distaste. 'Oh go away!' She loomed over Phyllis, dirty-nailed, dirty-faced, brilliant-eyed and dangerous. 'Go away! I didn't want you to come here, asking questions, nagging. I came here to have some peace. I don't want to see anyone. What do you want from me?'

'I want to help you.'

'Don't be so stupid. You help me? You're like a mad old woman battering at the prison gates when the hanging's due. All you really want is just to be in there watching. There's nothing here to watch. Just a fat woman eating. That's all. You can see them in any café, any day. They're all around.'

'You are very upset. Esther,' said Phyllis doggedly, 'I'm your friend. I'm very hurt you didn't turn to me when you were in trouble.'

Esther beat her head with her hand.

'That's what I mean! "*I'm very hurt!*" I can't stand it. What am I supposed to do now? Comfort your stupid little worries? What do you think it all is—some kind of game? This is our life, and it's the only one we're ever going to get, and it's a desperate business, and you come bleating to me about your being hurt because I, being near to death and madness, don't come bleating to you with—oh, he treats me so badly, oh, you know what he said, you know what he did—as if talking can make things different. Phyllis, will you please, for your own sake, go away and leave me alone?'

'No.'

Esther gave up.

'Then I will tell you all about it. And when you have drunk your fill of miseries, perhaps then you will feel satisfied and go away. I warn you, it will not be pleasant. You will become upset and angry. It is a story of patterns but no endings, meanings but no answers, and jokes where it would be nice if no jokes were. You have never heard a tale quite like this before and that in itself you will find hard to endure. Are you sitting comfortably?'

'Yes,' said Phyllis, putting her hands neatly together in her lap.

'Then I'll begin.'

* * *

Meanwhile, up in Hampstead, in an attic flat, two other women were talking. There was Susan, who was twenty-four, and Brenda, who was twenty-two. It was Susan's flat, and Brenda was staying in the absence of Susan's boy-friend. Just now Susan was painting a picture of Brenda: these days when she came home from the office she would put on a dun-coloured smock and take up her brush at once. She said it gave her life meaning.

Susan was tall, and slim to the point of gauntness. She had straight very thick fair hair, enigmatic slanty green eyes, high cheekbones, a bold nose and an intelligent expression. From time to time, as she worked, she would see herself in the mirror behind Brenda, and would like what she saw.

'It's a pity,' she said to Brenda, 'that your legs are so heavy. Otherwise you'd stop the traffic in the streets.'

Brenda had long legs and they were, in truth, fairly massive around the thighs. But seen sideways on she was almost as slim as Susan herself. She had a round face and an innocent look. She thought Susan lived a wild, fascinating, exciting life.

'What can I do about my legs?'

'Don't wear trousers,' said Susan.

'But trousers are no bother.'

'You're supposed to bother. You've got to bother if you're a woman. Otherwise you might as well be a man.'

'It's not fair. I didn't ask to be born with legs like pillars.'

'I dare say they are good for child-bearing.'

'Can I look?' Brenda lived in hope that one day Susan would paint a flattering portrait of her. Susan never did.

The telephone rang.

'You'd better answer it,' said Susan. 'If it's Alan I'm not at home. I've gone away for a month to the country.'

It wasn't Alan, but a wrong number.

'Perhaps you should ring him,' ventured Brenda. 'Then you wouldn't be so edgy.'

'I'm not edgy,' said Susan. 'I am upset. So we're all upset. Loving *is* upsetting. That's the point of it.'

'What about his wife? Is she upset?'

'I don't think she feels very much at all. Like fish feel no pain when you catch them. From what Alan says, her emotional extremities are primitive.'

'If I went out with a married man I'd feel awful,' said Brenda.

'Why?'

'I'd worry about his wife.'

'You are very different from me. You are fundamentally on the side of wife, and families. I don't like wives, on principle. I like to feel that any husband would prefer me to his wife. Wives are a dull, dreadful, boring, possessive lot by virtue of their state. I am all for sexual free enterprise. Let the best woman win.'

'If you were married,' said Brenda, 'you would not talk like that.'

'If I was married,' said Susan, 'which heaven forbid, I would make sure I outshone every other woman in the world. I wouldn't let myself go.'

'Alan didn't seem your type at all.'

'I don't have a type. You are very vulgar sometimes. You know nothing about sex or art or anything.'

'I don't know why you always want to paint me, then. You seem to have such a low opinion of me. It is very tiring.'

'You have a marvellous face,' said Susan. 'If only you would *do* something with it.'

'What do you mean, do something with it?'

'Give it a kind of style, or put an expression on it that suited it.'

'What would suit it?' Brenda was worried.

'I don't know. I'm getting very bored. Shall we go to the pub?'

'I don't like sitting about in pubs. All those smelly people, so full of drink they don't know what they're doing. Last time I was in a pub a man pee-ed himself, he was so drunk. How can you *talk* to anyone in a pub?'

'You go to pubs to enjoy yourself, not to talk. Communication is on a different level altogether. Sometimes I think you should run home to Mummy. You have no gift for living.'

'Oh all right, we'll go to the pub. But will you tell me all about Alan?'

'What about him? What do you want to know? You are very prurient.'

'I don't want to know all about that. I want to know what you *felt*. You make me feel so outclassed. Your relationships are so major, somehow. Nothing like that ever happens to me.'

'He was on a diet,' said Susan. 'That's a feminine kind of thing to be, really. On the whole masculine things are boring and feminine things are interesting.'

'Men don't bore me,' said Brenda. 'Everything else, but I've never been *bored* by a man.'

'Then you're lucky. But that wasn't what I was saying. You are very dim sometimes.'

Susan took off her smock. Brenda put on her shoes.

'You never know with men,' said Susan, pulling on an open lace-work dress over a flesh-coloured body-stocking. 'The ones who are most interesting before, are often the most boring afterwards, and vice versa.'

'In that case,' said Brenda, 'it would be absurd for a girl to marry a man she hadn't been to bed with, wouldn't it? Think of all those poor lovesick virgins in the past, all going starry-eyed to the altar and all destined for a lifetime's boredom. How terrible! And to think that my mother would wish to perpetuate such a system for ever!'

'All human activity,' remarked Susan, painting a rim of black around her eyes, 'is fairly absurd.'

Brenda put on her jockey's cap and they left. They were a ravishing pair. People stared after them.

Esther had a very pretty soft voice. It was one of the things that had first made Alan notice her. Now, as she recounted her tale, it floated so meekly out of her lips that it was quite an effort for Phyllis to catch what she was saying.

'Alan and I were accustomed to eating a great deal, of course. We all have our cushions against reality: we all have to have our little treats to look forward to. With Gerry it's looking forward to laying girls, and with you it's looking forward to enduring it, and with Alan and me it was eating food. So you can imagine how vulnerable a diet made us.'

'I wish you would stop using the past tense about you and Alan.'

'I know it is only four weeks ago but it might as well be forty years. My marriage with Alan is over. Please don't interrupt. I am explaining how food set the pattern of our days. All day in his grand office Alan would sip coffee and nibble biscuits and plan his canteen dockets and organise cold chicken and salad and wine for working lunches, and all day at home I would plan food, and buy food, and cook food, and serve food, and nibble and taste and stir and experiment and make sweeties and goodies and tasties for Alan to try out when he came home. I would feel cheated if we were asked out to dinner. I would spend the entire afternoon making myself as beautiful as my increasing age and girth would allow, but still I felt cheated.'

'You were a wonderful cook. Gerry used to say you were the best cook in England. When you two came to dinner I would go mad with worry. It would take me the whole day just producing something I wouldn't be ashamed of. And even then I usually was.'

'People who can't cook shouldn't try. It is a gift which you are either born with or you aren't. I used to quite enjoy coming to visit you two in spite of the food. You and Gerry would quarrel and bicker, and get at each other in subtle and not so subtle ways, and Alan and I would sit back, lulled by our full bellies into a sense of security, and really believe ourselves to be happy, content and well-matched. This day, four weeks ago, I really think I thought I was happy. There were little grey clouds, here and there, like Alan's writing, which was distracting him from his job, and Peter's precocity, and my boredom with the house and simply, I suppose growing older and fatter. In truth of course, they weren't little clouds at all. They were raging bloody crashing thunderstorms. But there is none so blind as those who are too stuffed full of food to see.'

'I don't really know what you are talking about.'

'You will come to understand, if you pay attention. You are sure you want me to go on with this story?'

'Yes. Oh Esther, you can't still be hungry!' Esther was taking frozen fish fingers from their pack.

'I have no intention, ever again, of doing without what I want. That was what Alan and I presumed to think we could do, that evening in your house when we decided to go on a diet.'

Phyllis Frazer's living-room was rich, uncluttered, pale, tidy and serene. Yet its tidiness, when the Sussmans arrived, seemed deceitful, and its serenity a fraud. And the Frazers, like their room, had an air of urbanity which was not quite believable. Phyllis's cheeks were too pink and Gerry's smile too wide. The doorbell, Esther assumed, had put a stop to a scene of either passion or rage. Gerry was a vigorous, noisy man, twice Phyllis's size. He was a successful civil engineer.

'I hope we're not early,' said Esther. 'We had to come by taxi. We have this new car, you see.' She was kissed first by Phyllis and then by Gerry, who took longer over the embrace than was necessary. Alan pecked Phyllis discreetly, and not without embarrassment, and shook hands with Gerry. When they sat down for their pre-dinner drinks Gerry could see the flesh of Esther's thighs swelling over the tops of her stockings. Esther was aware of this but did nothing about it. She looked, this evening, both monumental and magnificent. Her bright eyes flashed and her pale, large face was animated. Beside her, Alan appeared insignificant, although when he was away from her he stood out as a reasonably sized, reasonably endowed man. He had a thin, clever, craggy face and an urbane manner. His paunch sat uneasily on a frame not designed for it. He had worked in the same advertising agency for fifteen years, and was now in a position of trust and accorded much automatic respect. His title was 'Executive Creative Controller.'

'I know nothing about the insides of cars,' he now said, 'except that whenever I buy a new one it goes for a day and then stops. After that it's garages and guarantees and trouble until I wish I had bought a bicycle instead. I don't even know why I buy cars. It just seems to happen. I think perhaps I was sold this one by one of my own advertisements. I am a suggestible person.'

'You take things calmly,' said Gerry. 'If I bought a car which so much as faltered somebody's head would roll.'

'But you are a man of passions. I am a cerebral creature.'

'It's the British workman,' said Gerry. 'No amount of good design these days can counteract the criminal imbecility of the average British worker.'

'Oh please Gerry darling,' cried his wife. 'No! My heart sinks when I hear those terrible words "these days" and "British workman". I know it is going on for a full hour.'

'A man buys a new car. It costs a lot of money. If it breaks down it is only courtesy to give the matter a little attention, Phyllis.'

He was pouring everyone extremely large drinks—everyone, that is, except his wife.

'What about me?' she piped, trembling. 'I'se dry.'

Grudgingly he poured her a small drink, as a husband might pour one for an alcoholic wife. Phyllis very rarely drank to excess. For every bottle of Scotch her husband drank she would sip an inch or so of gin, on the principle that it would make her monthly period, which frequently bothered her, easier.

'All this talk of cars,' she said, emboldened by his kindness to her, 'I hate it. Don't you Esther? It's such a bore.'

'If you spend enough money on something, you can't afford to think it's a bore.'

'Your wife,' said Gerry, with a disparaging look towards his own, 'is a highly intelligent woman.'

Esther wriggled, showing a little more thigh for his benefit. They all drank rather deeply.

'Sometimes,' said Alan, 'I am afraid that Esther knows everything. At other times I am afraid she doesn't.'

'Why? Are you hiding something from her?' asked Phyllis.

'I have nothing to hide from my Esther.'

'You hide your writing from me. Or try to. You lock it away.'

'Writing?' they cried. 'Writing?'

'Alan has been writing a novel in secret. He sent it off to an agent last week. Now we wait. It makes him bad-tempered. Don't ask me what it's about.'

'What's it like? Are we in it?'

'No,' said Alan shortly. 'You are not.'

'He's the only one who's in it,' said Esther.

'How do you know?' he turned on her, fiercely.

'I was only guessing,' she said. 'Or working from first principles. Why? Are you?'

He did not reply, and presently they lost interest. Phyllis enquired brightly about Peter.

'He can't concentrate on his school work,' said Esther. 'His sex life is too complicated. But I don't think it makes any difference. He was born to pass exams and captain cricket teams. Failure is simply not in his nature.'

'Peter sails unafraid and uncomplicated through life,' said Alan. 'We take little notice of him, and he takes none of us.'

'Shall we eat,' said Phyllis, who appreciated Peter as a boy but not as a son.

'We're still drinking,' said her husband. 'Give us a moment's peace.'

'I'm afraid the beef will be overcooked.'

'Beef is sacred,' said Alan, so they went in to the dining-room, where the William Morris wallpaper contrasted prettily with the plain black of the tablecloth and the white of the Rosenthal china.

They sat around the table.

'Alan can't stand grey beef. He likes it to be red and bloody in the middle. He goes rather far, I think, toward the naked, unashamed flesh. But there we are. Beef is a matter of taste, not absolute values. At least I hope so.'

'Anyway, Gerry thinks if I cook something it is awful, and if you cook something it's lovely, Esther, so why bother.'

'I think you are a superb cook, Phyllis,' lied Esther.

'Or we wouldn't come here,' said Alan.

'Personally, in this house I would rather drink than eat any day,' said Gerry.

'I wish you would stop being horrid to your wife, Gerry,' said Esther, finally coming down on Phyllis's side. 'It makes her cross and everyone's gastric juices go sour. Why don't you just *appreciate* her?'

'She's quite right,' said Alan. 'Women are what their husbands expect them to be; no more and no less. The more you flatter them the more they thrive.'

'On lies?' enquired Gerry.

'If need be.'

Esther was disturbed. 'You are horrible,' she said. 'Can't we just get on with dinner?'

Phyllis passed the mayonnaise, where artichoke hearts, flaked fish, olives and eggs lay immersed. The mayonnaise was perhaps too thin and too salty. They helped themselves, with all the appearance of enthusiasm.

'It has been a hard day,' said Gerry mournfully.

'But rewarding?'

'A new office block to do, if I'm lucky. A new world to conquer.'

'And a new secretary,' said his wife. 'A luscious child, at least eighteen, and nubile for the last five years. Plump, biteable and ripe.'

'Alan has a new secretary,' said Esther. 'I don't know what she looks like. What does she look like, Alan? There she sits, day after day, part of your life but not of mine.' Her voice was wistful.

'She is slim like a willow. But she has curves here and there.' The appreciation in her husband's voice was not at all what Esther had bargained for.

'Oh dear. And I'm so fat. No thanks, Phyllis darling, no more.'

'I like you fat. I accept you fat. You are fat.'

'Not too fat?'

'Well perhaps,' said Alan, 'just a little too fat.'

'Oh,' moaned Esther, taken aback.

'What's the matter now?'

'You've never said that to me before.'

'You've never been as fat as this before.'

'I'm so thin,' complained Phyllis politely, 'I can't get fat. Do you like garlic bread?'

'Superb.'

'Well you can't spoil that, at least,' said Gerry.

'More, Alan?'

'Thank you.'

'Do you think you should?' asked Esther. 'Every time I sew your jacket buttons on I have to use stronger and stronger thread.'

'I admit your point. I am fat too. We are a horrid gross lot.'

'Eat, drink and fornicate,' boomed their host. 'There is too much abstinence going on.' His wife made apologetic faces at the guests.

'If you are fat you die sooner,' said Alan.

'Who cares?' asked his wife, but no one took any notice, so she said, 'Tell me about your secretary, Alan. Besides being so slim, but curvaceous with it, what is she like? Perhaps you wish she was me?'

'What is the matter with you?'

'It's us,' said Phyllis dismally. 'Discontent is catching.'

'I am not discontented. I just hope Alan isn't. Who am I to compete with a secretary fresh from a charm school, with a light in her eye and life in her loins?'

'Careful, Esther,' said Gerry. 'Those are Phil's lines, to be spoken in a plaintive female whine and guaranteed to drive a man straight into a mistress's arms.'

'One wonders which comes first,' she said, 'the mistress or the female whine. It would be interesting to do a study.'

Alan decided to bring the table back to order.

'You have no cause for concern whatsoever, Esther. To tell you the truth I can't even remember her name. It is entirely forgettable. I think it is Susan. She can't type to save herself. She is thin. She is temporary. I think she thinks she is not a typist by nature, but something far more mysterious and significant, but this is a normal delusion of temporary staff. She is in, I imagine, her early twenties. She keeps forgetting that I like plain chocolate biscuits, and dislike milk chocolate biscuits. Now you, Esther, never make mistakes like that. You have a clear notion of what is important in life. Namely money, comfort, food, order and stability.'

'You make me sound just like my mother. Is that what you really think of me?'

'No. I am merely trying to publicly affirm my faith in you, marriage and the established order, and to explain that I am content with my lot. I am a married man and I married of my own free will. I am a city man, and live in the city of my own free will. A company man, also of my own volition. So I should not be surprised to find myself, in middle-age, a middle-aged, married, company, city man—with no power in my muscles and precious little in my mind. Here in this sulphurous city I live and die, with as much peace and comfort as I can draw around me. Work, home, wife, child—this is my life and I am not aggrieved by it. I chose it. I know my place. I daresay I shall die as happy and fulfilled as most men.'

'It sounds perfectly horrible to me,' said Esther. 'However, I don't take you seriously because you have just sent your magnum opus to a publisher, and I know you are quite convinced you will spend your declining years in an aura of esteem and respect and creative endeavour. I believe also that somewhere down inside you lurks a rich fantasy life in which you travel to exotic places, conquer mountains, do any number of noble and heroic deeds, save battalions single-handed, and lay the world's most beautiful women right and left. There may well be a more perverse and morbid side to this, but I would rather not go into it here. And you, Gerry, tell me, do *you* not ever wish to do extreme and fearful things? Is your masculinity entirely channelled into lustful thoughts of the opposite sex? Do you not want to burn, savage, torture, kill? Or at any rate, like Alan, failing that, are you not seized with the desire to break all the best glasses, miss the basin when you pee, burn the sheets with cigarette ends, leave smelly socks about for your wife to pick up—'

'Women have their revenges too—' said Alan. 'They leave old sanitary towels around.'

Abruptly they all stopped talking. Alan crammed more garlic bread into his mouth. He bit upon a garlic clove and was obliged to spit it out. Everyone watched.

'We all talk too much,' said Esther to Phyllis in the kitchen a little later. 'One has to be careful with words. Words turn probabilities into facts, and by sheer force of definition translate tendencies into habits. Our home isn't half going to be messy from now on.'

When they returned to the kitchen with the second course, the murmur of men's voices stopped abruptly.

'What were you telling Alan to do?' Phyllis asked her husband. 'Go off with his secretary? For the sake of his red corpuscles?'

He did not reply, for this indeed had been the essence of his conversation.

'Esther,' was all Alan said, 'we are going on a diet, you and I. We are going to fight back middle-age. Hand in hand, with a stiff upper lip and an aching midriff, we are going to push back the enemy.'

'When?' asked Esther in alarm, looking at the mountains of food on the table—the crackling hot pottery dishes of vegetables, the bowls of sauces, the great oval platter on which the bloody beef reposed. 'Not now?'

'Of course not,' said Alan. 'Tomorrow we start.'

'New lives always begin tomorrow,' said Phyllis. 'Never now. That's right, isn't it, Gerry? Will you carve?'

Gerry sharpened the knife. It flashed to and fro under their noses. He carved.

'We're going to do it, Esther,' said Alan, watching the food piling on her plate. 'Look your last on all things lovely. We'll take a stone off apiece.'

'If you say so, darling,' said Esther. 'I'm all yours to command.'

'Oh she's a lovely woman,' said Gerry.

'You'll never stick it,' said Phyllis, jealously. 'You'll never be able to do it.'

'Of course we will,' said Esther. 'If we want to, we will. And we want to.'

'Doing without what you want is the hardest thing in the world,' said Phyllis. 'Isn't it, Gerry?'

'Incidentally,' said Esther to Phyllis four weeks later, 'there was too much salt in the mayonnaise that night, and too much in the gravy too. So we had to drink a lot. And the next day Alan and I had hangovers, and were cross and miserable even before we started our regime of abstinence.'

'You didn't say anything about too much salt at the time.'

'One doesn't. Or nobody would ever ask anyone to dinner any more. The middle classes would grind to a social halt. It wasn't a bad meal, for once, in fact. Which was just as well, because it was the last we had for some time.'

'After you two had gone,' said Phyllis, 'I went to sleep on the sofa. Gerry wouldn't stop visiting his ex-wife every Saturday, and I was upset and angry, and I thought he'd been behaving badly all evening, anyway. But in the middle of the night he hauled me into bed—he's much stronger than I am—and we were happy for a time. Until Saturday came again. Or at least he was happy. I'm not very good at that kind of thing. It's the gesture I appreciate, not the thing itself. I think.'

'And Alan and I went home and had cocoa and biscuits and went to sleep. We were tired. We'd been married, after all, for nearly twenty years.'

'But you and Alan were always touching each other,' said Phyllis, 'like young lovers. As if even after all those years you couldn't keep your hands off each other.'

'And we meant it,' said Esther crossly, 'in public. It was just when we got home we found we were tired. Once you are beyond a certain age sex isn't an instinct any more—it's a social convention.'

'Speak for yourself.'

'I am sorry, but you feel sexy because you know it's nice to feel sexy, not because you really are. Are you sure you wouldn't like coffee?'

'No,' said Phyllis. Then she added, urgently, 'Esther! Living here, alone, with no husband. No boy-friend. Surely you feel—at night—?'

'No. I live by myself. Just me. Self-sufficient, wanting no one, no other mind, no other body. I live with the truth. I need no protection from it.'

'Gerry and I,' said Phyllis. 'I am so miserable. We are chained together by our bed.'

'That is your misfortune,' said Esther, 'and why you are so unhappy. Bed is a very difficult habit to break. Now let us continue with my story, because yours is very ordinary and I am not concerned with it. In the morning Alan kissed me goodbye—on the doorstep so the neighbours could see—and went to his office. He had had no breakfast. He was feeling desperate and hungover, but dieting seemed to him to be a rich and positive thing. Perhaps that was why, this particular morning, his secretary made such an impression on him, and he on his secretary.'

Susan and Brenda sat in the pub, conscious of their youth and beauty, which indeed shone like a beacon in a boozy, beery world, and Susan gave Brenda her more detailed account of a morning which Esther could only guess at.

'The typing agency quite often sends me to Norman, Zo-Hailey—' said Susan, naming a large London advertising agency. 'They always need temporary staff. Girls never stay long. They think it's going to be glamorous and all they find is a lot of dull old research people plodding through statistics. Married ones, at that. And the pay's bad, so they hand in their notice. And then again, if they do get to the livelier departments, it soon transpires that men in advertising agencies hardly count as men. What man worth his salt would spend his life sitting in an office selling other people's goods, by proxy?'

'Alan seems to have behaved like a man, from what you say.'

'Alan was different. He was a creative person. Anyway they're all quite good at pretending to be men. They know all the rules. Their bodies, even, work as if they were men, but on the whole they're deceiving themselves and everyone else.'

'Perhaps you and I are only pretending to be women. How could we tell?'

'We are both flat-chested, it is true,' said Susan, 'and when I come to think of it, Alan had very pronounced nipples at the beginning of that fortnight. Almost what approached a bosom. It fascinated me. I had never encountered anything like it before. I began to wonder if I perhaps had lesbian tendencies.'

'It sounds perfectly revolting.'

'Not in the least. He has this thin face to counteract it. He was an important man at Zo's. Everyone seemed to think I ought to be pleased to work for him but all I did was make rather more mistakes than usual. He never got irritated. He just used to sigh and raise his eyebrows at me as if I was a naughty child but he would forgive me. In the end I began to feel quite like a daughter to him. And when one's father turns lascivious eyes upon one, that's that, isn't it? You get all stirred up inside. You begin to want to impress. You find yourself putting on make-up just to come to work. And he'd written this novel, and his agent rang up and raved about it, and I listened on the extension when I was getting the coffee in the outer office. I find there is something very erotic about literary men, don't you?'

'I really don't know. I haven't been in London long enough. Anyway, I thought you were supposed to be in love with William Macklesfield.' William Macklesfield was the middle-aged poet who had been seen occasionally on the television, and with whom, on and off, Susan had been sleeping for years.

'William and I are very close. We are best friends. We have a wonderful platonic relationship with sex lying, as it were, on top of it. But we are not in love. Not the kind of lightning love which suddenly flashes out of a clear sky and tumbles you on your back.'

'Good heavens. Things like that never happen to me.'

'It's your pillar-like legs,' said Susan. 'And your matriarchal destiny. Your time will come when you are sixty, surrounded by your grandchildren and bullying your sons. When I am an ageing drunken lush only fit for a mental home, then I daresay you will be glad that you are you and I am I. In the meantime I can fairly say that of the two of us, I have the more style.'

'Thank you very much, I'm sure.'

'Unless of course, I compromise, and marry. I might become a poet's wife. But poets I find, are often rather dull. They are in the habit of expressing themselves through the written word, and not through their bodies. William is awful in bed.'

'What *does* that mean?' asked Brenda. 'I thought it was the way a girl responded, not what the man did, that mattered. I never have any trouble. I always thought that girls saying men were bad in bed was just a way of making them feel nervous.'

'Oh you,' said Susan, 'you should write a column in a woman's magazine. I can see it happening yet.'

'You were talking,' said Brenda, devastated, 'about this lightning stroke which flung you back upon your bed with your knees apart.'

'I didn't say with my knees apart. Nor did I mention bed.'

'I thought it was what you meant.'

'You are not at all open to *forces*, are you?' said Susan. 'You are an artifact. You are not swayed by passions like me. Anyway, there I was, working in this great throbbing organisation, beginning to fancy my boss, and his wife would ring up every day and ask what he wanted for dinner. He would take her so seriously, I couldn't understand it. He would think and ponder, and sometimes he would ring her back later to give her a considered answer. It bespoke such intimacy. It drove me mad. She had such a soft, possessive voice. I wondered why he took so little notice of me. And why was there no one *I* could ring up, in the perfect security of knowing they would be home for dinner, come what may, and obliged to eat what I provided? William kept going back home to his wife for dinner and I found this most irritating. And why didn't Alan's wife ring up and ask him what did he want to do in bed that night, or something? Why was it always dinner? Poor man, I thought. Poor blind man. Here was I, young, clever and creative, with depths to plumb, able to take a constructive interest in what really interested him, sitting docile and waiting at his elbow, typing and all he'd do was let his eyes stray to my legs and back again. He was too busy telling his wife what he wanted for dinner. It was an insult to me. I wanted to ask about his novel but he seemed to want to keep it secret. He was so clever. Not just with words, but he loved painting, too. He used to be a painter before his wife got hold of him and destroyed him with boredom and responsibilities. Domesticity had him trapped. Can you imagine, he even kept photographs on his desk!'

'A commercial artist, do you mean?'

'No, I do not. He went to art school. He married her very young, on impulse, and had to give up all thought of being a proper painter. She drove him into advertising, and he ended up a kind of co-ordinator of words and pictures. A man with a great deal of power over people of no consequence whatsoever, and a long title on the plate on his door. How bitter! He should never have let her do it to him. Brenda, do stop making eyes at that Siamese gentleman.'

'He is not Siamese, I don't think. But he is very handsome.'

'I wonder why he seems to prefer you to me. Perhaps it's his nationality. Do you want me to go on with this story?'

'Yes.'

'Then try and concentrate. The first time he actually laid hands on me was the day he started his diet, the day he heard from his agent.'

On the first morning of the diet pigeons chose to strut about the window-sill and embarrass Alan with their intimacies. There was a red carpet on the office floor; red curtains at the window. The standard lamp was grey, and so was the upholstery of the arm-chairs. His desk was large, sleek, new and empty, except for a list of the day's engagements. He earned £6,000 a year and was not quite on the Board. It seemed doubtful, now, that he would ever get there. One younger, more energetic man had already used him as a footstool for a leap to Board level, and once a footstool, in Company terms, nearly always a footstool. And nothing would deter the pigeons.

Susan came in with a tray of coffee and biscuits. She wore a very short white skirt and a skimpy grey jersey.

'Mr Sussman—' said Susan, apologetically. She wore an enormous pair of spectacles. Her eyesight was normal, but the glasses combined frailty of flesh with aggression of spirit, and she enjoyed them. Alan sought for her features behind them. He was flushed after his telephone conversation with his agent.

'I am really very sorry—'

'Oh my God, what have you done now?' He spoke amiably, as well may a man who has just achieved, he thinks, a life-long ambition.

'It's just that I forgot about your biscuits again. I took the milk chocolate, not the plain. My gentleman friend always prefers milk, and I become confused.'

'Your gentleman friend?'

'How else would you have me describe him? My quasi-husband, my seducer, my lover, my fiancé? Take your pick. He is a poet.'

'It is too unsettled a relationship that you describe,' said Alan, 'for my peace of mind. Secretaries, however temporary, should maintain the illusion of being either virgins or well-married. Otherwise the mind begins to envisage possibilities. The girl takes on flesh and blood. You are a bad secretary.'

'I'm sorry about the biscuits.'

'I was not talking about the biscuits, and well you know it. It does not matter about the biscuits. I am not eating the biscuits.'

'Not eating the biscuits?'

'No. And no sugar in the coffee.'

'No sugar in the coffee?'

'Stop playing the little girl. You are a grown woman. I am on a diet.'

'Oh no!'

'Why not? I'm too fat.'

'People on diets become cross, bad-tempered. And desire fails. You are not too fat. Why do you want to be thin?'

'I want to be young again.'

'Why?'

'Because when I was young I had hopes and aspirations and I liked the feeling.'

'I think you are foolish. You don't have to be young to achieve things. I like an older man myself.'

'You do?'

'Oh yes.'

'All the same, take the biscuits away.'

'I will keep them for William.'

'The poet? I would rather you didn't.'

'Why not?' She took off her glasses to see him better.

'The thought confuses me. It is a relief your glasses have gone. Now I can see your face.'

'It is just a face like any other.'

'It is not. It is a remarkable face. I would like to paint it.'

'I do self-portraits, sometimes.'

'Do you paint?'

'Yes.'

'You're not really a secretary?'

'No.'

'They never are,' he said. 'They never are. All summer in the temporary season, they never are. That's why the typing is so bad. Get on with it.'

Routed, she sat and typed. He sat and read marketing reports and wondered whether to ring Esther and tell her his agent liked the novel. He decided against it. He feared she might prick the bubble of his self-esteem too soon.

'I am not a foolish girl,' said his secretary presently. 'You lead me on in order to make me look silly, but that is easy to do. It's rather cheap of you.'

'Oh good heavens,' Alan said. 'This is an office not a—'

'Not a what?'

'You go too far. You talk like a wife, full of reproaches. I warn you. You are a fantastic creature but you go too far.'

'Fantastic?' Her eyes were bright.

'You are very beautiful, or look so to me this morning.' He came to look over her shoulder, as if to see what she was typing. 'What scent are you wearing?'

'Madam Rochas. It's not too much?'

'Not at all. It is nourishing. Do you know what I had for breakfast? Two boiled eggs and some black coffee. Do you know what I shall have for lunch? Two boiled eggs and a grapefruit. And for dinner an omelet, and some black coffee, and guess what. A tomato.'

'Oh big deal!' she said. 'Do you expect me to be sorry for you?'

'No.' His hands, trembling, slid over her breasts. 'I am only explaining that I am light-headed and cannot be held responsible for my actions.'

The telephone rang. It was Esther. Did he want a herb omelet and a tomato, separate, or the tomato cooked in with the omelet? The former, he thought.

'She has a pretty voice,' said Susan. 'Is she pretty?'

But Alan was back at his desk. He seemed to have forgotten the past few minutes entirely. He was formal, brisk and cold.

'Get Andrew to come and see me,' he said, studying a folder of lay-outs launching a change in the formula of a dandruff shampoo. 'I don't know what is happening to Andrew's judgement.' Susan rang through and presently Andrew, a thin, well-born young man with a double first, came in to be chided. He reminded Alan of himself when young. Susan sulked and plotted.

'It was quite true,' said Susan to Brenda in the pub. 'He was already light-headed, otherwise I might never have got him to the point of touching me, from which all else stemmed. He was used at that hour of the morning to having a stomach full of cereal, eggs and bacon, toast and marmalade, tea, topped up by coffee and biscuits. And all of a sudden there was nothing inside him—only the vision of me, and the words I spun around him. If I spoke boldly, it was because that was what he responded to. He would never seduce, he would have to be seduced. But I trembled inside; it took every ounce of courage I had to speak to him the way I did. And when he touched me—'

'Lightning? You fell back upon the bed?'

'I was in an office, idiot. Had there been a bed, I would have. But he was not quite ready yet to fall on top of me, of course. I had further work to do.'

'I think you're making it all up, talking as if you did it all on purpose. Anyway men aren't manipulated like that. They either feel things for you or they don't. It's men who take the initiative. You keep talking about men the way men talk about women. It's rather disgusting.'

'You put things into their heads,' Susan insisted. 'You put beddish visions before their eyes.'

'I think that's a very old-fashioned view,' said Brenda. 'All this talk of seducing and being seduced. It's not like that at all. Everyone knows exactly what they're doing these days.'

'Well he didn't. He really didn't. He was too hungry for one thing.'

'You're older than me, almost of another generation. I expect that's why you take such an old-fashioned view.'

'You're drunk and you're jealous,' said Susan correctly. 'Let's go home.'

They rose to go. The man who came from the East rose too and followed them out into the street. He was following Brenda, not Susan.

'That morning when I rang and asked about the omelet,' said Esther to Phyllis in the basement, 'his voice sounded odd, and I had this sudden vision of his temporary secretary sitting there exhibiting her legs to him under the desk. He had described her the evening before at your place in altogether too detailed terms for my peace of mind. I was hungry and faint—what with the hangover and the black coffee—quarts of it—and cigarette after cigarette, and I was just standing looking out of the window, which was foolish because Juliet—that's the daily help—was polishing the floor and one shouldn't stand about being idle when other people are working hard. Especially when they're Juliet. Day One of the diet was a horrible day for me; although no doubt it was a delight to my husband.'

Esther's living-room was filled to the point of obsession with Victoriana. Sofas and chairs were buttoned and plump; walls were covered with pictures from ceiling to floor; occasional tables were almost hidden by lamps, clocks, figurines and vases. There was an embroidery frame where it was Esther's habit to sit in the evening, working minute stitches with her puffy hands. Everything in the room was dusted, polished and neat; but this was no thanks to Juliet, who this morning wildly and inefficiently polished the floor. Esther moved away from the window, steering her bulk with grace through the fragile bric-a-brac.

'Juliet,' said Esther, 'you'll never get a good shine if you don't sweep properly first. You'll just rub the dirt in and ruin the surface.'

Juliet put down her cloth and straightened up. She was thirty and short, with an hour-glass figure and a tendency to backache with which she excused her bad temper.

'Why aren't you in the kitchen?' Juliet's voice was accusing. 'You're always in the kitchen while I polish, cooking.'

'We are on a diet and there's nothing to cook.'

'Well don't take it out on me,' said Juliet, resuming her crouching position and the flailing of her arms.

'I'm not taking anything out on anybody. I'm just observing that if you rub grit into a parquet floor you spoil the surface.'

'The Hoover needs mending,' said Juliet. 'It doesn't take anything up any more. I told you about it weeks ago.'

'Well, you can sweep, can't you? Brooms were made before Hoovers.'

Juliet put down her cloth. 'What did you have for breakfast? Did you go without, or something?'

'I had a very good breakfast, thank you. I had eggs. And it's eggs for lunch, and eggs for dinner, and in two weeks I'll have lost a stone and a half.'

'You be careful. You can go too far. A friend of mine went on a diet and lost all appetite for food. They took her in at the hospital but it was too late, she died. Her stomach had shrunk to a dried pea—or was it walnut? One or the other, I do remember that.'

'This is a very well-tried diet, and very sensible. One should be able to control one's size, if one is going to control one's life.'

'What do you want to do it for? You're all right as you are. You've got a husband and a son and a house, even if it is filled up with all this junk, and someone to do your dirty work for you. What else do you want?'

'It's healthier to be thin.'

'Dieting ruins the health. Men like women nice and cosy. Their wives, anyway.'

'To tell you the truth I am really going through with it for Mr Sussman's sake. For my own part, I don't really worry. But it's easier for him if I do it too. You know what men are. They haven't got all that much willpower.'

'What you need is physical exercise. You ought to get down on your hands and knees more often, instead of just standing about.'

'When you have gone home, Juliet,' said Esther clearly, 'I often find I have to.'

She walked with determination into the kitchen, as if there was something there to busy her. Juliet peered after her, with an expression of quite serious malevolence on her face.

'You'll go too far,' said Juliet. 'One day you'll go too far.'

And she continued her manic, useless polishing.

The Sussmans' kitchen was full of herbs, spices, pestles and mortars and strings of onion and garlic, and jars of olive oil and cut-outs from early editions of Mrs Beeton. There scarcely seemed room in it for human beings, but that evening there they were, the two of them, Alan and Esther, their flesh squeezed between table and dresser, studying their diet sheet, and both bad-tempered.

'At least we can put herbs in the omelet,' said Alan. 'An *omelet aux fines herbes*, Delicious.'

Esther reached out for eggs and started breaking them into a basin. 'Oh big deal,' she said.

'Someone else said that to me today. I can't remember who.'

'Your secretary, I dare say. Since she spends so much time with you.'

'I think it was, now you come to mention it.'

Esther was suspicious. It did not suit her. Her eyes, usually luminous globes of expression, became smaller and mean. 'What were you and she talking about?'

'This diet, I think,' said Alan, allowing a certain weariness at Esther's bad behaviour to creep into his tone. 'I really can't remember. I've got to talk to somebody, haven't I?'

'This Susan seems to be quite your confidante. Do you discuss all your personal life with her?'

'Not particularly.'

'Do you discuss me?' She used her little-girl voice.

He used his angry one. 'As much, I dare say, as you discuss me with your window cleaner.'

'My window cleaner appears to be quite a randy man, for your information.'

'So, if you want to know, does my secretary.'

'What, a randy man?'

'No, a randy girl. Now you know.'

She chose not to believe him. She thought she had simply made him angrier than she had meant.

'I'm sorry,' she said. 'I'm being silly. It's because I'm hungry.'

'Yes you are being silly. Why are you dividing the whites from the yolks?'

'I'm making a fluffy omelet. It will go further.'

Esther's head, all of a sudden, felt very full and unpleasant. 'I feel awful.'

'I feel fine,' said Alan, with memories of Susan's forwardness and hugging to himself the knowledge of his agent's enthusiasm, which he felt Esther did not yet deserve to know. 'Lighter and emptier. I think this is what it felt like ten years ago.' He looked down at his paunch. It seemed to him to have shrunk.

'I've got a headache. I don't think I can face this omelet.' She laid her hands on her stomach. It was full and flabby. She was depressed.

'It says you must not on any account go without any of the food items mentioned. You just wait until spinach day!' He quoted from the diet sheet. '*The diet depends for its efficiency on a chemical process the body undergoes during the diet's course.* They may be good doctors but they're bloody awful writers of the King's English.'

'Queen's.'

'Why do you have this urge to find fault all the time?'

'That's very unfair.'

'What are you doing with that butter?' Alan's hand shot out to restrain Esther's. They both stared at their touching flesh, as if at something strange. Alan dropped her hand, quickly.

'You've got to have butter to make an omelet, silly.'

'It says on the diet sheet no dairy products whatsoever.'

'Don't be stupid,' She sneered quite visibly, her top lip curling over her tiny sharp teeth. 'How can you make an omelet without butter?'

'I don't know, but you've got to!'

'Then *you* do it!' She shouted at him. A glass mobile trembled, and the noise of its tinkling shamed her and pleased him. He seized the omelet mixture and poured it straight into the unbuttered pan. He took up the wooden spoon and scraped it off the bottom. It looked more like scrambled egg than omelet.

'There you see!' she cried, vindicated. 'You've made a mess of it the way you make a mess of everything.'

Alan decided it was time to bring the situation back into his control. 'Esther,' he said, 'either we do this diet or we don't. I think it is important that we should. We would both benefit by losing weight.'

'You mean *I* would. You don't find me attractive any more. You're ashamed to be seen out with me because I'm fat and horrible and you think people will be sorry for you because you're married to me.'

Alan still held the frying pan in his hand. The whites of his eyes glinted in the light from the oil lamp. It seemed for a moment that he was going to throw the omelet full in his wife's face, but at that moment his son Peter, came into the room, and he lowered the pan and rearranged his face into a less manic pattern. Esther for her part stopped cowering, straightened up and smiled maternally.

Peter was six foot two, some six inches taller than his father. He was pink-faced, blond, well-built and gave an immediate impression of health and cheerfulness. Otherwise he was very like his father. The school uniform he was obliged to wear did not succeed in making him look like a child.

'You two squabbling?' He strode to the refrigerator, plucked it open, and peered inside. 'Can I make myself some sausages and bacon? And fried bread?'

'You'll get fat,' said his mother.

'Not me. I've got youth on my side.'

'Your heredity's working against you, don't forget that,' said Alan, meaning Esther.

'You should learn dietary discipline now,' she said, 'so in the future you will be able to control your weight at will.'

'Hark who's talking. Really, Mum!'

'I'm sure I hope my children will do better than I. Because I am morally frail and weak-willed, this is no reason for you to be content to be the same. There is no possible point in procreation if one's children do not outstrip one in every respect. Put the bread away. Fried bread is going too far.'

'Why don't you two sit down and eat that omelet? You'd feel much better.'

They obeyed.

'Why is it,' he asked, as the smell of frying bacon filled the room, 'that people who are quite wilfully spoiling their own enjoyment cannot rest there but are also obsessively anxious to spoil other people's? "Put the bread away", indeed!'

'Stop trying to talk like your mother,' said Alan, scraping the last scrap of egg from his plate, adding, 'There's a very odd smell in here.'

'I can smell it too,' Esther had already finished and now sat, desolately, with her knife and fork neatly together on her bare plate. She turned her head like a questing dog, sniffing.

'It's the bacon,' said Peter. 'Incidentally, it is very thinly cut bacon. Why can't we get it thicker?'

'Because thin bacon is an excellent economy. It is the one economy I have. It's not the smell of bacon, I can assure you.'

'Oh of course,' said Peter. 'I forgot. It's aniseed.'

'Aniseed?'

'Aniseed?'

'From the buns. We're filling buns with aniseed. Then you throw them at the patrol dogs and they go after the buns, and not you.'

'Patrol dogs?'

'I could do with some more sausages.'

'Patrol dogs?' Alan's normally pale face was pink. As his colour heightened the resemblance between him and his son became more apparent.

'Down at Frampton. There's a biological warfare place down there. We're going down on a demo.'

'We?'

'Stephanie and me.'

'Stephanie?'

'You know Stephanie.' Another mouthful, and another bacon rasher disappeared. His parents watched.

'The one with the hair?'

'It's easier to look after like that. Cropped.'

'She could shave it right off and polish the skin,' said Esther. 'Then she could seal it, to preserve the shine.'

'That was not worthy of you, Mother.'

'I'm sorry,' she said, humbly, 'I am not at my best when hungry, and your father keeps getting at me—' Alan took out his cigarette, and failed to offer her one—'but she's a very nice girl, I know, and extremely bright. I like her. I understand she is very popular.'

'It is true,' said Peter nobly, 'that she does sometimes get mistaken for a boy, by the older generation. Never our own, however, and that is the most important thing. I do realise it is hard for people of your age to adjust yourselves to current values, and I appreciate the effort you both make. I mean really.'

'Tell me more about the patrol dogs,' said Alan.

'I don't like people who organise diseases for the benefit of humanity. I mean, do you? The least I feel I can do is register my protest. So I shall sit down on the ground in a field along with a couple of hundred others, until shifted by some force other than my own.'

'Oh youth, youth! said Alan, not altogether displeased. 'What good do you think it will do?'

'I don't know. None, probably. I don't much care. It will make me feel better,' Peter rose and cut himself a thick slice of bread. He spread it with butter, and covered it with apricot jam in which the apricots lay sugary and whole. 'Well I mean,' he went on, as his teeth slipped through the soft slice, 'you two went on marches once, didn't you? And left-wing meetings? You waved banners, along with the rest. You helped save the world. The world's the same as it always was, but what happened to you when you stopped trying to save it?'

'All that was a long time ago,' said Alan. 'Thank God.'

'We grew up,' said Esther. 'We gained a sense of reality.'

'You grew fat and cosy and comfortable, you mean,' said Peter. 'You changed sides, that's what happened to you!'

Esther jumped to her feet: she all but shouted. 'I am not fat and cosy and comfortable. Neither is Alan.'

'Oh Mum!' he said reproachfully, from his great rosy height. 'Oh Dad! Look at yourselves.'

Esther sat down again. Her heavy breasts drooped over the table. His paunch swelled beneath its top.

'I'm sorry I tried to cook that omelet in butter,' she said presently. 'It was stupid of me.'

'Oh forget it,' said her husband, who had no intention of doing so. 'Cigarette?'

Phyllis, listening to Esther's account of the first day of the diet, was beginning to feel hungry herself. She drank a cup of coffee and accepted a biscuit. 'You'll have to go on a diet again, Esther,' she said nibbling.

'But what's the point? What's the point?' Esther had stopped eating for the moment, and despair now rose up her gullet. 'There is only one virtue these days, and that is to be young. Everything is forgiven to the young—even fatness, and that is saying something. And I am no longer young. Nothing will be forgiven me. All I can hope is not to be noticed any more.'

'You're talking nonsense,' said Phyllis. 'You're just depressed. I know some very pretty and very elegant elderly ladies indeed. Most charming.'

'Har, har, har,' said Esther. 'And men laugh at them behind their backs for being old, in just the same spirit as men will laugh at girls with no ankles, and girls with spots, and girls with bad breath, because for all their efforts they fail to please. There's more dignity, if one is neither young nor beautiful, in simply giving up. Which is what, being middle-aged, I am finally allowed to do.'

'I think the way you sit and guzzle is most undignified. I think you should have more pride in yourself. It's your own opinion of yourself that counts, not other people's.

'Oh Miss Smarmy,' said Esther. 'I was telling you a story. If you don't want to hear it, go away.'

'Oh please go on. You haven't told me anything yet, really.'

'There are many things I want you to understand first. One of the terrible things about marriage is the dread of change that goes with it, as perhaps even you are aware in your own relationship with Gerry. Any change, and you begin to worry. Either Alan wanted me to be thin because he was fancying his secretary, or he wanted me to be thin because he was ashamed of me the way I was. Either way, he wanted me to be different from what I was, and this to me seemed the most devastating insult.'

'He'd had secretaries before. Why were you worrying about this one?'

'Her name was Susan. I've never like girls called Susan. I don't trust them. My mother's second name is Susan.'

'What does your mother say about your not being at home? She adores Alan.'

'I'll come to that later. She's been down here, you know, prying and spying.' Her voice, as always when Esther talked about her mother, became smaller and meaner, like her eyes.

'You're awful about your mother. She's such a wonderful person.'

'Oh yes. Of course. Any woman who gets past sixty is wonderful. I look forward to it, I'm sure. I hope to be dead by then.'

'And to suspect Alan of carrying on with his secretary because her name's the same as your mother's is just plain silly.'

'Well that's the way it goes, doesn't it. I didn't ask you to come down here, making me talk. I'm beginning to feel very upset. I was quite peaceful before. Now I'm all stirred up. I feel sick. I'm getting indigestion.'

'It's jealousy that gives me a pain,' said Phyllis, taking another biscuit. 'First I get the pain, and from that I know I'm jealous. It's down here.'

'Down here! Down here! In your womb, you silly barren bitch.'

'What a horrible thing to say. It's not in my womb, anyway. I know where my womb is. It's higher. I am not barren. Gerry and I simply can't decide whether or not we want children. Or rather, Gerry can't. And you've only got one child; why do you try to make out you're so fertile?'

'I don't. I'm not. I am wounded, through and through. Marriage is such a falling away. It hurts. When you go to the pictures you remember a time you used to hold hands. You go to bed in your curlers and remember a time you used to sleep in each other's arms. Nothing is ever as it was, in marriage.'

'I try to keep our love alive,' said Phyllis, her dolly eyes wide with virtue. 'Gerry's and mine. I wouldn't dream of going to bed in curlers.'

Esther quelled her irritation by unwrapping a chocolate and eating it. It was toffee and she had to speak now through jaws that had trouble in opening.

'Anyway that night we slept as far apart from each other as we could and Alan was late for work, and got closer to Susan as a result.'

'How do you know?'

'Because the more he fancied her the nastier he was to me. That's the way guilt takes him. He loads it on to me. He goads me into behaving badly so then he can consider himself justified. Kick the old nagger in the teeth, and cry "She drove me to it!" in the young one's bed. That's the way it goes.'

'I'm sure it wasn't. I think you're making it all up about Alan. He's very loyal to you. He loves you.'

'Love, shmove,' she said. 'Love, shmove!' and ate the last biscuit on the plate.

'Are you sure you want me to go on with the story?' asked Susan, when the two girls were back in the flat with the young man from abroad. He sat in the best chair sipping a cup of coffee, nodding benignly and watching every move that Brenda made. It was not clear whether or not he spoke English, since he said nothing. Susan was irritated by his presence, but could think of no good reason for objecting to it. 'Perhaps you would prefer me to go out or something, so you and this extraordinary person can be alone?'

'Good heavens no. What are you thinking of?' Brenda seemed surprised.

'Don't you want to get to know him better or something?'

'Not particularly.'

'Then why is he here?'

'Well, he just came, didn't he? It would seem inhospitable to turn him away. He is a stranger in a foreign land, after all.'

'I expect he comes from Bermondsey, if the truth was known. I don't want to go on if he can understand. It is all very personal to me.'

The two girls stared at him. He smiled and nodded, as if he would say something nice if only he knew how.

'Don't be silly,' said Brenda. 'You see! He doesn't understand a word we say. He's just a nice friendly man having a cup of coffee in a foreign land.'

'Very well. We'll leave it at that. But just don't let it go any further. You sometimes behave in a very eccentric way, Brenda. Your relationships can be very shallow.'

'Oh no. I'm a very conventional person, I'm afraid. I'm not brave, like you.'

They took their cups of coffee and sat by the gas fire—Brenda pulling her short skirt down to hide her stocking tops from her admirer as best she could—and Susan took up the story.

Alan was late at the office on the second day of the diet. Susan was watering the pot plants with a green and red watering-can from Heals, especially designed for watering pot plants. Alan was bad-tempered. His agent had appreciated his novel, but his life had not thereby been transformed, and he felt cheated.

'Oh, Mr Sussman!' said Susan, reproachfully. 'You're late.'

'Well?'

'You're late.'

'I am not late. I am just not as early as usual. If you can't be polite at least try to be accurate.'

'I suppose your being so often late is a protest against your coming to the office at all. I think it would be sensible for you to hand in your notice altogether. Why spend your days doing something you don't like? You only live once.'

'It is too early in the morning for this sort of conversation. I might as well be at home.' He hung his coat behind the provided curtain, and looked discreetly down at his stomach. It seemed much the same.

'It is not early for me. I've been up since five.'

'Whatever for?'

'The light is good at that time for painting. The whole world seems different, somehow, when everyone else is asleep. It's unobserved, and it shows.'

'You must show me some of your work, sometime.'

'I am very particular to whom I show my paintings.'

'You must try and be a little more particular about your typing,' was all he said, looking at the list of the day's engagements which she had typed.

She was wearing a white ribbed jersey, which seemed too small for her, an abbreviated skirt, and a leather belt which hung around her hips. He thought it scarcely seemed suitable attire for a secretary in an advertising agency. It would never have been allowed in a permanent girl.

'How can it be,' he said, 'that I have no meetings until late this afternoon?'

She sat down behind her typewriter and spoke coldly, for she had been snubbed.

'Today was the day you were supposed to be going to the Sussex shampoo factory. They waited as long as they could, and I rang Mrs Sussman and she said you'd only just left, so Mr Venery went in your place. That's why.'

'Oh.'

'They thought Mr Venery would do just as well.'

'Oh. Did they.'

'And I dare say they were right. He can be very impressive when he talks.'

'You are becoming quite impossible. I know you like to make it clear that you are not by nature a secretary. But since you are being paid, couldn't you at least act the role? It is very disconcerting to have a girl like you sitting about all day.'

'Thank you.' She smiled.

'I didn't mean that as a compliment, either. Offices are serious places, where work must always take precedence over everything else. I dare say to a girl as emancipated and free-thinking as you, the work we actually do must appear strange, even bizarre. I can see that to an outsider the vision of a group of grey-suited gentlemen of high moral principle and even higher income sitting round a table discussing the attitude of teenage girls to dandruff must seem somewhat ludicrous. But teenage girls have dandruff. And they need and like to have it cured. And a great many people work in factories making the cure, and others like us work at selling it in its most acceptable and cheapest form. It has its own kind of dignity, the work we do—if only because it is so open to mockery. It is easy enough to laugh at dandruff—just so long as you haven't got it.'

'You could use that as a headline. I wasn't laughing at dandruff in particular, as it happens, or at you. You've sold out, that's all, and I think it's sad. It's a waste of your potentiality. I'm sure if someone had said to you when you were fifteen that you'd end up selling dandruff cures you'd have committed suicide on the spot, and perhaps you would have been right to do so. People have a duty to their talents.'

'I have not "ended up", as you put it. And I sell a great many other things besides shampoo. And I think, incidentally, you are too old to be wearing that gear. It's for teenagers, not grown women.'

'Why do you feel the need to attack me? Why do you want to hurt my feelings all the time? Do my knees worry you so much?'

'No. It is not so much your knees, as you well know, but your thighs.'

'I am sorry,' she said. 'If it worries you I will wear skirts to my ankles. If you ask me to do anything, I will.'

'Good heavens,' he said, 'good heavens, it's much too early for this kind of thing.'

'I told you it didn't seem early to me. I've been up for hours.'

He circled her.

'What am I going to do for the rest of the day, with nothing arranged? And you quite wilfully tormenting me?'

'Act like the middle-aged company man you delude yourself you are. Spend a useful day stabilising your relations with the rest of the staff. Write memos to remind your superiors that you exist—it seems to be necessary. Go on a tour of inspection, there must be something to inspect. Ask your staff if they're happy.'

'Are you?'

'I'm always happy.'

'I don't believe you.'

'I always do what I want.'

'You are very fortunate, then.'

'Not fortunate. Sensible. I dreamt about you last night.'

'What?'

'It was very private. It was marvellous.'

'Good heavens,' he said, 'good heavens. What do you see in me? I'm a middle-aged man with a middle-aged mind. You are young, beautiful, talented, intelligent and truly, truly, remarkable.'

'You have a wonderful turn of phrase, just sometimes: did you know that? But a lot of the time you speak platitudes. What element in yourself is that you hide from? You use clichés as a shelter, and it is not necessary. I hope you don't use them when you write.'

'It is a lovely day. Shall we go for a walk in the park? How very irregular! But we could talk about books. Did you know I have just written a novel?'

'Yes, as a matter of fact.'

'Would you be interested in reading it?'

'Oh yes.'

'I haven't got a copy at the office. There are two at home, though. I'll bring one in. It might interest you. Many people might be shocked—but not, I think you.'

They put on the red 'engaged' light above his office door and went out, by different staircases, into the street and met in the park. He felt the same pleasure as when he had played truant as a child; she felt agreeably conspiratorial. The sun shone.

'What did you have for breakfast?' she asked.

'Eggs.'

'I don't think food is at all important, but I can see that for people who are used to it, going without would be most difficult. I don't think you ought to, actually. You are a shadowy enough figure as it is.'

'Shadowy?'

'You lack substance. Men do tend to lack substance in women's eyes. They are figments of lust, vague sources of despair. I think the least a man can do, in the circumstances, is to endeavour to exist well and truly in the flesh. I believe in you on account of your being so solid. It is the other way round with women. A woman has all too much substance in a man's eyes at the best of times. That is why men like women to be slim. Her lack of flesh negates her. The less of her there is, the less notice he need take of her. The more like a male she appears to be, the safer he feels.'

'My wife doesn't half fight back then.'

'Is she *very* fat?'

But he was silent.

'Did you used to be a painter?' she asked presently, returning to safer ground.

'Why do you ask?'

'From the way you pick up a pencil. From the way you scribble over bad layouts. You seem to know exactly what you're doing.'

'You are very quick. I did study once.'

'What happened?'

'I had a couple of shows. But it was hungry work. Then I married. You have to earn a living. Once you embark on family life it is too late to do anything else. Thoughts of self-expression fly out the window.'

'Not if you have courage. I think perhaps you lack courage.'

'If true courage lies in doing what you don't want to do, from a sense of duty, then I am a truly courageous man.'

'Not at all. True courage lies in doing what you want to do, and not caring whom you hurt.'

'True courage,' he said, 'lies in employing temporary secretaries with beautiful legs and wayward thoughts.'

He kissed her in the bushes where he was sure no one from the office could possibly see. She was vastly pleased, and took the afternoon off—

he could scarcely refuse—and went home and told William all about it.

And all the way home in his taxi that evening he brooded about Esther's malice in plotting to cook his omelet in butter the night before.

'It all sounds rather sordid to me,' said Brenda, sipping her coffee, 'secretary and boss and stolen idylls in the park. It's like the *News of the World*. My mother always said that men in offices were underemployed. That's why she would prefer me to marry a professional man. They are so worn out by work they don't cause trouble. She is very funny, my mother, in a sinister suburban way.'

'It was only a kiss,' said Susan, 'but afterwards all the colours in the park seemed stronger and the trees made strange shapes in the sky and when I went home and told William, I found my knees were trembling and so I knew I meant what I was saying. I was in love. The same man, not my boss, would probably have made no impression on me at all, I am honest enough to admit it. Status is a great aphrodisiac. His name was in black type on the telephone list and if you work for an organisation like Zo's, even temporarily, these things have the power to affect you.'

'What do you mean, told William?'

'I explained to him about Alan, and how it would be better for him to move out because it wouldn't be fair to him, me being in love with someone else. He quite understood. We have a very civilised relationship. He went home. It all seemed, at the time, to fit in very well.'

'You were presuming, weren't you? I mean that more would happen between you and Alan than just a kiss in the park? You were getting rid of William before you were sure of Alan. I mean next time you met him he might have pretended it never happened. I've met men like that before.'

The foreign gentleman held out his cup. Brenda filled it.

'His bladder will burst,' said Susan. 'How can any man drink so much coffee?'

'It's because he doesn't want to leave. The coffee is his excuse for staying. He is suffering greatly on our account.'

'Your account.'

'It is true,' said Brenda, 'that his eyes follow me, not you. I wonder why.'

'Perhaps in the country he comes from they like their women to have massive legs.'

'What country do you think it is?'

'The Lebanon?'

'Where's that?'

'I haven't the faintest idea.'

'Perhaps Ceylon or somewhere like that. He seems an educated man to me.'

'Now how do you deduce that?'

'He has a very intelligent expression in his eyes. Don't you think he's very attractive? I like a silent man.'

'I don't. I like words. Alan handles words beautifully.'

'Susan, if William is so civilised and understanding, why isn't he here now?'

'Because his wife's having a baby. I don't see why you're complaining. You're only here in the flat because he's not.'

'I'm sorry, I'm sure.'

'I didn't mean it like that. But naturally a girl prefers to live with a man.'

'What about all those Kensington secretaries, sharing flats with one another?'

'Cowards, or lesbians,' said Susan.

'Surely!' Brenda was disbelieving.

The foreign man closed his eyes. Brenda moved over and gently stroked his forehead, even as she protested.

'Brenda!' Susan was scandalised. 'You hardly know him!'

But Brenda stroked on. Susan rose and went back to the pub, leaving them together.

'By the fourth day of the diet I was in despair,' said Esther to Phyllis. 'I can't really bear to think about it. Shall we go and have some curry? It would do me good. I have hardly been out of this place for days.'

'You'll have to change,' said Phyllis. 'You can't go out like that.'

'Why not?'

'You're covered with soup.'

'If I don't care, why should you? I didn't bring anything with me when I left. I don't need clothes. I don't want anyone to look at me; it's their misfortune if they do. Are you ashamed to be seen out with me?'

'No.'

'You're lying. People have been ashamed to be seen out with me as long as I can remember. I was a very dirty little girl. My mother used to tell me so. She's a very small neat woman, as you know, and I by comparison, overflowed. I seemed to have more surfaces than she, and every single one of them picked up dirt. While I was married to Alan I tried very hard to be clean. I dusted and swept and polished myself as well as the house. I bathed every day, changed my clothes twice a day, bought new ones perpetually; had everything dry-cleaned. It is a very expensive business, being clean. I sewed on buttons, too. None of it was my true nature. In trying to be clean I contorted myself. This is what I am really like: I shall pretend no longer. If you are too ashamed to go into an Indian restaurant with me as I am, it doesn't matter to me in the least. I don't really want to go out anyway. I have lots of English curry in the cupboard.'

'You can't still be hungry.'

'It has nothing to do with hunger for God's sake.'

'It's psychological, you mean.'

Esther did not deign to reply. She picked out a tin of curry and a tin of savoury rice from the shelf.

'It's not real curry, this, of course. Real curry is very tricky to make. You use spices, added at precise intervals, and coconut milk. It's not just a matter of making a stew and adding curry powder and raisins and bananas. You have to devote a whole day to making a true curry. It is all a great waste of time and energy, but it keeps women occupied, and that's important. If they had a spare hour or two they might look at their husbands and laugh, mightn't they? I am glad you stopped me going out. If I leave this place goodness knows where my footsteps might not take me.'

'I didn't stop you going out. You stopped yourself.'

'Did I? How fortunate. Now where were we? One of the strange things about not eating is how clearly you begin to see things. By the end of a week I could see myself very clearly indeed, and it was not comfortable. My home was not comfortable either. It seemed a cold and chilly place, and I could see no point in the objects that filled it, that had to be eternally dusted and polished and cared for. Why? They were not human. They had no importance other than their appearance. They were bargains, that was their only merit. I had bought them cheap, yet I had more than enough money to spend, so where was the achievement? Those old things, picked up and rescued and put down on a shelf to be appreciated, were taking over my whole life. They were quaint, oh yes, and some were even pretty, but they were no justification for my being alive. Running a house is not a sensible occupation for a grown woman.

Dusting and sweeping, cooking and washing up—it is work for the sake of work, an eternal circle which lasts from the day you get married until the day you die, or are put into an old folks' home because you are too feeble to pick up some man's dirty clothes and wash them any more. For whose sake did I do it? Not my own, certainly. Not Peter's— he could as well have lived in a tree as in a house for all the notice he took of his surroundings. Not Alan's. Alan only searched for flaws: if he could not find dirt with which to chide me, if he could not find waste with which to rebuke me, then he was disappointed. And daily I tried to disappoint him. To spend my life waging war against Alan, which was what my housewifeliness amounted to, endeavouring to prove a female competence which was the last thing he wanted or needed to know about—what a waste of time this was! Was I to die still polishing and dusting, washing and ironing; seeking to find in this my fulfilment? Imprisoning Alan as well as myself in this structure of bricks and mortar we called our home? We would have been as happy, or as miserable, in a cave. We would have been freer and more our-selves, let's admit it, in *two* caves.'

'Caves are nasty damp places. You would have TB in no time. And I don't see Alan as a caveman. Now Gerry, I could see Gerry in a cave.'

'Oh, you are an inveterate little woman, aren't you? You love having a bully for a husband.'

'Gerry's not a bully. He is very strong-willed and not very good at controlling his emotions, and he speaks his mind, and he is very highly-sexed, but he's not a bully. And he needs me. And I like having the house nice when he comes home, and the smell of food cooking to welcome him and everything looking neat and tidy.'

'I bet you put on lipstick for the great home-coming, too. And a fresh dress and comb your hair, and put on a welcome-home-darling smile, just like in the women's magazines. God, what an almighty bore.'

'That's silly. He looks forward all day to coming home.'

'That's what he says, you make him say it; but what does he feel? What does he think? What do any of them think? When I looked at Alan during that week I saw a stranger, and a hostile stranger at that. Someone who conned me and betrayed me and laughed at me behind my back. All these years of marriage, I could see, he had been laughing at me, playing with me, using me and my money, and caring nothing for me at all. When he smiled at me it was to hide the sneer of derision on his lips; when he touched me and embraced me it was the worst insult of all, because he had to steel himself to do it. I knew he did. Because he touched me to keep me quiet. He lusted after someone half my age, and half my size.'

'Those are terrible feelings to have about anyone, let along a husband. And Alan's not like that. Alan's not a sly kind of person.'

'I'm not saying he is. I'm just saying that's what it felt like to me, that particular week. Juliet did what she could to make matters worse, too.'

On the seventh day of the diet Juliet sat at the living-room table polishing the silver with impudent inefficiency, and singing. Esther, in the adjoining kitchen, clattered pots and pans to indicate disapproval of her cleaner's merriment. The more she banged and crashed the sweeter Juliet sang. Then Esther appeared in the doorway, staring full at her, but Juliet sang on, and refrained from speeding up the rate of her polishing, or even of pressing harder upon the metal.

'Juliet, if you rubbed a little harder it would come up better.'

'Bad for the surface, Mrs Sussman, rubbing too hard. Gently does it, with the good stuff.'

'You just *say* that, Juliet. It's not true.'

Juliet put her cloth down. 'Are you saying I don't know how to polish silver?'

'Yes,' said Esther with desperation.

'Then perhaps you should find someone else to do it. To speak frankly, since you and Mr Sussman started not eating, this house has not been a pleasure to come into.'

'I would rather you didn't leave, Juliet.'

'You are quite right not to want me to go. You wouldn't get anyone else to work in a place like this. Things everywhere. Nothing new. Everything old-fashioned and dingy.'

'It's very fashionable, as it happens.'

'And the atmosphere! You wouldn't get anyone else to work in this kind of atmosphere.'

Esther was terrified. 'What do you mean?'

'Well,' said Juliet, in a more kindly fashion, 'I dare say it does take all sorts, and to be frank, your home is nothing to some I've seen.'

'You'll stay, you mean? Please do. Don't be upset.'

'I'll see you through a bit longer, because obviously you are not yourself. I think it is very foolish of you to ruin your health and your temper in this way, if you don't mind my saying so. Some of us are made fat and some of us are made thin, and that's all there is to it. You'll lose your husband if you carry on like this. He can't much fancy this glimpse of the Real You.'

'But it's he who makes me do it.'

'Not satisfied with what he's got? Is that it? That's husbands all over. Ungrateful pigs. You do everything for them, you bring up their kids, you cook their food, you wash their clothes, you warm their beds, you fuss over your face day after day so they'll fancy you, you wear yourself out to keep them happy and at the end of it all, what happens? They find someone else they fancy more. Someone young some man hasn't had the chance to wear out yet. Marriage is a con trick. A girl should marry a rich man, then at least she'd have a fur coat to keep her warm in her old age.'

'I don't know who you're talking about, Juliet, but it's certainly not *my* husband. If you do want to go on working for me, and I pay you eight shillings an hour, which is three shillings above market rates, I suggest you get on with it.'

'Oh go on, Mrs Sussman, just as we were getting on so nicely. Have a nice hot piece of toast with jam on it. And some nice milky coffee.'

'No, that would be cheating. Alan will kill me if I cheat.'

'You don't think he's cheating away at his office, wherever he is? What do you think he does when you're not looking?'

'Just get on with the polishing, Juliet.'

Juliet started singing. Esther went back to the kitchen, and tiny tears ran down her wide cheeks.

When Susan went back to her flat she found Brenda pacing the room in a dressing-gown. She seemed surprised: her large grey eyes were opened very wide. The man from overseas lay, fully clothed even to his carefully knotted tie, asleep on the hearth-rug.

'What an extraordinary thing,' said Brenda. 'How strange life is. They are right, love knows no boundaries of creed or colour. It strikes out of a clear sky. I am glad I left home. Things like this only happen in London.'

'I should be careful if I were you. Perhaps he has a strange disease.'

'Oh no, he's not like that at all. He is a very gentle, sensitive, discreet kind of person.'

'How do you know? He doesn't speak.'

'You can tell,' she said. 'You can tell from the way he breathes.'

'I think your behaviour is quite extraordinary. It might almost be called promiscuous. Please ask him to leave at once.'

'He's asleep. We'll have to wait until he wakes up, or it will be bad for his health. It is most unjust of you to call me names. You are always advocating free spontaneous behaviour, yet the slightest sign of life from me and you try to make me feel I have behaved badly. But I haven't, I really haven't. I have done nothing at all to be ashamed of. Everything I did, I did from love. It flowed out of me. It was a wonderful feeling, like being part of the earth.'

'What did happen exactly? I mean physically, not spiritually.'

'I can't remember, I really can't. Susan, have we any drink?'

She wandered out of the pool of light in the centre of the room into the darker perimeter, where Susan's paints and jars and brushes and clothing made black patches on the black floor.

'I feel awful all of a sudden,' she said, 'really I do. It is all your fault. I felt lovely until you came home. Free and happy and beautiful and taken by surprise. Now it's all nasty.'

'I am not your mother and you are not a little girl. I do think, however, that this kind of behaviour is not in your nature. It doesn't become you. You should go back home to Esther and marry a nice bank-clerk, and only fornicate, if absolutely necessary, with someone harmless like the milkman.'

'Supposing I'm pregnant?'

'Then you would be very foolish. Do you have his name and address?'

'No.'

'Then get it.'

'When he wakes. Will you go on telling me about Alan, and we can pretend he's not there?'

'You can't shut your eyes to realities. There is turps in that bottle, not wine.'

'Perhaps I should drink it. Perhaps death is what I deserve.'

'Death is a major and beautiful thing. What you have done was merely trivial and sordid. You should not speak about the two in the same sentence. Put the bottle down. You don't even deserve to die.'

'Don't talk to me like that. At least I don't go around trying to break up marriages.'

'I don't try to break up marriages. If marriages break up because of me that is scarcely my fault—it is the wife's fault for being my inferior. It may not appear fair on the surface, but it was what Christ was talking about when he said to them that hath shall be given, and from them that hath not shall be taken away.'

'But that's awful. I'm sure men value other things in their wives. I read in the paper about how Germans rate thrift in a wife as the most important thing, and then cleanliness, and then fidelity, and good looks came way down at the bottom of the list and intelligence last of all.'

'Do you want to marry a German?'

'No.'

'Well then.'

'But I don't want to get married and have my husband go off. I think it's wrong for girls to go with married men.'

'What about him?' The man on the hearth-rug stirred.

'I don't know if he's married. He hasn't said he's married.'

'I expect his wife is crying at home this very minute with the children sobbing at her knee. I expect that's why he hasn't bothered to learn English, in case anyone rebukes him with his wife and makes him feel bad.'

'Don't say such things. He's a gay young student, carefree and vital.'

'You reckon?'

'I just don't know. To tell you the truth, I don't know much more about him now than I did before. I wish he'd get up and go away and then I wouldn't have to worry.'

'Perhaps you take a very masculine attitude to sex. Perhaps that's what's wrong. The loving-and-leaving syndrome is not natural in a girl.'

'Alan was old enough to be your father. Perhaps you have a daughter-father syndrome.'

'Exactly, I don't deny it. He was so grey and middle-aged and clever and superior and in control, and his flies were so tightly buttoned, and the excitement of dissolving him and stripping away the veneer and turning him into a naked little boy again—and not even knowing whether I could do it—it was wonderfully exhilarating. And to be so frighteningly dependent, all of a sudden, quite against one's better judgement, upon someone else's good opinion; to want to impress; to want to attract; to want above all just to be noticed; to feel so nervous and insecure; to worry in case one's breath stank; these were all symp-

toms I had never known before. These were the symptoms of unre-
quited love, and they were both horrible and glorious. I felt truly alive
at last. I don't recommend it, Brenda, for you. You are not tough
enough to withstand pain; that is why you make sure your relationships
are always so shallow. Well, yours is one way of living. But I prefer
myself to enter wholeheartedly into whatever it is I'm doing, even if it
entails suffering. That is some of William's home-made elderberry
wine you are sniffing. It is not supposed to be drunk for another six
months, but I think we could open a jar, and drink to him and his baby,
and to Alan. And don't say I am breaking up William's marriage either,
because I'm not, or he wouldn't be back with his wife now, would he,
and you wouldn't be using my flat as a knocking shop, and none of any
of this upsetting business would have happened. We would all be as
happy as once we were.'

On the eighth day of the diet Alan sang, sitting in his chair in his
empty office with his feet on the desk. He was happy. There was an
almost empty bottle of champagne at his elbow. Susan came into his
office after lunch. She had been transferred, at Alan's request, to the
research department. It put her at a disadvantage.
    'Why are you singing?'
    'Because I'm happy.'
    'You've been drinking.'
    'I have been drinking but I do not have to drink in order to be happy.
Just occasionally I am happy, and then nothing can stop me, neither
flesh nor fowl nor drink nor wife nor even you, my dear.'
    'Why should you think I want to stop you being happy? I want you
to be happy.'
    'Oh no. *You* want to be happy.'
    'What are you going to do, Alan?'
    'Do?' Alan took his feet off the desk abruptly, dropped the cham-
pagne bottle into the wastepaper basket, and straightened his tie. 'Do?
About what?'
    'About us. Sometimes you make me feel like some vulgar office girl.
I think you do it on purpose.'
    'But you know you are not, don't you. You are a very fine and sen-
sitive person, with great talent and worthy of better than me. Yes?'
    'You are mocking me.'
    'You have no sense of humour. That is your whole problem. It is
quite remarkable.'

'And you are incapable of being serious about anything. That's much worse.'

'I am sorry. Am I being very disagreeable?'

'Yes.'

'I am hungry. I haven't really had much to drink. It is just that it's gone straight to my head, because my stomach is empty.'

'I don't know any longer what sort of person you want me to be.'

'I don't know what I want. I don't know anything except that I was happy before you came in, thinking about you. It is odd that when the reality of you appears all happiness should evaporate, to be replaced by feelings so resentful and defensive that I am now quite agitated. You are looking marvellous.'

'Are you coming round this evening? I need to know, so I can buy food.'

'I don't come to visit you to eat, do I? Remember I am a married man, and on a diet.'

'I wish you would eat more. You are nicer when you've eaten.'

'Come and sit on my knee.'

'I'm too heavy, and someone might come in.'

'True. Also, it is a vulgar habit between boss and secretary.'

'I just don't know what you think or feel about me. You talk as if you hated me and you act as if you loved me.'

'Be careful.'

'What of?'

'That word. It leads to more trouble than any other single word in the English language. Shouldn't you be working?'

'Tony White never comes back until half past three. He's always drunk. He smells. He leans over me and breathes into my ear. It's horrible.'

'Poor Susan.'

'Since you are being so disagreeable and strange I'm going back to my office. If you don't mind Tony White putting his hand up my skirt, why should I?'

'He's a dirty old man then, isn't he?'

'He's no older than you.'

'That's quite different. Oh Susan, I am a hungry man. The champagne has filled me with bubbles but bubbles are not food. Food is the supremest of pleasures.'

'Spoken to a mistress, that is not a compliment.'

'I am out of my mind. Am I thinner, Susan? Do I begin to lack the substance you want me to have? I dream all night, as I haven't dreamt since I was twenty. I dream of strange and marvellous things. I dream of fish and chips and bread and butter and cups of sweet tea. I dream of ship-loads of boiling jam cleaving their way through the polar ice-caps. I dream of—oh Susan, I have such dreams as life itself is made of.'

'You're laughing at me again.'

'Why not? I am allowed to have poetic fancies as well as you. I take you very seriously. When you sit and wave your legs at me they are the most beautiful legs I have ever seen. You make me young again. There is a gap between stocking top and knicker which excites me beyond belief. I want to eat it. I shall visit you this evening.'

'You are crude. You are only interested in my body.'

'And when you first waved your stocking tops at me, you did so more crudely than any other secretary I have ever had, and that is saying something. You had your way with me. But I must remind you that I am an old man. You are a child and you are playing with dangerous things. When children take their games seriously, it ends in tears. With grown ups, it ends in suicides, divorce, and delinquent children. Be careful what you do.'

'There is only twenty years between us. You are not old at all, just experienced.'

'Compared to you, I may say, I suspect that I am indeed young in experience. Yet I have my aims, my fancies. And I am older than you, much older, in years. Youth to me is a magic thing, although to you it may seem a burden. For I am a balding plump old man, and I don't want to be. I dream that you might rescue me, and infect me with youth and hope again and all the things I have lost through the years, along with ties and pocket handkerchiefs. But age wins in the end. It must. Age turns even lust to ashes. I am an honest man, and even though it goes against my interests, I warn you here and now that in a week or so I shall have a fit of coughing and take to my own warm familiar bed and forget all about yours. Yet perhaps I delude myself that this might hurt you? I know so little about your generation. All I can tell you is that my intentions towards you are entirely dishonourable. If you are likely to take me seriously, stop now. Stop waving your legs at me. I am not strong enough to withstand you. This diet weakens me. You are taking monstrous advantage of a poor weak hungry man. I never thought to be an adulterer.'

'You credit me with no feelings at all. You see me as some kind of sexual vulture preying upon your flesh. You are very old-fashioned.

You think that if a woman takes any kind of initiative she is cheap and worthless. In fact I have given up a great deal on your account, because I have faith in my own feelings and I am prepared to suffer for them— even your rejection of everything about me that isn't just my body. I offer you a great deal and you turn your back on it.'

'I hadn't noticed myself doing any such thing.'

'Please try and understand me.'

'Very well. What have you offered me?'

'My difference. Whatever it is that makes me different from every other woman in the world. You scorn it. You see me not as a person, just as a woman. I want to be a person.'

'Girls given to adulterous affairs must learn not to expect too much.'

'You try and hurt me in order to spare yourself. I have great faith in you, all the same. I think you are capable of more than sitting behind an office desk thinking about dandruff, and practising your silly defences on me. I am trying to rescue you. I am offering you a chance of escaping into a better richer honester life. It will hurt, but it will be better than what you have now, which is nothing, nothing, except boredom and dullness and sterility for the rest of your life.'

'I don't feel at all happy any more,' he said. 'I hope you are satisfied.'

She put her arms around his neck and snuffled his ear and told him everything was all right.

'When you stop talking,' he said, 'you are wonderful. You are a comforting delicious child, all peaches and cream. Your breasts are like melons, your breath is like honey, your hair is like—no, spun-silk is inedible.'

'Spun toffee?'

'Wonderful! I would rather make love to you than eat a dozen cream cakes, and that is the most sincere compliment you are ever likely to receive in your whole life. Now go and type for Tony White and tell him to keep his hands to himself, and kick him in the balls if he won't. Or threaten him with a memo in triplicate, which would hurt him even more.'

Susan was either crying or her eyes were watering with indignation. Brenda, who had never seen Susan cry, chose to think that it was the latter emotion. Susan put on a Sidney Bechet record and danced around the prostrate man on the floor. It was a solitary, lonely, despairing dance, sexual but entirely self-preoccupied, prompted by his existence but on the whole disparaging of it. Her body seemed composed of two disparate parts. Her top half swayed like a weak tree in a strong gale: her buttocks pumped up and down mechanically, like pistons. Brenda felt embarrassed by this exhibition of passion, and was glad when whatever madness it was left Susan, and she sat down, peacefully, and sipped elderberry wine.

'Love will always cause pain,' Susan observed, 'because the passion is so much nobler and greater than its objects. Men stand as trivial, flawed, puny things before the majesty of love. Love possesses one, but there is nothing fit for it to be released upon. So it is a perpetual agony.'

'Perhaps you should be a nun. Then you could be a bride of Christ, and then perhaps you would be satisfied.'

'I begin to understand nuns,' said Susan. 'I never thought I would. I suppose I can thank Alan for that. But I believe one has to be a virgin. And it would never do for me, anyway. I need men to define me: to give me an idea of what I am. If I didn't have boy-friends I don't think I would exist. I would fly apart in all directions. So I must live my life in perpetual pain, if I want to live at all.'

'I feel quite happy quite a lot of the time,' said Brenda, as one who apologises.

'Oh you! You are just a whore at heart. I was quite wrong about you and being a mother. Your thighs are money-makers, not creators.'

'It is a funny kind of love you talk about,' said Brenda, incensed. 'It seems to have nothing to do with the man loved. You have too much of it inside. It overflows and attaches itself at random, like a kind of bloodsucking slug. If I was a man I would most certainly want to brush it off.'

Susan looked at the painting on her easel. 'My painting makes me sick too. It just makes matters worse. There is no point in it. It's just more of me, spreading into another dimension. If you're a woman you never win. Look at it. It's so bloody fucking personal. I don't know why I bother.'

'Why are you sitting here listening to me?' asked Esther of Phyllis. 'Why aren't you at home warming Gerry's slippers, or sulking, or putting on a flimsy nightie to tempt him, or whatever you are accustomed to doing at this time of night?'

'He had to work late at the office, so I thought I wouldn't be there when he came home, just to show him.'

'Show him what?'

'That I can have a life of my own, too.'

'Do you play this game all the time, Phyllis, or only some of the time?'

'Game? It isn't a game. It's very serious, and very painful.'

'Supposing he comes home and finds you gone and goes straight out to revenge himself?'

'I know. It does happen. I suppose. It is very worrying. Perhaps I should go home.'

'I suggest you do.'

'You haven't told me a thing yet. You've just talked and talked. No, I don't think I should go home. Gerry must be taught a lesson.'

'No wonder he looks elsewhere.'

'It's not that Gerry *looks*. It's that unscrupulous women place themselves where he can't help seeing them. Some women are like that. And if he's angry with me—Gerry gets angry very easily—then terrible things happen.'

'Terrible for whom?'

'For me. And for Gerry. It complicates his life, and he has a strong sense of duty. He wouldn't keep seeing his wife otherwise.'

'You're his wife, Phyllis.'

'His ex-wife, I mean. It's hard to remember. I feel she's his real wife, you see, and I'm in the wrong to be living with him at all. Please go on with your story. Can I have some of that luncheon meat, please?'

Esther cut Phyllis a slab of luncheon meat, and another one for herself. They gnawed its pink flabbiness with pleasure.

'Talking of girls standing in the way to be looked at,' said Esther, 'it was exactly what this stupid child Susan Pierce was doing. Alan was not exactly a romantic figure, but he had written a book and that was enough to set her going. Her usual style, I gather, is any man of letters, preferably married, who has an assured future and frequent mentions in the Sunday papers. A very suburban creature, I thought her, and her true stereotyped self very easily got the upper hand. The slightest stirring in her loins—and Alan is remarkably good at the promise of pleasure, if not its fulfilment—and her suburban little heart cried love. And that was not what Alan meant at all.'

'What did he want, then?'

'He was hungry. A hungry man grabs what he can get.'

'But you were hungry too.'

'Hunger made him aggressive. It merely bored me. So much of my daily life had been taken up by shopping and cooking, and eating and washing-up after the cooking, and now it had all evaporated. There was nothing left to do in the long hungry hours but work myself up into a state about Alan's betrayal of me.'

'How did you know he had betrayed you? How could you tell?'

'The upheaval in my routine had left me paranoic, I admit. I would have suspected him of infidelity with his secretary, simply because she was temporary and named Susan, whether I had grounds for my suspicion or not. I had no grounds, but I suspected, and as it transpired, quite fortuitously, I was right.'

'I don't regard Gerry's affairs as a threat to my marriage. They are very trivial. He says so and I agree.'

'What other choice have you but to agree? Divorce? You are not brave enough to be a single woman. You are a coward. You have played at being helpless for so long that now you are. And Gerry knows it. He doesn't have to bother. Your friends are Gerry's friends, not yours at all. Your home is Gerry's home, bought with Gerry's money. You just don't exist without him. And again, a single woman over thirty is an object of pity, or so you think. So you agree with Gerry that such masculine affairs are trivial; you tell yourself it is not in a man's nature to be monogamous; but neither of these things are any more true of men than they are of women, and your misery is no one's fault but your own because you are craven and a betrayer of your sex. You suck up to the enemy. I despise you.'

'Thank you very much, I'm sure. I love Gerry, as it so happens.'

'You are incurable. You comfort yourself with words. I will continue. I was getting thinner. I had lost eight pounds in just over a week. I was pleased with myself, but no one would allow me comfort. I was tormented.'

On the ninth day of the diet Peter said to his mother, as he sat at the kitchen table eating steak pie and chips from the fish-and-chip shop round the corner, 'I think you are out of your mind.' His mother was eating three ounces of cottage cheese and two tablespoonfuls of spinach. Alan was not yet back from the office. 'Why don't you eat? No one cares whether you are fat or thin. Let's face it, you are out of the age group where it matters. You just be a nice cosy comfy mum and leave it at that! What more do you want? You've got a nice home and good husband and I'm no trouble to you, and an easy life—and when you think of the lives most women have to lead—seven children and a drunken husband—I think there's something rather awful about middle-aged middle-class people going on diets, when all over the world people are starving to death—literally—'

'My troubles are not outside me,' said Esther, 'They are inside me. Those are the worst troubles of all.'

That evening Alan and Esther lay in the double bed they had owned for eighteen years. It was five foot wide. Once they had occupied, happily, the two feet in the centre. Now they used the peripheries.

They lay staring up at the ceiling, hungry, and presently they began to talk, which was not their usual custom in bed.

'Steak and kidney pudding,' said Esther, 'with mushrooms and oysters and the gravy oozing out. And mashed potatoes and a cauliflower cheese, all golden and bubbling on top, with bits of green stalk right down at the bottom where the sauce is thinner and buttery.'

'Hare soup,' replied Alan, 'with fresh rolls and lots of butter. And then roast duck with roast potatoes and green peas. Followed by apple pie and cheese and biscuits. A Brie, I think, just at the right point of squishiness, with that slight and marvellous taste of something on the verge of going bad. Something you can suspect of being rotten, but you know you're allowed to eat.'

'I'd have apple pie. You break through the crust and it's juicy underneath. Chocolate mousse is nice of course, with chopped walnuts on top. With whipped cream flavoured with rum.'

'Or apricot crumble. My mother used to make that.'

'I know.'

'That's why I never get it, I suppose.'

'Don't be silly. We all know, of course, what a marvellous cook your mother was and how beautifully she kept her house. How the clean warm wind blew freshly through the windows, which were always opened in every bedroom at the same time every morning. That it was an Indian wind, of course, you forget. That there is nothing outside our windows but a fall of damp black soot from a sulphurous heaven you prefer to overlook. You still make faces at the closed bedroom windows. Men are very good at making faces over domestic details. They say nothing, but with the merest look they can drain all joy from any minimal sense of domestic achievement one may have painfully acquired.'

'You speak out of intimate knowledge of the domestic nature of dozens of men, I notice. You must have crammed a great deal into your life before you met me. And indeed, I may say, after.'

'I did. Another thing you forget is that your mother had some twelve Indian slaves whereas I have the dubious advantage of a daily help a couple of hours every day.'

'I was making no comparison between my mother and you. It was you who decided I had. All I said was that my mother made apricot crumble, and I liked it, and for some reason I never get it from you.'

'You could always cook it yourself.'

'Charming! Back from a hard day at the office to cook my own dinner. Why don't you ask me to sweep the floors too?'

'The more you complain about your hard day at the office, the less plausible it seems. Just sitting at a desk all day, talking, writing, lifting up the telephone, do you call that work?'

"People who have never worked in offices have no idea of the tensions, the decisions and the crises which attend one's every hour. I am worn out by mid-day, exhausted by the time I get home.'

'So I'd noticed.'

'What is that supposed to mean?'

'Oh never mind. I'm too fat and unattractive anyway. Unlike your— what's her name—Audrey? Janet? Susan? That's it. Susan. The willowy, artistic one.'

'For God's sake what do you want? We've been married nearly twenty years.'

'Oh don't pretend—'

'What is the matter with you?'

'I think she should leave. It's not fair to me.'

'Now what in the world—? What earthly reason have you—'

'You only talk about her when you're drunk, that's why. Not a mention of her when you're sober. You inhibit your conversation on her account. The only way I ever know anything about you is by listening to you when you're drunk, did you know that?'

'You speak as if I was some kind of alcoholic.'

'Perhaps you are. Anyway, there it is. You don't talk about Susan when you're sober.'

'I thought I was supposed never to be sober.'

'Don't be silly.'

'The truth is, of course, that I daren't talk about her. You are so impossibly jealous. You are mad. It is this diet. I think you had better give it up. I can't live with you while you're like this.'

'But you will carry on, of course, being so strong-willed and self-disciplined.'

'Yes.'

'Charming.' Esther sat upright in bed. The tops of her arms were flabby, but her flesh was still very white and smooth. 'So I've got to be fat and ugly while you get thin and carry on with your secretary.'

'You are quite impossible. It's no use trying to reason with you at all.'

Tears fell out of Esther's eyes.

'It's not fair to me. It's not fair. It's not my fault I'm fat.'

'Well it's certainly not mine. If it's not one thing it's another. Go to sleep. Stop behaving like a little girl. You'll feel better in the morning. Incidentally—'

'Yes—' said Esther, comforted by this exercise in luxurious authority, and wanting to hear more.

'Marriage isn't a prison. You remember what Gerry was saying the other evening? Unfaithful husbands are made by jealous wives.'

They lay silent for some minutes, both with their eyes open, carefully not touching, despite the dip in the middle of their marital mattress. Presently Esther stretched out her hand to lay it on his belly.

'Alan?'

'Go to sleep.'

'I'm sorry.'

'You always are, afterwards. Why do you start?'

'I don't know. I thought it was you who started. Anyway it doesn't matter. I love you.'

'Then I wish you would show it rather more. Why don't you trust me? You've got nothing to worry about. Can't we just leave it at that? You've always got to have something to worry about. I just wish you wouldn't make it my secretaries, because that makes me angry.'

'Alan—'

'Do we have to talk? The sooner we get to sleep the sooner breakfast will be.'

'You'll never really discuss anything, will you? I want to talk about everything and you want to keep silent about everything. Just suppose I was unfaithful to you, what would you do?'

'You have a great gift for forgetting things.'

'That was different, that was a long time ago. We were apart, of our own free wills, and it didn't count. But in general terms, if husbands get interested in other women, wives are supposed to be tactful and silent and not make scenes, and put on new corsets and get their hair done, and win their straying spouses back by patient loving endeavour. Now if *I* had a lover, would you try and win me back by behaving with restraint? Would you buy me roses and wash your feet and have your toe-nails manicured to please me better? Like hell you would!'

'What are you talking about now?'

'Just that there's one law for husbands and another for wives.'

'Of course there is. Wives need husbands more than husbands need wives.'

'What a terrible thing to say.'

'It is not terrible, it is simply true. Such is the structure of our society that women without husbands are scorned, and men without women admired. Provided they are known to be heterosexuals, of course. I notice an increasing tendency in women to label any unmarried man a queer, however; and to put about the damaging rumour that the fornicator is merely over-compensating, announcing to the world his sexual inadequacy. The male-female war is hotting up.'

'You are being flippant. It is not fair.'

'Of course it is not fair.'

'I wish I had been born a man.'

'You make that very apparent.'

'Now you are being unpleasant. Men are always accusing women of being unfeminine, and at the same time making sure that the feminine state is as unendurable as possible. You leave your dirty socks around for me to pick up. And your dirty pants. It's my place to pick them up, because I'm a woman. And if I don't, you accuse me of being unfeminine. It's my place to clean up your cigarette ash from the coffee cup where you've ground out your cigarette. I am only fit to serve you and to be used and to make your life pleasanter for you, in spite of such lip service as you may pay to equal rights for women. You may *know* that I am equal, with your reason, but you certainly don't *feel* that I am.'

'Quite the suffragette.'

'And that is still the worst term of abuse a man can think of to say to his wife.'

'I wouldn't like to see you join the ranks of the crusading women, I admit. It wouldn't make you any happier, and it is so unrestful.'

'You are so patronising. I hate men.'

'Ah, there we have it at last.'

'I don't hate you, personally. Only your race.'

'Don't worry too much about me. I'll survive. And you of course are free to go your own way.'

'You sound remarkably like Gerry, these days.'

'Thank you very much.'

'It is not altogether an insult. He is quite attractive in some ways.'

'He is a pompous bore.'

'He is very sexy.'

'He likes *young* girls, dear.'

'I am not as old and ugly as you think.'

'I don't think anything of the kind.' Alan sounded weary. 'You are a married woman with a grown-up child. Why can't you behave like one? You make yourself ridiculous with this kind of talk.'

'I feel hungry. I am all stirred up inside. I feel the way I did when I was eighteen. I don't know what I want but it's not this. I don't want to be this person, I don't want to be trapped in this body, in this house, in this marriage.'

'Thank you very much. You say the sweetest things.'

'Oh, let's go to sleep.'

'There's steamed fish tomorrow.'

'Charming,' she said. 'Life is so full of thrills.'

Alan, feeling that sleep was further than ever, got out of bed and stood upon the scales. He balanced from one foot to another to try and make the reading as low as possible. Proving to his own satisfaction that he had lost two pounds he said to Esther, 'There is something, however, that I haven't told you. If I have been behaving a little strangely, there is a reason for it.'

Esther opened her eyes, alarmed.

'My agent rang up last week,' he said. 'He likes my novel. He thinks it's going to make quite a splash. He's sent it to the publishers with a very strong recommendation. A pity you haven't read it. I would have liked to have discussed it with you.'

'Isn't that marvellous,' said Esther faintly. 'Isn't that wonderful! Why didn't you tell me earlier? We could have celebrated.'

'I didn't like Alan writing that novel,' said Esther to Phyllis. 'I didn't like it one little bit. And I liked it even less when he said his agent was enthusiastic.'

'I would have been proud,' said Phyllis. 'I'd think it was marvellous if Gerry could only do a thing like that. I wish I'd married a writer.

Writers stay at home most of the time. I could learn how to type and be a great help to him in his work.'

'I had no urge whatsoever to help Alan,' said Esther. 'Not in this respect. He'd come home from the office and have dinner and go into the bedroom and take out his typewriter and that would be that for the evening. I could sit staring into space for all he cared. And what would he have done if I'd gone off by myself and typed in the evenings? He wouldn't have stood for it. That's another of the rules of marriage. Husbands can snub wives but wives aren't allowed to indulge themselves in artistic endeavours: wives can only do so in secret, when husbands are out of the house. Wives are a miserable lot. I shall never be a wife again.'

'I think you should see a doctor. It's not right to think like that. It's perfectly natural for women to be wives, and to look after husbands who are not really fit to look after themselves, and it was very unfair of you to try and stop him writing. And most unwise. No wonder he looked elsewhere.'

'You have this extraordinary passion for simplifying things, Phyllis. I didn't try and stop him writing. I encouraged him. He was doing it just to annoy, anyway; to prove to me what a creative person he was and to demonstrate how I had stifled his talents and his personality. I knew from the way he would gobble down his dinner, pretending not to notice what he was eating, and then stand in the doorway and say, with his papers clutched in his hand—"I am going away to write now. I do not want to be disturbed—". He used such a challenging tone of voice that I quickly recognised the whole thing as an act of aggression. And he waited and waited for me to ask him what it was about, and I wouldn't, so he had to go on writing and almost before he knew what had happened, he had finished. So he ought to have been grateful to me. Instead, he preferred to believe he had done it all in spite of me, and not to spite me, as was the truth.'

'Didn't you want to know what he was writing? I would have died of curiosity.'

'If he wanted it to be a secret, why should I bother?'

'Poor Alan! Trampling on his creativity like that.'

'Poor Alan, indeed. When did Alan ever do anything except exactly what he wanted when he wanted?'

'Well that's men, isn't it?'

'You do reduce everything to a kind of comic-strip level, don't you? All this happened the night before Gerry called.'

Phyllis paused in the careful peeling of an apple.

'Gerry?'

'Yes. Didn't he tell you?'

'He didn't mention it.'

'It was quite a casual visit. Perhaps he thought it wasn't important—oh, don't look like that, Phyllis. You don't own the poor man.'

'I don't want to own him. I just want not to be hurt by him. I want it to be like it was when I was a child, when you thought the day you got married you lived happily ever after. Esther, I'm cold. You talk and talk and none of it matters and then you say something and it's real. Turn on the fire.'

Phyllis tossed the unbroken strip of peel from her apple into the air. It curled to make a 'C' on the floor.

'C. I wonder who that is? I wonder who in the world that is. Do you think I will ever meet someone who will make me happy? I wouldn't mind waiting until I was seventy. Just so long as some day I do.'

'Men don't make women happy. Men make women unhappy.'

Esther crouched in front of the gas-fire, making toast.

'Gerry used to make me happy. I was so very happy once,' said Phyllis.

'It is the memory of past happiness that makes the present so intolerable. Better never to be happy at all.'

'Tell me about Gerry. What did he say? Why did he visit you? What happened? Did you let him make love to you?'

Esther turned to stare at Phyllis in an unsmiling way, and the toast burned.

Brenda now lay on the bed in her nightgown with her hands clasped behind her head an an expression of beatitude on her face that quite tormented Susan.

'Did you really let that man make love to you?' asked Susan. 'Just like that? A foreigner? A pick-up in a pub?'

'Yes. Why not? Why are you so interested? What more do you want to know? I don't like discussing clinical details. He was different from an Englishman, really. There is no need to go on about his being a foreigner.'

'I don't understand how you can take such a thing so lightly.'

'You think you are the only person who ever feels anything. Who knows, perhaps he and me will get married.'

Susan looked at the prostrate figure on the floor. His watch was solid gold; his clothes must have cost a fortune in Carnaby Street; he had the smooth and silky skin of the protein-fed.

'You don't know his name,' she said. 'Or his income.'

'It doesn't matter. I feel I am in love. I have never been in love before. I want to feel like this for ever. My kind of love is not yours. Mine makes me happy. You say that that is being a whore. I think it's just being a normal, natural woman.'

'I think it's being a normal, natural man, more like. I think you have been born a boy.'

'My mother wanted me to be a boy. I am glad I am a woman, though, now. I feel wonderful.'

'You were feeling something quite different before. You were all anxious and worried.'

'When you came in looking so cross I felt I ought to apologise. The least I could do was not have enjoyed it. But now I am bored with pretending. I feel marvellous. I feel powerful. I think all I have to do is stretch out my little finger and men will fall down in front of me in droves. Do you ever feel like that?'

'Sometimes. Not often.'

'When I look back at the past I seem to have been so foolish. I worried about whether men would like me. But it doesn't matter, does it? What matters is whether I like them. What a revelation! Isn't life wonderful? I wonder what my mother would say. She'd have a fit.'

'She's probably in bed with the butcher at this very minute. Suburban widows are a randy lot.'

Brenda sat up.

'You have no right to say a thing like that. My mother loved my father very much and hasn't looked at a man since he died. She is a very good woman, and my father treated her very badly, which was what she wanted I'm afraid. She had to struggle very hard to bring me up, which she loved doing, and granted she isn't very intelligent, but she's a good woman, and very brave in the face of adversity—everyone says so; and the butcher is about eighty anyway. And I'll tell you another thing. I'm tired of being patronised by you. I don't think you know as much about love as you pretend. You may be kinky for artists and married men, but that doesn't mean you know everything about life.'

'Just because you've fallen into bed with a strange Asiatic and liked it doesn't mean you do, either. It was very unwise of you. I don't see him going down well in your family circle.'

'I won't really marry him. I will love him but never marry him, because East and West can never meet. He might be a Muslim, anyway, and his attitude to women not acceptable.'

'I hardly imagine he had marriage in mind when he followed you home from the pub. Or a union lasting not more than a quarter of an hour at the very most.'

'You make everything sound so sordid. We'll see when he wakes. I think your relationship with William is sordid, taking a man away from his pregnant wife. And you and Alan, that was sordid too. Fancy fancying a man because he'd written a book! I feel too happy to be really angry with you, however. You only say nasty things because you're jealous: because I have some capacity for happiness and you have none. I feel liberated. I thought I would have to marry a bank clerk or a doctor or a solicitor and have children and be a housewife, but now I see I needn't do any of these things. I shall never get married.'

'You will have to.'

'Why?'

'Children. You want children.'

'You don't have to be married to have children.'

'You'll grow old and ugly. Then you'll need to be married.'

'*You* don't mean to get married. Why should it be different for me?'

'Because you have a suburban soul.'

'I have not. Didn't I just go to bed with him? Is that being suburban?'

'Yes.'

'Oh.' Brenda's look of happiness died. 'You can't win, can you,' she said in a small voice. She turned her head on to the pillow and began to cry.

'Now what's the matter?' asked Susan.

'I'm all upset inside. I don't know what's the matter. Is there enough hot water for a bath?'

'Yes.'

'It won't make any difference though. I'll still feel sticky and horrible.'

'That's just guilt.'

'Why should I feel guilty?' Brenda stopped crying to enquire.

'Because you're not married, and you don't love him, and you don't want his children.'

'Do you have to want someone's children not to feel guilty about making love to them?'

'Yes.'

'You didn't want Alan's children.'

'Good God, no.'

'Then?'

'But then I didn't like Alan in bed either. I wasn't really interested in bed, just in his creative soul.'

Brenda got out of bed and knelt beside it and prayed.

'What on earth are you doing?'

'Praying.'

'To whom, for God's sake?'

'I don't know. Anyone.'

'What are you praying?'

'I'm just saying, "Dear God what shall we do to be saved?" '

'You are right to ask. I'll go away and leave you to your devotions.'

'Please don't. Don't go away until he does. If I shut my eyes, will you wake him up and get rid of him so that when I open my eyes he's gone?'

'Are you talking to me or to God?'

'You.'

Susan crossed to the sleeping man and kicked him. He grunted and stirred but he did not wake up. He was too drunk.

Esther scraped the toast into the sink. She looked with distaste at the black crumbs, and ran the tap to wash them away.

'I don't really eat,' she remarked. 'I scavenge. I am trying to clear up the mess that surrounds me, like a cat cleaning up after having kittens. Sometimes they eat the kittens too, by mistake.'

'You say horrible things,' said Phyllis, taking out her compact and staring at her face. 'Human beings are more than animals. I think you say these things just to shock me. But I am not easily shocked.'

'Where is Gerry now, do you think? At this very moment?'

'I don't know.'

'Why won't you answer my question?'

'It was an unworthy question.'

'What do you imagine Gerry is doing at this very minute? Let a vision come into your mind. I know what you see. You see him in bed with a woman. You don't know what she looks like, all you know is she isn't you. Perhaps she looks like me? Vaguely? He's just a vague shape too, isn't he? Your husband. You don't really believe he exists separately from you. At least I just eat food. You'd eat him, if you could. To incorporate him. That's a terrible way to be.'

'What are you talking about? I don't think Gerry is with another woman. And what horrible nonsense is all that other about eating him? What do you think I am? A cannibal?'

'You are shocked, aren't you. The truth is always shocking.'

'You're mad. What happened when Gerry came to see you?'

'What happened? What happened? Sexually? That's the only kind of happening you recognise. No wonder you fear growing old so much. But behaving and feeling as if you were fifteen won't stop your backbone shrivelling and your teeth falling out.'

'What happened? I begin to think you have something to hide.'

'Begin? You've been in a state of agitation ever since I said Gerry came to see me. Nothing happened, in the sense you mean.'

'I'm sorry to be silly. It's just he always fancied you. I don't know why. He'd go mad if I put on a pound, yet he liked you.'

'He came to let me know, on the excuse of passing by, that he had seen Alan lunching with Susan in Soho, and to tell me, under guise of denigrating her, just how young, beautiful, slim and intelligent she was.'

'But why would he do a thing like that?'

'Why do you think?'

'He's horrible! He's always fancied you. He thought you'd pay Alan out in his own coin.'

'You might be wrong. Perhaps it was all quite innocent. Perhaps he *was* just passing by. Perhaps he *did* think I knew about Susan having lunch with Alan. Perhaps he hoped for nothing at all. Perhaps it is all just in our minds, and not in his. We must be careful not to mistrust all men, just because they are our enemies.'

'You are so confusing. I know Gerry was after you, but I don't think men are my enemies. I like men.'

'So do I. But I don't think women should have anything more to do with men than they can possibly help. They should not try and ape them, either. I wish you would not wear trousers, Phyllis.'

'I like wearing trousers.'

'Women should aspire to be as different as possible from men. You should wear a skirt as a matter of principle. There must be apartheid between the sexes. Men and women should unite only for the purpose of rearing children. Any woman who struggles to be accepted in a man's world makes herself ridiculous. It is a world of folly, fantasy and self-indulgence and it is not worth aspiring to. We must create our own world. I will lend you a skirt, Phyllis.'

Phyllis shuddered in spite of herself.

'We were talking about your husband,' said Esther, 'on whose account you make yourself so wretched. I am not sorry for you on this account, since you married him with the full intention of being wretched. I will tell you the truth. Your husband came round and made a pass at me, although I am all of fourteen stone and five years older than him. Now why did he do a thing like that?'

'What did you do? Esther!' Poor Phyllis was trembling.

'I?' said Esther. 'What would a woman like me do when a man like that makes a pass at her? "I like", he said to me, "a woman I can get my teeth into". To which I replied, "I am not normally a mass of tooth-marks". That was quite witty, don't you think?'

'You're mad,' said Phyllis. She was standing up, pulling at her wedding ring, with her eyes so bright it was clear she was going to cry. 'You shouldn't talk to me about my husband like that. For pity's sake stop teasing me and tell me what happened. You are so clever and I am very stupid but it's not my fault. Please tell me!'

'I have already told you. Nothing happened that was of any account.'

'But what do you mean, "was of any account"? For all I know you'd go to bed with the Prime Minister and still say it wasn't "of any account." '

'Well, you know Gerry. It's all talk with him, isn't it.'

Phyllis started to cry. Mascara ran down her cheeks.

'Don't get hysterical,' said Esther. 'You wanted to hear this story. It's not my fault if it turns out to be something you don't want to hear.'

'Just tell me, Esther. I won't hold it against you.'

'Gerry and I did not make love,' said Esther, allowing Phyllis to see that her fingers were crossed. 'That night,' she added for good measure. 'Try and calm down, Phyllis. Why should you worry either way? What possible difference can it make to us, here and now, what happened to me a month or so ago? What matters is that your husband tried to upset me and succeeded.'

'All you can think of is yourself.'

'That is a charge that can fairly be levelled at every one of us. I wish you didn't have such trivial problems, Phyllis. You must learn to look outside them. Gerry's infidelity is merely a convenient hook on which to hang your anxieties. You would be better off as a peasant woman tilling the soil and trying to keep her family from starvation. Give any woman time to think and she's miserable at once. It is time you took up good works, Phyllis.'

'But you left Alan because he was unfaithful.'

'That is a gross simplification.'

'Well you didn't leave him just because he made you go on a diet.'

'He didn't make me go on a diet. We decided to do it. He quite wilfully set about depriving me. I quite wilfully set about depriving him. We conspired together to break our marriage, in fact. I was less whole-hearted about it than him. I would have retracted if I could. I made peace-offerings. I tried to cook him omelets in butter. He chose to see it as an act of aggression. He was determined not to be married to me any more.'

'I don't understand.'

'I will try and explain tomorrow. Don't worry about me and Gerry, it was all of no significance. You tempt me into being unpleasant to you, that's all. I am very tired. I want to go to sleep. You must go home, Phyllis, or to walk the streets if you are still determined to punish Gerry by staying out. Perhaps, who is to say, he does in fact have to work late in the office? The money you live on must come from somewhere.'

'I will see you tomorrow evening,' said Phyllis forlornly. 'You need me. You are going through a great crisis in your life.'

And she left the flat, found her way up the dark, broken steps, hailed a taxi and went home. Gerry was not there. She took four sleeping pills and lost consciousness.

2 The others slept badly. Esther was very sick at about four in the morning. A great mass of undigested food poured back out of her mouth into the lavatory basin: she could taste the different flavours as it passed. The soup, the toast, the curry, the cake, the nuts, the eggs, the fish fingers, the butter, the jam, the beans, the cake—the whole evening's intake reappeared in a spasmic flow. She had not realised that her stomach could contain so much. On the way back to bed, exhausted from retching to recover the last troublesome chunk of nut, she caught sight of her naked body in the mirror, and stopped to stare at the rolls of fat which swathed her body like a sari. She pulled the blankets over her—she had no sheets—and before going to sleep wondered if perhaps she had not gone too far? She had not really meant any of this to happen—as a child may feel who, setting light to a wastepaper basket to draw attention to himself, then has to watch his entire home go up in flames.

Susan woke at about two, afraid. She thought there was someone in the room. Then she was incensed because there wasn't. Somebody had obviously abandoned her. But who? She couldn't remember. She was lying on her back and found it difficult to breathe. She began to think she was immensely pregnant, and even when she moved her hands over her belly and found it flat as ever, she was not reassured. The feeling that there was a mountain beneath her breasts remained. The mountain, moreover, stirred and moved and heaved. William had thus once described his wife's pregnancy in a poem which he read aloud to Susan as they lay communicative after making love, and the image of the moving mountain still pursued her. Now, in the dark, Susan rolled up her eyes in anxiety: they peered into her brain and made her dizzy. She was pregnant. Something had gone wrong. She did not attribute her condition to a man—it had just happened. Or she had caught pregnancy like a disease from some other woman. Probably, through contact with William, from William's wife. She switched on the light, sat up, and felt more reasonable. 'I am Susan Pierce,' she told herself. 'Nothing is uncontrollable. Everything is controllable. There is nothing for me to be frightened of. I am not pregnant.' Now her reason was working again she felt quite lively. She wondered if perhaps women had a primitive group soul that linked them together. The pregnancy had been real enough; it had just turned out to be someone else's, that was all. Sympathy with her sex, she thought, could go too far. She must struggle against it.

In the next room Brenda slept voluptuously on the sofa dreaming of picnics in the grass, of elegant ruffled ladies and handsome peruked men: water tinkled from a fountain. A fish with her mother's face swam in the pool below. She lay on the grass and the earth moved to accommodate her limbs. She woke: she could not quite remember where she was or who she was. Presently she turned on the light and got out of bed and stood blinking, barefooted, and dressed in a pale-blue checked nightgown with a frill around the neck. The light woke the man on the floor, and he scrambled to his feet. Brenda's body, quite of its own volition, for her mind had not yet caught up with the events of the evening, made a kind of melting move towards him. But he took two pound notes from his pocket, handed them to her, bowed politely, and left. Brenda went and had a bath. She felt too humiliated to so much as cry.

In the morning they were all themselves again. Phyllis cooked Gerry's breakfast, with her face carefully made up, and composed into careful non-accusing lines. He ate heartily, and kissed her goodbye, for which she was grateful. Esther made herself a breakfast of porridge from a tin and evaporated milk, kipper from a plastic bag, already buttered, three Heinz tins called 'Junior Bacon and Egg Breakfast', toast, butter, marmalade, and coffee, to strengthen her after her illness. Then she began to feel sick again. Susan ate an apple, and some milk, took up her brush and painted. Brenda slept until eleven, and then blamed Susan for not waking her in time for her work as a receptionist in a Public Relations firm.

'I'm sorry,' said Susan, 'but I thought that now you'd started a career as a call-girl you would wish to give up your job.'

Brenda slammed the door and left, breakfastless.

All the same, they all went visiting that morning.

Esther went to visit a doctor; Phyllis went to visit Alan; Susan went to visit Peter; and Brenda rang up her mother and had lunch with her.

Esther's gynaecologist, when she went to see him, had changed. He was no longer the grey-haired respectable Englishman she remembered. He was bronzed, buoyant, slim-hipped, crew-cut, and wore a flowered shirt. The medical books that once had lined the walls had been swept away, and replaced by splodgy paintings.

'You've changed,' she said.

'One has to move with the times, Esther,' he said. 'These days London is a swinging city. Mini-skirted mothers give birth with cries of joy, not pain. Doctors—at any rate those not on the National Health—must train themselves to laugh, not commiserate. Now that we recognise that illness is self-induced, we must be brutal with our patients. The Medicine of Brutality is all the rage, and very profitable. *Erewhon* is upon us. The sick must go to prison and the criminals to hospital. What can I do for you? I warn you that many of my more elderly patients have transferred themselves elsewhere.'

'I was sick in the night,' said Esther, 'I am ill. Perhaps you should take it all away.'

'All what?'

'You know. Those parts inside me that I no longer use. I think they have fallen into decay and are poisoning me. Why else should I feel so sick all the time?'

'Because you are sickening yourself. Have you looked at yourself in the mirror lately?'

'Yes. Last night.'

'Then I suspect that that is why you are here. It is your guilt you wish to have excised, not your reproductive organs.'

'My guilt?'

'At so abusing the body God gave you. Correction,' he said, 'the body your parents gave you. You can't *like* being so fat.'

'I prefer it to other things, like being hungry. But I did not come here to discuss my size. I have a pain low down, and I feel sick all the time.'

'You make me feel sick too.' Having said it he smiled, seeming quite pleased with himself. Esther, feeling that in so freely indulging his rudeness he had achieved a lifetime's ambition, warmed to him just a little. 'You will have to lose some weight or I don't give twopence, not only for your reproductive organs, but for your life.'

'I'll tell you something,' she said, 'I don't give twopence for my life either. All the same, I don't wish to spend what remains of it in a state of nausea. Do you suggest I take my problems elsewhere?'

'My dear Esther,' he said, 'take them where you will. Wherever you go they will go too. I am merely pointing out that you wilfully aggravate matters by being so fat, and have done so as long as I have known you. You were a pretty girl, but much enveloped by blubber.'

'You live your sex life once. I chose to live mine emblubbered, that's all. And it's too late now, anyway.'

'I know your insides well, Esther, physically at any rate, but I have never been able to put my finger on the root of your spiritual discontent. Correction. Neurotic disorder.'

'Some people would have been better never born. I am one of them.'

'That is a silly thing to say.'

'It is what I believe. I should never have been born. I should have lived for ever in my mother's womb, where everything was dark and timeless, and I had no dimensions, and could not be seen, or judged. My mother, rot her, soon put an end to all that. She forced me out into the world, and I find it as hard to forgive her for this as she does me for fighting to stay inside, and giving her a bad labour. Things better should surely come after things good. And this is the whole of my discontent, that they don't. Since the moment I first found myself in this chilly, dangerous world things have gone from bad to worse. When I say I should never have been born, don't contradict me. Time goes so quickly, too. It frightens me. Once, for me, time was the measure of growth. Now it is the measure of decay.'

'If you are worrying about wrinkles I know an excellent cosmetic surgeon who can remove them. The eyelids can be tightened. That makes a lot of difference. There is nothing to be ashamed of in a woman wanting to go on looking young and attractive. Why not?'

'I came here to be cured of my sickness, not beautified. I don't care what I look like.'

'I have told you what to do. Stop sickening yourself.'

'Will you charge me for this consultation?'

'Most certainly.'

'But you haven't *done* anything.'

'My time is valuable, patients are queuing up to see me as they never used to when I was a more orthodox practitioner—and I have put up with your complaints.'

'I have friends to do that, free.'

'Oh yes. Mrs Frazer. I met her at dinner. I asked how you were and she replied, "Fat, and talkative". How is her bosom?'

'Bosom?'

'I assumed she would have told you. She went into considerable detail over the roast. She has had it lifted.'

'I didn't know she had any to lift.'

'That is not for me to say.'

'Crop the nose and lift the face,' said Esther. 'Tilt the breast and pin the ear—why do women do it?'

'To please men, I should think. All men, if they're in show-biz. One man, if they are neglected wives.'

'It is a degrading sport, this beauty hunting. Worse than chasing foxes. Undignified both for the doctors who do it, and the women who indulge in it.'

'Dignity is out of date—just look at me! My trousers are so tight I can scarcely sit down, and I am off to the Bahamas tomorrow. And surely, if a husband fancies his wife big-breasted, and the wife obliges, then the sum of human happiness has been increased, has it not?'

'Human sensation perhaps. Human happiness, no.'

'Don't delude yourself, they are the same thing.'

'It is true that Gerry Frazer likes large women,' said Esther. 'Or at any rate he claims to. I wonder why he ever married someone as skinny as Phyllis?'

'The change in his tastes may well accord with the change in him. Being fat now himself, he does not wish to court criticism and unkind comparisons.'

'You are really quite acute,' she said, 'in a dismal kind of way. You never used to be.'

'It is more profitable like this. Had you realised that infertility is a psychic, not a physical state?'

'Nothing surprises me,' she said, 'except doctors.'

'Aggression and obesity go together,' he said, and she wished she had never left her basement.

Phyllis rang Alan's office and was told he was in bed with flu. She called to see him, and sat by his bed.

'Poor darling Alan,' she said, 'I had to come. All alone with no one to look after you. Now tell me, what can I do?'

'You can leave me alone,' he said, but he was grateful to see her.

'You and Esther, you're as grumpy as a pair of pigs. You just can't get on without each other.'

'You've seen Esther?'

'Yes. Yesterday. No thanks to you, hiding her address like that. What are you trying to do to her? She's in trouble and she needs all the help she can get. Don't you care what happens to her?'

'No.'

'You only say that. When you've been married as long as you two have, of course you care.'

'Caring may be a habit, but it is not necessarily a good habit.'

'You've behaved very badly, Alan; she's very hurt and upset. I know how terribly bad I'd feel if Gerry got involved with his secretary.'

He raised his eyebrows at her.

'Marriage is a very hurtful business, I know,' she said in a small voice. 'At least it is for me, but there's no reason for you and Esther to fight. And I know you think I've got a nerve, interfering, but I do honestly want to see you both happy again. I admire Esther so much. She's everything I'm not. She's clever, and she's grown up. And it breaks my heart to see her like this.'

'I give you credit for your good intentions. I am afraid I am some-what rude. Times have been troublesome lately. Quite apart from any-thing else, the office bores me to hell, and Peter irritates me beyond belief. He has no idea of the seriousness of life: he is basically and deeply frivolous. It is Esther's fault. She bred cynicism in him. Wherever I look, I see nothing whatever to brighten my life.'

'There's your writing. That's a wonderful hobby to have. I wish Gerry was as clever as you.'

'Oh, yes,' he said with profound gloom, 'the novel.' He sank back into his pillows, as if struck by sudden feebleness. 'A hobby. Yes, I suppose that is what it was. How strange that I should have thought it to be the shaft of light which would illumine my whole life and give it meaning, and that in truth it is on a par with stamp-collecting and pigeon-fancying. There was a certain amount of confusion about the novel, to be frank. The agent attributed the wrong manuscript to me— the one he liked so much was written by a lady in Eccles. Mine, it turned out, he didn't like. It frightened him. He said it was cold and cruel and improper. Pornographic, even. I thought myself it was warm and friendly. How little one knows of oneself. Oh Phyllis, there must be something else in life than this?'

She was alarmed at such a question. 'Alan, I don't know what you're complaining about. You've got this divine home, and a clever wife who's a good cook, and a handsome clever son, and a good job and enough money, and why you suddenly want to spoil it all by taking up with a silly young girl who's just kinky for authors—'

'Who said so?'

'Esther.'

'Esther knows nothing about it.' He was cross.

'—because it's bound to upset everyone, isn't it? You should value what you've got and not go looking for something else all of a sudden. It's very immature of you. It's the way Gerry goes on, only he's like that all of the time, not just all of a sudden. And I can see you're upset about your novel, but people never do appreciate what's good, do they? The first thing you should do is go and ask Esther to come back. Then you can settle down again.'

'Why should I ask her back? She doesn't want to be here or she wouldn't have gone.'

'She's your wife.'

'You have this mystic faith in titles, Phyllis. It does you credit. No the home's broken up. Peter's gone. He lives during the week with crop-haired Stephanie. He's totally irresponsible and he expects me to pay his rent. He comes home at week-ends and sits doing his homework, and when he takes out his fountain pen packets of contraceptives fall out. He buys them with his pocket money. From a slot machine.'

'That's not irresponsible. That's responsible. He's a big boy now. He's a grown man. He's eighteen. It's not his fault if he's still at school. I expect he only does it to annoy you, anyway.'

'Perhaps he's not my son at all. How am I to know? I wasn't like that when I was his age. Only in my fantasies, not in real life.'

'Now you're being ridiculous.'

'Oh no I'm not. You don't know the half of it. There was a time in her life when Esther went mad. She cropped her hair, ate nothing but apples and went on the streets.'

'I don't believe you.'

'Well not quite the streets but the number of men visitors coming and going in her flat, it might as well have been the common pavement, and she lying in the gutter having it off with all and sundry.'

'Don't talk like that.'

'I'm sorry. Anyway, she calmed down and I accepted her back. But nothing she does surprises me any more. And why she should get in such a state because I like talking to my secretary and should so bitterly resent my feeble attempts to have a rewarding and pleasant relationship with another woman—it's not reasonable of her.'

'It didn't sound very platonic, the way Esther described it.'

'I never said it was platonic. But that was beside the point. Esther needed her freedom. When she got tired of it I had her back. I would have thought she could have afforded me the same courtesy and not left me here to die of influenza. I'll tell you another thing. Susan admired me. Esther never, in all her life, admired me. Esther is incapable of admiring a man.'

'She is so unhappy down there in her basement she would be ready to admire anyone.' Phyllis took off her little flowered hat and shook her curly hair free. 'And I'm sure she does admire you, Alan. How could anyone not? You're so clever and so good-looking. You have this kind of fine-boned sensitive face, and such deep eyes I think a woman could lose herself in them utterly. And you are so good at taking control of things. I do admire that in a man.'

'I suspect you,' said Alan. 'Why do you want Esther back here? Because of Gerry?'

She looked startled, and was too confused to reply.

'I know nothing about her and Gerry, mind you,' he went on, 'except I think Gerry must be out of his mind. Why can't he be happy with you? You're a proper feminine woman. I think the only one left in the entire world. You must excuse me. I feel weak. I have felt weak for a long time now. First it was lack of food, then it was lust, then it was literature, then it was Esther's hysteria, then Susan's neurotics, now it's flu. If it's not one thing it's another and it's a bit much. Everything suddenly boils over all at once, Phyllis, I am very weak and you are taking advantage of me.'

'Alan, what happened between Gerry and Esther?'

'So that's why you came to see me. Not because I was ill and not because you liked me but to get something out of me. I might have known. What difference does it make, Gerry and Esther, or Gerry and a dozen other women. None of it means a thing to him. One body or another, it's all the same.'

'Because Esther's my friend.'

'A fine friend. She'd sell you down the river a hundred times, the way she sold me. Why do you put up with Gerry? It's cold outside, Phyllis. Come into bed.'

Phyllis took off her flowered little-girl smock, and stood in her lacy stockings, her red brassiere and red suspender belt, by the bed. She had put on her best underwear for the visit. Alan, his eyes bright and his brow fevered, lay back on the pillows and watched.

'Everyone else does,' said Phyllis miserably, 'why shouldn't I?'

'Quite so,' said Alan. 'Those are my feelings exactly.' She took off what remained of her clothes and climbed into bed, where she lay inert and shivering.

'You are very cold,' he said. 'It's rather refreshing to encounter a woman like you.'

'You are very warm,' she said. 'I wish I wasn't so miserable. Why does Gerry get so much pleasure from going to bed with other women? If you don't feel affectionately towards someone, there's no pleasure in it, is there? At least that's what the books say. Perhaps he just manages to feel affectionate towards lots and lots of people. I've never been to bed with anyone in my entire life except Gerry and I don't understand what all the fuss is about. I am a frigid woman, you see. Unless it is that I have never met the right man. You are welcome to any comfort I can give you,' she added, lying more stiffly than ever.

'Please, please feel affectionately towards me,' he moaned. 'Someone has to.'

She did indeed, at that, feel a flicker of affection.

'You said I was a proper feminine woman. What did you mean by that?'

'You are gentle and docile and slim and pretty and neat, like a doll. You endure things. You don't try to be anything, ever, except what you are. You have pretty little eyes that never see more than they should. You are not in the least clever and you never say anything devastating. I should have married you.'

She began to feel quite cheerful.

'I even think I could make you happy,' he said, at which such feeling overwhelmed her that she turned towards him, and he clasped her, or rather clutched her, as if he was a drowning man and she the straw he sought for. She shut her eyes and pretended he was Gerry. There was very little difference between them, if she put her mind to believing it. She was pleased, anyway, to be the means of his pleasure, being grateful to him for his kind words. Afterwards a terrible thought occurred to her.

'You never actually *said* that Gerry and Esther made love.'

'No, I don't suppose I did.'

'Did they?'

'I don't know and I don't care. Do you?'

'You led me to believe they had. I think you were plotting to get me into bed with you.'

He considered. 'It's possible.'

'That was despicable of you.' She pulled away from him so that she no longer touched him, and immediately felt bereft. She hoped he would move nearer to her, but he did not do so.

'I think it would be despicable of you to make love to me simply because you wanted to be revenged on your husband.'

'It's not much revenge,' she said, and sounded disappointed. 'It doesn't add up to much, does it. People talk and talk about it, but in itself it's such an unimportant thing.'

He felt his temperature rising. He began to shiver.

'You bloody women,' he said, 'you're all the same. You're never satisfied.'

She got out of bed and dressed. He did not watch her. His head ached.

'It's not your fault,' she said, charitably, when she felt respectable again and had sprayed herself with scent. 'It's me. I'm frigid, you see. I was only trying to help you, and cheer you up. And really I enjoyed it very much.'

'I'm not a cream tea,' he groaned.

'We shouldn't really have done it,' she went on. 'How can I look Esther in the eye? I'll never be able to see her again, and I'm supposed to be calling this afternoon. Oh what will I do? What have I done?'

'Next time,' was all he said, 'please choose another man to inflict your frigidity upon.'

She cried, and said, 'I thought love was meant to make people happy. I was only trying to help.'

'Of course,' said Peter to Susan, 'Father is very upset. He is insanely jealous of me. It is often a problem when middle-aged men see their sons grow up and begin to have sex lives, and with Father the experience is proving quite traumatic. Apart from the length of your hair, you see, you are remarkably like Stephanie; who, again, is like my mother in her thinner moments. I think this was what attracted him to you in the first place. If I can sleep with Stephanie, why couldn't he sleep with you? It was unfortunate that Mother took it so seriously. If she had had any insight she would have understood him, and stayed, and waited for it to blow over. But again, when sons leave home, women tend to despair. What is there left for them? I am afraid the whole thing is my fault. Men have a menopause too, did you know? I think Father is suffering from it. Why exactly did you feel you had to come to see me?' He was dressed in black from head to foot. He was doing his homework. His school-books lay open on the purple velvet settee.

'Because I didn't want you to hold any of this against me. When two people fall in love it quite often happens that someone gets hurt. It is one of the tragedies of living.'

'Why should you care what I think?'

'Because you're of my own generation, I suppose.' Her long legs were crossed and she smoked a cigarette from a holder. Her nails were long and beautifully manicured.

'It's extraordinary,' he said, 'how like Stephanie you are. You would have made a smashing step-mother. In an incestuous kind of way.'

'I think that thought occurred to your father,' she said. 'It troubled him. It was one of the reasons—'

He looked doubtful. 'Did you really get as far as that? I don't think he really ever contemplated divorce. Men don't break marriages lightly. That's one of the reasons I'm not married to Stephanie. That, and me being at school. Have I said something wrong? You're looking all miserable.'

'Oh no,' she said, 'it's all right. It's just I take things seriously and I don't understand how other people can't. I am an artist, you see, and everything appears more real to me than it does to other people. And being more real is more painful. Your father found reality painful too, I think. He is a very sensitive person, in many ways, but confused, I suppose. You are very like him, but you have not been maltreated and twisted by life, as he has. You don't think women are things, do you? You believe they are people, don't you?'

'Of course.' He looked surprised. 'Didn't he?'

'No, not really. It is a common complaint with men of his generation. I keep having to batter away at their impregnability. It's a kind of compulsion. It never works. They still think I'm just a piece of decoration on a birthday cake, and get very angry if I so much as open my mouth to say anything except how marvellous they are. That's what I like about artists and poets and painters. They believe women are people. They don't mind getting hurt. I don't mind getting hurt, either. Your father hurt me.'

'I don't know why you take him so seriously. He's so old.'

'He's very fond of you. He thinks the world of you. That's because you look so much like him. He's a very good-looking man, you know. And very clever. But it's all no use. He's been destroyed by years of petit-bourgeois living: after all he's an ad-man. You'll never be an ad-man, will you?'

'I certainly hope not.'

'Because it destroys the soul, doesn't it? Your father says you write poetry. Can I see some?'

'I'd be delighted,' he said, blushing. 'You're a friend of William Macklesfield's, aren't you? He's one of my heroes. Poetry seems so simple when he writes it. So familiar, somehow.'

'He's a family man,' she said, not without bitterness. 'All the same, I know him well. I think I contribute something to his work. I wish I was more of a family woman. I get very tired of living the way I do, sometimes.'

'Perhaps you've never met the right man?' He was eager. 'I mean honestly, Dad wouldn't be right for you at all. He's much too old, and anyway he's married to Mother, so how could he have a whole-hearted relationship with you? I'm sure he would have if he could have, but being married, how could he? You mustn't let it upset you. You're not like Stephanie; she doesn't get upset by anything. I don't think that's right in a woman. I get the feeling I'm being used, if a girl's too cheerful about things. One welcomes a little intensity; I mean it's easy to be intense about politics, but a girl should be intense about sex too, to my way of thinking. I think the better of you for being upset, really I do.'

'All the other men I've met,' she said, 'only like me when I'm laughing. If I cry they go away. I suppose if one was married they wouldn't be able to so much. It is very refreshing to meet a man who doesn't mind one being miserable. Perhaps it's because you're so young. As you grow older and feel more like crying yourself you may be less well able to bear it.'

He put his arm around her, conscious that here his father's arm had been before him. He kissed her forehead.

'What about Stephanie?' she asked. 'I don't want to cause any more trouble. I'm older than you. I ought to be responsible.'

'She understands,' he said, steering her towards the couch. 'She is not at all possessive. All she ever does is laugh and cut her hair. Anyway she doesn't get back from work until seven. I get back from school at half past four, unless there's games. I'm in the school cricket team. It's a frightful bore but one can't let them down.'

'Thank God,' she said, succumbing, 'thank God you're not married. I can't stand married men. I can't stand competing with their wives.'

Under his weight, the unwanted gift pregnancy that still haunted her was beautifully flattened out, like a steak under a meat mallet. She pretended he was William Macklesfield. There was very little difference between them, if she put her mind to it. She was pleased, anyway, that someone so young, so handsome, so much his father's son, should afford her so much pleasure.

'You're not doing this,' he asked anxiously, 'to be revenged on my father or anything?'

'Revenged? Why should I want to be revenged?'

'Because he didn't take you seriously.'

'You've got it all wrong,' she said, 'it was I who didn't take him seriously.' And she crept under him again as if to hide.

'If you ask me,' said Brenda's mother, cutting through a *mille feuille* with a silver cake fork in the tea-rooms at the top of Dickens and Jones, 'inside your friend Susan, struggling to get out, is a dumpy little woman in a check apron with a rolling pin in the pocket. It is the only thing about her which reconciles me to your sharing that flat. And of course the knowledge that you are a sensible girl and aren't going to do anything silly. It is all talk with your friend Susan, all this sex and emancipation and art. It is quite obvious she just wants to be married but no one will ask her so she has to make do with free love. Who would want a girl like that, anyway?'

'Oh Mother,' said Brenda desperately, staring round the tables where well-dressed, middle-aged ladies with crocodile shoes and becoming hair-styles nibbled and sipped. 'Everything is so different nowadays. You don't understand.'

'Nothing changes. Women want to get married and have babies just as they always did. But your generation hasn't got the self-discipline ours had. My life with your father wasn't all roses, but I didn't complain. I stuck it out and I was very sorry when he died.'

'Well, his salary cheque stopped coming, didn't it. That was really the only difference I noticed. We never saw him.'

'Now why should you say a thing like that? London life makes you very rude. I don't imagine young men have changed so much since my day that they appreciate rudeness in a girl.'

'But Mother I don't much care what men think of me. No, don't look like that. I'm not a lesbian, it's all right. I just think it's as important what I think of men as what they think of me.'

'Well it's not, is it? Women have always tried to make themselves attractive to men, and you're not going to change a thing like that in a hurry. Look around you. All the women nicely groomed and attractive and good-looking, and the men no better than fat slugs, for the most part, or skinny runts. Unshaved and smelly as often as not. They get away with everything, men. They can do every disgusting thing they like and no one ever says a thing. Today is the seventh anniversary of your father's death.'

Her voice had risen, embarrassing Brenda, and there was a mad look in her eye with which Brenda was familiar, and with which she had lived for many years, and which was likely to lead to broken mirrors and china and her mother lying on her back raving amidst the debris. So the daughter, who never really gave up hope of extracting some soupçon of wisdom and enlightenment from the mother about the nature of true love, decided that now was not the time to seek it. She changed the subject to cream cakes and after tea they went down to the underwear department on the third floor and bought see-through nighties and frilly suspender belts for each other.

* * *

Presently Phyllis overcame her scruples sufficiently to visit Esther again. Esther lumbered to the door in her dressing-gown and having let Phyllis in, retreated back to bed.

'I am feeling rather sick,' she said.

'I am not surprised,' said Phyllis.

'Everyone says that. The trouble is, if I stop eating I feel even sicker than I do if I don't stop eating. I will have to learn to live with nausea, I suppose. I have done you a great wrong, Phyllis.'

'What do you mean? What have I done?' asked Phyllis, mis-hearing.

'You have done nothing. What are you feeling so guilty about? I have wronged you by trying to stop you grieving, by denying that you had any cause to grieve. You may grieve for all the wrong reasons, but grieve you do. Grief is a lovely word and a lovely thing. It heals, as resentment cannot. Grief must be admitted and lived through, or it turns into resentment, and continues to bother you for the rest of your life, rearing its depressed little head at all the wrong moments, so that one Sunday tea-time at the old lady's home you will unexpectedly begin to cry into your toasted tea-cake, and the nurses will say "Poor Mrs Frazer, that's the end", and will move you into the senile ward, when the truth of the matter is quite different. It's not senility, but grief grown uncheckable with age. Myself, I cry now and eat now, so as not to cry later, when it is yet more dangerous. I shall make a very cheerful old lady.'

'You're feeling better today, then,' said Phyllis.

'Better in my mind but sicker in my body. I am angry with you.'

Phyllis turned pale. 'Why?'

'It has come to my notice that you had your breasts enlarged.'

'I didn't want you to know. Not enlarged, anyway. Tip-tilted, is more like it.'

'Why did you keep it from me?'

'You're so odd about some things. I've done nothing to be ashamed of.'

'You ought to be ashamed. It was a degrading thing to do. To allow your body to be tampered with by a man, for the gratification of a man, conforming to a wholly masculine notion of what a woman's body ought to be. That you, a decent woman, should offer yourself up as a martyr to the great bosom-and-bum mystique; should pander to the male attempt to relate not to the woman as a whole, but to portions of the female anatomy; should be so seduced by masculine values that you allow your breasts to be slit open and stuffed with plastic. They are, let me remind you, mammary glands, milk producers.'

'Sometimes you are quite disgusting.'

'The truth is always disgusting to people like you. On the day you let that happen to you, Phyllis, you became less of a woman, for all your brand new bubbly bosom. Didn't it hurt?'

'Yes.'

'Serve you right.'

'I don't understand your attitude at all. I like to look nice. My clothes look better for a bit of bosom. And anyway you're always saying how awful it is to be a woman.'

'Never! It would be perfectly acceptable being a woman if only men didn't control the world. If only it were possible to accept their seed to create children, yet feel obliged neither to accept their standards nor their opinion of womankind, which is, let's face it, conditioned by fear, resentment and natural feelings of inferiority.'

'It's better when you eat than when you talk.'

'Why haven't you and Gerry got any children?'

Phyllis wondered whether perhaps Alan had made her pregnant, and decided, for no rational reason, that he had not.

'That wasn't an attack,' said Esther, 'I simply wondered. There is no reason for a woman to have children if she doesn't want to. But if your reason for not is the preservation of your figure for Gerry's benefit then I shall, indeed, think the less of you for it.'

Phyllis blushed, which made her look very pretty.

'Do you intend to go on like this for ever,' asked Esther, 'spending your entire life attempting to placate that fat selfish bully of a husband?'

'I love my husband. It's a pity you don't love yours a little more, letting him lie there ill with flu. You can talk and talk about woman's rights, but it doesn't seem to make you very happy. And you tease me about everything, and you won't even tell me about you and Gerry. It's not fair.'

'Nothing happened between me and Gerry. I sent him home.'

Phyllis was put out by this news, hoping now for Esther's misbehaviour to justify her own.

'I've only ever been to bed with Gerry,' she said.

'I went mad once,' said Esther. 'It was very interesting. I got very depressed after my father died and drank a bottle of bleach. It didn't kill

me but I couldn't swallow for months and I got quite thin, and I left
Alan to find out what the world was like—and do you know what? It
was full of men. So I went back to Alan. And do you know what?
Alan's no different from all the others. You live with them for years,
you clean and cook for them, you talk to them, you listen to them, you
share your children with them, and you achieve nothing. They are still
apart from you, suspicious of you, wishing and wishing you could be a
piece of docile flesh, no more. Juliet was trying to tell me that, I think.
She didn't mind about it. She didn't expect anything else. But we middle-class women are brought up with notions of partnership in marriage and that's why we all go mad and end up in bed with the plumber.
It's time to get on with the story.'

3 On the twelfth day of the diet Esther sat at her kitchen table and
drank black coffee. Her head was dizzy and her hands trembled.
Juliet sat opposite her and cleaned a copper saucepan, after a fashion.

'You've got to give them a good time haven't you,' said Juliet. 'You
can't grudge them their rights. They've got a right to expect certain
things. You-know-what, and a hot meal when they come home from
work. That keeps them quiet, and they don't interfere. What more do
you want?'

'It's not as easy as that.'

'You haven't got enough to do that's your trouble. You let things get
on top of you. I'm sorry for the husbands in all the houses I do for. All
these *thoughts* going on around them all the time. I'm never idle, that's
what it is. I'm always at it.'

'There doesn't seem anything to do any more, except fill in time.
Once I had a garden but I filled it in with concrete because it was
neater, and because I just didn't seem able to grow things any more. I'd
lost my touch.'

'You're not as young as you were. I mean, who of us is?'

'My world is so small. My body is shrivelling. Perhaps that's why I
need to be fat.' She held out her arm for Juliet to see. 'You see? I am
used to seeing my arm as it was when I was young—it was white and
firm. Now is is greyer, and flabby. I am going to die, Juliet.'

'Aren't we all? I don't know what the fuss is about. You should do a
little more, think a little less. I'm never idle, that's my secret. I'm always
busy.'

Esther raised her eyebrows in disbelief, and unfortunately Juliet saw.

'I should eat a biccy if I was you. It's silly, starving yourself like this.'

'I've lost ten pounds.'

'That's not much, is it. For a person your size. You could never tell. I hope you don't mind me saying so, but you could just never tell.'

'You could do with a bit off yourself, Juliet.'

'The difference between you and me is, of course, that I've never had any trouble with boys. If you start off popular you don't really care ever after. It didn't seem to matter what I looked like, they were always there, queuing up. I don't suppose it was like that for you, what with your size and all.'

'I don't do too badly, thank you, Juliet.'

Juliet held the saucepan under the tap, rubbed at it with Brillo, and talked over her shoulder to Esther.

'I can't seem to shift the stains on this pan. I think it's finished, Mrs Sussman, I really do. It needs throwing out.'

'No,' said Esther, with some passion. 'It is not finished.'

'All right. All right.'

'Old things ought to be cherished and looked after.'

'Throw them out. No use to anyone. Old ugly pans are like old ugly people. Once the children are grown up, they're no use to anyone.'

'Children always need their parents.'

'What, your Peter? He doesn't need anyone. Except a vicar to get him married. He's off now, anyway.'

'Off? What do you mean?'

'Your Peter. Sharing with Stephanie.'

'What are you talking about?'

'I heard him on the phone. Didn't he tell you? He's going to share that girl's flat. If she is a girl, with that hair. I don't mean to worry you, but I should find out. You can't have him growing up a pouf, can you.'

'Of course he told me,' lied Esther, her hands trembling even more. 'I don't know that it will come to anything, though. You know what children are, making plans.'

'Children!' said Juliet. 'I don't think you've taught him proper respect for women, that's the trouble. You'll be a grandmother any minute if you're not careful, six times over in the same month.'

'You're exaggerating.'

'A big boy like that, it's very unsettling in the house. The sooner he's on his own the better. For you, and Mr Sussman too. It puts ideas in the head, somehow.'

'I dare say.'

'This house is getting like a morgue. You can feel it when you come in through the door. It gives me the shivers.'

'I always used to bake in the mornings. Everything used to smell nice and homely. But it's wrong to cook. It makes us fat. Nothing I do is much use to anyone, is it?'

'Well, you said it, not me.'

Esther's hand crept out to the plate of biscuits which had been put out for Juliet. Then she drew it back.

'You don't even nag much any more,' said Juliet. 'You'll lose your standards and then where will you be? What'll you have left then?'

Esther's hand reached for the biscuit again. This time it got there. She put the biscuit to her lips. Juliet whirled round.

'I saw you! I'll tell him! I'll tell him what you've been up to. I saw you!' She was half-joking, half-malevolent.

'Get out of my house,' said Esther.

'But I haven't finished yet.'

'Get out of my house and don't come back,' said Esther, who after all had said too much to Juliet, and having distorted the balance of the relationship, now had no option but to finish it completely. 'I'm sick of you and your insolence and your spying. I'll do the work myself. Coming here, taking advantage of me day after day, listening to me, mocking me. Taking my money, giving me nothing in return—nothing—'

She was by now pale with anger. Juliet carefully and slowly took off her apron, as someone who has won a long-sought victory, and left. When she had gone, Esther leaned her head on the table and cried. She rang Alan for comfort but was told he had not been in the office that day.

'I don't understand why you have such trouble with your staff,' said Phyllis. 'Mine always stay. Yours always get out of hand.'

'It's because I can never see why other people should do my dirty work, and so I am apologetic about it. Or else I talk too much. There are so few people to talk to. When I rang Alan to tell him how horrible Juliet was and found he wasn't there I wished Juliet was back again so I could tell her all about it.'

'Where was he?'

'Well where do you think he was? He was with that silly slut Susan.'

'What's the matter with you?' Susan asked Brenda with some impatience. Brenda, back from work, lay on her back on the bed instead of cooking dinner.

'I am in love. I was too tired before to notice but now I know I am. It is distinguished by a strange breathless feeling under the ribs; a kind of pattering fluttering of feeling. I suppose if one was pregnant and the baby kicked it would feel like that. It is not a very pleasant feeling but it is very important. I can see that it would lead one to do all kinds of drastic things, like murder and divorce. It will only ever be still when I lie in a bed with my arms around him.'

'Who do you happen to be in love with?'

'That man who was here last night. Why should I have this feeling about a man I can't even speak to? It is not the union of two minds. Could it be the union of two bodies? Susan, why did he give me two pound notes and not his telephone number?'

'Because that's what they charge. How was he to know the difference? He could only judge you on your actions. You had no words to explain that you do not make a habit of such behaviour, if indeed you don't, which I am not in a position to know. Didn't you hand it back?'

'No. It was all too sudden. And I was grateful that he had given me something else. Besides himself, if you see what I mean. And then he was gone and I'm all upset and I want to see him again and if I don't I think I shall die. Tonight I will go to the pub and wait for him. I tried to talk to my mother but she had one of her mad fits right in the middle of Dickens and Jones and I nearly died of embarrassment. What I don't understand is why I should feel like this about this man when I haven't about any of the others. Actually there were only two, to tell you the truth, they were both very suitable, chosen by my mother. Perhaps that's why I couldn't fancy them. And they talked too much. The more they talked the more I saw them for what they were and I despised them. Isn't that terrible?'

'I expect they were too nice to you. It's easier to love people when they're unpleasant to you. You are coming on, I must say. A little suffering will do you a world of good. Let's have a drink. I saw Alan's son today.' Susan confided this almost shyly.

'You didn't! You have got a nerve.' They drank their sherry with relish.

'Well it annoys me the way men will try to get you all totally involved and at the same time try and confine you to a tiny part of their lives. If you're involved, they should be involved too, it's only reasonable. I don't understand why Peter's turned out so marvellous with such screw-ball parents.'

'How is he marvellous?'

'He is lovely. He is so simple. He is divine. I always knew he would be. Alan kept his picture on his desk. He's only eighteen and already he lives with this girl. He's much too young for me. Such lack of complication is a bit overpowering but what a body. What a body. One could become hooked on mere flesh and bones—had you thought of that? But of course you have. It's your forte. Perhaps you are right and a silent man is the only truly desirable man there is. From now on, everything's going to be different.'

'I think it's horrible. It's like incest. First father, then son.'

'Not at all. I find I do hope he tells his dad, all the same. Is that horrible of me?'

'Yes. What happened between you and Alan to make you so angry?'

'I will tell you. Perhaps if I can get it straight in my mind it will stop me feeling so awful. Except I don't know if I'm feeling awful about Alan or about William. I didn't think I cared about William but I find I miss him. He was so good to talk to, and we got on so well, and we had so much in common, and I don't understand why that silly stupid cow of a wife of his should have him just because she breeds all the time. What is this magic in reproduction? One gets it all the time. My wife, my child. My child's birthday. My wife's birthday. Someone's ill. Someone's speech day. It's Christmas. It's Whitsun. All the time this bloody fucking father-child husband-wife obsession. Can't men just exist by themselves for more than an hour at a time? Why do they have to have their appendages?'

'Then you shouldn't go with married men, should you?'

'You know what Peter's got? A cricket team. He hasn't got a wife. He hasn't got a child. But already, a cricket team. Sometimes I wish I was a lesbian.'

'I've told my mother I wasn't a lesbian. That's the worst fate she could imagine for me. Why do old people feel so strongly about these things?'

'It upsets them to think they may have lived their lives in error. That they could have had fun, and didn't. They had children instead.' She stood in front of the mirror, scraping back her blonde hair against her head, so that her cheekbones appeared bony and strong.

'Sometimes you remind me of a man.'

'Sometimes I feel like a man.'

'I wonder why my mother thinks there's a dumpy little hausfrau inside you trying to get out? I think it's more like a footballer.'

'What a horrible thing to say.'

'Which? The hausfrau or the footballer?'

'Both. I think such fantasies reflect badly upon both you and your mother. They say nothing about me—it simply indicates that your mother has lesbian tendencies and that you are kinky for brutish men. We already have evidence for both these suppositions, of course.'

'I don't think I like sharing a flat with you. All I want is time to think about how I love this man, and someone to talk to about him, and all I get from you is cynical, complicated, upsetting talk.'

'You needn't think I like sharing a flat with you, either. I wish William was here. William is the only person who has ever understood and appreciated me.'

'Nobody,' said Alan, 'has ever really appreciated me.' He lay on his back on the bed on the thirteenth day of the diet; the same bed where later Brenda was to lie and suffer, in her headlong flight from reality, the pangs of true love. Susan was in her artist's smock and stood at the easel with a paintbrush in her hand. 'All my life nobody has ever really appreciated me. All my life I have been used. My mother used me; she would dress me up in the same spirit as she dressed her poodle, in a little fur coat and red bootees, and take me out for walks. If you have a dog you never lack friends, she would say. Bloody beast, it nearly bit my nose right off. It's never been the same. It has this bump in the middle. Deformed.'

'It seems a very straight nose to me.'

'Do you think so? It's a funny thing, Peter has this same bump in his nose. What do you think that proves?'

'That he's your son, I suppose.'

'I don't mean that, I mean it would either imply that that bloody animal didn't in fact damage my nose to the degree I have always believed, or that Lysenko was right.'

'Lysenko?'

'Inheritance of acquired characteristics. You are fairly ignorant of facts, if nothing else. You are probably wise to be so. My father used me as a repository for useless information. What is the capital of Terra del Fuego, he would ask, or how many pennies would you have to put on the top of St Paul's in order to reach the moon. I don't know, I'd say, thus enabling him to pass the answer on to me—and make room in his own brain for some other piece of newer, fresher information he was anxious to acquire. Why, when I have made love to you, do I talk so much?'

'I like listening.'

'Esther doesn't listen. Esther doesn't appreciate me. She doesn't appreciate me in bed or out of it. Then she makes a fuss because I don't make love to her. But it's not love she wants, it's her rights.'

He had never talked about Esther to her before. Susan felt encouraged. It seemed possible that at last a man was going to abandon wife, family, home and all for sheer love of her—and think his world well lost for sake of Susan Pierce. Then, and only then, she felt, could she begin to live. She began to apply paint and became so interested in the process she almost forgot all about him.

'She was most unsympathetic about my writing,' he went on. 'She didn't want me to write. She didn't want me to express myself. She didn't say much but she exuded hostility into the air. I would wonder what she did want from me. She has some money of her own, you know.'

'Is that why you married her?'

'Certainly not.' He was shocked. 'She was a very pretty, plump, messy, intelligent, cultivated girl from a good middle-class family. I don't know why she married me—my father was a non-commissioned officer in the Indian army; we had pretensions but no style. She had style but no pretensions. I thought myself very lucky. We were both at art school. We were both trying to escape from our backgrounds.'

'And did you?'

'I did. I don't know about Esther. There was too much money in her family. Anyone can escape from class. Money is a harder conditioning. I lived on hers for a time. She's never forgiven me. But why did she offer? She said I should stay at home and paint, and she'd pay the bills. I tried for a full year. And do you know what? I didn't paint a thing. We spent too much time drunk or in bed. The situation was too humiliating, you see, for either of us to be anything or anywhere else. It's a year I prefer to forget. Then Peter was born and I went into advertising and we settled down. Yet although now I earn a lot of money she still believes that it's she who keeps me. She believes this not with her mind but with her feelings. That initial outrage on her femininity was too great. Yet she insisted, she insisted, that I rape her finer feelings. Why? You are a woman, can you tell me?'

She felt so like crying at this simple statement of fact that she could not reply. He did not notice, but went on talking.

'I think that women are determined to suffer at the hands of men. They will manipulate every situation in the world to ensure that they are in the right and the man is in the wrong. Show me a wronged woman and I will show you a baffled man, who wants no more than to eat, sleep, make love and procreate, and can't understand what all the fuss is about. That's what I like about you.'

'What?' she asked in alarm.

'You don't suffer. Not really. You pretend to for the sake of appearances but you are more like a man at heart. You take your pleasures simply and your relationships lightly.'

'Then I am afraid,' she said, 'that you are a homosexual at heart.' She put down her brush and sat with her head in her hands.

'Don't get upset. I intended it as a compliment and it in no way offends me that you should level accusations of homosexuality at me, since it is so patently untrue. I am a simple, natural man, and you are very beautiful, and let us face it, very easy.'

'Why don't you just go home to your wife?'

'I shall, presently when I am ready. I have just noticed that pipe on the mantelpiece. Does William the poet smoke a pipe?'

'Yes.'

'What a pretty domestic picture it makes in its arty kind of way. William's on one side of the fire with his head full of words and you on the other with your head full of symbols. Uniting, no doubt, on the hearth-rug from time to time. A pity you two don't have children. They might grow up to rule the world. But then of course William already has a wife, hasn't he, and prefers to have his children in wed-lock. And I dare say maternity would slow you down in your headlong career through the marriages of other men.'

'You have no right to talk to me in such terms. I asked William to go the day I met you. What more do you want? What sort of person do you think I am?'

'An easy lay.' He spoke sullenly, and they were silent for a bit.

'I am glad you're jealous,' she said presently.

'I'm not jealous. Why should I be jealous? Just get that fucking pipe out of my sight. You shouldn't keep other people's phallic symbols on the mantelpiece.'

She broke the pipe in half and put it on the fire and they were happy, after a fashion, for a while.

'Is the bulb growing yet?' he asked. He had bought her an expensive lily as a present. They had planted it together in a pot with some potting compost. She watered it lovingly but it showed no sign of green. The dull earth remained flat and undisturbed.

'No.'

'I'm afraid you forget to water it.'

'I don't forget. I water it faithfully but nothing happens. I haven't got green fingers.'

'Neither have I. Esther has, or used to have. After she ran away she had the back garden concreted over. She said it was tidier.'

'Ran away?'

'Never mind. You can't hold against people the things they do when they're mad. I wish she hadn't done that to the garden. I like looking at flowers, even though they seem to wilt if I so much as touch them. Go on painting. I like to sit here while you paint. I wonder why Esther couldn't bear me to paint? She would never leave me alone. She was forever offering me cups of coffee and biscuits and delicious new dishes. It was hardly surprising I got nothing done. When I was writing my book I locked it away but I left the key where she could find it. I wonder if she looked? I would write more and more extreme things; things that I knew would annoy her more than anything, to try and provoke her into taking some notice, but I don't know whether she even looked. When it's published she'll have to take notice, won't she. She'll have to read it then. Other people will force her into it.'

'How could you bear to live all those years without love?'

'I never said I didn't love Esther,' he said in some alarm. 'I do. I always have. She's part of my life. She's Peter's mother. The happiest time in my life was when Peter was a very little boy; we made our contacts with each other through him. A smile each to each above the tiny head—you know the sort of thing. But they were real smiles, you wouldn't know about that. Parenthood is a whole dimension of life which is meaningless to you.'

'You reproach me with having no children. But yet you wouldn't father a child on me. It's not fair.'

'Why do women always want things to be fair, I wonder. Nothing's fair. And I wasn't reproaching you, either. You have to be brave, mind you, to be a childless, husbandless woman. Women are only considered to exist through merit of their relationships. I admire you for being so brave.'

'It's very sad,' she said forlornly, 'that I should like and admire you so much as a person, and that you should like and admire me, I sometimes think, only as a female body. I thought for a time you were a serious kind of man, who could appreciate all of me and not just a bit of me. I don't want to be wrong about you. Don't make me be. You have been tied down in this hideous marriage of yours for so long I don't think you know what you're doing any more, or thinking, or saying, or feeling. I want to save you. I want to rescue you.'

'I don't want to discuss my marriage with you, Susan. Why do you insist? It will do you no good and only upset us both.'

'Because you've got to. You can't go on like this, living with someone who doesn't appreciate you. You need to be encouraged and loved and admired, and all your wife does is stultify every natural wholesome feeling you've got, until you're so full of defences you're just not capable of feeling properly any more.'

'I don't know why you have such a high opinion of me. Esther, who knows me better, has a very different view. I am her tame, despicable ad-man.'

'But that's what she's tried to make you. She seeks to despise you.'

'And you don't?'

'No.'

'I wish I could believe it. I say terrible things to you sometimes. Why do you put up with it? Other women wouldn't.'

'You try to drive me away, I know, because then everything would be simple and easier for you. But it's not what you really want.'

'I want food,' he said. 'I want pie and chips and HP sauce, the kind of food we had when I was a little boy. I can't raise my sights above my stomach. I'm sorry. I know I should, but really I can't take anything seriously but food.'

'Stop trying to get out of it. You've got to make some kind of decision. It's important. It's the turning point of your life. Your last chance.'

'Come here,' he said, 'body.'

Laying her on the bed he turned her unclothed body this way and that, and pumped her limbs here and there, penetrating every likely orifice that offered itself to his view. He slapped and bit her, pulled her breasts and tore her hair. It afforded no pleasure at all and she suffered a mounting sense of shock and outrage. This was not what she had meant at all when she embarked upon her career of cheerful sexual freedom. She cried, which interested him, but he did not desist. She was half on the bed, half on the floor, while Alan paused, searching his memory for details of vaguely remembered adolescent reading, when William let himself into the room. They covered themselves, separately, with blankets, and Susan flung herself weeping into William's arms. He put her in a chair, unmoved, and stroked his neat beard.

'I left my pipe,' he said. 'Where is it?'

'I threw it away,' she said. 'I'm sorry. He made me. Oh William, make him go away. He's being so horrible to me.'

'Good,' he said. 'You had no right to get rid of my pipe. One way and another you are no better than an animal. I am sorry I disturbed you at your antics. Pray continue. I am just going.'

'Oh don't go away. Don't leave me with him. Why did you go away when I asked you to? I didn't really want you to. We were so happy together, weren't we? Please don't leave me. Not now.'

'You've never cared twopence for anyone in your entire life,' said William, 'and I'll tell you something else. You're a lousy painter. Go back to your ad-man. You deserve each other. I hope you take better care of his property than you did of mine.' He nodded to Alan. 'Goodday.'

He left. Presently Alan laughed. Susan continued to weep.

'I'm sorry,' Alan said. 'But really I feel much better. You have a marvellous body, did you know?'

'I don't care about my body,' she said. 'What about me?'

'It's time you got married.'

She looked at him, instant hope mingling in her brain like instant coffee in boiling milk, but he shook his head at her and went back to his wife.

'Why do you bring me to life,' she cried out after him, 'if only to kill me again?'

'It's terrible to be used like a pound of butter,' said Susan to Brenda, 'because that's what he did. I won't go into details, you're too young, but he went all the way through the book of rules, bending me and him in every possible direction. What has love got to do with rules? Or positions?'

'If you want to be loved,' said Brenda piously, 'you have to love. If you had loved him enough you wouldn't have minded. You would have been glad to have afforded him some pleasure.'

'It wasn't anything to do with pleasure or with sex. It was just all his miserable rage and hatred coming out; he was humiliating me on purpose.'

'Do you think he's like that with his wife?'

'I am afraid not, with her no doubt he is more than reverent. That makes it worse. I was prepared to take him seriously and he was determined to treat me like a whore. If he had managed to have a decent relationship with me he might have been saved. Now he will have to be a dandruff shampoo man for the rest of his life. It's his loss, not mine. I learned about him in time. I shall never marry him. And it wasn't only what he did, it was what he said. In the morning his words were still all over me, like thorns.'

'You still haven't told me what made you leave Alan,' Phyllis was saying to Esther at about the same time. Nausea held Esther like a rapist's arms. She still ate, on the principle that she might as well give in and enjoy it, but the food in her mouth seemed offensive, and her very words tasted disagreeable. Phyllis stood at the stove stewing apples for her friend, having a vague notion that stewed apples had therapeutic powers. 'I can understand that when you go on a diet you would disturb all kinds of things you didn't know about, like shifting a heavy wardrobe and watching the little creatures scuffle away, and finding old beads and letters you'd forgotten about buried in the fluff. But wasn't being married to Alan something to cling to? I would have thought it was the one positive thing you had, being a wife. How could you ever know you were right to do such a thing?'

'I left Alan once before. That time it was easy. It was a positive act. I wanted sex, and life, and experience. I wanted things. I was young. I could hurt and destroy and not worry. I had excuses. This time it was different. I did it because the state I was in seemed intolerable, not because I hoped for anything better. And yes, it is true that this time I have been conscious of a sense of sin, not against Alan, but against the whole structure of society. It is a sin against Parent Teachers' Associations and the Stock Exchange and the Town Hall and Oxfam and the Mental Welfare Association and the Law Courts—'

'Do you feel sicker, Esther? Should I call the doctor?'

'No. I have lost my faith in doctors—it was a wilful sin against all those human organisations that stand between us and chaos, marriage being one of them. My mother was very shocked when she rang home and found me gone. She followed me down here.'

Esther's mother, Sylvia Susan, was small, neat, pretty and sixty-five. She was flirtatious, and wore clothes so up-to-date that people, never having seen anything like them before, would stare after her in the street. Now she wore a grey denim smock with matching kerchief in her hair. Her legs were thin and knotted. Esther was able to look at her own with something approaching approval. She sat at the table biting her finger-nails, which was something she only did when in her mother's company.

'I wish you wouldn't worry me so,' said Sylvia. 'It is not fair of you. Am I not due for a little peace? Could I not be allowed, for once, the luxury of not worrying about you?'

'I am not worried about myself, so I see no reason for you to be worried.'

'Look at you! You're in a terrible state. You've got soup all down your front. You always were a messy child. I don't know who you got it from. It wasn't me. I did all I could to train you but you were very stubborn. You were too clever, that was the trouble. You could read when you were three, and type when you were four.'

'A pity it all came to nothing.'

'It made me uneasy at the time, and I was right. None of my side of the family had brains. You got them from your father. And your body became overgrown in its attempt to keep up with your brain. Your father would stimulate you, that was the trouble. He encouraged you to think when what you needed was the exact opposite.'

'I don't think you ever really gave the matter two thoughts, Mother, you were too busy.'

'I know you have this view of me as a frivolous party-going woman, goodness knows why. If I went to parties when you were a child it was simply to help your father. Giving parties was an expensive and tiring occupation. But his business depended on his social contacts.'

'You were good at those.'

'Now what do you mean? Esther, what is the matter with you? Come home with me. What you need is a rest, and some proper looking after and then you will go back to Alan. You are in one of your states, and it's no use taking any notice of the things you say or do. I shan't let them hurt me. I know you too well. You are my daughter, when all is said and done.'

'What is the matter, Mother? What is all this talk of daughter? Have you decided you are lonely, after all these years? I prefer it down here, thank you very much. And I am not going back to Alan.'

'Now, you are being ridiculous. Now listen, Esther. You remember the doctor you saw last time, who did you so much good—'

'I am not mad. I know you want to think I am, but I'm not. I had a nervous breakdown fifteen years ago, from which I am quite recovered. At least I suppose it was a nervous breakdown. That's what people said. It seems, in retrospect, more like a fit of sanity, from which happy state you and your doctors wrenched me, forcibly. By the time you'd drugged me and shocked me I was in no state to do anything but go back to Alan. Why should one necessarily be mad just because one prefers not to live with one's husband? I am not mad now.'

'No one is saying you are, darling, just overtired and overstrained. And I'm sorry, I know it's hard for you to admit it, but you were definitely off your head then, the last time. You had no reason for leaving Alan. You couldn't give one. He was earning good money, at last. Your marriage had got off to a shaky start, I can tell you now I cried nightly all that first year when he was living off you, sponging off you, but then all of a sudden he changed, and he was doing marvellously, and we could all see what a wonderful future you both had. It was Peter's birth that did it, of course. It was all Alan needed, a sense of responsibility. I don't know why you had to go to that art school. You should have gone to the University and done something with your brain, since you had one, instead of hanging around with that extraordinary crowd. But by some miracle, which I will never understand, it all turned out all right in the end, until you suddenly take it into your head to walk out on your child and husband for no reason. If that's not madness, what is?'

'I could see where it would all end, that's all.'

'What do you mean?'

'Like this.'

'Like what? And, what has happened between you and Alan if it is more than just your neurosis? Is it another woman?'

'Yes and no.'

'I'm sorry dear, but it's yes or no. There are no half ways where these things are concerned.'

'I am afraid there are.'

'No doubt that's very modern of you. But let us try to get at the truth. Is he being unfaithful to you?'

'Mother, will you let me and Alan run our own marriage, or ruin it, as the case may be? I'm a grown girl now.'

'One would hardly think it. Look at it, this room. Look at the state you're living in! It's disgusting.'

'You didn't run your own life any too successfully.'

'Now what can you mean by that? I was a good wife and your father was a good husband. I am lonely now. You are all I have in the world. But he left me well provided for.'

'You never cared a fig for him. You went away on your holidays leaving him all alone with only me to look after him—'

'I was very delicate. I was never strong. What would you have me do? I'd have been no use to either of you if my health was broken.'

'And I used to dread you coming back and sneering at me, which is what you did, for being ugly and fat. But it was your fault that I was ugly and fat. And if I wasn't good at looking after Father, I was only a child, wasn't I? Or meant to be.'

'You should have aired the sheets. You were twelve. That's quite big. You knew sheets ought to be aired. It was damp sheets that gave him rheumatic fever. The doctor said so.'

'It's an old wives' tale about damp sheets and rheumatic fever. You held that over me for years. You ought to be ashamed of yourself.'

'And it was his weak heart after the rheumatic fever that killed him. I've never said it as plainly as that before but it's in my heart, and it ought to come out.'

'Don't you worry, it's been leaking out of your heart for the last fifteen years. I know what you think. But it's your own guilt speaking. Who were you off with on your medically recommended holidays in the South of France? Who? What were you doing, and who with? That's what killed father, not my damp sheets, but your adulterous ones.'

'You are out of your mind, Esther. Don't let's quarrel. We haven't quarrelled like this for years. If I'd had a son we wouldn't ever have quarrelled. Daughters are so possessive about their fathers, that's the trouble. I did what I could in the face of my own nature, which is the best any woman can do. But it's all in the past now. I am getting old. You seem young to me still, a child, but in the eyes of the world I suppose that even you are no longer young. You won't marry again, who would want you? You are too gross. You must stay married to Alan. I beg of you. You have some money of your own, but it is folly,

folly, to throw away your security, and your status, and the respect the world accords you as a married woman and a mother, and your husband's income, and presently his pension, which will be generous. Three-quarters of his salary I understand.'

'Women of your generation seem to regard men as meal-tickets. It's not very nice.'

'It's a great deal less painful than regarding them in any other way. And it is practical. Youth goes so quickly. It is such a short span in one's life. When it is over you recognise that comfort, status and money in the bank are really more important to a woman than anything else. And her family, of course. Esther, you are my family.'

'The thing about my mother,' said Esther to Phyllis, 'is that she never thought anything was important except her bank balance in her entire life. This lover she had in the South of France gave her jewels and money. That was why she went to him, not for love. And my poor father died trying to keep up with her demands—her financial demands, not her sexual ones, she didn't have those. I don't understand how I came to be born, nor, I think, does she. He was such a gentle clever man. All he ever wanted to do was sit in his study reading old law reports, with me to dust and bring him coffee and cook his dinner, but she insisted. She insisted. She made him go out into the world and entertain clients and steer so near the edge of the law he lived in dread of falling over, and ending up in prison. I think prison would have been a relief to him, in fact. He could have been the librarian and pottered.'

'Did he like Alan?'

'He liked him at first, when Alan refused to keep me or make a home or do anything but paint. I think he admired him for being so strong. I liked Alan at that time, too, except that my mother went on and on so about him using up all my money. Then Peter was born, anyway, and everything changed. And father became ill with his heart, because of the rheumatic fever and then he died, so I don't know what he was thinking, in the end. I had a feeling he turned against Alan when Alan went respectable and that's another reason I felt allowed, that time, to leave. This time I have no one's judgement but my own to go by. I used to be terrified I would end up like my mother. Many women do. They turn into their mothers far more easily than sons turn into their fathers.'

'You take these little holidays from your husband, all the same, the way your mother did from your father. Perhaps if you were seven stone lighter you would be more like her than you imagine.'

'Out of the mouths of babes and sucklings—'

'I am not as young as all that. I am thirty. That's a terrible age to be. There are wrinkles beginning to show around my eyes. And as for breast-feeding, it fills me with horror, the very thought of it. I don't want to be like a cow, with a baby draining away my strength. That's another reason I don't have a baby. I've never dared to tell anyone that before. Don't let Gerry know.'

'You can always give them bottles.'

'But that's not right. That's failure. Babies should be breast-fed. They force you to, in hospitals.'

'That is only the latest revenge of the doctors. A more subtle torment than just any old birth pains, which have too short a duration for their liking. You are right to fear maternity wards. Every resentment against the fecund female grows rampant there, like weeds, strangling common-sense and kindness. Any hospital is a place of myths and legends, and a maternity one is worst of all. When Peter was born bottles were considered more hygienic than dugs and breast-feeding a damaging habit; but then to compensate one was obliged to underfeed one's child, to keep it perpetually thin and pale and crying, if of course it was not too weak to cry at all. You must never pick your child up and cuddle it, was what they said then, that's spoiling, and interrupts its routine. But what they meant was, you shall not enjoy this baby you have had the presumption to have. We shall never, ever, let you.'

'Peter's not thin and weak now. He's a well-built boy. He takes after his father.'

'I took no notice of them. I fed him when I wanted and when he wanted. We were happy. Then my father died. I have been in mourning ever since. He seemed more like Peter's father to me than Alan ever did.'

'You still have not told me why you left Alan. The apples are cooked. Will you try them?'

'Thank you. With sugar and cream. I begin to feel a little better. I hope Peter is all right. But why should he not be? He has his compensations, he does not need me. He is more like Alan than he thinks.'

'I think you should be worrying about your husband.'

'My husband is an attractive man. There will always be women to look after him. He will use them while it suits his purpose, then he will damage them and send them away.'

'He is not like that at all. You wrong him.'

'You seem very possessive of my husband, Phyllis, all of a sudden, and to know a great deal about him. Do you fancy him?'

'What a thing to say.'

'Because you're welcome.'

Phyllis blushed crimson and spilt the sugar.

Esther watched her sweeping up the elusive grains with pleasure.

'Your trousers are too tight,' Esther said, 'you're getting fat. Gerry won't like it. He likes his wives to be small and his women to be fat, like me.'

When Phyllis straightened up there was a look of despair on her face.

'You are awful,' she said, 'I just don't know what to think or what to feel any more. There aren't any rules left.'

'Calm down, and I'll go on with this story, which you so rashly wanted to hear. Peter came to visit me a couple of days ago. I was more pleased to see him than I was to see my mother.'

'Oh Mum,' said Peter. 'I wish you would come home. It is very upsetting. Just because I leave home, doesn't mean you have to too. It is very embarrassing explaining to people, and it's not very nice in this room, is it? Everything is usually so tidy at home, how can you bear to live like this? It makes me think you must be depressed. It is very worrying for me—I shouldn't be hindered with worries at my age. It is bad enough being captain of a cricket team, and having duties and responsibilities towards Stephanie, without having to feel responsible for a miserable mother, too. That should be Father's business. He's taken to cooking. Recipe books everywhere. "Hi there, Mrs Sussman I presume", I said to him the other day, when I was home for the week-end, "slaving away over a hot stove again I see", but he didn't think it was funny. He doesn't think anything is funny, nowadays. Oh Mum, come home. It is all so dreary like this.'

'But you have your own home now, Peter. Choose to use your former home as a week-end hotel, by all means, but kindly do not insist on cheerful chambermaids. Or indeed on resident ones. This is where I live. You live somewhere else. Your father lives in yet another place. How you and your father choose to behave is now entirely your affair. Thank God I am not around to witness it.'

'Mother, you begrudge me any sex life. It isn't fair.'

'I most certainly do not. Have it off with all and sundry, male, female, bald-headed as you will. The pair of you.'

'Dad behaved very foolishly, I know, but don't take it out on me. She is a female fatale, Mother. He couldn't help it. There are these women about, you know. Insatiable and irresistible. It was just bad luck he happened to encounter her when both your spirits were so low. You should never have stopped eating, either of you. In middle-age, food is far less troublesome than sex. There is something terrible, tragic, monumental, in thinking of Father with that beautiful, beautiful girl—'

'Have you seen her, then? Where? How?'

'She called to visit me. To apologise for breaking up my home. I was trying to get on with my homework and waiting for Stephanie to come back from work when there was this knock at the door, and there she was. This vision. So unhappy, so distressed. I think there is a kind of kinship between us. She understands so much. She has so very, very much feeling. Women with feeling are very rare, Mother. But it is all over between them now. She has grown out of the stage of looking at older men. She prefers her own generation. That is maturity.'

'I see. What does Stephanie think about this?'

'One of the nice things about Stephanie is that she doesn't really think at all—after school it is such a relief, all this non-thinking. As a schoolboy one has to use one's brain all day; even playing cricket demands great mental concentration. I really do need you at home to talk to, you know. I am fairly grown up for my age but every now and then I become confused. If girls didn't like me I can see I would lead a narrower life, but it would be a more peaceful one, wouldn't it, and not so alarming. I mean, see how it confused Dad's life, simply fancying a girl as one could fancy a dish of strawberries and cream. Because that is how it was with Dad and her—he saw her as a symbol of delight, not a person. It was most distressing for her. Mother, somebody has to look after her. She is not good at looking after herself.'

'She's older than you. You're the one who needs looking after.'

'You are perfectly right,' he was triumphant. 'That is exactly what I have been trying to say. Oh Mother, come home.'

'There he was, you see,' said Esther to Phyllis, 'playing with fire and frightened of getting burned. All set for an affair with suburban Susan, coming to me to be protected from himself, hoping that my outrage would be strong enough to turn him back from the incestuous paths to which he had set his face. Going to bed with Daddy's mistress it's far too near for comfort to going to bed with Daddy's wife. I used to fancy my mother's rich lover, I remember, being too scared to actually fancy my Dad. But now I refused to be outraged. I had given him the eighteen years a mother has to give a son. Now he was on his own. I wanted to save my outrage for myself. Not waste it on a child who had youth on his side to save him from the direr penalties of obsessive fornication. I was older than him, and needed my outrage if I was to escape my husband.'

'Perhaps your mother was right, Esther. Please try and think rationally about things. When you talk like this I get upset. Nothing is as I thought it was; you make my whole world rock. You should see a doctor. An old-fashioned, physical one, I mean. Things have gone too far with you. You can have your frontal lobes cut, do you know, and then you never worry about a thing. You're just happy all the time. All the time.'

'Poor Phyllis. Is that next for you? If cutting your breasts open and stuffing them doesn't work, try cutting open the brain? You don't half pursue happiness to extremes. You'll corner it somewhere, won't you. In a little dark corner of your coffin, I dare say, finally you'll corner happiness.'

'I assure you I am very happy. It is you I worry about, Esther. You shouldn't think of that lovely boy Peter in those terms, much less reject his pleas for help. He wanted to be saved from Susan Pierce. It was your duty as a mother to save him. You should have packed and gone home there and then.'

'Well I didn't. If Alan doesn't ask me to return I never will. And even if he does, I won't. I have my pride. Did I tell you Susan Pierce has just been to see me? She brought me a flower-pot.'

'What an odd thing to do.'

'It was a present Alan had given her. She said she couldn't make things grow, but she thought I could, and she couldn't bear to leave that lily to wither up and die. It was just an excuse to see me. It was as if she wanted the entire family. Not content with the father, and then the son, I really think she would have welcomed a lesbian relationship with me.'

'Oh really Esther! She's no dyke. She's just sex-mad.'

'You mean I have been talking to you all this time and you still see human relationships in terms of sex? It had nothing to do with sex. The sexual urge is concerned with the reproduction of the species. She just wanted to wriggle back, somehow, anyhow, into a family situation. That she chose a genital method of doing so was merely coincidental. She could have done it more simply by doing our charring for us. It was a great misfortune that Alan had his family pictures on his desk. It was me she had been reaching out for all the time. I realised it when she handed me that flower-pot full of dried up earth. It was Mummy's and Daddy's bed she wanted to be in. She wanted to know what happened there. She wanted to be included in the mysteries. A pity that the mysteries, when at last discovered, should prove so trivial. A matter of plungings and positions. And yet the dark that shrouds all sexual intercourse, the dark of spirit and emotion, and the black cloak of love that makes one decent, leads one always to believe that there is something yet to be discovered. It is very aggravating, and responsible for a good deal of domestic confusion.'

'What are you talking about? You are a pagan. You are not decent. You are obscene!'

'Now what have I said to upset you so? I am telling you what you were curious about. About why Susan came to see me.'

'I felt so nervous about coming here' said Susan to Esther. 'But I thought I ought to try and explain things, and make them better. I wouldn't wish you to have hard feelings about me, or about your husband. He is an artist, you see. And artists are not like other people. The ordinary rules of morality do not apply to them.'

'Their immorality appears to me to be as dull and sordid as any ordinary person's. Alan is not, in fact, an artist, he is an advertising man, by profession, and by paucity of soul. That is to say he is talented, and intelligent, plausible and attractive, trivial to the bottom of his heart, and pathetic in his aspirations to a different way of life. That, however, is as may be. I may take a more jaundiced view of my husband, by virtue of my years with him, those chaste and temperate years, than you do by virtue of the couple of weeks, and the varied and various shaggings which no doubt you have shared with him.'

'You are not,' said Susan, sitting down, 'what I expected at all. For a wife you are very vocal.'

'I am sure it is most admirable of you, to come visiting to explain things to me. People ought to do it more often. What a coming and going there would be, week in, week out. What a knocking on doors, day and night, up and down the land. But there'd never be a woman at

home when the knock came. She'd be out on the town herself—
explaining.'

'You are taking advantage of me. I have been very upset by your
husband.'

'Well don't come complaining to me.'

'And I am afraid he is unhappy, and it is my fault. And you are
unhappy, and it is my fault. And Peter is unhappy because you two
aren't together. It is very upsetting for him. Please Mrs Sussman, go
home to your husband. We have all behaved so badly, I know. But
there is only one person who can put things right, and that is you, by
going home.'

'I would like to make something clear. My leaving Alan is nothing to
do with you. You are welcome to him, I promise you. Anyone is. And
probably are. When Alan embarked on this manic association with
you, he was in a sad psychic state. You were a symptom, not a cause. A
chicken-pox spot, if you like, but not the virus. You itched him, so he
scratched. Now the spots have subsided, but the virus, I am afraid,
remains. It is the unhappiness and discontent attendant on having too
much leisure, too much choice, too little pain. And none of it is anything to do with you. Kindly stop indulging yourself, and go away.'

'You are making things very difficult for me. It is not easy, I know,
for a non-artist, like yourself, to understand and forgive. It must all
seem strange to you, if you cannot comprehend the suddenness, the
awfulness, of love when it strikes. The helplessness which overcomes
one, the misery when it all goes wrong, when one offers so much and is
turned away.'

Her face had changed. She looked younger and uglier. She cried.
Esther began to feel more kindly towards her. 'Mrs Sussman, he didn't
want me at all. He wanted you.'

'He didn't have to want either of us, did he. He might have wanted
the moon, or the Pope or the Queen. I am afraid the intensity of your
rivalry with me prevented you from noticing anything of the kind.
This knowledge might, perhaps, make you feel better. It is not that I
have vanquished you. It is that we have both been wounded in a battle
which we should never have embarked upon because it didn't concern
us at all. People will make sex an excuse for anything. What is it that
you are carrying in your hand and watering, so sweetly, with your
tears?'

'A present.'

'A pot of earth. For me? How delightful.'

'Don't laugh at me. It is not a pot of earth, it is a pot plant. There is a lily down there. Alan gave it to me.'

'How sweet!' Esther peered at it elaborately. 'Alan's and your baby, as it were. It's not very advanced for its age though, is it?'

'Stop being so nasty. You were being nice before. I wish we could be friends. There is so much I don't know about things, and the more that happens to me the less I know. I only want to love someone and be loved back. Nothing I do goes right, it's like the lily. It won't grow for me. That's why I brought it to you. I thought you could make it grow. Something has to come out of all this. It must. If only a bloody pot plant.'

'Peter quite fancies you.'

A look of horror appeared on Susan's face.

'You know about that? I don't know how it happened, I really don't.'

'He wants to look after you.'

'Does he really? You don't mind?'

'Stop behaving like a little girl. You go all to pieces in the face of your elders, don't you. You become infantile at once. If I was you I should go and throw yourself at Peter's mercy and ask him to explain everything. He has a very neat version of the world, my son, far placider and tidier than mine. You can sop up his little boy helplessness when the dregs of it trickle out of his ears. And he can sop up your little girlishness when it flows and pours out of your every orifice. Play at mummies and daddies and daughters and sons in every conceivable combination you can imagine, but just leave me in peace.'

'I had no idea you were so clever. I wish my mother had been like you.'

Esther heaved herself out of her chair and turned Susan out, first snatching the flower-pot. She watered it tenderly with luke-warm water from a milk bottle, and sang it a little lullaby. But the earth didn't stir.

'That terrible woman,' said Susan, ungratefully, to Brenda. 'She's more or less pushing me into bed with her son. Any decent woman would have been shocked and scandalised at the very idea. She is very, very odd. No wonder Alan looked elsewhere.'

'Perhaps,' said Brenda, 'she wanted to be revenged on Alan. I mean to say, what an uncomfortable position for him. Supposing you and Peter got married. You having a former lover for a father-in-law. He a mistress for a daughter-in-law, and everyone knowing.'

'It would all be rather cosy,' said Susan. 'And companionable. I think I should like that. I'll walk down with you to the pub, and while you lie in wait for that silent man I'll go and call on Peter. It's Wednesday, and crop-haired Stephanie has a boy-friend she visits on Wednesdays.'

'What are those bruises on your neck?' Phyllis asked Esther. Esther, having told Phyllis about Susan's visit, had been violently sick into the lavatory. She returned to lie upon her bed, and opened her collar so that the old yellowing bruises on her neck could be seen.

'It's where Alan tried to strangle me.'

'He didn't. He never did!'

Phyllis put her hands to her own neck, grateful for a lucky escape. 'I am sure Gerry would never try to strangle me. I am sure he wouldn't. *How* did he try to strangle you?'

'He put his hands around my neck and he pressed and he squeezed and he tried to kill me. To put an end to me altogether. As if that would have solved his problems. I think, mind you, that I would strangle me if I was him. It must be a fearful thing to be a man and have a wife. Never to be able to do what you want without feeling guilty. Always feeling in the wrong, because wives are always in the right. I feel quite sorry for men sometimes.'

'But to try and strangle you!'

'I did call him an impotent old man. An impotent balding old man.'

'Perhaps you were angry.'

'But you see, it was the truth. He was spiritually impotent, totally, and physically impotent, partially. Once I had told him the truth, I had to go. There could be nothing left between us. Lies are never dangerous, not by comparison with the truth.'

'Esther, Esther,' cried Alan on the evening of the final day of the diet. 'I've lost another pound!' The weighing machine now had a permanent position in the living-room. It was eleven o'clock at night, and the diet ended at twelve. Alan was in his dressing-gown, which now had an appreciably greater overlap than before.

'Esther, Esther!' he called in the direction of the kitchen, but no one answered. 'Another pound. Think of that! Of course I've been taking a lot of exercise. I'm sure that helps. But twelve whole pounds.'

There came a small rustling furtive noise from the kitchen. He leapt from the scales, so that the dial swung wildly, and flung the kitchen door open. Esther crouched in a corner, like a woman taken in adultery. She was eating a biscuit. Rage overwhelmed Alan.

'You cheat,' he cried. 'You cheat! You're eating.'

'You're the one who cheats,' she hissed. She seemed half mad. 'You always cheat me.'

'What are you talking about?' He tried to snatch the biscuit from her. She resisted.

'Please,' she begged, 'please let me keep it. It's nearly midnight. The whole nightmare is nearly over. I must eat it. I must.'

He got hold of the biscuit and threw it to the other side of the room.

'You take everything,' she said. 'You take everything, and you give me nothing. You take my life and you throw it away.'

'You're mad. You're mad again. They never really cured you, did they.'

'You made me mad.'

'You have no self-control. You are despicable. You can't even stop eating for a couple of weeks. You have to nibble, and cheat, and go behind my back, and lie, and twist, and cheat, and cheat, and cheat again.'

'I have nothing else to do but eat. What else have I got? You give me nothing. No love, no affection, no sex, nothing.'

'Take a look at yourself. You are disgusting. What do you expect?'

'I have given you everything. All my years, all my life. Everything I ever had all wasted. Every bit of love I ever had I gave to you. And now you just throw me away.'

'Like an old glove?' he enquired. She raised her hand as if to strike him, but he dodged. 'Oh calm down,' he said. 'All this fuss about an old biscuit. You're hysterical. Why do I always end up with hysterical women?'

'Is Susan hysterical too, then?'

'Here we go again. What *is* it you want, Esther? Why can't you be satisfied? You've got a home, and a child, and security, and a husband who comes home every night. I support you. I'm polite to you. I don't beat you. You're luckier than almost every other woman in the world.'

'I'll tell you my discontent. It's this. I think that if you found me ill and lying in the gutter you wouldn't bother to pick me up and take me home, you'd just pass by.'

'You're a fair weight to pick up. Ha-ha.'

'You can't resist being funny at other people's expense, can you? How they must hate you at the office.'

'Oh, cut yourself a slice of cake. I'm going to get dressed and go out.' He moved towards the door. Esther moved to intercept him.

'Where?'

'That is none of your business.'

Esther stood with her back against the door, barring his way.

'Where, I asked.'

'Where I want. Anywhere in this world to get away from you. You make me sick. You want to keep me in prison. I can't even to go bed when I want any more, because I hear your prissy little voice calling down the stairs like some teenager.' He mimicked her soft voice, ' "Oh Alan, Alan, beddy-byes". What sort of life do you think I have, sitting in a bloody office day after day, getting nowhere, doing nothing, with only "Alan, beddy-byes" at the end of it? This is the only life I'm going to have. I'll be dead soon. And you make me live like this. I was born a *man*, and now look at me. I am scarcely human any more. I tell you, the day I married you was the end of my life. You squeezed my talents out of me. You depleted me utterly with your demands and your naggings, you turned me into a poor grey dried up company man with an income and pension. It's not me, and it's your fault. I hate you. You've cheated me of my freedom, and my life. You've stolen it.'

'You're a poor balding impotent old man. A dirty old man. I read what you wrote. All your sexual fantasies. You'd be mad to think anyone would publish them. They were the sick ravings of a lunatic.'

'You're the lunatic, not me. I don't *want* you in bed. How could I?'

'I despise you too much. I pity you.'

'Get out of my way.' He tried to push past her.

'No. Where are you going? To your Susan?'

'Yes. Are you surprised? You have driven me to it. You have played your cards all wrong, Mrs Sussman.'

'Perhaps you haven't played your cards so well either. Perhaps I have somewhere to go too. Men don't think of that. Do you think I just sit quietly at home, and take what you deal out to me?'

'What do you mean?' But a bland self-satisfied smile just crossed Esther's face and vanished again. 'What do you mean? Who would want you? Who in the world would want you?'

'You must be feeling very guilty,' said Esther, 'to assume my guilt when I haven't said a thing. Not a thing.'

'You fat slut.' He tried to move her from the door, but she spread her arms against it as if crucified. Noiselessly, they struggled. He was stronger than she, for all her size, and it was evident that he would get the door open in time, but she would not give in. Her face kept appearing, almost wilfully, in the path of his fists. He slapped her hand on the side of her face, and she tore at his cheeks, with her nails. He put his hands around her neck and squeezed. When she sank to the floor he let go. He opened the door and left the kitchen. Esther, still crouching on the floor, heard him go up to the bedroom, dress, collect his coat, come down the stairs and let himself out of the front door. Presently she raised her head and surveyed the kitchen. She stood up, ran a finger along a dusty ledge and cursed Juliet. She took a couple of biscuits, and poured some milk into a pan, and started to make herself cocoa.

'The night she walked out on him,' said Susan to Brenda in the pub, 'he came to see me. He'd never been in the night before, only in office lunch-hours and on the way home after work. I didn't let him in. I didn't want to be treated like that again; like an old dustbin for all his old rubbish. And anyway I kept thinking William might turn up—isn't that your silent friend coming in?'

Brenda blushed and lowered her eyes. The man from the night before saw her, looked surprised, and then, gratified, crossed to sit beside her. Susan rose. 'I'll be off then,' she said, 'to see Peter. Make sure he buys your drinks, and not the other way round.'

'I can't speak to him, so I can't make him do anything. I'll just have to accept him as he is, won't I.'

'Put your charges up. Then he'll value you more.'

'I do live a very dull life,' said Phyllis to Esther. 'Gerry never tries to strangle me, and his girl-friends never come to visit me. Perhaps he doesn't have as many as he would like to think; perhaps in fact it *is* all talk with him—' she looked hopefully at Esther, but Esther made no sign of either assent or dissent—'or perhaps it's just all over so soon they never get round to finding out my address. I think as soon as he gets what he wants he loses all interest.'

'That's right,' said Esther. 'It's in, out, and off. That's Gerry. Very boring, and not worth discussing.'

Phyllis fell silent. Then she ate a biscuit.

'Funny thing,' said Esther. 'I don't feel hungry any more. I think your horrible doctor was right. I was sickening myself. Now I'm purged, and I'm better. Eat up, Phyllis, it will do you good. You know the thing that disconcerted me most about Susan's visit? It was the way she called me Mrs Sussman, but Alan by his Christian name, I realised how small a part of his life I was, or ever had been. It was hard to stomach.'

'What are you going to do next?'

'Nothing. Stay here. Eat, read books. Die. Be buried. Rot. Be finished.'

'That's silly.'

'It is true,' said Esther. 'I am finished. I am over. It is very simple, really. I am a woman and so I am an animal. All women are animals. They have no control over themselves. They feel compelled to have children—there is no merit in it, there is no cause for self-congratulation, it is blind instinct. When I was a girl I searched for a man to father my children. My eye lighted on Alan. I had my child. Now the child is grown up and I have no further need of the man. I shuffle him off. And he has no need of me, because women age faster than men, and I am no longer a fit mother for his possible children. Let him beget more if he can, and start the whole thing over again with someone else. That's his affair, not mine. The drive is finished in me. I am dried up. I am useless. I am a burden, I wait to die. Phyllis, I am making myself feel hungry again.'

'I am not an animal.'

'You coward. You prissy miss, with your curls and your sexy little suits. You're an animal. You said to me once you were chained to your bed. Well so you are. Because you're a female animal, and your brain and your mind and and all your fine feelings are no help to you at all. You're just a female animal body, fit to bear children and then be thrown away. And if you don't have children, you'll be on the rubbish heap all the sooner, and being stamped on like an empty milk carton to boot. So watch it.'

'You're still not well.'

'I don't expect to be well.'

'There's someone coming down the steps,' said Phyllis, who was sitting near the window. She craned her head upwards. 'Oh good heavens, it's Alan. It's your husband.' She turned to her friend, panic-stricken, and trembling.

'Don't get so panicky,' said Esther. 'I know all about you and him.'

'How? What do you mean?'

'It has been evident from your manner all day. It doesn't matter in the least. I doubt that either of you enjoyed it. A simple matter of tit for tat. And you can think about *that* phrase a little longer, and repeat it to your bosom doctor, from me.' She crossed to the door to let her husband in. He loomed crossly through the doorway.

'What are *you* doing here?' he said to Phyllis. 'What mischief are you making now?'

'Esther is very ill,' said Phyllis. 'She needs help. I'm glad you've come—she says the oddest things.'

'What are you playing at, Esther? It's absurd, living in two places at once. I thought you'd come to your senses sooner and come home. Your behaviour is very inconvenient for everyone. Have you calmed down enough to come home, do you think?'

'I don't want you down here, nagging, go away. You're a pompous old bore.'

'Peter needs you. He's very upset these days. He's emotionally imma-ture. He's unstable.'

'I think he'll be all right.'

'It's you he needs.'

'I have needs too, you know.'

'My face is beginning to heal, at last. It has been most embarrassing. It went septic. Your nails must have been dirty.'

'Oh you poor thing,' said his wife.

'You really must try not to be so hysterical. It does a lot of damage. You can't go on living in this pig-sty. How much do they charge you?'

'Five pounds a week.'

'It's robbery. It's damp. It's a slum. I haven't seen anything like this since I was a child.'

'We lived in a room like this the first year we were married.'

'And a terrible place it was, I remember. You've got fatter, you don't look at all well.'

'I'm back to where I was before I started that terrible diet of yours.'

'I was on it too,' said Alan.

'Is that an apology?'

'What have I got to apologise for? Let's just forget it all. Come home, Esther, don't be silly.'

'I like it here. No one nags. I can breathe better, too, now the swelling on my throat has gone down.'

'Throat?'

'Where you tried to strangle me.'

'You drove me to it. You goaded me.'

'I'd better be going,' said Phyllis brightly.

'Oh don't,' cried Esther falsely. 'Do stay to tea, Phyllis darling. You'd love her to stay to tea, wouldn't you, Alan?'

'And you can stop that here and now,' he said. 'If you walk out on me you can take the consequences.'

'What about Susan?'

'What about her?'

'I was with you then. I had done nothing wrong.'

'I was on a diet. I was very upset. There was all that terrible business with the agent and the publishers. It was very humiliating for me, Esther, and you didn't help at all. Susan was a nothing.'

'Poor Susan then. Just a nothing. I think she will be revenged.'

'How?'

'Never mind. That's another story. I will tell it one day.'

'Wives always win in the end,' said Phyllis hopefully; she had moved into profile against the light, so that her new and improved breasts stood out to advantage. It was for Alan's benefit but he took no notice. 'All they have to do is hold out long enough.'

'You silly prissy smarmy common bitch,' said Esther. 'I don't think I can stand you much longer, Phyllis. Will you please take yourself and your bosom away, and this nagging bore of a man with you?'

'But it's true,' Phyllis persisted, with a note of hysteria in her voice. 'Wives win.'

'And what a victory, over what.'

'Please will you both calm down,' said Alan. 'There is no point in you staying here wasting money. You can't be happy here. You might as well be at home where you can be of some use.'

Esther put her head in her hands. She appeared to be defeated.

'No,' she said, 'we mustn't waste money, I suppose I might as well be there as here. It doesn't seem to make much difference where one is.'

Phyllis began to grizzle.

'Oh shut up Phyllis,' said Alan. 'Why do you keep butting in on other people's family quarrels? I hope you haven't got much luggage, Esther, I only brought the Mini.'

'Just what I took with me. A few old clothes. I'll leave the paperbacks. And that stupid pot plant. We'll leave that.'

'The plant is growing,' said Phyllis. 'Can I have it?' Esther got up, crossed to the window sill and peered into the flower pot. A little sprig of green disturbed the dusty surface. She was inordinately pleased.

'Good heavens! Do you mean to say I did that? Do you mean to say it's growing for me? Alan, look!'

But Alan did not turn round. He was looking with amazement into the food cupboards.

She shrugged.

On the other side of London Susan cried happily into Peter's shoulder and recited tales of domestic living with William and sexual adventures with Alan, while Peter lovingly blancoed his cricket pads. And in the pub Brenda held hands with the man she couldn't speak to, and was overwhelmed with such a sweet surge of love and gratitude that tears came into her eyes. He wiped them away, gently, with his very white pocket handkerchief thinking she had been drinking too much and that he must take her home quickly in case she fell asleep.

About the Author

Fay Weldon is the author of several novels, including *Down Among the Women, Female Friends, Praxis*, and most recently *Puffball*. She has also written three plays and many television scripts. Ms. Weldon lives in London and Somerset, England.